THE YANGTZE RUN

What started as a straightforward collection soon became a nightmare for Harry Lord as the unwitting pawn in a four-sided struggle for two tons of gold bullion. Far from counting his $50,000 fee, he found himself fighting for his life, and for that of Annie Kim, whom he had promised to take out of Shanghai. Lord rarely made promises, but those he made he kept . . .

Patrick O'Hara

The Yangtze Run

CORGI BOOKS
A DIVISION OF TRANSWORLD PUBLISHERS LTD

THE YANGTZE RUN

A CORGI BOOK 0 552 10730 1

Originally published in Great Britain by
Arlington Books (Publishers) Ltd.

PRINTING HISTORY
Arlington Books edition published 1977
Corgi edition published 1978

Corgi Books are published by
Transworld Publishers Ltd,
Century House, 61–63 Uxbridge Road,
Ealing, London W5 5SA

Made and printed in Great Britain by
Cox & Wyman Ltd., London, Reading and Fakenham

The Yangtze Run

SHANGHAI

Friday, May 20th, 1949

THE night was dark and the light breeze out of the north-east ruffled the bank of kunai grass that rose around the inlet where the *Jacaranda* lay hidden on the south shore two miles above the village of Chen-kou. The river was lost in darkness and a dank fog trailed westward with the breeze from the north bank that was Kiangsu province. The river was the Yangtze Kiang – The Great – and it rolled its waters down across three thousand, four hundred and thirty miles of the most spectacular scenery ever looked at by man, from distant Tibet, from the melting snows of the Himalayas.

But this night the only scenery of any interest to Harry Lord was the lemon-misted carbide lights of a Communist motor junk as it prepared to begin its outward run toward midstream from a point a little way below the village. Lying flat on the dew-wet foredeck, he put the night-glasses on the junk and watched her lights swing around below the blacked-out huddle of greystone houses, then start back toward midstream. When he looked at his watch he saw the hands read precisely 1.00 a.m. At normal patrol speed it was going to take the junk at least twenty minutes to reach midstream, and settling down to wait, he suddenly distinguished another sound above the slop and gurgle of the river. Easing his head around the portside of the low, raked cockpit, he saw a hunched figure in a white sharkskin suit and Panama hat at the port gunwale in the stern-quarters. 'Hey, you!' he called aft. 'Get the fuck back under that tarp and keep your yellow head down.'

Startled, the man turned and scuttled back under the tarpaulin without even darting a backward glance in the direction of the foredeck.

Watching him disappear, Harry Lord thought; slopeheads, bloody slopeheads.

On this trip he had seen everything, even a Chinaman who found time to take a leak across the side while a stream of puttee-legged Communist troops armed to the teeth were headed by on the bank fifty yards to the rear, on their way to Shanghai sixty miles to southward. If it hadn't been so pathetic it might have been funny. Further, it was a trip that had gone wrong right from the outset, a trip he hadn't wanted to make in the first place, until Old Heinie Sztykgold talked him into it. Worse, he supposed Sztykgold was at that moment sitting with a nightcap brandy in the Shanghai Yacht Club, safe as houses, on the Soochow Creek. And from the way things were going, he wondered if he was destined to ever see the old Soochow Creek again.

He had come in above Chen-kou with darkness at 2.00 a.m. on the morning of Wednesday 18th, and there had only been three of them waiting. Two others had arrived just before dawn, both of them old men, with two villagers carrying one of them on a make-shift stretcher. By then it had been too late to start back downriver and he had hauled the *Jacaranda* around behind some boulders scattered across the mouth of a shallow inlet where she was screened from the bank in rear by a clump of willows, and settled down to wait for darkness the following evening.

It had remained quiet until just before noon, when Communist troops on their way south from the crossing at Kiangyin began to pass intermittently on the path along the bank in squads of two hundred or more at a time. Unable to make any move, they had been forced to sweat it out until dusk fell, when the other three refugees arrived with a guide from the village. Even then, one of them, the twenty-four years old son of a Nanking broker, had had the gall to arrive dressed in a white sharkskin suit, Panama hat, and carrying a briefcase as if he had been on his way to a board meeting.

Two hours later, when ready to pull out, a Communist motor junk had suddenly come downriver to take up station off Chen-kou. Bad as it was, anger and frustration had knotted inside Harry Lord's stomach when she had begun a night-long patrol of the river, during which time she had shot up two sampans and a river junk attempting to make a dash downriver to southward. In the end he had been left with no alternative but to wait over for a further day in the hope that the junk would move on before nightfall. Instead she had remained on station off Chen-kou all during daylight, and to further complicate matters the old man who arrived on the stretcher the previous day had lost consciousness toward late afternoon. With that, an even more oppressive sense of gloom had settled over the launch.

But now, Harry Lord put the night-glasses back at where the lemon-misted lights of the junk showed about a quarter of a mile out from the shore, and a look of bleak determination etched itself on his tough, dark face. Having already timed the junk over the same trip on the four previous occasions she had made it earlier that night, he knew exactly what he was going to do. On the outward trip she took just over twenty minutes, losing some three-quarters of a mile downriver against the current, and then she would come about and start back toward her point of departure, making up the distance she had lost downstream on the return trip. So when she reached the outward limit of her patrol, he would start the motors and head upstream in a wide arc to northward that would take him out across the river. Once out in midstream the junk would by then be well toward the shore on the return trip, and it would be simply a matter of cutting the motors and allowing the *Jacaranda* to drift downriver with the current.

When he next put the night-glasses on the junk she was still headed out, losing way against the current, the searchlight in her bows twitching around in the misted darkness. Satisfied with her progress, he turned his attention to the stern-quarters. All was silent. 'Hey, back there. How's the old man making out?'

'His condition hasn't changed any, Captain, sir.' It was Mr Wall Street, the irrepressible up-and-coming broker from Nanking who answered.

'Then keep putting those compresses on him.'

'Yes, *sir*, Captain, sir!'

Harry Lord shook his head in dumb wonder. Two hundred bucks apiece for this lot, he thought; *Jesus H. Christ*.

All eight of them were from Nanking, having been caught in and around Chen-kou when Communist troops had bypassed the final columns of refugees headed south toward Shanghai. After that it had taken them several weeks to get word south about their plight, to set the wheels in motion for friends or relatives to arrange with Heinrich Sztykgold to buy their passage downriver.

Harry Lord glanced at his watch again, then jerked suddenly upright, ears straining. The distant sound of marching feet was unmistakable. Turning to peer through the tangled clump of willows, he saw a line of carbide lanterns approaching from northward along the bank in rear, moving like some giant illuminated caterpillar following the undulations of the shore. Lying flat, with the big Gibbs ·505 in his hand, he watched them go on by, faces blurred in the light of the lanterns. Almost ten minutes elapsed before the end of the column disappeared into the hollow toward the village.

Arming the sweat from his face, he returned his attention to the river. The junk had meantime made steady progress and now showed well out toward midstream. Deciding it was time to make a move, he climbed to his feet and took another look to northward but could see no sign of any further lanterns in sight. Standing there in the open, he made a big shadow up on the foredeck. Although he wasn't tall, only five-ten, he was made to appear even shorter by the bulk of his upper body. Despite this bulk, when he dropped down into the cockpit it was almost noiselessly.

Leaving the Gibbs and night-glasses on the dashboard where the sawn-off ·38 Smith & Wesson Police Special was already stashed, he shrugged his old US Army combat jacket aside, then swung out across the starboard gunwale. When he hit the river bed he landed knee-deep in soft mud and water. Making his way forward under the long raked bows in the darkness, he put a bulky shoulder against the flare and heard her suck free under the pressure, and he went out with her until the water reached his shoulders, then hauled himself back inboard. Going quickly forrard, he grabbed a boathook on the foredeck as the current lifted the stern clear, fended the bows off a slab of granite, then nudged them out from under the tangle of dipping willow branches.

'You want a hand, Captain, sir?' Mr Wall Street called forrard from beneath the tarpaulin.

Harry Lord turned on him with a low growl as the current carried them out clear of the inlet and on down broadside toward the blacked-out village. 'Another word out of you and I'll crack you across the skull with this fucking boathook.'

They had drifted the better part of two hundred yards downriver when he thumbed the electric starter to bring the twin Issotta Fraschini motors to life with a roar that sounded loud enough to wake Peking. Quickly throttling them back, he watched the shore, the village, and the outgoing junk all at the same time. But when the anticipated shout or rifle crack failed to materialize, he put the motors in gear and opened the throttles over to bring her head around against the current. She went easily ahead against the current and the shore coasted smoothly by, the boulders, the clump of willows dipping their branches across the inlet where they had lain up for the past two days, and then they were up past it and he edged her out away from the immediate shoreline.

A mile to northward he opened the throttles over further and swung their head around toward midstream. He felt a glow of relief to be under way again, to feel the deck alive beneath his feet. To southward the junk was now on her way back toward the shore, and out in midstream he brought their head around downriver, throttled the motors all the way back, and let her drift with the current. The mist lay more thinly out in midstream and the quiet was disturbed only by the swirl of the water along the hull and the hum of idling motors.

'How are we doing, Captain, sir?'

Harry Lord scowled back astern and saw the bright-eyed blur of Mr Wall Street's face looking back at him from beneath the edge of the tarpaulin. It occurred to him that if he were to throw him across the side he wouldn't be any loss; the man was born to be a pain in the arse to somebody somewhere anyway. 'Open your mouth again and you get out and walk.'

Mr Wall Street's face vanished instantly, and taking the night-glasses from the dashboard, Harry Lord screwed the junk into focus. They were no more than a half mile to northward of her, and she was still headed serenely in toward the shore. Then lowering the night-glasses, he suddenly found himself staring into a wall of steel plates looming up out of the darkness right ahead. Startled, he couldn't think what the hell it was at first, then he saw she was an old LCI, her plates scoured and rusted, headed diagonally across the river from the north bank toward Chen-kou. His immediate reaction was to make a run for it, but before he could hook the motors up a searchlight back astern of the pillar-box wheelhouse snapped on to trap him full in its glare. In the following instant the night erupted. Örlikon, machine gun and rifle-fire shattered the quiet. Multicoloured lights arced, waltzed, and floated around the *Jacaranda*'s low superstructure, and as the motors hooked with an urgent roar and upflung cloud of broken wash and exhaust, the windshield fragmented and disappeared.

Blinded by the glare of light, he had no alternative but to skid her around on her stern off the LCI's starboard side and head back upriver. It took a twisting, zig-zag run back toward the south shore before he eventually lost the searchlight, but even then, when he looked astern he saw the LCI headed upriver in his wash. And disturbed by the commotion, the junk had also come about and was headed back out toward the LCI, so that between the two searchlights the river was lit up a bright misted lemon. Spinning the wheel to starboard, he brought the bows around sharply and headed out across the river in a bid to escape the glow of light.

He had covered no more then two hundred yards when a growing roar filled the night; like the sound of an approaching express locomotive. Then it faded, cut out altogether, and seconds later a huge column of water mushroomed into the air. Right behind it followed another. They had come from the south shore, somewhere close by to northward, 75 or 105 millimetre rounds. Bathed in the glow of light to southward, the *Jacaranda* was a sitting target for the gunners further upriver. And in that instant he knew there was only one way to go, and that was *downriver*.

With the throttles full open, he spun the wheel back around to starboard as another large calibre shell hit the river astern, the concussion of displaced air cracking across the surface with the blast of a furnace door thrown open. When he came around downriver it was to be confronted by the LCI and the junk lying about a half-mile apart and still closing on him. Without hesitation he pointed the bows directly into the space between them, and with the revolutions building to full power, the slipstream buffeting through the empty windshield, and the wheel shuddering with the reverberations, he headed south. With the roar of the motors drowning all other sound now, all he saw was fountaining water and the criss-cross of tracer shells converging on him from the LCI and the junk.

Crouching low in the cockpit with the bows ripping a dazzling wash high up astern, he went down and on through the diminishing gap with tracer shells passing all around the low, raked cockpit. And then out on the south side of the rapidly failing glow of light he saw a sampan with three soldiers in it suddenly materialize out of nowhere. More incredibly, he saw one of the soldiers in the stern climb to his feet and aim his rifle, and in the next instant the *Jacaranda*'s raked bows cut the sampan apart, passed through her without even a tremor. Hitting close to forty knots and with the revolutions still building, it was like the Luichow Express running down a handcart left on the track while she made top speed on the down gradient out of Changsha on a dark night.

Holding top power, he quickly left the glow of light off Chen-kou behind, and passed to starboard the blacked out villages of Fushan and Hupukow on the south shore. With no further challenge issuing from the darkness, they were soon well to southward, and easing the throttles, he looked back into the stern-quarters. 'You all right back there?'

First one apprehensive face, then another, lifted itself from beneath the edge of the tarpaulin. For the first time since boarding the *Jacaranda*, Mr Wall Street was lost for words. Nor was he the only one to find it incredible that he was still alive. It was the old man who spoke. Pushing the tarpaulin back, he climbed unsteadily to his feet. Very quietly, he said, 'I think Old Chang is dead.'

Harry Lord motioned to him. 'Come here.'

When the old man came forrard, Harry Lord saw he was badly shaken, not only by the shooting, but from the physical hammering he had taken from the motors while lying flat on the duckboards in the stern-quarters. Throttling the motors back further until there was just enough way on the *Jacaranda* to prevent her from swinging with the current, he put the old man's hands on the wheel. 'Hold her just like that.'

Going aft, he pulled the tarpaulin aside and found the old man staring up at him with wide open sightless eyes. Glancing forrard, he said, 'What did you say his name was?'

The old man at the wheel answered quietly, 'Old Chang. I knew him in Nanking. We used to dine in the evenings at the same restaurant. He was a tailor.'

'Any idea where he was headed?'

'He mentioned a brother, also a tailor. I believe he has a business somewhere on the Nanking Road.'

'Well we can't take him into Shanghai dead.'

The old man turned his eyes to the river. 'I don't think Old Chang would mind what became of him. He didn't at any time give the impression of being a vain man.'

Harry Lord cast a glance around the other six impassive faces in the stern, but none of them offered any objection, and lifting the old man in his arms, he laid him into the water over the port gunwale. For a brief moment he floated placidly on his back, then turned twice with the current like a length of timber, and was lost in the darkness.

And Harry thought; all this for two hundred bucks apiece. He really *was* mad.

* * *

It was 2.00 a.m. when the aircraft picked up the glow of light in the sky that was Shanghai. It came in from the north-west, an old US Air Force transport bearing the White Sun insignia of Nationalist China Airways. On a direct flight from Chungking, it carried thirty-four passengers crammed into its utility seating. Among them, seated at a port midway along the fuselage, was a noted Chinese banker named Henry Wan. In the seat next to him was his wife, and directly behind her, in the seat next to the aisle, sat their bodyguard Tzu Hsun.

While the aircraft drummed across the north-western suburbs, Henry Wan watched with mild interest as the lights of Shanghai gradually settled into a geometric pattern beyond the port wing. Although it was fourteen years since he had last visited the city, certain parts of Greater Shanghai were still indentifiable to him. The old International Settlement, the business and banking quarter, was betrayed by the glare of light reflected from its floodlit buildings. The fairy lights of Chapei, the old Japanese quarter, lay to northward, on the further side of the narrow silver ribbon that was the Soochow Creek, bounded to eastward by the angular cuts of the Hongkew Creek, almost opposite Pootung Point to southward. To westward was the old French Concession with its tree-lined avenues and pavement cafés; and beyond, the Old Chinese City in Nantao. Also visible was the glint of steel rails where they converged on the North and South railway stations. To southward the glitter of the Whangpoo River bisected the city, the south shore ablaze with the lights of Pootung, Tienningshih, and Tungkow to eastward where the river flowed down to join the Yangtze fourteen miles away at Woosung. And scattered amid the blaze of light was the glow of several fires burning in various northern parts of the city.

Zephyrine Wan leaned past her husband for a closer look at the pattern of lights spread out below them. With a small note of anxiety in her voice, she said, 'Do you suppose those fires are the result of a bombing raid?'

Henry Wan bent his face to the port. 'They're too widespread. They look more like the work of the People's Militia to me.'

Zephyrine Wan leaned back into the iron frame and canvas seat, her delicate Szechuanese features shadowed by the glow of light outside the port, her thoughts impenetrable.

From his seat in rear, Tzu Hsun leaned casually forward. In a whispered voice, he said, 'Don't be in any hurry to disembark. And stay right with me. I want to keep an eye on these people.' Sitting back, he then resumed his interest in an American magazine, perfectly at ease.

Of slim, athletic build, the former Kealo Secret Society gunman was twenty-seven years old. Although he was only an inch or two taller than Henry Wan, he cut a much more impressive figure, physically. And like Henry Wan's wife, also being from Szechuan province, his face bore the distinctive features of that area. Yet there was an odd chill in his looks, although he was still handsome, and his hair, meticulously barbered, was combed straight back away from his forehead. To anybody meeting him for the first time, there was nothing to indicate that he had been responsible for the cold-blooded slaying of seven men. Yet tucked beneath the dove grey cloth over his left breast was a medium calibre pistol, and concealed by the right sleeve of his coat, a broad-bladed knife affixed to his arm with a strap so that the knife lay flat along the inside of the forearm.

Now, folding the magazine aside, he buttoned his coat as the aircraft swept in across the glitter of the Whangpoo River toward the approach lights of Zero Three runway at Lunghwa Airport, and turning in his seat, he made another guarded scrutiny of their fellow passengers as they crowded their faces to the ports in a bid to catch a glimpse of the lights along the river. Then he felt the bounce and screech of tyres as the undercarriage touched down, and relaxing back into his seat, he watched the string of runway lights outside the port gradually lose pace.

It was 2.20 a.m. South China Time when the first passengers descended the ramp into a morning damp with dew and smelling of the nearby river. Minutes later, with the throng of people beginning to make their way across the asphalt toward the terminal building, Henry Wan and his wife fell casually in behind Tzu Hsun, and when they entered the Arrival Lounge to await their baggage being unloaded, he led them to a corner which gave an unhindered view of the big room, and at the same time overlooked the Baggage Hall.

After a wait of some ten minutes, Tzu Hsun saw their three pieces of luggage arrive at the checking counter and he caught the attention of a porter, and still clutching the black metal document case which he hadn't allowed out of his grasp since leaving the house out at Ta Er Wo the previous evening, he led the way out of the building to where several Green Cab Company taxicabs were waiting in the cab rank outside on the Lunghwa Road.

In that same moment a man wearing a rumpled blue lightweight suit casually emerged from a nearby washroom and strolled to the news-stand in the main hall where he bought an early edition of the *Shanghai Morning Post*. Idly, he assumed a stance beside the counter and folded the newspaper over open. To all appearances he was merely a bystander engrossed in the latest news when the taxicab bearing the Wans moved away in the direction of the city with Tzu Hsun's face at the rear window. Only then, as the taxicab disappeared outside the glow of light that issued from the terminal building, did he show any haste, when he walked toward the rank of waiting taxicabs.

3.10 a.m. showed on Tzu Hsun's watch when they arrived at the Great Eastern Mansions on the Nanking Road. While one of the plum-coated Sikhs on the entrance collected the three pieces of luggage from the taxicab, he turned to lead the way across the marble foyer to reception. It took Henry Wan several minutes to decide which suite they wanted to rent, and after questioning the clerk on the merits regarding the quiet and solitude of those available, he finally decided to take the Peking Suite on the hotel's eighth floor. Meanwhile Tzu Hsun's attention was taken up with a collection of jewellery on display in a strip-lighted showcase close by, although he was more interested in the tinted mirror lining the case behind the blue velvet cushions than in any one particular piece of jewellery. And it was here, while Henry Wan was signing the register, that he saw the reflected image of a man enter the foyer from the street and sit into a chair near the entrance to unfold a copy of the *Shanghai Morning Post*. Then, as the Wans were being led to the elevator, he straightened up from the showcase to follow them without as much as a cursory glance at the foyer.

Only when the wrought-iron gate of the elevator slid shut behind them did he come suddenly to life, thrusting the document case into Henry Wan's hand. 'The man with the newspaper,' he said in a low whisper.

The startlement on Henry Wan's face changed instantly to shock. Physically, he wilted, and all trace of earlier confidence vanished. 'A man? What man?' he stammered.

At her husband's side, Zephyrine Wan's features hardened and her eyes narrowed. 'I saw him, yes,' she said.

In the same low whisper so that the elevator boy couldn't overhear, Tzu Hsun said, 'He was on the flight from Chungking.'

A flash of panic crossed Zephyrine Wan's face. 'Are you sure?'

In answer, Tzu Hsun reached out an arm and stopped the elevator on the first floor, stepped out into the hall and said in through the gate as he slid it shut behind him, 'Go right up. You know what to do.'

Returning downstairs by the service stairway, he reached the foyer to find it empty. Quickening his stride, he went outside and glanced both ways along the roadway. The man was on his way northward in the direction of the Shanghai Racecourse, newspaper folded in his hand, in no apparent hurry.

He was waiting patiently on the corner of Cathedral Road for the flow of traffic to ease when Tzu Hsun caught up with him. Stepping in behind him, he had the knife shielded in his right hand, but at the instant when he went to bring it up under the rib-cage, the man stepped out from the kerb.

Nonetheless he felt it go in, heard the man give a grunt of pain and surprise, and saw him half stagger to his knees with blood spouting from the wound. Then the man's natural reflex for survival appeared to overcome his shock and pain, and dropping the newspaper under the wheels of a passing truck, he changed direction and started across the Nanking Road in the face of swerving traffic, stumbling toward the darkness of the Racecourse.

Two minutes elapsed before Tzu Hsun was able to make his way across the roadway, and discarding the knife in favour of the pistol, he plunged into the shrubbery at the point where the man had disappeared. Immediately he began to beat around in the undergrowth, tried first in one direction, then in another, and eventually came up against the white rails marking the perimeter of the racecourse. Momentarily he was undecided about which direction to take, then started along the rails further into the park. He covered quarter of a mile and came on nothing more sinister than a couple making love under some bushes. When he saw it was going to be impossible to find his quarry in such conditions, unless he was lucky enough to blunder into him if he was hiding in any of the bushes he was beating his way through, he gave up and started back toward the Nanking Road.

Henry Wan knew the instant he unlocked the door, after hearing the three distinct raps, that it hadn't gone as expected. With his face the colour of a corpse, he said, 'What happened? Didn't you find him?'

Tzu Hsun pushed past into the room. 'He got away.'

Panic seized Henry Wan. 'Didn't you go after him?'

Tzu Hsun lifted a bottle of Scotch from the liquor cabinet, broke the seal, tipped a glass full, and swallowed most of it over in a single gulp. 'Of course I went after him. I got the knife in too, but he still got away. I lost him on the Racecourse.'

Hope lighted in Henry Wan's eyes. 'Was he hurt badly?'

'I'm sure of it. But he stepped off the kerb just when I put the knife in. Only I couldn't follow him across the road because of the traffic. When I did, he was gone.'

Zephyrine Wan spoke for the first time. In an uncertain voice, she said, 'Maybe we're reading too much into this. Couldn't it just be a coincidence that he happened to come here?'

Tzu Hsun flashed a sharp look at her. 'I *know* when I'm being followed.'

In a hollow voice, Henry Wan said, 'What Tzu says is true.' He sank into a nearby chair and ran a nervous hand across his forehead. 'Let's think about this.' He looked again at Tzu Hsun. 'Do you suppose he could have been a policeman – a Blueshirt?'

Tzu Hsun grimaced, shrugged his shoulders. 'It's difficult to say. He could have been anybody. Not all policemen look like policemen these days. But I can't say I ever saw him around Chungking. Not that it means anything. Chungking was swarming with cops.'

'What if we moved somewhere else?' Henry Wan was gradually beginning to regain control of his shaken emotions.

Tzu Hsun said emphatically, 'Changing hotels isn't the answer. If it's somebody who knows why we're in town then he'll also know that we intend to contact only one of two or three people. It would be a simple matter of elimination.'

'I feel inclined to go along with that.' Zephyrine Wan's face was as grave as her voice.

Henry Wan glanced at her, deep in thought. He had to agree; Tzu Hsun's experience in such matters was unquestionable, and had been proved so on more than one occasion. And it was for that specific reason that he had acquired Tzu's aid in the first place. What he said made sound sense. He said quietly, 'You're certain that there was just this one man alone?'

'He was alone.' Tzu Hsun remained as emphatic as previous. 'I remember him during the flight. He sat toward the rear of the aircraft, on the opposite side of the aisle to us. I made a note of everybody. And he was the only unattached person on board. But I didn't see anything at all suspicious about him, not until he entered the hotel here.'

Henry Wan frowned, pulled at the sagging flesh of his jaw. A feeling of nausea lay uncomfortably high in his chest. He said, 'Then what do you suggest?'

Tzu Hsun brought a package of cigarettes from his coat, and lit one. He drew on it deeply, then drained the Scotch remaining in his glass. 'Well it's still my opinion that we're safer here than anywhere else. Nobody running from the police is likely to take up residence in a place like this. Yes, I know. We're not running as yet, but we will be if we don't get out of here before Tuesday at the very latest. And this fellow, if he is a cop, can only be waiting to see what's going to transpire in the next couple of days. And if he isn't a cop, then he could be somebody who's heard rumours in Chungking. So either way it makes little difference. He has to be got out of the way, permanently. In which case I'll go back and check out that Racecourse again when it begins to get light. I can't believe he was able to get far. Afterward we can decide the next step we should take, depending on what I find.'

* * *

Captain Hop finished buttoning his uniform coat and glanced up to see the girl watching him from the rumpled bed. She was studying him with calm detachment over the mounds of her breasts, eyes heavy-lidded, as if she was trying to make up her mind about something she now saw in him for the first time. Her breasts jutted spectacularly, even lying on her back. He found difficulty in removing his eyes from them. Their nipples put him in mind of acorns. But now there was a crude and blatant suggestiveness in her posture that put him in mind of a sated cow. Her mouth was slack and sulky, her legs spread askew to expose the crevice between her sturdy dancer's thighs, the hair around it a tangle of damp curls. It was as if she was deliberately playing the part of a $5 whore and finding immense satisfaction in it, and from the resultant embarrassment it created in him. And this awkwardness and embarrassment he always felt afterward was something he had never been able to hide, and it made him feel at a disadvantage, vulnerable.

Taking two cigarettes from a jade-inlaid case, he lit them, thrusting one into her mouth. Unable to suppress his irritation, he said, 'Must you lie around like that? – like a bitch on heat?'

She turned her swollen face dramatically toward him and blew a stream of smoke ceilingward. With the movement, her honey-coloured hair glinted highlights on the pillow. 'But I'm always on heat, Captain.' Her lips reflected wetly the harsh light cast by the naked electric bulb in the ceiling. 'Didn't you know that?'

He stared down at her dispassionately and said without

inflexion, 'I'll remember to tell the porter on my way out.'

She moved her head around and looked him deliberately upward from the black polished riding-boots. 'I believe you, Captain.' Her voice was heavy with an accent which added its own allure to her exotic body and its tawny colouring of honey and cream.

Captain Hop made no effort to reply. Instead he devoted himself to his cigarette. He had first seen her dancing in Le Patronat across in the old International Settlement. She was billed as Princess Kopa, was twenty-two years old, and White Russian. There was no disputing the fact that she was White Russian, but he was sceptical about the *princess* part. According to what she told him, her grandfather was of Russian nobility and had fled to Manchuria to escape the aftermath of the Revolution when the Dark People had been running bloodthirsty through the streets of St Petersburg. Not that any of it mattered to him. All that had ever interested him were those twin mounds of luscious flesh and the urge to get his hands around them. And it hadn't been difficult.

She had commenced work on him in the taxicab crossing town, when she had hitched up her cheongsam so unashamedly that the driver had almost put the taxicab into the Soochow Creek. Then the moment they entered the room she had grabbed him with both hands and her mouth so that they had made love the first time in a frenzy on the floor with their clothes still on, with her biting and wailing as if she hadn't experienced a man inside her in months. Later they had undressed and gone to bed to repeat the performance at a more leisurely pace.

But now that he had satisfied himself he found the smell of sweat and love-making in the cheap room with its harsh yellow light and soiled bed-linen rank and distasteful to him. It was as if he had betrayed himself.

She watched him crush his cigarette into the ashtray by the bed, reaching out a hand to his arm. 'Was it worthwhile, Captain?'

Disengaging her hand, he avoided her searching gaze and retrieved his cap, gloves, and riding-crop from where they still lay on the floor amongst her scattered clothing. He flicked a speck of dust from his cap and adjusted it on his head, trying to control the impetuous urge of his limbs to get him out of that room and away. With effort he forced a smile. 'What do you think?'

She lay back, smiling at him over her spectacular breasts. 'And tonight?'

'We'll see.' Smiling thinly, he placed the tip of the riding-crop in her groin. 'Why don't you cover yourself up? Catch a running nose and it won't do business any good.'

Before she was able to decide whether or not this last remark was intended as a sexual rebuff, he had put the light out and gone out and closed the door. For a long moment she continued to stare at the closed door, then turned over on her side with a shrug to find the ashtray in the darkness. It didn't really matter one way or the other. It was all experience. She had never been taken to bed before by one of Chiang's dreaded Blueshirts, and she basked in the thrill of it.

4.00 a.m. was tolling in the late darkness when he left the Kwangtung Hotel on Fu Yam Terrace in the old Japanese quarter of Chapei. He walked quickly, as if his only desire now was to get as far away from the area as possible. In the cool air the heat rose off his body and he felt disgust with himself when he caught the musky scent of her sweat and sex. Worse, he could taste her mouth on his lips and feel the rubbery brush of her nipples on the palms of his hands. A prickle of sweat broke on his forehead and he quickened his pace. When he came to the footbridge across the Soochow Creek at the end of the Sze Chuen Road, he grasped the rail with both hands and gulped down several deep breaths of cool air, trying to quell the rising nausea in his throat.

After some minutes, when his nausea had receded, he pulled his cigarette case from a pocket of his uniform coat and lit a cigarette, relishing the harsh taste of the tobacco on the back of his throat. Each time it was the same, and produced the same nightmarish after-effects. The following days would be filled with torment and revulsion, until the event gradually faded from memory. To seek release from the tensions and frustrations of pursuing ambition in the flesh of a woman was a weakness that he was unable to forgive himself. Yet when breaking point was reached he became like the alcoholic searching in desperation for the nearest bar ready to debase himself for a drink in way of release from the inner self, and he despised himself for it bitterly.

His ambition was one of the most difficult for any man to realize; that of becoming rich. Had he been lucky enough to be born the son of a warlord, then it might have been so much easier, but instead he had been born the fifth son of a huakan man in Pihsien, the collection centre for the vast opium-growing area extending down through the foothills into Sikiang province. In 1932, at the age of fourteen, he had applied successfully for enlistment in the Kuomintang Army in a bid to escape following in his father's footsteps, and because of his zeal and unquestioning loyalty was rewarded with a transfer to the coveted ranks of the Kuomintang Secret Service in August 1939.

For a young man of his obscure background, it was a spectacular attainment, especially in view of the fact that the ranks of the KSS were composed mainly of the sons of influential men drawn from the elite Whangpoo Officers Club. And here too his fervour and devotion to duty didn't go unnoticed, and in May 1941 he was promoted Sergeant and moved to Kunming as Political Interrogator with offices in the main railway station. In July 1945 he was brought back to Chungking to serve for two years with the Political Division, and in September 1947 promoted Captain and transferred to Shanghai as Senior Officer in charge of the 3rd District.

At a time when widespread graft and corruption was at its peak throughout the country, he was pleasantly surprised to find that the 3rd District was the most sought after prefecture in the city for the rich pickings is offered. In the first months his share of 'squeeze' wasn't only the most he had so far earned, but also the easiest, and he set out to make up for lost time, aware that with the Communists sweeping down from the north it was a situation not destined to last indefinitely. Now, tonight, with the Communists massing on the northern perimeter of the city, he knew that its future could be counted in hours. But with a small fortune in money and jewellery already transferred to the vaults of the Yunnan Bank in distant Kunming, he was in the enviable position of being ready to leave the moment that the Communist artillery opened up on the city defences. Meanwhile there was still time to put those remaining hours to good use, and leaning on the rail of the footbridge with the city spread out before him, he felt his old determination begin to build again, like a wall built brick by brick. One day he would be as rich as any of those foreigners whose lavish buildings crowded the broad shoulder of the Shanghai Bund; he swore it.

When his taxicab arrived at the complex housing the Headquarters of the Kuomintang Secret Service and Shanghai Police Department on Drury Road in the old International Settlement, he went straight to his office on the third floor.

He was in the office only a few moments when his aide arrived with a sheaf of correspondence collected from the Orderly Office some minutes earlier. Surprised at finding his superior in the office at such an early hour of the morning, the slouch vanished from Sergeant Kee's shoulders instantly. Stiffly, he clicked his heels. 'Good morning, Captain.'

Captain Hop removed his gloves, placed them inside his upturned cap on the desk, but made no effort to return the greeting. Instead he glanced at the sheaf of correspondence in Sergeant Kee's hand. 'What's the latest news?'

Sergeant Kee made a pained grimace. 'I'm afraid it's getting worse by the hour, Captain. There are reports here of shooting around the Hankow Park and Hsiangying Road areas, while the People's Militia succeeded in setting alight to the Loyang Flour Mills.'

Captain Hop turned his back to the room. Outside the window towered the floodlit mass of buildings he had earlier stared at so intently from across the Soochow Creek. 'Yes,' he remarked without interest. 'They also burned down the Political Detention Quarters on the Sassoon Road. I saw the fires from Chapei.' He felt no sympathy for the Anglo-Chinese Corporation of faceless men, rich beyond most other men's dreams, who owned the Loyang Flour Mills and a dozen others, at one time spread throughout China. Like most other Western businessmen they had left Shanghai months earlier for the safety of Paris, London, New York, or Chicago. That was something else he had learned; the rich never took risks where their own well-being was at stake. They tended to succumb from over-indulgence, cirrhosis of the liver, or from heart seizure, in plush apartments or secluded estates.

Behind him he heard Sergeant Kee shuffle his feet uneasily. He turned away from the window. Despite himself, a fleeting image passed before his eyes, of Princess Kopa earlier lying on her back gazing approvingly at him through her spread open legs above her while she waited impatiently for him. 'Is something worrying you – eh, Kee?' he asked, his annoyance with himself for his moment's weakness showing in his words.

Sergeant Kee blanched visibly, stammered, 'No, sir. Not at all. I was just wondering if you had something special in mind for this morning.'

Captain Hop's annoyance with himself receded. He took a cigarette from his case and lit it unhurriedly, his handsome face as impassive as marble. He had to find something that would divert his thoughts from his encounter with the girl. Thoughtfully, he said. 'Perhaps we should get the car out and pay Lunghwa Airport a visit. What do you say to that, Kee? Some of those passenger lists ought to make interesting reading.'

Sergeant Kee responded enthusiastically with a smile of approval. 'Yes, Captain.' Only the previous afternoon they had taken the Dane Svend Bohr, owner of the Condor Club, one of the old International Settlement's few remaining plush bars with a rich Western clientele, off a flight for Manila and held him over on the pretext of questioning him on the movements of a regular customer known to be a Communist sympathizer. Although Bohr had known it was merely an act of harrassment, he had gladly parted with $1,300, the only US currency he was carrying, to be allowed to go on his way. 'I'll have Choy bring the car around front immediately,' he declared vigorously, and was reaching for the phone when interrupted by a knock at the door.

Captain Hop threw it an irritable glance. 'What is it?'

A dapper, balding figure clad in a wrinkled blue KSS uniform coat, entered the room hesitantly. Sergeant Pao was the Duty Orderly Sergeant of the night-shift, and he glanced self-consciously at Captain Hop's frosty countenance. He had always found the man's self-confidence and elegance disconcerting to the point of actually putting fear into him.

Captain Hop crushed out his cigarette in the base of a brass 75 millimetre artillery shell which served as an ashtray. 'What is it, Pao? I hope you haven't come to bother me with some ridiculous triviality at this hour of the morning.'

With a pained smile, Sergeant Pao held his ground in the face of the clearly implied threat. As Duty Orderly Sergeant any worthwhile snippets of news usually reached his ears first, and over the years he had accumulated a small fortune by selling them off to senior officers on the understanding that he was rewarded when any of his tit-bits reaped a dividend. 'I wouldn't like to think that anything I had to pass on was exactly trivial, sir.' He dropped a deliberate glance at the small brown linen bag in his hand which normally was used to contain a suspect's personal effects after his apprehension. 'As a matter of fact, I have something here that I'm sure will interest you.' Opening the neck of the bag, he tipped the contents on to the desk. Amongst the sprinkle of loose coins, a cheap leather wallet, a bulky manilla envelope, and a 9 millimetre Browning thudded on to the desk top.

Captain Hop was unimpressed. 'What is it – an arrest?'

Sergeant Pao's pained smile gathered in confidence. 'No, sir. This stuff belongs to a man one of our patrols brought in about an hour ago. They found him wandering around in a state of collapse beside the Racecourse. He claimed to be a KSS lieutenant.'

'And of what particular interest should that be to me?' Captain Hop's voice was acid.

Sergeant Pao looked at him shrewdly. He said tentatively, 'Maybe if you were to take a look inside the wallet, sir.'

Captain Hop's gaze bore an icy threat as he reached for the wallet and flipped it open. The celluloid pocket contained the official KSS red warrant card: LIEUTENANT HUANG CHAO-YUNG KUOMINTANG SECRET SERVICE 1ST DISTRICT CHUNGKING. Accompanying it was a photograph of a gaunt head with the number 31/887 printed underneath. The other two compartments yielded $47 in US currency, and the receipt for a radio bought from a shop in Chungking's Tin Lok Road.

Sergeant Pao moistened his lips, confident in the knowledge of his own secret. 'The envelope – try the envelope, sir.'

When he opened the envelope, Captain Hop evinced real interest for the first time. Inside was $1,000 in US currency, in crisp new $50 bills.

Sergeant Pao smiled at his success, face aglow. 'He was covered in blood when they brought him in. They said he mentioned the Great Eastern Mansions several times on the way here. It was all that made any sense to them.'

Captain Hop and Sergeant Kee exchanged sharp glances; the Great Eastern Mansions and money had long been synonymous, an oasis for the rich.

Sergeant Pao braced his shoulders, felt he hadn't only justified his intrusion, but had also found favour. 'He's in the infirmary if you want to take a look at him. I've just come from there. The doctor's busy on him right not.'

Captain Hop offered an opaque smile by way of apology for his earlier misjudgement. 'Good. But who else knows about this?'

Sergeant Pao answered eagerly, 'Only myself, sir. And the patrol, of course. But naturally they didn't go through his pockets. They know better than to try and pull something like that with me.'

Captain Hop nodded. 'And the doctor? What does he know about it?'

Sergeant Pao drew himself up another two inches, smiling. 'Just that he was brought in hurt. I don't believe in letting people like that know too much.'

'Of course, Pao.' Captain Hop gathered the envelope and wallet from the desk and returned them to the bag along with the Browning and loose coins, before locking it away in a drawer of the desk. 'Naturally we'll keep this to ourselves for the time being – eh, Pao?'

Sergeant Pao grinned conspiratorially. 'Whatever you say, sir.'

Captain Hop and Sergeant Kee went downstairs to the infirmary on the ground floor and were met by a young doctor wearing the light tan uniform of a 2nd Lieutenant of the Shanghai Police.

Captain Hop said brusquely, 'I'm informed you had a man brought in about an hour ago.'

'Yes, Captain,' the doctor affirmed politely. 'But I'm afraid he's in a bad way.'

Captain Hop's shoulders stiffened. 'So?'

The doctor saw the hopelessness of argument, shrugged, and turned down the hall.

The shaded light in the small, curtained side room cast a dim glow across the waxy face of a man who in the past few hours had aged considerably. Captain Hop and Sergeant Kee stared at the bed incuriously. The man's breathing was so shallow it was barely discernible. Captain Hop glanced in the doctor's direction. 'What was it?'

'A knife,' the doctor replied with professional detachment. 'In the back.'

'Will he live?'

The doctor shrugged. 'I shouldn't think for more than a few hours. There are serious internal complications.'

Captain Hop studied the young doctor intently. 'Has he said anything?'

'No, Captain. At least nothing that made any sense.'

'Can he be made to talk? Can you give him something?'

2nd Lieutenant Hsu glanced away from Captain Hop's intent gaze. In a short and so far undistinguished career with the Shanghai Police Department he had learned never to offer argument to anybody above his own rank, and certainly not to an officer of the KSS. Besides it didn't mean anything to him if the man died in peace or not. People were dying in the most atrocious circumstances these days and at least this one was in bed. He turned to open the doors of a nearby medicine cabinet.

Captain Hop looked on with indifference as 2nd Lieutenant Hsu brought a hypodermic and probed the unconscious man's arm. Then he made a dismissive gesture with the silver-tipped riding-crop. 'Thank you, doctor. That'll be all meantime.'

Something like eight minutes elapsed before Lieutenant Huang's eyes fluttered open.

Captain Hop leaned over the bed. 'Lieutenant Huang? Can you hear me, Lieutenant?'

Again the eyes fluttered and the mouth exposed a bloody tongue.

Captain Hop said directly into the waxy face, 'You're in the infirmary at KSS Headquarters in Shanghai, Lieutenant. Do you understand what I'm saying?'

The eyes strained to focus on the cold, handsome face above the bed. 'Yes – yes, I hear you.' The voice was little more than a faint whisper.

Captain Hop bent his face closer. 'Then my name's Hop – Captain Hop. If you want to tell me what you're doing here in Shanghai then I may be able to help in some way.'

'This morning – I arrived this morning – Flight 129 from

Chungking—' Lieutenant Huang's voice broke, and he licked at his bloodied lips.

Captain Hop gave an impatient snap of his fingers. 'Water!'

Sergeant Kee leapt to his superior's command, poured a glass full from a carafe, and saw it seized and touched to Lieutenant Huang's mouth.

'The knife. Who used the knife on you, Lieutenant?'

In a more audible whisper than previously, Lieutenant Huang said, 'Tzu Hsun caught me in the street. I hid in that park around the Racecourse until I saw one of your patrols go by.'

'Tell me about this Tzu Hsun. Who is he?'

Lieutenant Huang swallowed noisily, raising a hand to pluck weakly at Captain Hop's sleeve. 'I'm going to be all right?'

'You're going to be fine, but somewhat indisposed for a little while.'

His agitation intensifying, Lieutenant Huang struggled to raise his head from the pillow. 'You swear I'll get my share of whatever we get out of it if I tell you? And get me out of here with you before the Communists arrive?'

Captain Hop answered placatingly, 'Whatever you say. You have my word. My aides and I already have it arranged to leave Shanghai. Taking you with us would be no problem. But what's so important? What about this Tzu Hsun?'

With a weary sigh, Lieutenant Huang sank back on to the pillow. Several seconds passed before he regained the strength to speak again. 'Tzu is bodyguard to Henry Wan and his wife. I followed them from Chungking last night. They rented the Peking Suite in the Great Eastern Mansions.'

The shadow of profound thought darkened Captain Hop's forehead. *Henry Wan;* somehow the name had a familiar ring to it, jogged his memory. Then he remembered it again out of the years he had spent in Chungking. 'Is this the banker? Henry Wan the banker? The Wan Merchant Bank of Chungking?'

Lieutenant Huang gave affirmation of the fact with a weak movement of his head. 'I've been watching him since back in January when a man called David Kow came to see me, a director of the bank. I'd known him for some years. There had always been animosity between him and Wan on account of something that happened in the past, and he told me he believed Wan was planning to appropriate certain bank funds and smuggle them out to the West. He said he had discovered Wan had been converting certain securities and bonds into bullion on the blackmarket and that it was secreted in one of the vaults which Wan requisitioned for his own personal use.'

'And you reported this?' Captain Hop's eyes had assumed a strange glow.

Lieutenant Huang's answer was a frail smile. 'I had plans of my own. I set out to learn all I could about Wan. There was only his wife and Tzu to worry about – and Tzu was humping her stupid. It wasn't difficult to find that out.'

Captain Hop sent a glance at Sergeant Kee whose face had the look of a man who wanted desperately to believe what he was hearing, yet was afraid to trust his ears. He nodded to Lieutenant Huang. 'Listen,' he said assuredly. 'You can depend on us for any help that's needed, absolutely. And you're going to need help while you're laid up here in bed for the next few days.'

Lieutenant Huang's gaze probed the handsome face above him. 'Is that your promise?'

'I've already given you my word,' Captain Hop impressed. 'You can trust me.'

Lieutenant Huang sighed wearily, and in the same strained whisper said, 'All right, I'll tell you it all. I began to watch Wan around the clock from the very day David Kow called on me, snatching a few hours sleep only when I knew that he was unlikely to make any move. It didn't take me long to discover that what Kow suspected was true – that Wan was converting the bank's securities and bonds into bullion on the blackmarket with Tzu's help. But to enable me to go ahead with my own plans I told Kow that progress was slow and that I would need time to prove anything for certain.

'And all during that time I was waiting for Wan to show his hand in some way as to how he planned to get the bullion out of Chungking. Then on February 15th Wan and Tzu visited the bank during the early hours of the morning. Shortly afterward a man called Liang and his four sons arrived with a truck. Liang was a junkmaster who used to ship opium for the Kealo Secret Society, and as Tzu at one time carried a gun for them it wasn't difficult to see how they knew each other. Anyway, when the truck left the bank courtyard I followed it out to a derelict godown on the North Bank above Shuan Hao Pa. This time the Liangs were accompanied by Tzu, and when it finally pulled away from there – it was empty,' he concluded significantly.

Captain Hop smiled encouragement, leaned his eager face closer to the pillow. 'Go on,' he urged.

Lieutenant Huang struggled to find fresh reserves of strength. 'That day I hid in a nearby loft where a fanlight gave a view of the godown and the adjoining wharf. At one o'clock the following morning Liang's junk – the *Tungting Explorer* – arrived at the wharf, and along with Tzu, he and his four sons transferred a number of bullion cases to the junk. When through, they cast off and dropped downriver to take on a cargo of wool at the Circular Quay. Eventually they pulled out at a little after two o'clock that same afternoon – the afternoon of the 16th. When I checked on her I found she was slated for Kiangling.'

'But destined for Shanghai instead – is that it?' Captain Hop was barely able to contain his excitement.

'Yes, but something went wrong,' Lieutenant Huang continued. 'Since that afternoon I practically lived out at Ta Er Wo waiting for Wan to leave for Shanghai when word reached him of the bullion's safe arrival, but he didn't. Instead he became a worried man, as did Tzu. I had already formed the opinion that the Communists must have captured the junk, then last night, just after dusk, I saw the eldest Liang boy arrive out at the house. He was there for almost an hour, and when he left I stopped him on the road back to town. He had $1,000 on him. At first he wouldn't talk, but when I put my gun on him he changed his mind. He said he'd returned to tell Wan that they had run into a Communist crossing of the river below Chingkiang and had been forced to take refuge on the south shore—' suddenly he gagged and broke into a bubbling cough.

Captain Hop anxiously touched the glass to the parched mouth. '*And the junk?*' he urgently stressed. '*Where's the junk lying?*'

'Lang Dok – she's lying at Lang Dok. They buried the bullion on shore to hide it from the Communists when they found they couldn't get downriver.'

'How much bullion, Huang?' Captain Hop found it impossible to restrain his mounting excitement. *'How much?'*

'I'm not sure – but David Kow believed it had to be somewhere in excess of three million dollars in US currency.'

Captain Hop and Sergeant Kee exchanged incredulous glances. And suddenly the danger of loose tongues occurred to Captain Hop. 'What about the Liang boy?'

Lieutenant Huang gave a shallow sigh, his voice wavering. 'I clubbed him to death with a boulder and hid his body in a ditch.'

'Then what?'

'After I got rid of the boy I went back to Ta Er Wo and arrived just in time to follow the Wans and Tzu when they left. They drove into Chungking, abandoning their car in the parking lot of the Canton Hotel, then made their way along the North Bank to the Circular Quay where they took a sampan out to Shaun Hao Pa. It was obvious they were headed for the airport, and when I put a call through to it I was told there was a flight later in the evening to Shanghai. Then I called David Kow at home and asked him to meet me, that I had news for him. When he arrived I had him drive me out to Electric Hill where I shot him, then dumped his body in the river.' The height of the drug-induced talkativeness had passed and Lieutenant Huang's strength was beginning to ebb visibly. His face was bathed in a cold sweat and his breathing made a hoarse sound in his throat that made his words increasingly difficult to interpret. 'There wasn't much time left then and I just made it out to Shaun Hao Pa to board the aircraft a few seconds before the Wans.'

Captain Hop straightened slowly upright beside the bed, feeling easier in his mind knowing that David Kow was also dead. 'And now they're in Shanghai to try and arrange to get the bullion downriver,' he concluded to his own satisfaction.

Lieutenant Huang didn't answer. Suddenly finding the strength to raise himself up from the pillow, eyes staring into the light with failing vision, a shadow passed lightly across his face and with blood streaming from the corners of his mouth, he gave a small shiver and relaxed back into death without even a sigh.

On the other side of the small, curtained room, Sergeant Kee was staring at the bed with a dazed, disbelieving expression on his sallow face. It was the first time that he had ever heard anybody talk in terms of *millions* of dollars, and he couldn't bring himself to believe it was true. He was afraid even to think about it. After some minutes he sneaked a glance at Captain Hop who was staring at the dead face beneath the shaded light from a great distance, his handsome features frozen with the intensity of his thoughts. Eventually he expelled a long breath and turned away from the bed. Sergeant Kee followed him with his eyes, and in a hushed voice, as if afraid to chance breaking his superior's train of thought, said, 'Do you really think what he's just said is true, Captain? I mean about so much bullion?'

Captain Hop turned to look at him, like a man suddenly aware that he was in company. 'Why not?'

'But three million dollars!' Sergeant Kee's tone expressed persistent disbelief.

Captain Hop ventured a faint smile. '*I* believe him,' he said simply.

'But even so,' Sergeant Kee argued. 'How could anybody hope to collect such a cargo from a place like Lang Dok? It's forty miles from here, at least. The Communists are dug in all along that stretch of shore.'

'You think I don't know that?' Captain Hop was already beginning to see it all clearly, exceedingly clearly. 'You seem to forget that there's always somebody in Shanghai prepared to risk his life for the right inducement.'

A dawning look of comprehension spread across Sergeant Kee's face when he considered the remark. 'Sztykgold?'

Captain Hop was experiencing a lightness in his chest he had never experienced before. $3,000,000; he had been waiting all his life for just such an opportunity to present itself, and he didn't propose to pass it up. 'Sztykgold's the natural choice,' he stated confidently. 'So too is Harry Lord. He has the fastest craft left around the river. There's nobody else would be any good for such a job.' He had already decided what he was going to do, the very first step that had to be taken. Replacing his cap, he left the room and found the doctor in the hall outside. 'He's dead,' he tersely informed him. 'Now I want him dressed exactly as he was when he arrived. I also want all traces of medical treatment removed from the body. Understood?'

2nd Lieutenant Hsu didn't understand any of it, but there wasn't a doctor in Shanghai foolish enough to question the orders of the KSS. He answered with a servile nod, 'Just as you wish, Captain.'

Captain Hop said flatly, 'And five minutes, doctor. I want him ready in *five* minutes.'

Captain Hop's confidence was infectious, and as they started back upstairs to his third floor office, Sergeant Kee began to share his superior's enthusiasm. He knew from experience that there wasn't a single problem which Captain Hop's mind couldn't cope with adequately. He had an extremely adaptable mind, as well as being cunning, and it didn't work more brilliantly than when it was concerned with matters likely to lead to his own financial gain. When they reached the third floor hall, he said, 'What do you have in mind, Captain?'

Captain Hop didn't pause in his stride. 'We're going to get Huang back on to that Racecourse. It's just possible this fellow Tzu is going to take another look around that park with daylight.'

Sergeant Kee's face was a study of enlightenment when they entered the office to find Corporal Choy awaiting them. 'Is the car ready?' he asked as they came through the door.

Corporal Choy stood heavily to his feet, perplexed by so much enthusiasm and activity so early in the day. He said vacantly, 'Yes, the car's ready. Do you want me to bring it around front?'

Captain Hop said impatiently, 'No. Leave it in the garage. We'll be taking a passenger with us when we leave.' Without further explanation, he snatched the phone to his ear and rang the Orderly Room. 'Pao?' he said into it. 'Then listen. Find out what you can about a man called Henry Wan. He's a banker – the Wan Merchant Bank of Chungking. And, Pao, discreetly. Yes. Let me know the moment you have anything.' He rang off and unlocked the desk drawer, then emptied the brown linen bag on to the top of the desk. The manilla envelope containing the money Huang had obviously taken from the murdered Liang boy the previous evening in Chungking, he put away in the breast pocket of his uniform coat, then from the wallet he extracted the warrant card and the receipt from the radio shop and returned them to the bag along with the Browning. The $47 he left intact, and swept the wallet across the desk along with the sprinkle of loose coins toward Sergeant Kee. 'Put that back on the body. And make certain there are no other means of identification left anywhere about him.'

Corporal Choy looked on with a heavy frown darkening his hawked, North China face.

Captain Hop fixed him with a level stare. He considered Choy little more than an animal, a moron. Yet since having recruited him from Hu Tsungnan's 2nd Kuomintang Guards as his second aide and driver he had proven a useful acquisition. Of massive build and tremendous strength, he had once seen him break a man's back with a single blow of a fist. But women were his speciality. There was nothing he wouldn't do to a woman, or persuade a woman to do to him. But he had found there was always something peculiar to people of Choy's type; there were occasions when they were inclined to allow their mouths to run away with them. He said to him sternly, 'There's something I want you to hear and remember, Choy. For the next few days we're going to be working on a matter that's going to require the greatest degree of secrecy if we're going to gain from it, so I don't want you to go talking about it with anybody. Is that clear?'

Corporal Chou shifted his massive frame awkwardly under his superior's stern scrutiny and glowered sullenly at the desk top like a scolded child. 'Yes, Captain,' he grunted. 'I don't say anything to anybody.'

'Good. Now go along with Kee and give him a hand to get our passenger downstairs to the car – he has some difficulty walking. And remember, we don't have a great deal of time, it'll be getting light soon.'

Alone, Captain Hop sat for some minutes in silence, shaping his thoughts into order, deciding the necessary steps that would have to be taken, the manicured fingers of his right hand drumming on the desk top. Then the phone rang. 'Hop,' he said crisply.

'Sergeant Pao here, Captain,' the voice the other end of the line informed him. 'I've just been through the files of the Political Division. The only stuff they have on Wan is unclassified, nothing at all of any importance. He's entered as managing director of the Wan Merchant Bank of Chungking. Has a house at Ta Er Wo, and is married. His wife's own name is Zephyrine Yeh, sister of lawyer George Yeh, former member of the board of the Wan Merchant Bank of Chungking, but now deceased. There are no dependents on either husband or wife's side. If there's anything more on him other than that, Captain, then it isn't on record.'

'Thank you, Pao. That's all I wanted to know. But if in the next few days anything should come through from Chungking concerning this man, then let me know immediately.'

When Captain Hop returned the phone to its cradle, he paused only long enough to collect his cap, gloves, and riding-crop.

* * *

It was still dark when Harry Lord swung the *Jacaranda* around upriver past the hulk of the old Panamanian freighter *Cameroon Highlander* where she had gone aground and broken her back during typhoon VERA the previous September. Since entering the Whangpoo River from the Yangtze he had passed only an occasional river junk making way downriver in a fog that lay thick across the south shore. To northward he saw the misted lights of traffic occasionally arc and sweep on the bends of the Chungkung Road where it led down to Woosung, but to southward he could see nothing in the fog that carried the pungent smell of river debris and rotting vegetation.

Continuing upriver, he passed several ocean-going junks moored close to the shore awaiting daylight, their carbide lanterns hazed in the fog. The fog drifted from northward, heavy and wetting as drizzle, glinted on the *Jacaranda*'s superstructure and trickled down the side windows of the low, raked cockpit. The *Jacaranda* ran close to the shore and the low rumble of her twin Issotta Fraschini motors reverberated through her hull as she thrust her way upriver on quarter power against the current.

When he was up clear of the wreck buoys he watched the Tungkow waterfront ghost down the port side, passed the storage tanks of the Standard Vacuum Oil Company, then eased the throttles over when he came up on the twin orange beacons of the Luk Keong Godown Wharf in east Tienningshih. Glancing back into the stern-quarters, he saw the blurred faces beneath the tarpaulin stare out at him apprehensively. 'You better start making ready,' he told them.

Several faces turned to peer at the fog-wreathed shore, and one man half rose to his feet. 'Now, Captain, sir?' Mr Wall Street's voice was only just audible above the throttled back rumble of the motors.

'I'll tell you when,' Harry Lord told him, as he passed off the end of the wharf preparatory to bringing the bows around against the current.

When he came around in against the pilings he motioned at an iron ladder that rose sheer on the wharf. 'Okay,' He told them. 'Make it quick. Once you're clear of the wharf turn upriver on the front and you'll see the Tienningshih Ferry concourse right ahead. You'll get wherever you're going from there.'

Mr Wall Street hesitated as the others began to go over the port gunwale, took a step toward the bulky shadow in the cockpit. 'I'd like to thank you—'

Harry Lord turned a black scowl on him. 'You paid your money,' he told him. 'Now get the fuck off here.'

Hurriedly, Mr Wall Street clambered on to the ladder to lose himself in the orange-misted gloom, and Harry Lord, backing the *Jacaranda* out stern first, swung the bows around upriver. He wasn't worried about anybody seeing his cargo go ashore; it was just that he thought the less anybody *did* see, then the less it was likely to grieve them. And now he was rid of them he opened the throttles up so that the bows nosed upward and the stern thrust into the flat black water to raise up a fountaining wash to gleam phosphorescently astern.

Wiping the fog from his face with his sleeve, he pulled a cigarette from a crumpled package in the pocket of his old combat jacket and lit a match to it while he held the *Jacaranda* off the Tienningshih shore. Ahead to northward the lights of Greater Shanghai made a big glow in the sky, while further northward he saw patches of angry brilliance he knew were fires. As near as he could judge they lay somewhere beyond the shanty district of Yangtzepoo, somewhere in the vicinity of the Hankow Park and Hsiangying Road, and another one, a big one, over north of the old International Settlement, beyond Bubbling Well Road, maybe on the Soochow Creek. It was three days since he left for Chen-kou and things had been bad then, but now they appeared close to getting out of hand.

When he was above Tienningshih, on the Pootung shore, he saw the upper stretches of the river on the Hongkew Bund side were deserted, even the usually busy Ropewalk Wharves. Then his attention was caught by the mass of the Pootung Ferry *Morning Star* up ahead, slanted in toward the Pootung shore with her strings of fairy lights lending her the appearance of a floating bank block on the Shanghai Bund. Easing the throttles over and running the wheel to port, he turned in downriver of the *Morning Star*, in around the beacons out over the end of the Carfax Oil Depot dock, and crept in under the swivel reels with their wound fuelling hoses. Up on the dock the Fuelling Master was waiting, brought from his office by the sound of approaching motors, and after he threw him the bow and stern lines he went back to the cockpit and put the big Gibbs .505 back in its clips beneath the dashboard and locked the facia down.

Tan-chu had a dark frown on his face when Harry Lord climbed up on to the dock. 'What happened?' he asked, eyes darting over the *Jacaranda*'s shattered windshield and splintered hull.

'I ran into a little trouble off Chen-kou.' Harry Lord started across the dock to where the lighted window showed in the Fuelling Master's office, with Tan-chu at his side.

When they entered the office Tan-chu took a steaming pot of coffee from the charcoal brazier and poured two cups full. 'Things must now be very difficult on the river.'

Harry Lord took the cup and sat on to the edge of the desk. 'Three times over,' he remarked off-handedly.

Tan-chu sipped at his coffee. Although he had always been on the friendliest terms with Mad Harry Lord, he never cared to pursue any line of questioning, however innocent, and he was content to sit and sip at his coffee and let the other man do the talking, if he was going to, which was seldom the case if past experience was any measure. The man was something of a celebrity along the river, if celebrity was the right word. He knew about the cannon that was spoken about in whispers too, the monster gun he kept locked out of sight. There were a great many stories told about Mad Harry Lord, and he could believe them, all of them. He had known him almost three years, since his arrival in June 1946, and he frankly was prepared to believe anything anybody told about him. He had known a great many men who had made the Yangtze Run, but Mad Harry Lord had made it his own.

Harry Lord glowered over his cup. 'How much do I owe you?'

Tan-chu rose out of the rattan chair and reached a ledger

down off a shelf. 'Three hundred and ten dollars.' Somehow it sounded almost like an apology.

Harry Lord brought a wad of US currency from a pocket of his combat jacket and counted off $310, then put another $40 on the desk which he paid Tan-chu once a month for keeping an eye on the *Jacaranda* when she was in dock.

While Tan-chu pocketed the $40 and locked the rest into the safe, Harry Lord gulped at his coffee, his face dark, brooding, and unshaven. 'Any idea what those fires were I saw coming upriver?'

Tan-chu shrugged. 'I don't know. They are all in the north. But the Communists have bombed in daylight the last two days. Yesterday morning it was Yangtzepoo, then Woosung just before nightfall.'

Harry Lord stared out of the window across the dock at the lights of Greater Shanghai, his dark face thoughtful, a crumpled cigarette dangling from a corner of his mouth. 'Do you suppose they're finally going to launch that offensive we've been hearing so much about?'

Tan-chu said quietly, 'If they are – then I don't intend to be sitting around here when it starts.'

'Oh,' Harry Lord said. 'What do you have in mind?'

Tan-chu dropped his eyes to his cup. 'I have plans, Mr Lord.'

Harry Lord rubbed a hand across his stubbled jaw. 'I guess it's about time I started to make some myself.' Setting his cup on the desk, he stood to his feet. 'If you give me a hand to refuel I'll check her over in case I've got to move out in a hurry.'

Tan-chu said, 'Do you want I get breakfast from the Kweilin Restaurant?'

'Thanks, but I'll eat when I'm through, before I head across town.'

* * *

Henry Wan alternately paced the deep carpet of the big room and drank brandy while his wife sat in a corner of the huge upholstered sofa which occupied almost one complete wall. Since Tzu Hsun left to take another look around the Racecourse they had exchanged words only occasionally, for reasons more out of a sense of mutual nervousness than anything else, but pointedly avoiding any reference to the reason for their presence in Shanghai, or to the mysterious passenger who had accompanied them on the flight from Chungking.

After a time Zephyrine Wan commented absently, 'It hasn't changed much.'

Henry Wan stopped pacing and looked at her, his face vacant.

'Shanghai,' she explained. 'What I've seen of it.'

Henry Wan resumed his measured pacing. He didn't see any reason to reply to such an inane statement. He couldn't have cared less how much Shanghai had changed, or hadn't changed, or if it would indeed change any in the foreseeable future. Shanghai was the least of *his* problems.

Zephyrine Wan dropped her gaze to her long slim hands. An exceptionally beautiful woman, she was tall for a Chinese, several inches taller than both her husband and Tzu Hsun, a physical asset that at times alluded to a feeling of superiority and dominance, although it had always been of a more sexual nature than a psychological one. Her figure was also striking, her limbs long and shapely. Although her breasts were somewhat large, they were full and firm, and the elegance with which she carried herself drew any undue attention from them. But her face was the most arresting feature about her, its delicate bone structure and flawless white flesh having the appearance of the finest and most fragile porcelain, a stark contrast to her thick black hair and dark eyes. She knew how to make the best of her looks too, and her hair was combed high and shone like polished black jade. She still wore the neat black Paris suit and court shoes she had dressed herself in the previous evening, one of the two suits and three dresses she had brought with her.

While Henry Wan continued his restless prowling, she tried to interest herself in the decor of the room in a bid to take her mind from the awkward and fractious air that had come to exist between them. There were curlicues on the ceiling and around the chandelier where it was attached to the ceiling. The walls were coloured a rich cerise and decorated with silk prints in gilt frames, and numerous mirrors also in gilt frames. The liquor cabinet her husband had ordered to be sent up was also gilded. There were brocade cushions on the huge blue velvet upholstered sofa, and the deep cerise carpet was scattered with white fur rugs. But she found she couldn't interest herself in the decor; the gilt and cerise was too overpowering. Also, she was too pent up with the complexity of emotion she had experienced during the past few hours even to be able to interest herself in her own thoughts; and she knew that only sex would bring her any relief.

Finally she rose without looking at her husband and said, 'I think I'll go and bathe.'

Henry Wan stared at the glass in his hand, swilled the amber liquid around its sides, and swallowed it over while he listened to her leave the room to put the light on in the main bedroom. He waited a minute then sent a sly glance across the room. Through the partly open bedroom door he saw a glimpse of white flesh and the cheek of one breast as his wife undressed. His haggard face showed a strange, amused cynicism while he stood watching her, and then it was gone, and he was again the inscrutable grey spectre.

Very deliberately he poured himself another drink, and very deliberately avoiding the bedroom door, he carried it out on to the balcony. The morning air carried a chill, still damp with falling dew. He leaned on the parapet, inhaling deeply, welcoming the coolness. Below him the Nanking Road was a chasm of garish light. He sipped at his drink and stared brooding down at the miniature figures moving on the pavements and the streams of traffic moving in opposite directions either side of the roadway. Then he lifted his gaze out across the darkness of the Racecourse, the mass of trees a black inked shadow against the glow of light beyond. Somewhere out there, he prayed, was the body of a man who might have threatened him with total personal disaster.

It was incredible now even to consider remotely the possibility that ill-fortune could overtake him. It wasn't as if he hadn't taken every precaution. He had always been a careful man, attentive to details. It stemmed from childhood and his early working life, when he had worked for various brokers in Mukden and Tientsin, until at twenty-three he found a post with the Harbin branch of the Banque Russo-Asiatique. Motivated by a need for power and recognition he always felt was destined for him, he had lived and ate frugally, disdaining social interests, investing every cent he was able to lay hands on. In 1929, at the age of thirty-four, his employers had paid tribute to his ability and dedication by offering him an agency for the bank of Chungking, and a year later he had taken the opportunity to form a company of his own called the Wan Finance and Development Company; the first step in an ambitious programme to achieving his ultimate goal of self-independence.

However, it wasn't until 1932 that good fortune again took a hand in subscribing to his eventual destiny, when a company calling itself Chungking Holdings, the controlling company of the Loong Merchant Bank of Chungking, was faced with a financial crisis. On investigation he discovered Chungking Holdings to be a sister company of the Chungking-Shanghai Investment Trust, located in Shanghai. Three days later he was in Shanghai where he obtained an appointment with its board of directors, who after listening to his proposition, agreed to part with Chungking Holdings if he would assume liability for a £53,000 debt it had previously incurred. Delighted with the deal, he in turn, through his connection with the Banque Russo-Asiatique, received from it £53,000 in credit. Then both his companies, Wan Finance and Development Company, and Chungking Holdings, applied to other banks for loans, which in turn enabled him to buy large amounts of stock belonging to the Loong Merchant Bank of Chungking on the open market. A month later, he was managing director of the bank, an ambition realized at a total cost in cash of £1,000, the money subscribed when he had formed his new investment.

Not fully satisfied with his achievement, he had then set to work in an effort to make the bank wholly his own personal possession. First he discovered that every one of his fellow directors held loans granted against the collateral of their stock in the bank. He checked them out, dwelling over the certificates like a lascivious old man dwelling over the robust body of a young woman. From there on the rest was child's play. Six weeks from the date of his discovery, the Loong Merchant Bank of Chungking's shares fell abruptly on the stock exchange of China and Hong Kong, so that as the bank's collateral officer he was duly forced to inform his associates that as the shares were worth less than the value of their loans, then more security was required to insure the loans or the bank would be forced to sell their certificates.

His fellow directors treated the matter if not with merriment, certainly with an unhealthy degree of blithesome disregard; all except David Kow, who out of a sense of impending disaster, immediately set about raising the necessary security to insure his loan. Quietly confident, Henry Wan, a week prior to the day when it became legally right to sell the stock in question, kept an appointment with a young broker acquaintance, a man called Charles Yeh who a year earlier had moved from Harbin to open his own business in Chungking. Over dinner Charles Yeh had given him the necessary commitment to sell to him personally the exact amount of shares of stock as the directors possessed, and a week later, while his former associates looked on in astonishment and disbelief, he had sat down to compose a new board of directors, among whom was Charles Yeh, and the vigilant David Kow.

Now, it was this same old confidence and ingenuity he knew he had to draw on if he was to win through, along with a measure of good luck. But good luck had always been an integral part of his existence, had always been on his side ever since childhood. It was this same good luck that had been instrumental in bringing him into contact with Tzu Hsun, without whose help and underworld contacts he would never have succeeded in accruing the fortune in bullion which had been smuggled south with the aid of the *Tungting Explorer*. And now Tzu Hsun was out somewhere on the Racecourse looking for the body of a man who had threatened their possible destruction, and he would also have to be carefully watched, for nobody knew better than Henry Wan just how dangerous were the vices of ambition and greed. And standing on this balcony alone waiting for a dawn that would be the most crucial in his life, the thought brought the pallor of a smile to his grey lips, the same indecipherable smile with which he had watched his wife undress.

* * *

Between them Sergeant Kee and Corporal Choy carried Lieutenant Huang's body into the park around the Racecourse and laid it down beneath some shrubbery. The park was fresh and green in the half-light of false dawn, the foliage wet with overnight dew.

When through they arranged themselves in a wing of the grandstand, a vantage point which overlooked the entire scene. A thin mist hung across the deserted stretch of shaved turf that was the actual racecourse, and the quiet was disturbed only by the muted sound of traffic passing on the Nanking Road.

They had been in the grandstand little more than ten minutes when Sergeant Kee caught a glimpse of a figure pass between some trees. 'Here comes somebody now.'

While they watched, the man emerged from a screen of shrubbery, paused in his tracks, and looked carefully about him.

Captain Hop nodded as the figure moved on again through the undergrowth. 'This looks like our man all right.'

They watched him cross a path and resume his search on the other side, eyes combing the undergrowth.

In a hoarse whisper, Corporal Choy said, 'He's getting close to it.'

Some yards farther on the man stopped abruptly in his tracks as he came suddenly on Lieutenant Huang's sprawled body. Giving a furtive glance about him, he bent down and turned the body over on to its back. Next he went through the pockets of the suit, found the wallet, ran his hands lightly over the limbs, then glancing about him again, started hurriedly back in the direction of the Nanking Road.

Captain Hop watched until he lost sight of the man among the trees, a thin smile on his handsome face. 'So that was Mr Tzu,' he remarked.

Sergeant Kee glanced at him questioningly. 'And now, Captain?'

'Now we're in business,' Captain Hop stated categorically.

Corporal Choy motioned at Lieutenant Huang's sprawled body. 'What about him?' he asked.

'Get him back into the car,' Captain Hop instructed. 'We can dump him in the river off the Yangtzepoo front.'

* * *

The three raps came at the door at a few minutes after 6.00 a.m. The instant Henry Wan saw Tzu Hsun's face he knew that he had met with success.

Tzu Hsun entered the suite grinning. 'I knew I had him good,' he announced.

The strain and anxiety flooded out of Henry Wan's face. 'I don't mind admitting I was worried.'

Zephyrine Wan, disturbed by the commotion, emerged from the main bedroom wrapped in a large blue bathtowel. She glanced questioningly from her husband to Tzu Hsun. 'What happened?'

Henry Wan glanced at her brightly. 'There's nothing to worry about. Tzu found him.'

She started toward them, an eager smile on her face. 'Tell me about it.'

Tzu Hsun said with pride, 'He never made it out of the park. He was lying beneath some shrubbery. I must've been close to falling over him last night.'

'Dead?' Zephyrine Wan felt she required confirmation of the fact in the actual word itself being uttered.

Tzu Hsun said, 'What do you think?'

With time to think, Henry Wan's mind was already alive to the more critical aspects of the matter. 'Was there anything to identify him?'

Tzu Hsun flipped the wallet across the room. 'There's forty-seven dollars in there. Apart from that there was only some loose change in his pockets.'

Henry Wan was suspicious. Frowning, he said, 'Nothing else?'

'Nothing else,' Tzu Hsun confirmed.

Henry Wan turned the wallet slowly over in his hand, then passed it back to Tzu Hsun. 'You better get rid of it.'

Zephyrine Wan stood watching the two men, a frown puckering her brow. 'Then his coming here the way he did was just a coincidence after all.'

In the circumstances Tzu Hsun now felt inclined to the same opinion. 'I was certain that he followed us – but well – close up he didn't look anything at all. And I certainly never saw him anywhere around Chungking.'

A shadow of uncertainty still clouded Zephyrine Wan's face. 'And what do you think?' she asked.

Tzu Hsun shrugged. 'I don't know. It doesn't really explain anything.'

'Only that he's dead,' Henry Wan observed.

'Yes,' Tzu Hsun agreed. 'Only that he's dead. And there's no more permanent a solution than *that*, whoever he was.'

In his silence Henry Wan's haggard face was inscrutable; the grey spectre. Then he reached a decision. 'I think we better get down to business and get out of here.' Draining his brandy glass, he walked to the phone and gave a number to the operator on the hotel switchboard. Seconds later he heard the ringing of a phone in an apartment on the Avenue Lafayette across town in the old French Concession.

A male Chinese voice answered briefly, 'Yes?'

Henry Wan felt the tension rise up in him again, aware that if his call failed, then his whole future was in serious jeopardy. 'Mr Heinrich Sztykgold?'

'What do you want?' The voice gave nothing away.

Henry Wan said, 'I'd like to talk to him. It's a matter of some urgency.'

'Does he know you?' the voice queried suspiciously.

Henry Wan began to sweat. At his back Tzu Hsun glanced at Zephyrine Wan's intensely set face as she drew the bath-towel more tightly around her so that the bumps of her nipples showed hard against the soft material they pressed against. Meanwhile Henry Wan was saying patiently, trying to hold anxiety and impatience in check, 'If you would kindly tell him that it's business – important business – I'm sure that he will want to talk with me.'

The voice hesitated, then said curtly, 'I'll speak to him.'

Henry Wan expelled a pent-up sigh of relief when he heard the receiver being laid down, and a brief period later heard it being picked up again.

'Who is this?' The voice carried a marked trace of annoyance, as if its owner had something more important to do with his time than answer the phone.

In an apologetic tone, Henry Wan said quickly, 'I'm sorry to disturb you so early in the morning, Mr Sztykgold. But I have some important business I would like to discuss with you – a matter I believe only you can help me with.'

The voice said, 'Who gave you my number? It isn't in any directory.'

'A former business acquaintance gave it to me. Marcel Julot. I spoke with him recently from Chungking.'

The voice reflected with some surprise, 'Yes – I know Julot. And your name?'

'Henry Wan.'

'I don't know you.' The voice appeared to lose any former interest.

Henry Wan felt his heart beat against his chest. 'No, Mr Sztykgold. Not yet.'

'Then what do you want?'

'I'd rather not go into details on the phone. I'm sure you understand the position. But if you care to talk to Julot I instructed him to answer any questions you may wish to ask concerning me. I'm certain you will find it to your financial advantage – even a man like yourself, Mr Sztykgold – if we can arrange a meeting.'

A discernible change occurred on the other end of the line. 'Where can you be reached?'

Henry Wan glanced across his shoulder with a triumphant smile at his wife and Tzu Hsun. 'The Great Eastern Mansions. Perhaps if you'd care to accept an invitation to breakfast we can go into the matter in more detail then – if Julot answers any questions to your satisfaction,' he quietly concluded.

The man on the other end of the line took a long moment to answer, then in a restrained tone which gave no promise of anything, said, 'I see. Very well. I'll think about it.' And hung up.

* * *

Heinrich Sztykgold replaced the receiver in his apartment on the Avenue Lafayette and stared at it reflectively. He had been disturbed while shaving and his long grey face still bore traces of lather. 'Marcel Julot,' he murmured. It was some time since he had heard of Julot, and at least three, if not four months since he had seen him. Marcel Julot had been a reasonably prosperous buyer for a time after the War, when the woollen business had been getting back on to its true commercial basis. However, the last two years had seen a decline set in owing to increasing Communist involvement and interference, and Julot was now in his sixties and his time as a leading European representative had quickly run out. But no matter how he tried, he couldn't imagine a man like him to be involved in a matter of intrigue. Nonetheless his curiosity was aroused.

Opening a telephone directory on to the table, he riffled the pages over until he arrived at the letter J. He ran his finger down the page and found both the name and address. Tossing the directory aside, he started back through the apartment to the bathroom. On the way he called out, 'Sato – get in here!'

He was patting cologne on to his shaved face when Sato Tadatoshi put his head around the door. 'Tell Yasugi to get ready. Then see to the car. We're going out.'

Ten minutes later, dressed in a dark grey suit, cream silk shirt, red silk knitted necktie, and gleaming black shoes, Heinrich Sztykgold presented himself to the outside world with the assurance of a man in business who couldn't, and never had, made a wrong step. He went down in the elevator with Nakamura and found Tadatoshi waiting on the newly hosed pavement with the Mercedes parked outside the entrance, its black bodywork glinting in the early sunlight. So equally well dressed were the two Japanese bodyguards they might have passed for business associates of their employer if it hadn't been for their bulk and hard-eyed faces.

'The rue Condé,' Sztykgold instructed.

Sato Tadatoshi obediently swung the limousine crisply around on the wide roadway and headed north on the avenue. He drove two blocks until he came to the rue Castiglione, turned on to it, and headed west toward the Old Chinese City in Nantao. Eight minutes later he was driving along the rue Condé with its dirty plaster frontages and shabby cafés.

'Here.' Sztykgold indicated a café-*tabac* sandwiched between a pawnshop and a hand-wash laundry.

Tadatoshi pulled the limousine into the kerb and got out to open the door for Sztykgold. The street had the sad air of wilful neglect and decay, and even the few trees imprisoned within the railinged park appeared disillusioned with their environment.

Sztykgold started across the pavement with both men closely accompanying him one on either side, their footfalls carrying through the building when they climbed the stairs. On the second floor Sztykgold stopped and peered in the gloom at a slip of cardboard pasted to a door. His knock echoed through the building like a drum-beat. 'Julot,' he said against the door.

Several minutes elapsed before the door was edged open by a man clad in wrinkled green pyjamas. His red-flecked eyes registered only the merest hint of surprise when he saw who his visitors were.

Sztykgold smiled. 'You remember me then, Marcel?'

Marcel Julot nodded. 'Who could forget you, Heinrich?'

Smoothing the shock of white hair back from his forehead, he opened the door further and stood aside. 'Come in – as long as you don't mind the disarray.'

Sztykgold entered the room with the bodyguards at his back. It was a one-bed apartment, cluttered with soiled clothing and empty bottles. 'You look as if you've had a rough night, Marcel.'

Marcel Julot gave him a long sad look of regret. 'And I'm afraid they're getting to be further and further between.'

Studying the veined face, Sztykgold changed the subject. 'You didn't seem surprised to see me.'

Marcel Julot sank down on the rumpled bed with a tired shrug. 'A man of my years isn't easily surprised, Heinrich.'

Sztykgold stared back at him impassively. 'Then you know why I'm here?'

'I had a call from Chungking last evening, if that's what you mean.'

'Then you're a friend of this fellow Wan?'

'Not exactly a friend – more of an acquaintance through business.'

'And what did he have to say?'

Marcel Julot said simply, 'That I was to tell you anything you wanted to know.'

'And what can you tell me that's so interesting?'

Marcel Julot stared up at Sztykgold's long grey face. He was still the same Old Heinie Sztykgold, aloof and condescending, as supremely egotistical as ever, and even now, in these last hours, eager to grab the opportunity to make an easy dollar out of somebody else's misfortune. But then Sztykgold had always enjoyed more than his fair share of luck. While interned in the Ward Road Gaol by the Japanese occupation troops, he had watched Sztykgold, through the good fortune of his nationality, make a meteoric rise in Shanghai's business world. But then certain people seemed born to succeed, while others were born to meet with abysmal failure whatever their efforts and intentions. 'Obviously you don't know Henry Wan,' he observed.

Sztykgold answered flippantly, 'I've never heard of him – at least not until he called me this morning.'

Marcel Julot smiled. 'Then perhaps the Wan Merchant Bank of Chungking rings a bell?'

Sztykgold's grey face expressed instant approval. 'The same?'

With a trembling hand, Marcel reached out and tipped the dregs from a vermouth bottle into a glass and gulped them down. 'I thought that might do the trick.'

Sztykgold remained waiting.

'There's not a great deal to tell,' Marcel Julot continued at length. 'He called last evening to say he remembered certain stories I'd told over dinner in the old days. He wanted to know if you were still around. Apparently he's under the impression that you may be able to help him in some way.'

'In what way?'

'I don't know. He didn't say.'

Sztykgold glanced at his two stolid-faced companions. 'How well do you know him?'

'Well enough to know he wouldn't waste your time. For my help in the matter he said there would be a thousand dollars deposited in the French Indo-China Bank in my name this afternoon.'

'In that case I assume there's a great deal more money involved than a mere thousand dollars,' mused Sztykgold. 'What do you say?'

'I wouldn't know, Heinrich.' Marcel Julot's smile was humourless. 'But he's a banker – he doesn't deal in water-buffalo.'

Sztykgold decided he had heard enough. He made a motion to his two companions that he was ready to leave.

Marcel Julot stood wearily up from the bed. 'Oh, Heinrich. Give Henry my regards when you see him, and tell him I plan to utilize that thousand dollars by acquiring a plane ticket to Hong Kong. Who knows but that the wool business may be in better shape there than here.'

When they returned downstairs to the street, Sztykgold settled himself in the rear of the limousine along with Nakamura and to Tadatoshi said, 'Make our next stop the Nanking Road.'

* * *

Zephyrine Wan stood by the open doors to the balcony and watched the sun rise through the mists of Kiangsu province, out beyond Woosung and Tsungming Tao where they lay hazed on the Yangtze. Then, still wrapped in the bathtowel that trailed around her bare feet, she turned and walked back across the room, glancing at her husband where he stood beside the liquor cabinet alone with his thoughts. She found it difficult to believe that a mere few months could have taken such a devastating toll of him physically; his haggard face with its sallow skin hanging loose in folds around his chin was that of an incredibly old and worried man. Even his hair had become thin and lifeless. She watched him lift his drink to his mouth and saw his hand shake, and a feeling of revulsion rose in her.

She looked away, and saw Tzu Hsun walk to the sofa and seat himself, lighting a cigarette. And as she did so, the old and familiar charge of nervous energy rushed through her, leaving her body quivering in every muscle and sinew. Between her thighs the flesh literally tingled. Then suddenly she was aware that her husband was watching her, his old man's face inscrutable. For an instant she was afraid he had been able to read her thoughts. She smiled quickly, and walked across to join him beside the liquor cabinet. She put a splash of tonic water into a glass and sipped at it. 'Do you really think this man Sztykgold will check with Julot?' The question was instigated purely by guilt.

Henry Wan stirred himself from his thoughts. Above the dark pouches on his face his eyes moved listlessly. 'We ought to know soon enough, one way or the other.'

From the other side of the room, Tzu Hsun interjected, 'And if he doesn't, we can always call on him. I've found it's sometimes an advantage to confront a man personally.'

Henry Wan drained his brandy glass. 'Julot will interest him,' he confidently predicted. 'There's time enough to get worried.'

Zephyrine Wan glanced at him sharply. 'But isn't time what we have least of?' she queried archly.

Henry Wan smiled deprecatingly. 'Are you telling *me* that, my dear?' There was no rebuke in his voice, just the hollow echo of an old man's disappointment.

'One thing I don't think we ought to do,' Tzu Hsun put in, 'is to mention anything about our late friend on the flight from Chungking. We don't want to frighten him away.'

'Yes, I agree,' Henry Wan said quietly. Then setting his glass down, he glanced at his watch. 'I'm going to shave and change.'

Zephyrine Wan watched him cross the room and close the door of the main bedroom behind him without a backward glance, aware that her limbs had begun to tremble in anticipation of being left alone with Tzu Hsun. When the door remained closed, she turned quickly across the room, the flesh of her thighs touching against itself electrically, her face fevered by an intense penetrating expression which grew out of her eyes. She met Tzu Hsun as he rose out of the sofa, threw her arms around him and searched for his mouth hungrily with her own, her body straining against his.

'No!' he hissed sharply into her face, trying to disengage himself from her. 'This is insane!'

'He's a fool!' she whispered urgently. 'He doesn't suspect anything!' Seizing his hand, she drew it up between her thighs and imprisoned it firmly. 'For a moment – just a moment!' she pleaded, pushing her lower body against his imprisoned hand while she grabbed at his crotch, feeling the roll of muscle begin to uncoil under the persistent kneading of her fingers.

He withdrew his hand roughly and grabbed her by the shoulders, held her firmly away from him. 'Stop this idiocy!' he whispered harshly into her thrown back face. 'We can't afford to take chances like this!'

She flared up angrily. 'Then kill him – *now*!'

He shook her roughly by the shoulders. 'Don't be a fool! Just as we couldn't leave him behind in Chungking, we can't afford to get rid of him here either until we know what's going to happen with Sztykgold. Listen to reason. I know what I'm doing.'

Zephyrine Wan stared at him, and her anger subsided. 'All right, but before we leave Shanghai. I can't go on like this.'

'Yes, but leave it to me. We need him to carry through the necessary arrangements. See it my way. It can only take another day or two at most. Now go and get dressed. We don't want him to start suspecting anything at this stage.'

For an instant Zephyrine Wan appeared prepared to argue, then started reluctantly across the room. When she entered the main bedroom she found her husband seated at the dressing-table, freshly shaved, adjusting his necktie in the mirror. 'I stayed on the balcony to watch the morning come in,' she commented. 'One can get such a superb view of the city from out there.'

Henry Wan studied her reflection in the mirror, noted the

flush on her face and the sparkle in her eyes. In an even, perfectly controlled voice, he said, 'Hadn't you better start thinking about getting dressed? There's no telling when this man Sztykgold may decide to put in an appearance.'

* * *

With the roads still relatively quiet the ride across town was accomplished with the minimum of delay, so that it was still a few minutes short of 7.30 a.m. when they arrived on the Nanking Road. Parking the limousine on Silversmith Street, they walked back toward the Great Eastern Mansions where Heinrich Sztykgold inquired at reception for Henry Wan, Two minutes later they were at the door of the Peking Suite on the hotel's eighth floor.

Tzu Hsun answered the door to find himself confronted by Tadatoshi's impassive face. Behind him stood Nakamura, their combined bulk effectively shielding the gaunt figure of Sztykgold.

Tadatoshi said curtly, 'Mr Sztykgold to see Mr Wan.'

Tzu Hsun saw Henry Wan incline his head, and opened the door wide.

The two muscular Japanese were first to enter the suite, their professional gaze instantly registering its contents. Satisfied it was inhabited only by Henry Wan and a woman obviously his wife, they stood aside to reveal Sztykgold close behind them.

Pleasantly surprised to find himself looking at a distinguished and elegantly attired man who looked more like a financier than the most notorious manipulator the Shanghai underworld had ever known, Henry Wan stepped forward to meet him, trying to conceal his anxiety that everything should meet with Sztykgold's approval. 'I'm delighted to see you managed to accept my invitation, Mr Sztykgold.'

Sztykgold studied Henry Wan speculatively before accepting his proffered hand. 'Nothing ventured, nothing gained, I believe the saying has it.'

A quick, nervous smile flitted across Henry Wan's face. 'Quite.' He glanced across the room. 'This is my wife – Zephyrine,' he explained.

Sztykgold gave a polite inclination of his head, immediately aware that she was a woman who possessed more than just ordinary good looks. 'Delighted,' he intoned.

Although the unexpected presence of the two Japanese bodyguards had taken them unprepared, Zephyrine Wan recovered her composure under Sztykgold's somewhat frank appraisal, and smiled at him, putting all her considerable charm into it. 'I'm sorry if we should have inconvenienced you so early in the morning, Mr Sztykgold.'

Sztykgold answered with a dismissive gesture of his hand, smiling. 'Please don't concern yourself about it unduly,' he informed her politely. 'Besides, this is the first time I've been beyond the dining-room and bar of the Great Eastern Mansions.' He paused, glanced around the room with unmistakable distaste. 'Now I'm not sure that I missed anything by it. It is rather ostentatious – don't you think?'

Zephyrine Wan's smile was equally charming. 'Yes, my thoughts entirely, Mr Sztykgold.'

Sztykgold thought he had never seen a woman's eyes sparkle with such vitality. Nor was she muffled in any of the usual shapeless gowns favoured by upper class Chinese women, but instead wore a simple smoke-grey cheongsam which complemented a figure of which she was obviously proud.

Henry Wan stood silently on the other side of the room, uncertain of how to broach the subject of business. Ordinarily it would have been no problem, but now the moment had arrived he felt enervated by the very nature of it. When the conversation faltered he said self-consciously, 'A table for three has already been set on the balcony but now that you've brought friends—' he concluded awkwardly.

'It's of no importance,' Sztykgold commented absently. 'They can remain here with your man.'

Embarrassed, Henry Wan said, 'Forgive me – I forgot to make the introduction. His name's Tzu Hsun.'

Sztykgold didn't even bother to glance in Tzu Hsun's direction; with two capable bodyguards of his own it was obvious that he considered the former Kealo gunman of no significant consequence.

Meanwhile Zephyrine Wan went to the phone and rang down the dining-room. When she replaced the receiver, she smiled at Sztykgold. 'Breakfast will be here in a few minutes. Shall we go outside?'

The table was laid with the hotel's monogrammed white linen and silverware, while a dark green awning fringed with white cast a pleasant shade over the balcony. The air had warmed with the sun, although it still retained the fresh smell of the early morning. The city to southward was spread out below them and the trees were very green and the river sparkled in the sunlight. Nobody made further conversation until breakfast was served by two white-coated waiters.

Zephyrine Wan was pouring coffee when Sztykgold himself broached the subject of business, mentioning her husband's earlier phone call. 'And what exactly is the nature of your problem, Mr Wan?'

Henry Wan sat in silence, stared back at Sztykgold steadily across the table. He sipped at his coffee, in no hurry to answer, knowing that once he took this step there would be no turning back, and he didn't quite know as yet if he was really prepared to trust Sztykgold.

Sztykgold lit a Turkish cigarette. When he spoke he might have been reading Henry Wan's unvoiced thoughts 'Please,' he said in a quiet and sincere tone, the aroma of Turkish tobacco drifting across the table. 'I know the matter in question must be extremely important to you – but really – we aren't going to get anywhere like this. If we're going to do business then there must be trust on both sides. For myself, you have my assurance that you can talk to me in confidence and anything you say will be respected.' He sat very straight in the chair, holding Henry Wan's uncertain gaze steadily. 'After all,' he continued in the same quiet and sincere tone. 'I would never have survived in business all these years if I wasn't the soul of discretion. And in that time I've been commissioned by some of the most respected names in China, and outside of it. So do feel at ease.'

It took Henry Wan a full minute before he finally committed himself, aware that, after all, there was really no alternative. What it simply amounted to was taking yet another risk in what over the past few months had become a never-ending line of risks. Also he knew he had to make any move quickly if he wasn't to extend that same line of risks longer than necessary. He said cautiously, 'Julot told you about me?'

Sztykgold had already decided to take his own time, to show no undue inquisitiveness. Almost absently, he said, 'He explained who you were.'

Henry Wan glanced at his wife's intent, listening face, and seemed to reach the all-important decision. In a strained voice, alert for Sztykgold's reaction, he said, 'I have upward of three million dollars' worth of gold bullion stuck in the Yangtze, Mr Sztykgold. I want it brought downriver.'

If he expected some dramatic reaction from Sztykgold, he was disappointed; not even the flicker of a muscle registered on the long grey face. It was almost as if he received the same request every other day of the week. And when Sztykgold did speak, it was to utter an unexpected question. Rubbing his cigarette out in the ashtray, looking directly into Henry Wan's face, he said, 'Your own – or the bank's?'

Henry Wan sat up very straight in his chair with indignation.

Sztykgold quickly smiled and waved a hand to silence the forthcoming protest. 'It makes no difference to me, so don't let there be any misunderstanding. I ask only because of the possibility that the police may be involved.'

Henry Wan glanced fleetingly at his wife, and shook his head. 'No, the police are in no way involved. But I would like to be clear of Shanghai by Monday evening at the latest – if it can so be arranged.'

Sztykgold studied him shrewdly across the table. 'Then the bullion belongs to the bank.' And again silenced Henry Wan with a quick gesture. 'I told you, it makes no difference to me. I simply like to know where I stand. But you said upward of three million dollars. That might mean anything, Mr Wan. Is that calculated at forty dollars an ounce – or a hundred?'

Henry Wan quickly realized that Sztykgold was far from being a fool. He knew that only an honest reply would suffice. 'It was bought on the blackmarket, or the largest portion of it was acquired in that manner.'

Sztykgold smiled at Henry Wan's reluctance to fully commit himself. 'It's the weight – the approximate weight that I'm interested in, Mr Wan.'

Henry Wan said reluctantly, 'A little over two tons.'

Again Sztykgold smiled, knowingly. 'So you're calculating it at the rock-bottom price of forty dollars the ounce? You know, of course, that it could be worth anything from one hundred and ten to one hundred and sixty on the open market?'

Henry Wan sat frozen upright in his chair, but offered no argument.

Sztykgold drained his coffee cup unhurriedly. 'Don't let it worry you, Mr Wan. I have a naturally inquisitive mind. I always like to have all the facts at hand. Now perhaps you'll be kind enough to explain just how the bullion came to be stuck in the Yangtze?'

'It left Chungking by river junk on the afternoon of February 16th,' Henry Wan explained in a quiet, somewhat leaden voice, 'concealed under a cargo of wool bound for Kiangling.'

'But destined instead for Shanghai?' mused Sztykgold.

Henry Wan nodded affirmatively.

'And that's fully three months ago. Just what happened to her?'

Henry Wan refilled his coffee cup, offering the pot to Sztykgold, who declined it. 'Frankly, we had almost given up hope of ever hearing from her again. We didn't really know what to think. I suppose we were afraid that the Communists had captured her – at least until last evening when one of the crew arrived to tell us they had been caught in a Communist crossing of the river the same day that the British frigate *Amethyst* was attacked. However, he assured us that they had found refuge on the south shore and buried the bullion somewhere nearby to prevent it falling into Communist hands. That's about it.'

Sztykgold remained contemplatively silent for a long moment, his mind active. The *Amethyst* had been imprisoned on the Yangtze up by Ta-sha since April 20th; more than four weeks. It was a long time. 'I assume you know this to be an unquestionable fact?'

'Absolutely.' Henry Wan was emphatic.

Sztykgold didn't share the same blind faith. 'A great deal can happen on the Yangtze in four days, Mr Wan – never mind four weeks.' Yet he allowed it to pass, toyed with his empty coffee cup, his professional mind at work. 'Tell me,' he mused. 'Is the junk caught up above, or below the *Amethyst*?'

Henry Wan hesitated. The *Tungting Explorer*'s position was one of his few safeguards.

Sztykgold's smile was one of sympathetic understanding. 'Look,' he said. 'I'm not asking you to divulge her exact position at this stage, but I must have an answer to my question. It's something I need to know.'

Henry Wan said hollowly, 'Then it's below the *Amethyst* – not very far from here – in terms of distance.'

Sztykgold lit another of his Turkish cigarettes, then looked back across the table at Henry Wan. 'But still behind Communist lines.' He leaned back in the chair. 'You know that it'll be difficult to arrange its passage downriver – extremely difficult.' He saw dismay cloud both the Wans' faces and added with a smile. 'But don't misunderstand me – I didn't say it would be altogether impossible. Yet we certainly don't have time on our side.'

The Wans were unable to conceal their mounting anxiety. 'But you'll be able to do it,' Zephyrine Wan said without conviction.

Sztykgold's reply was carefully non-committal. 'Perhaps.' He was in no hurry to continue. His mind was already functioning along other lines. 'You understand that if I accept this commission there'll be others involved? I may perhaps be able to make the necessary arrangements, but I don't pretend to be so desperate for money to risk my own neck making the Yangtze Run.' He paused to force a self-effacing smile. 'That sort of thing I leave to others of more determined character.'

'But you'll be able to do it,' Zephyrine Wan reiterated in her anxiety.

Sztykgold glanced away, looked out across the river. There was only one cog in his plans over which he could exert no direct control, and it was the most vital one, the one without which nothing else could function; Harry Lord. And he knew Harry Lord would prove both stubborn and difficult. It had already taken all his powers of persuasion to get him to agree to make the trip to Chen-kou, and he knew he couldn't commit himself, not even to himself. He pushed the chair back from the table. 'I'm afraid I must first make a phone call before I can give you any sort of answer, and even then the final decision won't rest with me.'

'Very well.' Henry Wan quickly rose to lead the way back inside.

The three bodyguards eyed Sztykgold curiously when he walked to the phone. The number which he gave the switchboard operator was that of the Yangtzepoo Pilot House. A minute later he was speaking to one of the River Commissioners in a low voice, his back to the room. 'Sztykgold here,' he told the man. 'I was expecting the *Jacaranda* in sometime yesterday.'

The reply came back promptly. 'She came upriver shortly after four this morning. I watched her put in to the Carfax Oil Depot.'

Sztykgold politely thanked the government official who had been on his payroll for eleven years, and rang off. He said nothing to Henry Wan until they returned to the balcony and resumed their seats at the breakfast table where Zephyrine Wan was awaiting them anxiously. 'There's a chance,' he told them. 'But beyond that I don't want to commit myself. It's going to depend on yourselves when the time arrives.'

Henry Wan frowned, perplexed by Sztykgold's concluding remark. 'I don't understand.'

Sztykgold knew that the circumstances demanded he reveal more of the actual details involved in the possible operation than when he dealt with a client normally. Otherwise the whole thing could prove impossible to get off the ground. Altogether different tactics would have to be employed with Harry Lord on this occasion if he was to stand any chance at all of success. He would confront him with the Wans themselves, so that he himself would appear to be playing only a secondary role. 'Look, I'll be frank with you. There's only one man in Shanghai these days who can make a trip like this now the Communists are on both sides of the river above Woosung. Therefore what I propose to do is to arrange a meeting between you. But I warn you now, he's going to require a very great deal of convincing – moneywise.'

'Then arrange it,' Henry Wan said eagerly. 'Arrange it for as soon as possible.'

'All right,' Sztykgold agreed. 'I'll try to arrange something for later today, when I've been able to get in touch with the man in question.'

Henry Wan smiled, felt as if a vast burden had been lifted from his shoulders, although his anxiety remained as keen as ever. 'And the cost, Mr Sztykgold?'

Sztykgold sat back. It was obvious that both the Wans were aware the situation was ideal for blackmail, whereby the circumstances would allow him to name almost any price that came to mind. Instead, he said, 'My normal fee has always been ten per cent. I see no reason now to change that.' He almost smiled when he saw the relief flood the two anxious faces opposite. 'No, I've never believed in taking advantage of my fellow-man's misfortunes.'

'And the other man?' Henry Wan inquired anxiously. 'The man who will make the trip?'

Sztykgold heaved a sigh. 'Ah, yes. That's quite a different question. Shall we begin at twenty-five thousand? You can improve on that by tens depending on his reactions.'

Henry Wan brightened even more perceptibly. 'That sounds perfectly reasonable to me.'

'Good.' Sztykgold chain-smoked another Turkish cigarette. 'But one other thing – if he asks the weight of the cargo tell him it's around *one* ton, that you paid eighty dollars the ounce. The reason I'm telling you this is because he runs a fast launch and I've never known him shift anything like two tons of cargo, and he may feel uneasy about undertaking something like that now with the way things are out on the river. But if he doesn't ask, then don't go into details. Leave everything to me.'

Henry Wan said anxiously, 'But you're sure he can ship a cargo like that?'

'Yes, I'm sure of it – and he only has to ship it one way, downriver.'

'But is he honest?' Zephyrine Wan interrupted. 'I mean that's a great deal of bullion, Mr Sztykgold.'

Sztykgold put his head back and laughed. 'Let's be frank, Mrs Wan. You have to take the chance whether you believe him honest or not – if you're to have any hope of getting that bullion downriver. But, yes, I believe he's honest. He's worked for me for several years now and he's never yet run off with anything.' He sat forward, leaned across the table to lend emphasis to another point he wished to make. 'And that's something I want to impress on you both – we're going to have to trust each other implicitly while working together. I must have all the details concerning the junk, her crew, and her exact position before I can make any sort of move whatever. Also you must be prepared to act only on my instructions. There can be no interference from you once I begin making arrangements. And if you aren't prepared to accept these conditions then I see no point in our discussing the matter further. Have I made myself clear?'

Henry Wan, trying to conceal the hopeless sense of resignation which he felt, said gravely. 'There isn't any alternative, is there, Mr Sztykgold?'

Sztykgold relaxed back in the chair. 'No, I'm afraid there isn't, unless you feel inclined to abandon the bullion altogether. But don't worry. You'll be kept informed of every step I take.'

'There is one other thing, Mr Sztykgold,' Zephyrine Wan quietly put forward. 'As my husband has already said, we want to get to Hong Kong when everything has been completed. Would it be possible for you to arrange that too?'

Sztykgold answered her with a comforting smile of assurance. 'I don't see any problem there, Mrs Wan. I have a contact at Lunghwa who runs his own airfreight company, a man called André Passel. I'll have it arranged for you to be on your way to Hong Kong the moment we have the bullion off-loaded.' And then, with it all thought out in considerable detail, he moved his coffee cup aside and leaned, still smiling assuredly, back across the table. 'Now what do you say we get down to real business, Mr Wan?'

* * *

The time was 8.00 a.m. when Harry Lord climbed up into the cockpit from the motor space. A product of London's Golders Green, he had wandered far during his twenty-eight years. A week after completing his apprenticeship as an engineer in a Millwall diesel shop he had shipped out from the Pool on a Panamanian freighter bound for Buenos Aires. Over the years he had changed berths countless times, had sailed into ports everywhere around the world from Bombay to Sydney and Valparaiso to Cape Town. He could take care of himself too. Although he wasn't tall, he was a big man, powerfully built, his upper body heavily muscled. Black hair matted his chest and grew down his arms and along the backs of his hands. But the most disquieting feature about him were his eyes; they were blue, of such a shattering contrast to his swarthy darkness that anybody meeting him for the first time received an uncanny and embarrassing jolt. His smile was also crooked, so that when he grinned it gave him a somewhat mad, crazy air. More disturbing, he could make the same grin disappear like magic, leaving in its place a look of blank, ominous violence. It wasn't difficult. Mad Harry Lord was ugly; that same peculiar ugliness which so many women find irresistible.

In the after end of the cockpit he stood up wiping his hands on a wad of cotton waste. The two Chinese carpenters had fitted a new windshield while he was below, and the smell of fresh paint hung in the oily air of the dock. Crossing to the starboard gunwale, he saw they had hauled their sampan close aft while they finished patching and spotting the shrapnel splinters in the hull with grey paint. 'Is she okay?' he asked across the side.

Both men nodded affirmatively. 'Number One, Mr Lord. We're just finished.'

'You've done a good job on her,' Harry Lord told them; and it wasn't the first job they had done on her either. 'Here.' Peeling several bills from a roll of US currency, he paid them across the gunwale.

As the two carpenters started sculling the sampan across the dock, he took a look around the freshly scrubbed cockpit and stern-quarters and felt satisfied with his morning's work. But the real satisfaction he always found in her lay below deck in the gleaming motors he tended like a mother tended her baby. He was a born genius where machinery was concerned. He loved every second below deck, the touch of polished steel, the hammer of the motors, and the hot, humid smell of oil and gasoline. He was never happier than when covered with grease and oil and with a spanner in his hand.

Almost four years had elapsed since he had seen the launch lying abandoned on the beach below Cabo Engaño on Luzon, at a point some eight miles east of Aparri. He had seen her as they sailed by, sleek and powerful, even shot up. In the late days of 1945, beaches everywhere were littered with the debris of war, but he had known on first sight she was something different. He had been Second Engineer on board the MV *Pueblo Hundido* out of Valparaiso at the time, and when he went ashore that evening in Aparri he had walked out to the beach to take a closer look at the launch. Critically damaged as she was, she was beautiful, a sailor's dream. But what had impressed him most were the twin Issotta Fraschini motors, the best prewar gasoline motors in the world, and there hadn't been a scratch on them. She had been beached only because of structural damage sustained from a near-miss bomb. And although wearing the red Japanese insignia on her bows and foredeck along with the numerals P 27, she had been custom-built in Italy for some wealthy Far East customer, and subsequently commandeered at some time by the Japanese during the War and put to use as a high-powered patrol craft, although she was devoid of any armament.

When the *Pueblo Hundido* sailed next afternoon he had lain on the beach and watched her put out into the bay without the faintest regret. Six weeks later the launch was seaworthy enough to be towed into Aparri, and after a further two months of hard work had made her first trial run in the bay. Afterward, at a time when everybody in the Far East was involved in some illegal postwar scheme to make themselves a fortune out of the upheaval affecting the overall economy, work wasn't difficult to find with a fast well-equipped launch.

One customer with whom he regularly did business was a Chinese general merchant in Aparri called Old Sun who as a side-line also ran a boarding-house down on the front. He was already prospering when in February of 1946 a young Chinese arrived at the boarding-house and rented a room across the hall from him. Wong Peng Yin, as it subsequently transpired, had come down from Shanghai for reasons known only to himself. Always friendly with Harry Lord, he had commented one afternoon while they were seated on the dock, 'With a boat like that you could make plenty of money Chinaside.'

Harry Lord had looked at him hard. 'How come?'

'Have you never heard of the Yangtze Run?' Wong Peng Yin had asked.

In return Harry Lord had grinned his magic grin. 'No – but I've got a feeling I'm going to.'

'I was working the Yangtze Run when I was thirteen years old,' Wong Peng Yin had stated proudly. 'It's that stretch of the Yangtze Kiang between Shanghai and Nanking. If you understand, everything that isn't supposed to come downriver arrives at Nanking, and everything that isn't supposed to go upriver arrives at Shanghai, so in between it has to make the Yangtze Run. It's very simple.'

Harry Lord had never heard of anything being simple in his life. 'And no doubt very illegal.'

'Naturally,' Wong Peng Yin had confirmed with enthusiasm. 'And with a boat like that you can make a fortune so long as you can take care of yourself.'

Harry Lord had replied judiciously, 'So what're you doing here?'

Wong Peng Yin had given a philosophical shrug. 'We ran into a little trouble about a year ago and I thought it would be safer to get away from Chinaside for a time. You see, I worked for the Kang brothers. Along with Po-han they were amongst the most successful junk-owners making the Yangtze Run. Then they and Po-han decided to pirate the Baines & Hyland steamer *Kanchow* when she left Nanking. Shortly afterward we caught her pulling out for Shanghai one night and we sailed her up to Poyang hu. She had seventy-six passengers on board and we held her for ransom of a hundred thousand dollars.'

'Did you get the money?'

Wong Pen Yin had displayed a complete set of gold dentures in his smile. 'Oh, yes, we got the money. The German acted as intermediary.'

Harry Lord had been curious. 'So what went wrong?'

'Well the police were never able to prove anything against Po-han, but the Kang brothers were hanged last November in the Ward Road Gaol.'

Harry Lord had nodded sagely. 'And now you're on the run from the cops.'

Wong Peng Yin had answered unperturbed, 'Anybody can make a mistake. But there's still plenty of money to be made, plenty of money with a boat like that. All you have to do is meet The German. He will make you money in no time.'

Harry Lord had been intrigued. 'Just how would I get in touch with him?'

Wong Peng Yin had smiled and spread his hands. 'Ask. Everybody in Shanghai knows The German.'

As a result of this conversation with Wong Peng Yin, Harry Lord had run the *Jacaranda* up along the Hongkew waterfront in early June to get his first look at the famous Shanghai Bund. And now, standing in the after end of the cockpit gazing wistfully out across the river, he was aware that the end of yet another era of his life was close at hand,

and that he would have to find somewhere else to go. That was something else he had to think about; the future.

Twenty minutes later he was in the Ferry House eating breakfast at a table overlooking the river. On the way up from the Carfax Oil Depot he had bought the morning newspapers. The *Shanghai Morning Post* was an English language newspaper composed mainly of Associated Press, Reuters, and Chinese-American News Alliance reports combed throughout the Far East, heavily influenced by American sympathy for Chiang Kiashek and the Kuomintang Nationalist Government. The front page concerned itself with the abduction of an American businessman the previous afternoon: US BUSINESSMAN KIDNAPPED Howard K. Lenison, Vice-President of American-Asiatic Holdings Inc., had been stopped when leaving a taxicab to keep an appointment at the Cathay Hotel with Kuomintang financial advistors. So far none of the kidnappers had been apprehended, although two of them had been identified by witnesses as known Communist sympathizers. As Harry Lord didn't hold any stock in American-Asiatic Holdings Inc., he read on, skipping the nine pages of world stock market quotations, the American sport results, and found the only reference to the besieged city in an unobtrusive item on the back page which stated that Communist troops and artillery were believed to have reinforced troops already dug-in on the sector between Luikiahang and Yangkiachen to north and north-west of Shanghai. Apart from *that*, the Communists might have been a thousand miles away.

The *Shanghai Standard* was written partly in English and partly in Chinese. Its news came from unconfirmed and unidentified sources and was generally regarded as being as near the truth as it was possible to get without betraying connections with the wrong people. Accordingly, unidentified sources in Nanking reported that the Communist RED DRAGON OFFENSIVE was expected to be launched within a matter of days. Marshal Tseng, Governing-General Communist Liberation Forces South China was believed to be with Generals Li, Chao and Chen, respectively commanding the Second, Fifth and Seventh Field Armies at Field Headquarters on the Nine Towers Estate fourteen miles north of Luikiahang making final preparations for the drive south and west against remaining Kuomintang territory.

It was all depressing stuff. Folding the newspapers aside, he tipped them across the rail into the river and settled back with another cup of coffee to wait for the *Morning Star* ferry-boat to put in from the old International Settlement. The sunlight was now hard and brittle and the buildings on the Shanghai Bund were a sharp angular mass, and downriver he saw the Tienningshih Vehicular Ferry headed in toward the Hongkew Steps above the Yangtzepoo Pilot House. And further downriver he saw something else that brought the magic grin to his stubbled face. *The Ladybird* was headed upstream about a half mile below the China Navigation building, her stovepipe smokestack laying a tar-black smoke-screen along the shoreline, She was the craziest vessel he had ever set eyes on; a floating wedding cake. A paddle-steamer, she was so out of proportion from the various pieces which had been added to her superstructure from time to time that she defied all known laws of both buoyancy and gravity. Of no more than three hundred tons, she was short, squat, top heavy and her paddles made so much noise that she could be heard five miles away on a dark night. She was also afflicted with a permanent ten degree list to starboard, while her stovepipe smokestack with its fringed cowl listed to port as if in effort to remain perpendicular to the surface. Even more eccentric in appearance was her Master, an old Dutch woman called Mary Drees, better known along the Yangtze as Dutch Mary.

Like *The Ladybird*, Dutch Mary was a legend in her own lifetime. Together they had plied the Yangtze for some thirty years, mainly out of Nanking. Some stories claimed that Dutch Mary hadn't set foot ashore in those same thirty years either. Whether there was any credence in them or not it was difficult to gauge, but there was no denying her eccentricity, and even the Japanese had given her a wide berth during their occupation of South China. Harry Lord had first met her shortly after arriving in Shanghai, when on his first trip to Nanking he had come across *The Ladybird* hard aground on the shifting bottom of the River Gate Mud Flats in heavy fog. After towing her free, Dutch Mary had felt indebted to the extent that everytime afterward when he was in Nanking she had summoned him on board for dinner and a drink.

It was only after the Communists entered Nanking that

she finally pulled out and dropped downriver to Shanghai where she had since spent her time shipping refugees south to Ningpo at $10 a head, the cheapest escape route from Shanghai. It was also a trip that was regarded as the voyage of a lifetime, for due to *The Ladybird*'s highly temperamental engines there was no such thing as a hard and fast timetable, although with the current astern she made the trip downriver in considerably less time than it took her to perform the return journey.

The Ladybird was still making heavy way against the current when he saw the *Morning Star* head in toward the Pootung shore from across the river, and paying his bill, he went out and found a telephone kiosk on the dock and called a number across in the old French Concession but received no answer.

And Harry Lord thought; where the hell is that bastard? – the heel-clicking prick.

* * *

Captain Hop entered the Great Eastern Mansions at a few minutes before 9.00 a.m. He walked directly to the reception desk where the clerk stumbled over his own feet as he hurried to attend to him.

Captain Hop was to the point. 'I believe you have a Mr Wan staying here.'

The clerk bobbed his head. 'Yes, sir. Mr Wan, sir. He arrived this morning and took the Peking Suite.'

Captain Hop's gaze roamed the polished foyer with its bustle of breakfast waiters, porters and bell-hops. 'What about visitors? Has he had any so far?'

The clerk answered ingratiatingly, 'Yes, sir. As a matter of fact, a gentleman calling himself Heinrich Sztykgold arrived with two associates about an hour and a half ago, just after seven-thirty.'

Captain nodded briefly. 'Anybody else?'

'No, sir. Nobody else.'

'Naturally you'll make no mention of my inquiries to anybody.'

The clerk felt the icy draught of Captain Hop's voice. He swallowed, blinked rapidly behind his spectacles. The Captain stood as straight as the blade of a rapier and seemed to exude about as much emotion. 'Naturally, sir.' His gaze fastened on the riding-crop which Captain Hop tapped ominously against the polished length of his riding-boot. 'I haven't seen nor heard anything, sir. You can be assured of that.'

Captain Hop left the Great Eastern Mansions and walked the half block westward to where the big open car was parked. Everything was going just as he had envisaged it would. Right from the outset he had known it would be Sztykgold, just like it would be Harry Lord who would make the trip. Time was the only worry. They would have to move quickly, before the Communists launched their offensive. But Sztykgold would be actively alive to that particular problem too.

When he arrived back at the car he found Sergeant Kee and Corporal Choy awaiting his return expectantly. 'Just as I thought,' he told them. 'Sztykgold's been with Mr Wan since just after seven-thirty. It can only be a matter of time before Harry Lord becomes involved.' As he settled himself into the deep upholstery he felt supremely confident, convinced that no morning had ever showed so much promise. 'Let's get back across town and check with the Marine Police to see if they have any news on Harry Lord. It's three days now since he went downriver for Chen-kou.'

* * *

Along toward the Racecourse, Harry Lord stopped and took another look at the buildings both sides of the roadway but saw no sign anywhere of Chang's name. He lit a cigarette and wondered if it was worth going to any further trouble. The Nanking Road was a busy thoroughfare at the best of times, and he had only been an old man, and what was one old man, more or less, in China these days, he reasoned. Besides, the only thing he knew about him was his name and that he had a brother who was supposed to own a tailoring business somewhere on the Nanking Road. It wasn't a great deal to go on, whichever way he looked at it, and with the lack of success which his earlier phone call had met he wasn't in the best of humour. But he knew that sort of thinking wasn't going to help him find Mr Chang, if Mr Chang was still around. For all he knew Mr Chang might have already left town. Everybody with any sense was leaving town, or trying to. Just about everybody was on the move, one way or another.

He flipped the butt of his cigarette into the gutter and was still temporizing when he saw two high-class French whores wearing smoked spectacles leave the offices of the Swallow Tourist Agency and start up the road toward the Racecourse looking for a taxicab. Even from a distance of a hundred yards it was obvious that they were wearing nothing beneath their chic Paris suits. He watched them out of curiosity as they went on up the road disdaining the covert grins of the downtown slopeheads who, he reasoned, stood about as much chance of making time with them as they had of growing wings and migrating to Hong Kong. By the look of them he guessed they were probably from the Cathay or the Picardie, the recognized hang-outs for visiting politicians and generals, and in which case they probably sported more campaign medals than a veteran of the Boxer Uprising.

Eventually he started up the road again with the magic grin on his dark stubbled face thinking about all the bed-occupied back rooms there had to be in travel agencies around town with a continual parade of whores queuing up to make a personal down payment on a rail or steamer ticket, although there were no longer many steamers leaving anymore. Yet it was a good indication of just how bad things had become in Shanghai. When a whore left town then its future was something of a foregone conclusion, and there was nothing more conclusively foregone at that moment than Shanghai's future.

Corporal Choy slowed the big open car so abruptly that it took Captain Hop unawares. Sitting upright, he surveyed the crowded roadway with a dark scowl. 'What the hell are you stopping for?'

Corporal Choy gestured southward. 'Over there, Captain.'

Captain Hop and Sergeant Kee saw Harry Lord in the same instant. Captain Hop relaxed back into the upholstery, tapped the riding crop in the gloved palm of his hand thoughtfully. 'So he's back in town,' he mused. 'That saves us a journey. But what's he doing in the Nanking Road at this time of the morning?'

Sergeant Kee said hopefully, 'Do you suppose Sztykgold's been in touch with him already?'

Captain Hop shook his head. 'I doubt it. He looks as if he's got something else on his mind.'

'He seems to be looking for something, Captain,' Corporal Choy commented dourly.

They saw Harry Lord stop outside a bar called The Kimona, glance around him at the buildings both sides of the roadway, then turn away.

Corporal Choy sat upright behind the wheel. 'He's going into that bar.'

Captain Hop watched Harry Lord shoulder his way in through the swing glass door. 'Come on – this could be interesting.'

Sergeant Kee remained in his seat, hesitating. 'Do you think that's wise, Captain? I mean what if he should become suspicious about anything later?'

Captain Hop laughed Kee's fears aside. 'I think you tend to overestimate him. You've been listening to too many stories. What do you say, Choy?'

Corporal Choy showed his teeth in a yellow grin. 'He doesn't worry *me*, Captain.'

Sergeant Kee felt inclined to argue, but changed his mind. Yet he didn't feel easy with their unwarranted display of confidence, believed it misplaced. Indeed he had always considered this confidence of Captain Hop's something of a weakness. It worried him, and there had been other times when he wished he had shown a little more discretion, now especially, with upwards of $3,000,000's worth of bullion at stake.

It was cool in the bar after the glare and bustle of the roadway outside. Harry Lord's gaze took in the glitter of bottles lining the shelves, and the Japanese cock calendar from which no obscene detail had been omitted. Striking a match to light another cigarette, he glanced along the bar. The bartender, who was little more than a boy, was preoccupied with his thoughts, polishing a glass with such a rapt expression on his face that it conveyed the impression he might be seriously contemplating how best to spend the money had just won with first prize in the city lottery. 'Hey, you. What're you running here – some kind of Christian Aid Mission?'

The boy turned startled, hurrying the length of the bar. 'I'm sorry, sir,' he said. 'What can I get you?'

'The Green Label. Give me a bottle of Green Label.'

As the boy brought the bottle from the ice-box his gaze registered the huge frame and rumpled clothing, and when the man put his hand into his pocket he wouldn't have been surprised to have seen him haul out a gun and found himself shot stone cold dead.

Harry Lord took a swallow of beer and leaned on to the bar. The beer was so cold it jarred his head. But it was the Japanese cock calendar that claimed his attention. He had never realized there were so many novel ways in which a man could cohabit. If Mao had arrived at that moment the kid behind the bar and whoever owned the place would have found themselves condemned to twenty years apiece in the Ward Road Gaol for the corruption of public morals. Then the door down the end of the bar opened and he watched with his glass raised halfway to his mouth as Captain Hop and his two aides entered. Jesus H. Christ, he thought; he needed Captain Hop about as much as he needed a wooden leg.

'Well, well,' Captain Hop said, affecting surprise. 'If it isn't my old friend Harry Lord.'

Harry Lord met his gaze with all the emotion of a brick wall. 'I didn't know you had friends, Captain.'

Ignoring the remark, Captain Hop removed his gloves and placed them on the bar along with his riding-crop and cap. 'You look as if you haven't been to bed for a week. What is it – your friend Sztykgold been keeping you busy?'

'I'm still making the odd buck, if that's what you mean,' Harry Lord answered easily. 'But what're you doing here – you come to arrest somebody?'

While Sergeant Kee snapped his fingers to the bartender and ordered three beers, Captain Hop replied in a superior tone, 'I wonder why it is that everybody immediately presumes that the moment a policeman appears it's his intention to arrest somebody?'

Harry Lord was well aware of the many people unfortunate enough to have made Captain Hop's acquaintance through no fault of their own. 'Maybe they know you,' he said with a grin that contrived to appear somewhat crazy, while his unnerving blue eyes remained unblinking.

Behind them Corporal Choy stood up off the bar with a challenging grunt.

Only Harry Lord's eyes moved as he remained slouched

at the bar. 'I thought you only let *him* out on a chain.'

A brutal frown darkened Corporal Choy's face as Captain Hop stepped smartly between the two men, saying thinly, 'Still the joker, eh, Lord?'

Harry Lord said nothing. He knew all about Captain Hop. Nor was his riding-crop an affectation either, for if a Fascist dictatorship depended on one thing more than anything else for survival, it was respect.

Captain Hop reached for his beer, sipped at it as if nothing had happened. Although he had never had any direct dealings with Harry Lord he knew that at least some of the stories told about him couldn't be entirely without foundation, and that he really *was* mad. Nobody would have taunted Choy as he had done if in their right mind, even to taking delight in it. He decided to try a pacifying tact, and said casually, 'And what brings you to the Nanking Road at this time of the morning – couldn't you sleep?'

Harry Lord dug a matchstick into his ear and appeared surprised at what it unearthed. 'I thought I'd take a last look at the sights.'

Captain Hop nodded his understanding, 'Yes, it's a pity that the end must always spoil everything. But when I hadn't seen you around these past few days I thought you had already left town.'

Captain Hop didn't fool Harry Lord. Captain Hop knew everything there was worth knowing. He said, 'I can't say I haven't thought about it.' And, pursued by curiosity, began a tentative excavation of his other ear.

Captain Hop said amiably, 'Perhaps it would be in our best interests if we *all* left town. I don't know if you've heard or not, but there's a rumour that we can expect the Communists to launch their offensive at almost any hour. But then perhaps you don't read the newspapers.'

Harry Lord said off-handedly, 'Only the Unclaimed Money columns.'

Leaning off the bar, Captain Hop restrained a sudden flush of irritation. With effort he forged a smile. 'That, unfortunately, is what most of us Chinese lack – a sense of humour.'

Harry Lord thought; listen to this fucking yo-yo. And in wooden agreement said, 'Among other things, Captain.'

Captain Hop smiled, but only with his mouth. Mad as the

man undoubtedly was, he had an infuriating habit of being able to turn everything to his own advantage without apparent effort. And despite the fact that he had never experienced any dealings with him personally, it was obvious that he wasn't in the least impressed by authority. Nor was he easily frightened, and he had always harboured an obscure wonder and resentment of such people. He also knew that there were any number of policemen who would gladly have arranged his disappearance if it hadn't been for Heinrich Sztykgold's financial arrangements with the Kuomintang hierarchy in Chungking. Sztykgold paid good money for the privilege of not only having his own activities overlooked, but also those of his employees, and that, unfortunately, included Harry Lord. Frankly, he hated Sztykgold as much as he now hated Harry Lord. He had maintained an envious eye on the Sztykgold protection contract ever since his arrival in Shanghai to take charge of the 3rd District. Sztykgold had one of the most lucrative businesses in South China, and it irked him to be unable to move in on any of his various activities. But that was something else he intended to rectify.

At his side Sergeant Kee said pointedly, looking at his watch, 'That appointment, Captain. We will need our time.'

Captain Hop's sharp glance conveyed his irritation. He knew Kee was offering him the opportunity to back out of the meeting without belittling himself, but he had already decided to stand his ground. He had no intention of losing face to anybody, let alone to a madman of Harry Lord's calibre. He said conversationally, 'I suppose you're still living at the Red Fortune Hotel?'

The red bell of suspicion began to clang in Harry Lord's brain. Captain Hop had never *supposed* anything in his life. He knew he had been living at the Red Fortune Hotel ever since his arrival in Shanghai. For some inexplicable reason he had reverted to small-talk. Something was wrong. He was being quietly hustled; he knew it intuitively. With a crazy-mad grin, he said, 'Why – you thinking about putting it in quarantine?'

Captain Hop was forced to acknowledge the fact that he wasn't going to get anywhere with Harry Lord. As a result it required considerable effort on his part to keep his exasperation in check. 'Not at all,' he said stiffly. 'It's just the policy of the Kuomintang Government that its police shall at all times endeavour to maintain surveillance on all aliens who may become a source of embarrassment to it.'

Harry Lord's face at once assumed an expression of childlike innocence. 'I never knew you regarded me as being likely convertible material Communistwise, Captain.'

Captain Hop was near to the limits of his patience. He said coolly, 'Just as times are changing – then so are certain people's politics.'

With the same childlike innocence, Harry Lord said, 'Then maybe you should report your suspicions to Chungking. Old Heinie Sztykgold has a lot of influential friends up there who'd be happy to have your report.'

For an instant Captain Hop's anger boiled on the point of eruption. And then he drew a deep breath, asserted control of himself. He could wait. Within the matter of a few hours he would have the last laugh not only on Harry Lord, but also on Sztykgold. With exaggerated nonchalance he replaced his gloves and gathered his riding-crop and cap from the bar. Smiling thinly, he said, 'Some day I'm afraid that you're going to over-reach yourself, Mr Lord. Some day—'

Harry Lord stared after them with narrow blue eyes as they marched toward the door. There was something odd about it all and he didn't like it; he didn't like anything in which Captain Hop was involved. He had a reputation known throughout South China. Yet he couldn't fathom just what the hell it had all been about, and it worried him, left a nagging doubt at the back of his mind.

He finished his beer and down the end of the bar saw that the bartender had returned to his financial problems. 'Hey, you – Gulbenkian. Ever heard of a slopehead around here called Chang? He's supposed to be in the tailoring business.'

The boy answered politely, 'There was a man called Chang who had a place somewhere around the corner of the Kwong Lee Road. But I haven't seen him in more than two weeks now.'

Harry Lord nodded his thanks, and on the way out stopped by the pay telephone at the door and called a number across in the old French Concession only to meet with the same lack of success as he had done earlier in the day.

Outside he turned right and started toward the Racecourse. From the intersection with the Kwong Lee Road he saw the roof of the Racecourse grandstand and the green of the trees around it, while on the corner of the road stood a bar called the Top Hat, and over it the offices of the Nippon Steam Navigation Company, and over these something calling itself SU-LING'S SPECIALITY RUBBER GOODS FITTED FREE WALK RIGHT IN NO APPOINTMENTS NECESSARY printed on a piece of cardboard stuck in a window.

He tried around the corner and found Chang's name midway up the list of tenants. The office was on the third floor with Chang's name in peeling gilt on a pane of frosted glass set into the door. He knocked and waited while a tramcar went by outside and set the entire building trembling. When nobody answered he knocked again, and this time he saw a shadow flit across the glass panel in the door. 'Hey, you in there,' he said.

A hesitant whisper from inside said, 'Who is that?'

'Marco fucking Polo,' Harry Lord said hitting the door again.

While he waited the bolt was withdrawn and the door edged open to reveal a scrawny Chinaman peering our apprehensively. 'What do you want?'

Harry Lord put his foot in the door. 'Is your name Chang?'

The Chinaman's eyes narrowed. He couldn't believe it; the man looked eight feet tall and big as a house. But before he could answer, Harry Lord put his shoulder to the door and pushed inside past him, leaving him to secure the door quickly and scuttle around behind the desk at the window.

'I asked your name or are you deaf?'

The Chinaman blinked, stared up at the huge figure looming across the desk. 'Yes, my name's Chang.'

'The same Chang as had a brother in Chen-kou?'

Mr Chang paled, tugged at the collar of his shirt irresolutely. 'What do you want with me? Why do you come here like this? I've never seen you before.'

Harry Lord said, 'I'm asking the questions – or hadn't you noticed?'

Mr Chang gaped open-mouthed. Whoever the man was he looked as if he had slept the previous week in a rice-paddy. But he wasn't a policeman; anybody would have seen at first glance that he wasn't a policeman. In a dry whisper, he said, 'Yes, I have a brother in Chen-kou.'

'And you paid Sztykgold to get him out?'
Mr Chang frowned. 'How do *you* know that?'
'Because I shipped him out this morning.'
Mr Chang brightened. 'He's here – in Shanghai?'
Harry Lord stood back off the desk. 'That's what I came to tell you about.'
Mr Chang's face fell. 'Is something wrong?'
'He's dead,' Harry Lord said simply. 'He died coming downriver. He was in a bad way when he came on board.'
Mr Chang sank back into the chair behind the desk. Like age, life only became progressively more bitter to accept as it moved relentlessly and impartially toward the end. First it had been his wife after only two years of marriage, then his parents, and now his eldest brother. It was as if the whole world had turned against him.
'There wasn't anything could be done for him.'
Mr Chang lifted despairing eyes. 'And his body?'
'The river,' Harry Lord said. 'If he'd had anything of value I'd have brought it along but all he had was what he was wearing.'
Mr Chang sighed resignedly, 'Despite my urgings he refused to leave Nanking until the last moment. It was only ten days ago that I learned he had been caught in Chen-kou when Communist troops overran the final columns of refugees.'
'Well you couldn't very well have stayed on here in Shanghai either,' Harry Lord observed.
Mr Chang spread his hands above the desk. 'It was our intention to join our youngest brother in Hong Kong. Over the past two months we transferred our business there. I only remained behind to clear up one or two business contracts and await our eldest brother's arrival from Nanking.'
Harry Lord sent a glance around the airless room. Apart from a few odd bolts of cloth and two racks lined with samples of women's clothes, the place was empty. 'Then there's no reason for you waiting around any longer.'
Mr Chang's shoulders slumped. 'It isn't quite as easy as that,' he said sadly.
Harry Lord looked at him. 'What do you mean?'
Mr Chang lifted his shoulders in a gesture of resignation. 'The police have been watching me for the past week. They're never far away.'

Harry Lord immediately pushed past the desk to take a look from the window and found his worst fears fully justified. The ex-US Army jeep with the White Sun emblem of the Kuomintang painted on its bonnet was parked near the intersection with the Nanking Road, and it it were a Lieutenant and Sergeant of the Shanghai Police idly watching the people passing by on the pavements. 'Fuck,' he said. It was just about what he might have expected for doing somebody a good turn when it had been much against his better judgement in the first place.

Mr Chang peered past his shoulder. 'There – I told you,' he breathed in an awed whisper. 'That's Lieutenant Yang and Sergeant Soon.'

Harry Lord backed away from the window, face dark with ominous violence. 'What the hell's it all about?'

'They've been watching me ever since I withdrew the last of my money and bullion from the bank,' Mr Chang explained. 'Now they're waiting for when I try to leave town so they can arrest me when they know I'll have everything with me. Only last week the same thing happened to a watchmaker friend of mine from Nantao. They arrested him for being a suspected Communist agent when he tried to board an aircraft at Lunghwa Airport.'

Harry Lord quietly studied the ashen face with great oily beads of sweat rolling down it to disappear under the limp collar of the shirt, and he knew Chang had told the truth. They were all at it, from the lowest traffic cop to the highest-ranking Blueshirt, each with his own pet scheme to grab everything and anything of value before the Communists arrived. He motioned at the window. 'Any idea how long they've been down there?'

Mr Chang shook his head. 'I'm not sure – but they weren't there when you arrived. I was watching from the window when you knocked on the door.'

Harry Lord relaxed. For a moment he had been afraid they might have seen him enter the building. But now Mr Chang was his big problem. If the police got to him he would gabble anything that came into his head, and Mr Chang was a born gabbler if ever he had seen one. 'Listen,' he said. 'Just how did you intend to leave town with those two cops breathing down your neck?'

Mr Chang ran a nervous hand across his mouth, eyes

wide, staring. 'I thought perhaps I might take a train – board it outside of town. If I could get to Sungkiang or Kashing.'

'Forget it,' Harry Lord growled. 'You've got as much chance nailing yourself in a crate and going air-freight.' And then he thought about his own neck and had a sudden inspiration. 'Tell me, have you got everything you're taking with you here?' He was in a hurry now, a decision reached.

Mr Chang hesitated. 'Yes, but—'

'Never mind the buts,' Harry Lord told him. 'Get it – and make sure it isn't much. This isn't Cook's you're dealing with.'

Hesitantly, Mr Chang stooped to remove a length of board from the floor behind the desk, extracted two bundles of bank notes and several small bars of gold bullion, putting them away in a brief-case.

'Forget the case. We don't want to be seen with any case. Just load that stuff in your pockets.'

Mr Chang didn't pause to argue. It was either Lieutenant Yang or this hulking Westerner, and he decided that the latter was the lesser of the two evils, despite his appearance.

Harry Lord took another look at the street, saw Lieutenant Yang and Sergeant Soon still in the jeep, and took the heavy, sawn-off .38 Police Special from his waistband.

Mr Chang's eyes widened. In a frightened whisper, he said, 'What do we want with a gun?'

'What do you think?' Harry Lord started for the door. 'Come on – before you get your arse shot off.'

At the end of the top floor hall a door gave on to a flat tarred roof. Harry Lord led the way down across the roof-tops of the Kwong Lee Road until he came to an open fan-light. Lying flat on the roof he took a look at the hall below, then grabbed Mr Chang by the collar and lowered him through the opening before he could argue. Relinquishing his grip, he saw him hit the floor and sit down winded, then dropped lightly down to join him. The only sound to reach his ears was the clack of mahjong counters from somewhere below.

'Whatever happens, you keep going,' he said into Mr Chang's ashen face.

The mahjong game was on the third floor and they went on down past the open door and on down again with Mr Chang lumbering along in rear, his weighted pockets flopping around his knees.

They were on the second floor when a woman wearing a pink housecoat appeared in one of the doorways. Her face lit up instantly, Harry Lord claiming her attention. 'Hey, Joe,' she said. 'Are you looking for me?'

She was the last person on earth Harry Lord was looking for, and hustling Mr Chang on past him, he sent him on downstairs. 'It seems we've got the wrong house,' he told her.

She started after him. 'Listen – wait.'

Harry Lord kept on going.

'Hey,' she called after him. 'Look.' Opening her housecoat, she jounced her breasts at him. 'How do you like that?'

'Never seen better,' Harry Lord said over his shoulder, and caught up with Mr Chang in the downstairs hall where his legs had given out on him. He stopped only long enough to grab him to his feet before he jostled him out across a courtyard and into an adjoining alleyway. When they emerged on to the Tonkin Road a taxicab was headed toward them. Flagging it down, Harry Lord bundled Mr Chang into it ahead of him. 'The Yokohama Specie Bank,' he instructed the driver.

Mr Chang gaped at him inanely. 'What do we want with a bank?'

Harry Lord glanced back out of the rear window as the taxicab turned on to Delbert Road. 'Shut your mouth and enjoy the ride. If those two cops have seen us it could be your last.'

When they drew up outside the tall glass and concrete building Harry Lord glanced back along the palm-lined stretch of the Shanghai Bund, then with Mr Chang on his heels, walked in through one door across the black marble foyer and out through another door on to Latimer Drive in time to hail a taxicab leaving the Pearl of the Orient. Assurance Company building.

Crossing the Garden Bridge five minutes later, he found his magic grin again when he saw *The Ladybird*'s smokestack jutting into the skyline above the Ropewalk Wharves. 'This'll do,' he told the driver.

At first glance it seemed as if half the population of Shanghai was gathered around *The Ladybird*'s bow. Grabbing Mr Chang, he elbowed his way through the crowd to the brow where Dutch Mary's First Officer was trying to keep control while the deck crew hosed coal dust from the deck and superstructure where it had collected in sooty drifts when she had taken on bunkers at the McBrayne Coaling Wharf in west Yangtzepoo.

Ling's face lighted when he saw Harry Lord force his way through the crowd around the brow. 'Hello, Mr Lord. We thought you had pulled out for good when we saw you go downriver earlier in the week.'

'Oh, I've been around. Where's Mary?'

Ling stood aside. 'In the wheelhouse. Go on up.'

Harry Lord nudged Mr Chang up the brow ahead of him. Once on board he turned forrard along the starboard outer companionway until he came to the midship screen door, then led the way up the main stairway forrard to the upper cabin deck and saloon where two waiters were wiping down the tables. The wheelhouse was right forrard, almost directly over the bows, some thirty feet above the waterline. Harry Lord knocked on the stout teak door above which was a worn brass plaque which read GLASGOW 1892.

Dutch Mary herself answered the door, a cloud of smoke billowing out into the saloon from the inevitable Dutch panatella she smoked. At the sight of Harry Lord her face broke into a welcoming smile. 'By Gott!' she exploded in an accent which indicated she might only have left Rotterdam for the first time in her life a fortnight earlier. 'And I was thinking you were gone and having left us.'

Harry Lord gave her his magic grin. 'I came in from Chenkou earlier this morning. I was having breakfast in the Ferry House when I saw you come upriver.'

Dutch Mary stood aside, gestured with the glass of gin she held. 'Then in you come and join me in a drink I was having—' Her voice faltered when she became aware of Mr Chang for the first time. 'And who this is?'

In that off-hand way of his which Dutch Mary knew from past experience constituted trouble ninety-nine times out of a hundred, Harry Lord said, 'It's okay. He's a friend of mine.'

Dutch Mary's eyebrows knitted together as she glanced Mr Chang over. 'Yes?' she mused with doubt in her mild grey eyes. 'What sort of friend?'

Harry Lord hesitated. 'Well it's a long sort of story.'

Dutch Mary shook her ringleted grey head. 'Always they

are long stories where Harry Lord concerned is.' She motioned at the bottle of Dutch gin sitting on the ledge forrard of the huge, brass-handled wheel. 'Help yourself.'

Harry Lord poured a glass full. Out through the string of open windows the river glittered in the hard straight sunlight. *The Ladybird* lay astern of a battered freighter out of Hong Kong; the *Elgin Castle* had made the regular South China run to Shanghai and back for almost as long as Dutch Mary had sailed out of Nanking.

Built on much the same lines as *The Ladybird*, and equally as durable, Dutch Mary sipped at her gin and returned her attention to Mr Chang. 'Listen,' she said. 'Just who this friend is?'

Harry Lord sank half the glass of lukewarm gin, leaned his shoulder against the wheel, and briefly outlined the circumstances of his meeting with Mr Chang.

When he was through, Dutch Mary wore a dark scowl. 'You think those cops have seen you maybe?'

Harry Lord grimaced. 'I doubt it. Only I didn't feel like leaving my friend here behind.'

Dutch Marry nodded agreement. Everybody had troubles these days, never mind somebody like Harry Lord to whom trouble was something of a second nature in any case. 'Then you want him I take to Ningpo?'

Harry Lord swallowed another mouthful of gin. 'I'd be more than grateful if you could, Mary.'

Dutch Mary found she couldn't take her eyes off Mr Chang. 'Say – what in his pockets he has got?'

'That's his fare,' Harry Lord explained.

Looking nervously on, Mr Chang sweated profusely.

Dutch Mary thought Mr Chang had all the characteristics of a man waiting resignedly for Fate to catch up with him. She had seen numerous Mr Changs during her years in China, some after they had leapt in front of tram-cars, others after they had been cut down, some after they had been fished out of rivers; and this particular specimen, she decided, looked as if he had all the hallmarks of a hanging job.

Mr Chang suddenly delved a hand into a pocket of his coat. 'I can pay!' he blurted. 'I can pay anything you want – see?' He showed two small bars of bullion, his hand trembling.

Embarrassed by the stench of unashamed fear, Dutch

Mary said quietly, 'Away you put that. That stuff here we do not need.'

'No!' Mr Chang insisted. 'You take it! You take it all – everything!'

Harry Lord leaned off the wheel. 'Forget it. The Captain's doing you a favour.'

'Sure,' Dutch Mary adjoined. 'When tomorrow morning we to Ningo get I fix for you a Hong Kong sailing also. There still is plenty traffic for Hong Kong leaving Ningpo.'

'You hear that?' Harry Lord said. 'Do what the Captain says and you'll be all right.'

'Yes,' Dutch Mary affirmed. 'In a cabin you stay and to no harm you come.'

Tears of gratitude brimmed in Mr Chang's eyes. 'I'm so grateful I don't know what to say,' he mumbled.

Embarrassed, Harry Lord said, 'Then don't say anything. Just do what I told you.' Finishing his gin, his eye caught sight of the clock on the after bulkhead. 'Well I guess I'd better make a move. I want to see Heinie Sztykgold sometime today.' Opening the door to the saloon, he glanced back at Mr Chang. 'S'long,' he told him. 'Take care of yourself.'

Dutch Mary walked aft with him through the saloon and upper cabin deck. 'You have yet decided what you do when you leave?' she asked out of genuine curiosity as they descended the main stairway.

Harry Lord shrugged. 'I haven't given it much thought yet.'

Dutch Mary shook her head. It was all too typical of Harry Lord's haphazard approach to life. It seemed to her that he always got where he was going more by luck than design, almost as if he was motivated by some invisible force which looked after its own. 'Well start thinking before too late it becomes. Otherwise one morning you wake and find them under the door the *Red Star Bulletin* are shoving.'

'And what do you have in mind?' Harry Lord wanted to know.

'Indo-China.' Dutch Mary stopped and leaned on the capping in the outer starboard companionway. 'Saigon,' she said. 'Where a war is there are people to help also. About life that much I have learn if nothing else.'

'Saigon,' Harry Lord mused. 'Like that, huh?'

Dutch Mary looked into his face, perplexed. 'Sure – why not?'

'You mean you really intend sailing *The Ladybird* all the way to Saigon?'

Dutch Mary's perplexity changed to outright wonder. 'Out here from Glasgow she got.'

Harry Lord ran a hand rasping across his stubbled jaw. 'But that's no guarantee she could back there get.'

Dutch Mary laughed aloud with him as they looked out across the Hongkew waterfront, a stretch of dinghy riverside below the mouth of the Hongkew Creek cluttered with gloomy buildings and a maze of wharves and jetties that had become oddly deserted over the past few weeks, like most of the rest of the river. She studied the smouldering stub of the panatella, then let it fall and watched it spiral down between the battered plates of the hull and the wharf to fizzle out in the water that sucked and slid around the weed-grown pilings. 'This my next to last trip will be from Shanghai,' she explained. 'When from Ningpo we get back it will be to collect the crews' families. Even then during darkness I want in and away to get. Since those Communists bombing in daylight started things are not so comfortable before they used to be.'

Harry Lord's gaze drifted out across the broken eaves of Hongkew. 'All the way to Saigon.'

'All the way,' Dutch Mary confirmed.

Harry Lord struck a match to a cigarette. He hadn't thought about Saigon; hadn't thought about anywhere really. 'I'll keep that in mind.'

Dutch Mary extended a hand. 'Yourself you take care. And remember – around here things will bad get pretty soon.'

'Sure,' Harry Lord acknowledged. 'I'll remember that too. And thanks for getting Chu Chin Chow off my back. It's greatly appreciated.'

'That you never mind. But before on the Yangtze your neck you risk again, then twice you think. You hear? Not for money even it is worth.'

Harry Lord started down the prow. 'You can bank on that, Mary,' he promised.

On the dock he passed Ling issuing tickets from a machine around his neck like a tram-car conductor as the crowd of waiting refugees started to surge on board *The Ladybird*. He raised a casual hand to the companionway as he strode out westward. And in the starboard companionway Dutch

Mary leaned on the capping and watched him swing along the front. She had given up count of the hardcases she had met in her time, but she would always remember Harry Lord. She watched him go on along the front with that confident and aggressive gait that was purely his own. Purposeful; she supposed that was the true descriptive word. No matter where he was going he always somehow looked as if he was on his way to rob a bank.

But she knew there was more to Harry Lord than just a natural toughness; he was looking for something, she was convinced of it. He was like some mediaeval knight in rusty armour destined to wander the world all his days in search of something that he would only know when he found it. He was on earth for a specific purpose; that she was also convinced about. More than once she had considered that there was every possibility he might be some Messenger sent by the Avenging Angel to test the souls of the Damned before they were summoned for Final Judgement. And she was by no means a religious woman. Nor did she believe that it was such a far-fetched theory. Harry Lord could push a man to his limits without expending the least effort. Yet there was another side to him; she had seen that too. And so had Mr Chang.

She shook her grey ringleted head in wonder. 'By Gott. That boy and trouble both brothers are,' she mused aloud.

Harry Lord crossed the Hongkew Bund and made his way along the front toward the Red Fortune Hotel. The hotel was situated on the corner of the Bund and Sai Woo Lane, an old plasterwork building which consisted of four floors and overlooked the river. He had moved in after he collected his first pay cheque from Sztykgold. Although it had none of the attractions of the modern establishments found uptown, like the plush cocktail bars and the inevitable bar-girls, it was situated on the waterfront within easy reach of the ferries and the Carfax Oil Depot across in Pootung.

The front hall was empty when he arrived. He called down the bar, 'Is anybody home?'

The beaded curtain at the far end parted and Old Po put his head out, saw who it was, and gave a toothless smile. 'Where have you been – Hong Kong?' He started along the bar as though moving on castors, with a bottle of Haig & Haig and a glass, the long braided pig-tail draped over one shoulder and the black silk skull-cap pulled down on his head. 'Old Po was getting worried. You said you would be away no longer than two days at most.'

Harry Lord opened the bottle of Haig & Haig and poured a drink. 'I ran into a little trouble on the way.'

Old Po looked at him but said nothing. He belonged to an almost forgotten China of Imperialism, feudal war lords, and ancient custom, and Harry Lord's total indifference to everything at times gave him cause for the greatest wonder and alarm. 'There has also been trouble here since you left. Those Communists now bomb in daylight and always it's downriver here.' He smiled ruefully. 'I suppose Old Po should have had his hotel upriver in Nantao. In Nantao there's nothing worth for them to bomb.'

Harry Lord grinned, saw Old Po's argument as another example of age-old Chinese logic. 'Has anybody been asking for me while I've been away?'

'Only Mr Sztykgold. He called three times today.' Old Po spoke like a ventriloquist, only his white whiskers moving. 'He said he heard that you came upriver early this morning and he wanted to talk to you, to see you.'

Harry Lord was curious; Sztykgold had been calling him but his own calls to the Avenue Lafayette had received no reply. 'Did he say where he was calling from?'

'No, he just said he would call again later and that it was important.'

'When was the last time he called?'

'About an hour ago.'

Harry Lord knew the only thing that was important to Sztykgold was making another dollar, and so he was obviously out somewhere on business, big business if he had called three times. But this time he wasn't interested. He was through, finished. He was getting out. Like Dutch Mary had said, it was time to get his hat and coat on and get to hell out before things got any worse. But first he was going to collect his money for the Chen-kou trip. Eight slopeheads, including the old man who had died, at $200 the head amounted to $1,600, and he didn't intend leaving that sort of loose change behind, even if it was going to benefit the Hongkew Unmarried Mothers' Association.

Old Po fussed with the bar. 'You want I fix you something to eat?' he asked.

Harry Lord ran a hand across his stubbled jaw. 'Not right now. I think I'll go and get cleaned up first. If Sztykgold calls again put him through upstairs.'

Harry Lord's rooms were on the top floor. One of them was a big room with rattan furnishings and a rush mat covered floor. The veranda overlooked the Bund and the river, afforded a view of the whole south shore. Off to the left of the veranda was the bedroom. Pushing open the veranda doors, he took the .38 Police Special from his waistband and went through and put it beneath a pillow on the bed. He had bought the gun across in Tienningshih after his arrival in Shanghai, like the big .505 Gibbs. It wasn't much of a gun as far as guns went, and it wasn't too reliable beyond a distance of eight to ten yards. But when it went off it went off with such a hell of a bang that it scared the shit out of every living thing within a half mile radius.

When he returned from the bedroom he stood for a moment staring reflectively out through the veranda doors across the upturned eaves of Hongkew and Yangtzepoo to eastward. He wasn't at all certain about Saigon. The truth of it was he was weary of all the wheeling and dealing of big business, the con men, back-stabbers, the heavy water brain specialists, and the uniformed cut-throats who now seemed to infest every square inch of China. Besides, with what he had put away in the bank in Keelung he could afford to pull out and take it easy for a time. He wondered if maybe he should head south somewhere, maybe down somewhere around the Philippines again, laze around on some beach with nothing more strenuous to do than watch the rollers boom in once in a while. The trouble was there was always something seemed to happen to prevent him giving the subject any real thought. But this time, before the night was out, he would give it all the thought it required.

An hour later, bathed and shaved, he carried the bottle of Haig & Haig out to the veranda in time to hear a raucous blast of noise echo across the river as *The Ladybird* pulled away from the Ropewalk Wharves under a tarry plume of smoke. So crowded were her decks it seemed half the population of Shanghai had managed to climb on board. Taking a drink from the bottle, he watched her swing around cut in midstream, around the buoy directly off shore from the British Consulate building, her two paddle wheels and stern paddle threshing the river up white around her stern. She really didn't look so much like a ship, but more like a floating three-tiered wedding cake; the Ark departing in face of the pending flood.

With the current astern she began to pick up speed as she moved down along the Tienningshih waterfront while she kept a parallel course with the Chungkung Road below Yangtzepoo on her port side. He watched her go on downriver on the south shore toward Tungkow and the Yangtze out beyond the forts at Woosung fourteen miles downriver, and a mental picture of Mr Chang peering out from a cabin window deep in *The Ladybird*'s bowels while he waited for one of Chiang's gunboats to haul alongside passed before his eyes. Then the phone in the room rang and he went in and took the receiver from its hook. Old Po put the call through.

It was Sztykgold's questioning, slightly anxious voice that came across the line. 'Is that you, Lord?'

'Who the fuck you suppose it is?' If one thing about Sztykgold rankled Harry Lord it was his constant allusion to secretiveness. He flatly doubted if Sztykgold divulged to himself when he intended taking a bath in case he tried to drown himself.

Indecisive silence followed. Then: 'What is it? – is something wrong?'

Harry Lord said, 'I've been calling you most of the morning, that's what's wrong.'

In an apologetic voice Sztykgold answered, 'I'm afraid I was out on business. But I did try calling you several times at the hotel. Didn't anybody tell you? I knew you came upriver earlier in the morning.'

'Forget it,' Harry Lord growled. 'More important – what about the Chen-kou trip?'

'I'll have the money with me tonight.' Sztykgold now sounded as if his honesty was being regarded as suspect.

'Where?'

'Le Patronat. Can you get over there?'

Harry Lord said, 'For sixteen hundred bucks I'll get over the moon.'

Sztykgold laughed indulgently. 'Excellent.' He had

quickly regained his confidence. 'I'll be with some friends I think you'll want to meet.'

Harry Lord said cautiously, 'Yeah – what sort of friends?'

'You'll see when you get there,' Sztykgold now sounded mysterious.

Harry Lord stared hard at the receiver. 'Well don't count on hiring me out for anything. I'm not going to get my arse shot off by some trigger-happy slopehead at a time like this. I'm getting out just as soon's as I make the arrangements.'

Sztykgold answered evenly, 'And what do you think I intend doing?'

'Just so long's you know,' Harry Lord said flatly.

'Of course,' Sztykgold said. 'I'll be at Le Patronat around midnight. See you then.'

Harry Lord looked at the receiver and hung it back on the wall. Two minutes later he was climbing into bed, his brain fogged with lack of sleep and half the contents of the bottle of Haig & Haig.

* * *

At 4.15 that same afternoon Captain Hop and his two aides were sitting in the big open car beneath the trees lining the Avenue Lafayette in the old French Concession. From their vantage point to northward they had maintained a discreet watch on the Roebaud Apartment building since noon when they had followed Heinrich Sztykgold and his two Japanese bodyguards back across town from the Great Eastern Mansions. Now, after four hours of inactivity Sergeant Kee was restless. He spoke out of boredom, to nobody in particular. 'What do you suppose they're doing up there?'

Captain Hop lifted his gaze to the windows of the sixth floor apartment that showed through the branching foliage of the trees. 'Sztykgold will be making his arrangements,' he confidently predicted. 'It all takes time – even with a brain like his.'

Sergeant Kee shifted his morose gaze to the busy avenue. 'Waiting around like this never did agree with me.'

Captain Hop's handsome face showed a sudden flash of irritation. He said coldly, 'Then you better resign yourself to waiting around a lot more because from now on patience is going to be a prime necessity if we intend to bring off this little trick. If you want the plums you have to shake the tree. Do you think they'll fall into your cap otherwise?'

Sergeant Kee lapsed into sullen silence while Corporal Choy turned in his seat to look back at them. 'Time's getting on, Captain.'

'Forget the time,' Captain Hop told him sharply. 'Time's of no concern now.' He shifted his position, extracted a cigarette from his inlaid case, and applied the flame of a chunky gold lighter to it. He liked to think both the case and lighter were among the necessary possessions of a man of position. Possessions had always mattered a great deal to him, and the impression they created. His watch too was gold, Swiss and expensive. He had confiscated it from a prisoner in Kunming whom he had shot through the head after he had persistently refused to sign a confession to the effect that he was a subversive agent. He could never recall the man's name, not even when he looked at the watch. 'Personally I'm inclined to agree with the gentleman who offered the opinion that time and space are but hallucinations,' he said expansively.

'Confucius?' Corporal Choy with an ebullient smile suggested eagerly.

Captain Hop smiled at him tolerantly. 'My dear, Choy. If Confucious had said everything that's generally attributed to him he would never have had time to get his pants down.'

Corporal Choy's smile immediately lost its ebullience. Slighted by the remark, he turned away to sit glowering balefully at the avenue. By no means intelligent, he nonetheless possessed the dullard's sensitivity to intellectual disparagement of his ignorance. He was still brooding over being exploited in front of Sergeant Kee when he caught sight of Sztykgold and his two bodyguards emerge from the apartment building. 'Here they come,' he called back over his shoulder, feeling in an obscure way that he had restored himself by being the first to see them.

They watched the three men climb into the long black limousine and saw it swing out into the flow of late afternoon traffic. It headed south on the avenue, turned right on to the Avenue Bertrand Aubusson then left toward the river, away from the old International Settlement, westward.

Corporal Choy moved the big open car along half a block in rear, followed it around on to the Nantao Bund, then headed westward in pursuit.

Sergeant Kee was grateful to be on the move again. Sitting upright, he watched the limousine up ahead eagerly. 'It looks as if they're headed for Lunghwa.'

'It would seem so,' Captain Hop agreed; then to Choy said: 'Be careful. We don't want to arouse their suspicions.'

Twenty minutes later Corporal Choy pulled into the kerb on the Lunghwa Road when he saw the limousine glide to a halt on the opposite side of the roadway up ahead.

Seconds later Sztykgold started across the pavement to the offices of the Pheonix Airfreight Company with Tadatoshi in close attendance while Nakamura remained at the wheel of the limousine. Captain Hop watched the scene with interest. He knew all about the Pheonix Airfreight Company, and its owner André Passel. Like all operators involved in the running of a business not strictly legitimate, the Frenchman made certain donations to individuals of the KSS in order to have his activities overlooked, and in this instance the individual to whom Passel made his donation was Captain Hop. And unlike in the case of Sztykgold, he was therefore in a position to exert direct influence on Passel.

Leaning forward, he tapped Choy on the shoulder, and the massive figure nodded, put the motor in gear and drove the car into the parking lot of the Oceanic office building overlooking the Lunghwa Road.

Fifteen minutes elapsed before Sztykgold and Tadatoshi returned to the limousine, and watching, Captain Hop saw it turn around and start back in the direction of the city. He waited until it was lost to view, then threw his cigarette aside and glanced at Sergeant Kee.

André Passel was so busily intent on emptying the contents of his desk that he didn't hear them enter the office.

Captain Hop said conversationally, 'Going somewhere, André?'

Passel turned startled. 'Oh – it's you, Captain.' It took him every effort to conceal his dismay. With a sick smile he dropped the papers he was holding to the floor, paying no heed to the direction they took. He glanced from one to the other of the two impassive faces, dismay and uneasiness mounting with the passing tick of every second. And he knew, with Sztykgold having just left, that Captain Hop's unannounced appearance was more than just a coincidence.

He dropped his gaze to the paper-littered floor, gestured at it weakly. 'I was just clearing things out before making ready to leave.'

'Mm-hmm,' Captain Hop mused. 'So should everybody with any sense.' Tapping the riding-crop against the polished length of his right boot, he surveyed the scene with the indifference of a man who had seen it all before. 'And where do you intend going, André?'

Passel shuffled his feet with ever-mounting apprehension. He knew that Captain Hop didn't make social calls. 'I thought I'd try my luck in Singapore.' His own attempt at casual indifference failed miserably.

'Singapore – eh?' Captain Hop strode to the window to look incuriously out at the precincts of the airfield, the slap of the riding-crop against his boot sounding even more ominous in the strained silence which had descended on the room.

André Passel waited, feeling his heart beat erratically. 'Is there something I can do for you, Captain?' he asked when he could withstand the strain no longer.

Captain Hop turned away from the window with an austere smile. 'Your visitor – what did he want?'

Passel dabbed at his balding forehead with a crumpled handkerchief. He said lamely, 'You mean Sztykgold, Captain?'

Captain Hop's smile became even more austere. 'Come now, André. Who else would I mean?'

Passel felt himself grow cold. He knew better than to attempt to lie to a man like Captain Hop, yet he was also afraid of Sztykgold. He had seen the results of his bodyguards' handiwork before, and it didn't inspire betrayal. He licked at his dry mouth. 'Listen, Captain,' he pleaded. 'You know Sztykgold. Think what he would do if he found out I had told you anything.'

Captain Hop's austere smile suddenly became a reassuring one. 'I wouldn't worry about Sztykgold, André. He won't trouble you.'

Passel hesitated, but only for a brief moment. There was absolutely no way out, and he acknowledged the situation with a forlorn sigh. 'He wanted to hire an aircraft.'

Captain Hop went right on staring back at him. 'Why?'

Passel gave a helpless shrug. 'I don't know. He didn't say.

He just said it was to stand by in readiness. I couldn't very well say no. You know how we've done business over the past few years.'

'When is the aircraft to be made ready?'

'Tomorrow evening – Saturday evening. He said his intentions meantime were to leave sometime before daylight on Sunday morning. He didn't give an exact time. He said he was waiting last minute developments concerning some business deal.'

'Did he say where he was going?'

In exasperation, Passel said, 'You know Sztykgold, Captain. He wouldn't tell his own mother what he had in mind.'

'What else did he say?'

Passel glanced at a bottle of Martell on the desk. 'Is it all right with you?'

'Go ahead,' Captain Hop said, at the same time declining a drink with a motion of his white-gloved hand.

Passel gulped the cognac straight down. 'He said that if a man called Henry Wan got in touch with me I was to tell him everything's arranged for Hong Kong the moment he's ready.'

Captain Hop met Sergeant Kee's questioning gaze across the room. Both had understood immediately the significance of Passel's statement; Sztykgold intended the aircraft for his own use, and its destination obviously wasn't Hong Kong. Mr Henry Wan was about to lose a fortune in two directions at the same time.

Captain Hop said, 'Who's piloting the aircraft?'

'I am – that was the deal.'

Sergeant Kee spoke for the first time. 'Where is it to be standing by?'

Passel helped himself to another cognac. 'At the southerly end of Zero Two runway.'

'Did Sztykgold mention anything about a proposed cargo?'

Passel shook his head. 'No – nothing.'

'And what do you think about all this?' Captain Hop asked matter-of-factly.

Passel shrugged, murmured, 'I don't know what to think, Captain.'

Captain Hop smiled. 'That's what I like about you, André – you don't think when you're not supposed to. That's one of the reasons why we've always got along so well together.'

'Yes, Captain.'

'And, André. If Sztykgold gets in touch with you about any change in plans – then you call me immediately through Sergeant Pao at Headquarters. Understood?'

'Of course, Captain. Anything you say.'

'Naturally. *Anything* I say.' Captain Hop paused, watching Passel's face. He was a man with a wife and two children, therefore vulnerable. 'And don't think the safest way out of this situation is to leave Shanghai tonight. You have a charming wife and two pretty daughters—'

Passel's already pale and sweating face turned white. 'You don't have to worry about me doing anything like that, Captain. You have my word.'

They left André Passel staring after them with beaten eyes, shoulders sagging over the desk.

Outside Captain Hop climbed into the waiting car followed by Sergeant Kee. 'Back to the Avenue Lafayette,' he instructed Choy.

As the car started back along the Lunghwa Road, Sergeant Kee said worriedly, 'It's obvious that Sztykgold intends to run out with the bullion himself.'

'He wouldn't be Sztykgold if he didn't,' Captain Hop answered calmly.

'Then what do you think his next move's going to be?' Sergeant Kee eagerly inquired.

'His first task's going to be to get somebody through to Lang Dok to warn the people there to get the bullion ready for shipping downriver. If it has to be dug out of the ground then they're going to need time to get everything ready. To avoid any chance of trouble Lord will have to get in and away as quickly as possible.'

Sergeant Kee leaned back into the deep upholstery with a feeling of increasing uneasiness. The sun was going down beyond the distant waters of Tai hu and the long black shadows became indistinct as dusk crept over the city from eastward. After a time he said, 'With us being unable to exert any direct influence on what's happening it could well become complicated, Captain. Is there nothing at all that we can do about it?'

Captain Hop stared fixedly ahead. It was impossible to tell whether he had heard Kee or not; his thoughts were preoccupied with a more important matter. He was regretting not having asked Lieutenant Huang at which rate David Kow had affixed the value of the bullion. On the open market he had known it fetch as much as $160s the ounce. Again, he could have based his estimate on a much lower figure. In which case the bullion could be worth considerably more than $3,000,000. What he ought to have asked him was if he knew the approximate weight of the bullion. The possibility that it might be worth an even more impressive sum intrigued him.

Eventually he said in reply to Kee, calmly meeting his anxious gaze, 'At this stage the important thing is we stay close to Sztykgold so that we know every move he makes. Let him make all the arrangements. If you remember – I said earlier that patience would be a prime necessity.'

In the encroaching darkness their headlights swept out across the river as they turned on to the Nantao Bund and headed east in the direction of the old French Concession.

SHANGHAI

Saturday, May 21st, 1949

S–TYR–E

It was already midnight when Harry Lord awakened. The first thing he did was check with Old Po that there hadn't been any further calls for him while he was asleep. Afterward he lit a cigarette and got out of bed to find the one suit he owned and a set of underclothes folded across the back of a chair freshly laundered, even his shoes cleaned ready for him. While he dressed he decided that the best move he had ever made was to move into the Red Fortune Hotel. Right from the first day Old Po had taken care of him like a son. It was something he would miss when he moved out. After he was dressed he took the .38 Police Special from beneath the pillow and put it in the pocket of his coat.

When he went downstairs he caught a cruising taxicab on the Bund a little way west of the hotel. It was quiet all along the front as they headed uptown toward the old International Settlement with its lurid glow of light reflected in the sky overhead, the buildings along the Shanghai Bund tall, angular, and white under their floodlights; the Yokohama Specie Bank, the Oriental Banking Corporation, and the Mercantile Bank of India, London, and China clearly identifiable. Outwardly there was no real evidence that the revolution had directly affected the business quarter of the city, although one noticeable change which had taken place in the past few days was the almost complete lack of evidence of the White Sun Flag of the Kuomintang. So sparsely did it now show above the rooftops it seemed that only Chiang and his immediate associates were confident of continuing survival.

Passing the old Russian Consulate, the taxicab crossed the Soochow Creek and turned westward along the left bank, the water black and unmoving, scored by the fairy lights of Hongkew and Chapei on the far bank, the world-famous Willow Pattern houses sculptured against the sky. Further on they passed the new Kuomintang Government Administration building with its windows still boarded after being dynamited by the People's Militia the day after its official opening by Chiang. Next they turned on to Bubbling Well

Road and headed south past the Police Barracks which lay within its grounds to westward. When they drew level with the barracks Harry Lord saw the glint of light reflect from the machine guns mounted on the roof, while out front of the high-railinged parade ground policemen patrolled in pairs with Thompson guns. He couldn't understand anybody wanting to invade a police barracks, not even the People's Militia.

The club Le Patronat was on the Yenching Road, on the northerly fringe of the old French Concession. Held to be one of the more superior places of entertainment by Shanghai society-goers, it was owned by a Frenchman called Jacques Roullet. Harry Lord had first met Roullet shortly after his arrival in Shanghai, when Sztykgold arranged for him to make a trip to Nanking on Roullet's behalf. That was when he discovered that Roullet was intrenched in more lucrative ventures than running a fashionable nightclub. The club was in fact merely the headquarters for the re-routing westward of the poppy which found its way into Shanghai from the north. That had always been the way of it in Shanghai: only the very unlucky or the very naïve didn't have some illegitimate venture going for them.

Le Patronat was crowded as always when he arrived, the humid air smelling of cigar and cigarette smoke, alcohol, French perfume, and starched linen. He stood up inside the entrance, cast a searching look across the heads of the diners at the tables around the dance floor, saw no sign of Sztykgold, then turned his attention to the bar. He recognized several faces. In a huddle by themselves were eight or ten English journalists who had been in Shanghai since the Royal Navy frigate *Amethyst* was shelled and trapped on the Yangtze when attempting to navigate the river in the face of a Communist crossing on the morning of April 20th. The survivors and wounded who had managed to struggle ashore had been arriving in Shanghai by various routes for the past four weeks and the journalists had been waiting to relay first-hand accounts of the hardships they had faced. It appeared they would be around Shanghai for sometime to come for the *Amethyst* was still held fast under the Communist guns off Tan Sha below Nanking.

'I'm glad to see you finally made it.'

Harry Lord turned to see Sztykgold at his side. He looked

older, greyer, and more nervous than ever. Harry Lord knew by the look of him that something more important than a $2 deal was in the air. 'What's wrong, Heinie?' he grinned. 'Your shoes too tight?'

Sztykgold chose to ignore the jibe. He said dryly, 'I happen to be rather tired at the moment – that's all.'

Glancing around him, Harry Lord saw no sign of the two habitual bodyguards, the arrogant Sato Tadatoshi and the hulking Yusagi Nakamura. 'Where's Flanagan and Allen to-night?'

Sztykgold's high grey forehead puckered with a frown. '*Who?*' he said.

'Forget it,' Harry Lord said.

Sztykgold said coolly, 'Let me buy you a drink.' And turned to lead the way across the room.

There were three of them sitting at the table, Chinamen. Both men wore black silk evening suits. One of them was an elegant cigar-smoking individual somewhere in his fifties, worried-looking. His companion was considerably younger, of athletic build, and confident in a physical sort of way. Harry Lord didn't like him, instinctively. He had a theory that a slopehead hatchetman always liked to play the part on the assumption that if they were to play it toughly enough the opposition would keel over with psychogenic fright.

The woman was something different. She wasn't only coolly sophisticated, but also beautiful. And on further inspection he decided he hadn't seen such a classic piece of Chink arse in a long time. She knew it too, he thought; looked ready to drop her knickers at the first cough.

Sztykgold made the introductions. 'Allow me to introduce Mr Lord.'

Neither of the Chinamen rose from the table, although the cigar-smoking individual gave a polite smile while his gaze remained coolly calculating.

Sztykgold went on to explain silkily, 'This is Henry Wan – and his wife.'

Harry Lord glanced at Henry Wan, his wife, then at the other man. 'And who's he – Kublai Khan?'

Tzu Hsun's eyes hardened and he started to his feet only to check himself when Henry Wan laid a hand on his arm. 'I'm certain that Mr Lord means no offence, Tzu.' Henry Wan had a mechanical bland smile.

Grinning, Harry Lord stared pointedly at the bulge the pistol made under the left breast of Tzu Hsun's evening coat. 'You want to watch that shooter doesn't drop out your coat and break your foot.'

Tzu Hsun's jaws tightened, their muscles prominent as whipcord, and his eyes flashed.

Sztykgold trembled with relief when he saw Tzu Hsun again relax under the insistent pressure of Henry Wan's grip on his arm, then reluctantly resume his seat, his face the colour of wax paper; and he turned quickly on Harry Lord in an attempt to avert further possible disaster. It was always the same where Harry Lord was concerned, none of it ever went as planned. 'Will you join us in that drink?'

Harry Lord hesitated, undecided, then hauled out a chair and slouched into it. 'What about the money?' he asked. Among the few things he believed in was in not wasting time, especially not *his* time.

Sztykgold covered his embarrassment with a sickly smile and passed the envelope he brought from an inside coat pocket across the table.

Harry Lord took it, looked in it, then put it away in his inside coat pocket without comment.

Henry Wan watched the transaction with interest. Then Sztykgold said, 'How did the trip go? I expected you back a couple of days ago, yesterday at the latest.'

Harry Lord said, 'If I thought you were interested I'd tell you.'

Henry Wan beckoned a waiter. 'What can I get you, Mr Lord?'

Harry Lord looked across the table at him. He wasn't impressed by any of them, although he had an open mind where the woman was concerned. 'Who's paying?' he asked.

Henry Wan laughed, and Sztykgold found a dyspeptic smile. 'I'm afraid you'll have to excuse Mr Lord's sense of humour – it takes some time to become accustomed to it.'

Henry Wan studied Harry Lord candidly. He had already reached a decision. 'You don't have to apologize in anyway for Mr Lord. I find his forthrightness refreshing. What's more, I appreciate a man with a sense of humour.' After giving the waiter an order, he turned back to the table and made a motion of approval in Sztykgold's direction.

In turn Sztykgold glanced at the occupants of the nearest

tables, then leaned forward. In a low whisper he said, 'Mr Wan has a proposition he wishes to put to you.'

Harry Lord was unimpressed. 'I'm not interested.'

Sztykgold's face lengthened. 'Not even enough to hear how much it would be worth to you?'

Harry Lord eyed him dubiously. He had known since hearing of Sztykgold's three earlier phone calls to the Red Fortune Hotel that there was something more than a $2 deal in the air, otherwise he could never have looked as ill as he did.

Henry Wan showed sudden anxiety. 'Perhaps if you explained the nature of our business to Mr Lord.'

Sztykgold wetted his mouth and leaned even closer across the table. 'Bullion,' he whispered. 'From upriver.'

The magic grin at once spread its crooked way across Harry Lord's dark face. 'You're joking.'

'I don't think that one as a rule makes jokes about something like upwards of three million dollar's worth of bullion, Mr Lord,' Henry Wan assured him solemnly.

Harry Lord studied him contemplatively. Henry Wan was serious. He had probably never been so serious in his life as he was at that moment. Harry Lord recognized the look of a man who wasn't only serious, but also desperate. He said, 'I don't know if you're aware of it or not, but they're shooting at everything on sight out there. I was lucky to get back downriver yesterday morning in one piece.'

'It would be worth twenty-five thousand dollars to you.' Sztykgold sounded as if his shirt collar was choking him.

Harry Lord's unnerving blue eyes showed absolutely nothing. But he reasoned that if they were offering $25,000 for openers then it was worth waiting around, if only out of curiosity. Then across the table Zephyrine Wan reached for her glass and presented him with a deliberate glimpse of an exquisitely shaved armpit. Sipping at her drink, she exchanged a fleeting glance with Tzu Hsun whose handsome features were still set in a grim, resentful line. And watching them, Harry Lord's magic grin widened even further. He had known intuitively that there was something odd about the situation, and the glance that had passed between Zephyrine Wan and Tzu Hsun clearly indicated that somebody was banging somebody and that it wasn't Old Cigar-Smoking Henry Wan who was on the lucky end of it. And they were worried, almost as much as Henry Wan. Yet something told him that Henry Wan wasn't as ignorant of the situation as he appeared, and that maybe he had something else on his mind besides the bullion.

Suddenly aware that Harry Lord was still watching her, Zephyrine Wan smiled a smile across the rim of her glass that promised the moon. Harry Lord stared back at her levelly, the magic, crazy-mad grin still on his face, and decided she had somehow formed the impression that he had been dropped on his head while a baby. Then Zephyrine Wan put her glass back down on the table and very deliberately crossed a pair of thighs that appeared to travel on forever. And in a very soft, mysterious voice full of insinuating promise, said, 'It could perhaps be worth a great deal more to you, Mr Lord.'

Grinning crazily, Harry Lord said, 'It could well be, Mrs Wan – but you don't have to show me your knickers to prove it.'

His voice had cut across the table like a surgeon's scalpel, freezing Zephyrine Wan instantly. And on the other side of the table Sztykgold choked on his drink as Tzu Hsun rose up out of his chair as if scalded. Only Henry Wan and Harry Lord remained easy where they sat.

Tzu Hsun's face was masked with fury. 'I heard what you said!' he hissed.

Harry Lord looked up out of his chair at him, unperturbed. 'Make one move, Kublai, and I'll hit you so hard you'll hear bells for a fortnight.'

Henry Wan suddenly smiled, broke into a low chuckle. 'I think it would be advisable if you were to sit down, Tzu.' Then turning back to Harry Lord, he said, 'Fifty thousand, Mr Lord. You hear? – *fifty thousand*.'

Harry Lord wondered if he heard correctly. His hearing had never failed him where money was concerned, certainly not the sort of money Henry Wan talked. He said cautiously, 'How far upriver would I have to go?'

'I'm afraid that's something we can only discuss if you agree to make the trip,' Henry Wan quietly explained through a cloud of cigar smoke.

Sztykgold, his face still white from the shock of a few moments earlier, whispered, 'I can say you won't have to go as far as Chen-kou.'

'Fifty thousand – huh?' Harry Lord wondered what $50,000 would look like in folding money and if he would need a handcart to wheel it on board the *Jacaranda*.

Henry Wan watched him anxiously. 'Guaranteed, Mr Lord.'

Sweat began to bead on Sztykgold's high grey brow. 'Well – what do you say?'

Harry Lord let them wait. Across the table Zephyrine Wan and Tzu Hsun sat through it as if turned to stone.

'You won't regret it,' Henry Wan promised.

Harry Lord leaned forward on to the table, looked long and hard at him. 'You want to hope not – for *your* sake.'

Sztykgold heaved an audible sigh of relief. 'There's only one condition – and that is you make the trip tomorrow night.'

Harry Lord felt he was wasting his time again. 'What's wrong with tonight? I can be headed downriver inside an hour.'

Sztykgold shook his head. 'I'm afraid that's impossible. First I've got to get word through the Communist lines to the people concerned, and that's going to take time. But by tomorrow evening everything should be arranged.'

Harry Lord saw his reasoning. 'All right,' he conceded. 'But where's the stuff going. That's something I have to know in case I've got to take on extra gas.'

'The cargo will be delivered here to Shanghai,' Henry Wan informed him. 'I think that's all you need know for the moment. Mr Sztykgold will give you all the relevant details before you leave tomorrow. That's our arrangement. Surely you can see that I must take certain safeguards.'

Harry Lord nodded. 'Okay – you made your point.'

Henry Wan finished his drink and rose from the table accompanied by his wife and Tzu Hsun, their faces exuding about as much warmth as a morgue slab. 'Thank you for your cooperation, Mr Lord. I'm certain you're an efficient as well as an enterprising young man. You ought to go far in this world.'

Harry Lord said solemnly, 'With fifty thousand bucks I'll make a point of it.'

'Then I trust that you'll have an uneventful trip, Mr Lord. Good evening, gentlemen.'

Harry Lord watched them make their way through the

crowd around the bar toward the door. 'You know, Heinie,' he said. 'I'll lay odds that Tzu's banging the arse off that piece four, five times a day. And I'll also lay odds that old Henry Wan knows about it too.'

Sztykgold shrugged immaculate shoulders, afraid to think how close everything had come to disaster despite the care he had taken. There was no doubt but that the man was mad, *wholly* mad. 'What do you say that we let them attend to their own problems?'

'As long as they don't become ours,' Harry Lord countered. 'All I'm in this to do is bring the stuff downriver, nothing else.'

Sztykgold thought what he said might well be true, but he couldn't see any of it reaching out to them. 'Don't worry about it any. I'll take care of everything this end.'

Harry Lord was curious. 'Who the hell is he anyway? I've never seen him around town.'

Sztykgold saw no reason not to let him in on at least some of it. 'Have you ever heard of the Wan Merchant Bank of Chungking?'

Harry Lord said, 'That's him?'

Sztykgold nodded.

Harry Lord began to see some of the implications. 'And the bullion?'

'It belongs to the bank,' Sztykgold explained. 'Not that it matters any to us. He arranged for it through Tzu to be smuggled out of Chungking on board a junk slated for Kiangling with a cargo of wool, only it was headed for Shanghai.'

'So that's it?'

'Yes, and the junk managed to get itself caught up in a crossing of the river that day the *Amethyst* was hit and the crew took refuge on the south shore. Since then it's been impossible for them to make any sort of move without attracting Communist attention.'

Harry Lord's curiosity gave way to doubt. 'Christ, that's a hell of a long time to have stuff like that lying on the river. How come he waits this long before trying to bring it down?'

'Because he didn't know what had happened to the junk until one of the crew returned with the news to Chungking last Thursday evening.'

'You're telling me this junk's been sitting upriver all this time loaded to the gunwales with bullion?' Harry Lord said, finding it hard to believe.

'Not exactly. When the crew saw it was going to be impossible for them to continue downriver they buried it on shore. But don't worry about it. I went into everything in detail before I allowed myself to become involved. All you have to do is collect the stuff and bring it downriver. Everything will be ready. Leave it to me.'

Harry Lord sat back, and lighting a cigarette, caught sight of Captain Hop at the bar. Instantly he was alert, naturally suspicious. 'Listen,' he said. 'You don't suppose the cops could know anything about Mr Wan and his problems?'

Sztykgold glanced at him sharply. 'What do you mean?'

Harry Lord flicked his eyes toward the bar. 'Captain Hop – and we both know how he's got sixth sense where money's concerned.'

Sztykgold stiffened, edged a glance toward the bar. Like Harry Lord, he also harboured a natural aversion to Captain Hop and he knew that it was only his long-established connections with the Kuomintang hierarchy in Chungking that prevented Hop from attempting to move in on his activities. 'But I don't see how he can possibly know anything. Wan didn't arrive in town until yesterday morning.'

Harry Lord was unconvinced. He never trusted cops at anytime, especially not slopehead cops. 'Maybe he heard a whisper somewhere.'

'I can't truly believe that,' Sztykgold disputed. 'Surely if the Chungking police had suspicions about Wan they would never have allowed him to leave town.'

'Maybe,' Harry Lord conceded reluctantly.

Sztykgold was arguably less doubtful. 'But the town's swarming with strangers at the moment. People are coming and going everywhere and even Hop can't know everything that's going on.'

'No?' Harry Lord remained unconvinced. 'I wouldn't underestimate him any. He already shook me down yesterday morning in the Nanking Road.'

'Why?'

'I don't know. That's what bothered me.'

Sztykgold took a long calculating look at Captain Hop where he stood alone at the bar. There was nothing about him to arouse suspicions. He was alone, with a drink, apparently preoccupied with his own thoughts. He hadn't glanced even once in the direction of their table all the while he had been watching him. 'Nonetheless I'm certain you're wrong about this,' he declared with spirit. 'Although knowing him I don't entirely blame you for being suspicious. I've always felt about as comfortable in his presence as I would with a cobra.'

'Well I hope you're right,' Harry Lord brooded.

Suddenly Sztykgold relaxed, said in a voice that showed relief despite his outward confidence. 'Somehow I think he has more on his mind than money tonight.'

Harry Lord followed Sztykgold's gaze and saw Captain Hop now hovering on the edge of the dance floor where a striking White Russian girl was cavorting around near nude.

'Well?' Sztykgold smiled. 'What do you have to say about that?'

Harry Lord replied unenthusiastically, 'Only that she's wearing those tits like maybe they're her old man's medals.'

Sztykgold's smile was equally without enthusiasm as he reached his brief-case out from beneath the table.

'What's wrong, Heinie? – in a hurry?'

Sztykgold eased himself stiffly from beneath the table. 'If it's of any interest to you I still happen to have a great deal of unfinished business to get through tonight. Maybe you'll arrange to be at the Avenue Lafayette at noon. Now if you'll kindly excuse me.'

Harry Lord watched him push his way through the crowd around the bar toward the door. Obviously the most important item on Sztykgold's agenda had to be in finding a way to get word north to the crew of the junk wherever it was they were holed up so that everything would be arranged for his arrival.

''Allo 'Arree.'

Harry Lord turned in his chair to find Jacques Roullet at his shoulder. 'Hello, Jack. How are you?'

Jacques Roullet pulled out Sztykgold's vacated chair and sat into it. 'Fine, fine,' he announced. Short, middle-aged, and with a paunch concealed beneath an expensive black silk evening suit of a shantung weave, his black hair was oiled into waves and he wore a pencil thin moustache; typically French. 'I was surprised to see you were still around.'

'I won't be much longer,' Harry Lord assured him.

'Best thing too.' At the table opposite a Chinese couple smiled across, and Roullet politely returned it. 'Madame – Monsieur,' he purred. Then returning his attention to Harry Lord all trace of stage French vanished. 'I'm going to get the fuck out of here myself tonight, Harry-boy.'

'Then I hope you have it arranged good.'

Roullet nodded understandingly. 'I'm confident. I hired a plane from Hong Kong. It's coming in from Hangchow later in the morning.'

'You want to be careful the cops don't know anything about it.'

'I'm leaving right from the club when it closes – right to Lunghwa.'

'Well you keep an eye open for the cops just the same,' Harry Lord warned. 'I met a slopehead today who had similar problems. And especially you want to watch *that* bastard.'

Roullet sent a glance across the room to where Captain Hop lounged on the edge of the dance floor with his drink. 'I know what you mean, Harry-boy.'

'By the way, how long's he been hanging around here?'

'The last couple of nights, since I hired that Russky piece, Princess Kopa.'

'Is she really a princess?' Harry Lord asked out of vague interest.

Roullet shrugged. 'You know these Russky pieces, Harry-boy. They're *all* princesses.'

The *maître d'hôtel* appeared while he was talking, and excusing himself, whispered a word into his ear.

Roullet looked back across the table apologetically. 'I'm sorry, Harry-boy. I'll have to leave you now. We have two of Chiang's friends in the house, and if I know these two boys our Captain Hop could well go home alone this morning.' Returning the chair beneath the table, he leaned close to Harry Lord's ear. 'Look me up if you're ever in Hong Kong. I already have two places working for me there. Try the Trois Canards in Victoria Central.'

'I'll do that, Jack,' Harry Lord promised.

'And look after yourself, Harry-boy.'

'You too.'

Harry Lord sat for another few minutes, finished his

drink, then got up and made his way toward the door unhurriedly. Once outside he slipped into the shadows and waited to watch the entrance and the roadway with its bustle of night traffic, half expecting to see Captain Hop follow him outside. But when he failed to appear, he turned shrugging his worries aside and walked out to the pavement to hail a taxicab and tell the driver the Red Fortune Hotel.

* * *

Sergeant Kee watched Harry Lord hail a taxicab from the darkness of a rooftop across the roadway, then descended to the ground in time to meet Captain Hop as he emerged from the side entrance which gave access to Le Patronat's dressing-rooms. He grinned happily at his approaching superior in the gloom. 'You were right, Captain. He waited to see if he was followed.'

'He'll have put his mind at rest,' Captain Hop said blandly. 'And Sztykgold?'

'He caught a taxicab and headed back in the direction of the Avenue Lafayette.'

It was proceeding exactly as Captain Hop had envisaged. He nodded approvingly. 'Good. Now let's get back and join Choy.'

Together they walked back to where they had left the car in the parking lot of the Hotel Ferdinand.

At 1.35 a.m. they parked the car a block to southward of the Roebaud Apartment building, in the tree-shadowed drive of the sedate Versailles Club, the exclusive refuge of the more wealthy French residents of Shanghai, and walked back to join Corporal Choy where he stood watching the lighted windows of the apartment building from the shadows on the north side of the avenue.

Captain Hop glanced up at the lighted windows on the sixth floor. 'How's everything been?'

'Quiet, Captain. Everything's quiet.' Choy's bulk occupied almost the entire doorway into which they were crowded. 'Sztykgold arrived back twenty minutes ago.'

'And the bodyguards?'

'They didn't set foot outside after you left to follow Sztykgold.'

'Yes,' Captain Hop mused, his gaze still on the lighted windows on the sixth floor. 'He most probably decided to keep them out of sight for the time being in case they made Wan uneasy.'

Sergeant Kee, interrupting, said. 'There's Sztykgold now.'

On the opposite side of the avenue they saw Sztykgold approach one of the lighted windows on the sixth floor and stand for several moments examining the greenly lighted expanse of the tree-lined roadway.

'It looks as if he's waiting for somebody to arrive,' Sergeant Kee observed.

In the same instant Corporal Choy laid a massive hand on Captain Hop's arm. 'This could be somebody coming now, Captain.'

Crowding back into the doorway, they watched the Green Cab Company taxicab pull into the entrance to the apartment building. Two men alighted on to the pavement. Both were powerfully built, although the taller of the two easily outweighed his companion by forty or fifty pounds. He had a round shaved skull which gleamed in the light, and enormous sloping shoulders; the build of a Sumo wrestler. The shorter man was the younger and had vigorous good-looks. Both wore light-coloured suits and were self-possessed and formidable.

The three men crowded into the doorway on the other side of the avenue knew them both by sight. The tall man's name was Po-han, and the other man, Yang Sen, was his cousin. They were both of Manchurian blood, and employed by Sztykgold when they weren't devoting their time and cunning to their own conspiracies. They also possessed extensive police records, and although the courts had never been able to prove it, they were still regarded as something of celebrities in the criminal world for the part they had played in the *Kanchow* affair in early 1946, when with the Kang brothers they had pirated the Baines & Hyland steamer one night leaving Nanking and sailed her up to the waters of Poyang hu where they had successfully held her to ransom for $100,000. For the past two years Po-han had owned an ocean-going motorized junk called the *Sungari* and during that period was suspected of several other acts of piracy and murder in the waters of the Yangtze Estuary and Hangchow Bay, although again nothing had ever been proved successfully.

Captain Hop was surprised by their presence on the

Avenue Lafayette, but not unduly concerned. As the taxicab drew away, he watched the two men turn into the building, then saw Sztykgold withdraw from the window where he had been watching.

Consternation clouded Sergeant Kee's face as he stared after the two men. 'What are they doing here?'

'I'd say that Sztykgold obviously intends to use the *Sungari* in some way or another.' Captain Hop was calmly examining the deserted expanse of the tree-lined avenue. 'Although I seriously doubt if Harry Lord knows anything about it or else he'd also be up there.'

'I don't like it,' Sergeant Kee said heavily.

'Nor do I,' Captain Hop calmly admitted. 'But it's something we can take care of later. Right now I'm more interested to learn who's going north to Lang Dok. One thing is certain, it won't be Po-han and the *Sungari*. She'd be blown out of the water before she'd made a couple of miles up-river.'

It wasn't until 2.05 a.m. that any further developments occurred, when Po-han and Yang Sen emerged from the apartment building entrance, with Sztykgold's two bodyguards, Tadatoshi and Nakamura, close behind them. The startling fact was that the latter were dressed in the rough garb of peasants, Tadatoshi with a broad sweat-band knotted around his forehead, and Nakamura clad in a tattered black work-suit. For a moment all four men scrutinized the darkly shadowed avenue before starting hurriedly southward.

Corporal Choy stared after them, a heavy frown of perplexity darkening his hawked, North China face. 'What are they doing dressed like that?'

Captain Hop ignored him. His attention was focused on a lighted window six floors above where Sztykgold was watching the avenue in an effort to make certain that nobody was on hand to follow the four men. Captain Hop knew it had to be Tzu Hsun Sztykgold was looking for, aware that Henry Wan would undoubtedly have decided to take the precaution of keeping an eye on him. But he knew where Tadatoshi and Nakamura were headed; he had half suspected it would happen this way, that Sztykgold wouldn't be inclined to take a chance with anybody outside his own trusted circle with so much at stake. With his attention still focused on the sixth floor, he said quietly to Choy, 'I think we'll find those two are on their way to Lang Dok.'

Corporal Choy's dull, hawked face didn't alter as he stared after the four men hurrying south on the avenue.

Meanwhile Captain Hop was still watching the sixth floor, but his thoughts now centred on Po-han and Yang Sen. He was ninety-nine per cent certain in his own mind about the part that Sztykgold intended them to play, but the one remaining per cent still worried him. He had never felt easy about leaving anything to chance and there was only one way to make certain there were no mistakes made. Then Sztykgold, obviously satisfied that nobody was lurking outside, drew away from the window, and with a glance at the avenue, Captain Hop saw that the four men had walked almost two blocks. 'Come on!' Keeping close to the shadows along the building-line, he started back toward the Versailles Club where the car was parked, Sergeant Kee and Corporal Choy following close behind. They were almost at the drive when they saw Tadatoshi and Nakamura wave down a passing taxicab near the intersection with the Avenue Bertrand Aubusson and leave Po-han and Yang Sen walking south toward the Shanghai Bund and the river.

Corporal Choy caught up with the unsuspecting taxicab as it left the old French Concession, then drifted back into the stream of traffic to follow it north across town.

Sergeant Kee sat brooding in the rear, his gaze fixed on the taxicab up ahead. 'If they're on their way to Lang Dok then I hope they know what they're doing. I'd hate to think of them getting shot going through those Communist lines.'

Captain Hop countered evenly, 'Those two have the luck for anything.' Adding significantly: 'At the moment.'

But Sergeant Kee remained uneasy despite his superior's confidence. What had happened the previous morning was something that happened only once in a lifetime. In fact, he still couldn't quite bring himself to believe it; $3,000,000 – in bullion. It was something a man only dreamed about. True, he had some money put away along with Captain Hop in Kunming, an enterprise on Hop's part which could, in the circumstances, be their salvation in the forthcoming capitulation of the Kuomintang régime when it would be every man for himself. It wasn't much, twenty per cent of the 'squeeze' they took out of the 3rd District over the calendar month, but at forty-six it was enough to insure himself against the immediate future. But $3,000,000; he felt weak at the thought of it.

The dashboard clock showed the time was 2.25 a.m. when Corporal Choy brought the car to a halt on the west side of the Loyang Bridge where it spanned the Soochow Creek. Captain Hop and Sergeant Kee alighted hurriedly and scrambled down the bank to the cover of some scrub as Tadatoshi and Nakamura started across the bridge. On the far side they saw them turn west along the north bank to where several canal junks and sampans lay huddled close to the shore, their carbide lamps throwing shadows from their wicker living-quarters to light on the flat black water. Minutes later a sampan glided out from the shore with the bulky figures of the two men filling the stern-quarters, then turned upstream to lose itself in the darkness.

Captain Hop emerged from the clump of scrub looking thoughtfully after it. 'If everything goes as I expect it will, then they should be safely through those Communist lines by daylight.'

Sergeant Kee stared into the darkness along with him, although he was no longer thinking about Tadatoshi and Nakamura. What was now worrying him was his superior's confidence. This time they were involved with Chungking property, and if word of what was happening reached Chungking, then it would be a bullet in the neck and no questions asked. Sometimes he wished he was as thick in the head as Choy.

'Come on, let's get back to the car.' When Captain Hop started back up the bank he knew exactly the next step he was going to take in a bid to eradicate that remaining one per cent of lingering doubt which still troubled him.

When they climbed into the car, Choy turned looking at them inquiringly.

'The Tienningshih Vehicular Ferry,' Captain Hop instructed him. 'Let's see if we can find Yang Sen. They ought to be back across river by now.'

Corporal Choy drove the big open car down the ramp from the vehicular ferry-boat on to the Tienningshih Bund at 3.00 a.m. Turning left on the Bund, he then drove eastward through the bustle of night traffic on the long stretch of roadway bordered by a bank of sampans and river junks on one side, and on the other by a jumble of squalid bars, hotels, and eating-houses. Ten minutes later he doused the headlights and pulled the car into the shadows on the Tungkow Bund where it overlooked Henning's Wharf.

Among the ocean-going junks moored around the jetty the *Sungari* was easily recognizable by the dragon's head painted on her high flared bows. Taking the Zeiss glasses from the glove compartment. Captain Hop focused them on the junk's well-deck where three figures were seated around a brazier. Although Po-han had his back to the shore his shaved skull and bulky silhouette were unmistakable. Studying the other two faces in the reflected glow of light as they passed a bottle between themselves, he saw that neither of them was Yang Sen. Returning the glasses to the glove compartment, he looked back at the jumble of bars along the Tungkow waterfront. 'Let's see if he's around any of these places.'

Fifteen minutes later Sergeant Kee found Yang Sen in a bar to eastward, then returned along the front where he met Captain Hop and Corporal Choy covering the hovels among the alleyways running southward. 'He's back there – in the Lemon Tree Bar.'

'Alone?' Captain Hop asked.

'He's at the bar alone.'

Captain Hop turned on Corporal Choy. 'Get the car.'

Corporal Choy went for the car and they drove eastward along the front until Sergeant Kee pointed out the bar up ahead. Captain Hop indicated a nearby alleyway, and Corporal Choy turned the car and backed it into the narrow black tunnel and extinguished the headlights.

At 3.50 a.m. Captain Hop jolted into life when the light-suited figure passed the mouth of the alleyway. 'There he is – alone!'

Corporal Choy immediately left the driving seat and moved swiftly down the alleyway. By the time he disappeared around the corner on to the Bund Sergeant Kee had taken his place at the wheel. Without wasting time, he put the motor in gear and eased the big car gently out on to the broad stretch of cobbles and turned upriver toward Henning's Wharf.

The first Yang Sen knew that something was wrong was

when the car slid alongside him at walking pace. As he started to turn toward it he was immediately encircled by an enormous pair of arms from behind, and the next thing he knew he was lying in the rear of the car with the muzzle of Captain Hop's revolver staring him between the eyes. When he tried to sit up, Captain Hop said, 'Don't move a muscle.'

Genuinely puzzled by his abduction, Yang Sen lay still while the car picked up speed, slithered around corners on the dew-wet cobbles, and sped down streets and across intersections leaving him ignorant of the true direction they took. Only when the car slowed to a halt and Corporal Choy wrenched him upright by the lapels of his coat did he recognize the long deserted tunnel they were in as Godown Way, an area of engineering workshops, paint stores, and ship riggers over behind the International Dock. But before he could regain his breath he was bundled out of the car and slammed up against a corrugated iron wall.

Captain Hop moved in behind him with his revolver while Corporal Choy put his shoulder to a nearby door and sent it back off its hinges. 'Move!' Captain Hop grabbed Yang Sen around and shoved him headlong through the doorway.

Yang Sen lay where he fell, knowing by the smell and the taste of the dirt in his mouth that they were in some kind of engineering workshop.

While Corporal Choy wedged the door back shut Sergeant Kee found the light switch, and when the single low-watt light came on Yang Sen saw they were in a walled cubicle under a high dark roof. Sheets of steel plate, beams, rods and tin plate patterns were racked on the walls either side of a heavy pattern-maker's bench.

Captain Hop gestured with the revolver. 'On your feet.'

Yang Sen hesitated, then hoisted himself warily to his feet. 'What do you want with me? I haven't been any trouble to you. You're from across in the old International Settlement.'

Captain Hop holstered the revolver. He said casually, 'That may well be so – but you were with Po-han at Heinrich Sztykgold's apartment earlier this morning and I want to know everything that was said.'

A slow, dawning look of comprehension overtook Yang Sen's face, although he made no effort to answer.

Captain Hop gave vent to a sigh of weary resignation, and before Yang Sen knew what was happening, Sergeant Kee and Corporal Choy moved in on either side of him, pinning him back across the end of the bench. 'You had better know now that we don't intend to waste time.' Captain Hop's voice was softly venomous.

Yang Sen gritted his teeth. 'I don't know what you're talking about.'

Captain Hop found a length of cord on the dirt-packed floor and threw it to Sergeant Kee. 'Then perhaps we can help you remember.'

Yang Sen lay passive under Corporal Choy's weight while Sergeant Kee pulled his legs apart and secured his feet to a leg either side of the bench.

'Well?' Captain Hop stood waiting.

When Yang Sen again made no effort to answer, Sergeant Kee bent quickly down and wrenched his trousers open. Smiling calmly, Captain Hop stepped close and prodded Yang Sen's exposed belly and private parts with the steel tip of the riding-crop, like a coolie prodding a sow with a stick. 'And how many women has that thing frightened?'

Corporal Choy, leaning his weight across Yang Sen's upper body, craned his neck for a better view, and guffawed loudly.

With theatrical care, Captain Hop extracted a cigarette from his inlaid case, lighted it, then drew on it until the end glowed. Yang Sen watched with horrified fascination while his mouth dried up and sweat began to ooze down his flanks. 'What – what are you going to do?' he croaked, his eyes staring.

In answer Captain Hop stepped close and brought the glowing end of the cigarette down. Yang Sen's scream was instantly choked to a gurgle when Corporal Choy clamped a hand around his throat.

Drawing calmly on the cigarette again, Captain Hop said, 'I'm asking you once more – what was said in Sztykgold's apartment?'

Yang Sen felt the hand ease its strangulating grip on his throat and he fought to pull air down into his lungs, sweat streaming down his face, pain and nausea coursing through his body.

When Captain Hop next brought the cigarette down he

held it in place despite the violent convulsions of Yang Sen's straining body. Again the scream was choked off by Corporal Choy's hand, while the eyes stared far out of their sockets. Yet Yang Sen gave no indication of being ready to talk when Corporal Choy removed his hand.

Angered by this show of stubbornness, Captain Hop threw the cigarette aside and snapped a flame to his gold lighter.

This time the scream that issued from the contorted face was choked off with vomit, and it required the combined strength of both Sergeant Kee and Corporal Choy to keep the flailing body pinned to the bench.

Captain Hop snapped the lighter shut at that split-second when unconsciousness is almost met, and when he stepped back clear, Sergeant Kee and Corporal Choy released their grip on Yang Sen and allowed his body to slump forward on to the dirt-packed floor.

Several minutes elapsed before Yang Sen stirred. With a whimpered groan he finally rolled on to his side and covered his groin with his hands.

'Cut him loose,' Captain Hop instructed Sergeant Kee, and when his feet were free, smiled down at him serenely. 'Perhaps now you see the world in a somewhat different light.'

Yang Sen lay with his face buried against the dirt floor. In a whimper he said, 'They'll kill me if I say anything.'

Captain Hop said calmly, 'And I'll kill you if you don't.'

Yang Sen swallowed hard, spat vomit from his mouth weakly on to the floor. 'And afterward – if I talk?'

'Afterward's of no importance to me. All I'm interested in was what was said in Sztykgold's apartment.'

Yang Sen decided his only chance of remaining alive was to talk. With his face still against the dirt floor, he said, 'Harry Lord's going to be at Lang Dok tonight around eight o'clock. Tadatoshi and Nakamura will be there waiting for him. When they come downriver the bullion's going to be transferred to the *Sungari* at Tsungming Tao. Then she's going south to Hangchow Bay, to put into Gough Hill Cove north of Ningpo. Sztykgold will be waiting there on Sunday morning. He has it arranged with André Passel to fly him down. That's all I know – I swear it!'

Captain Hop nodded approvingly; all they would have to do was wait for Sztykgold to leave for Lunghwa Airport either sometime late that night or else early Sunday morning. But one thing remained to trouble him, the unpredictability of Harry Lord. He dug the riding-crop into Yang Sen's ribs. 'And what were Lord's instructions?'

'I only know what Sztykgold told us,' Yang Sen answered painfully. 'He said Lord believes that the bullion's headed for Shanghai, that he's going to tell him it's arranged he docks at the old Henderson Wharf out at Lunghwa.'

Captain Hop thought it sounded reasonable. Then another thought occurred to him. 'Did Sztykgold mention anything about the amount of bullion involved?'

'He said we were to expect something like two tons, and that it would be packed into cases.'

Captain Hop's heart missed a beat. *'Two tons!'*

'That's what Sztykgold said,' Yang Sen affirmed.

Captain Hop was both staggered and elated; evidently David Kow had estimated it at a figure that had to be somewhere around the lowest level of exchange, when in fact, even on the open market, two tons of bullion could fetch something in the region of $8,000,000, or even $9,000,000.

'Is something wrong, Captain?'

He turned to find Sergeant Kee watching him anxiously. He decided against telling him anything. 'No, nothing.' Then snapping the riding-crop down along the length of his riding boot with the sound of an exploding pistol, he said. 'Get him outside!'

Corporal Choy grabbed Yang Sen to his feet, hauled the door open, and bundled him out into the night air. Yang Sen stumbled, fell, then climbed to his feet again. When he saw them make no further move to harm him an expression of disbelief registered on his pain-wracked face, and he began to back away uncertainly, clasping his groin with one hand while he held up his trousers with the other, then he turned into an obscene shuffle, his gaze still on them.

Ignoring him, Captain Hop climbed into the car followed by Corporal Choy and Sergeant Kee. When they were settled he glanced back down the roadway and saw Yang Sen break into a run and be quickly swallowed up in the darkness. '*Now*!' he said.

Corporal Choy started the motor and turned the car around in the roadway. When the car came around the headlights picked up Yang Sen far down the walled tunnel.

They saw him stop and look back, and pinned in the headlights he appeared to be in two minds about what to do. As they started toward him he turned again and broke into a run, and they saw him stumble and begin to weave from side to side of the roadway in a bid to escape the headlights. But when they caught up with him he turned suddenly into the headlights and flung both arms up to cover his face. Just before they hit him he screamed and they saw his trousers fall down around his knees. He went under the fender and the car passed over him with a jolt. Twenty yards farther on Corporal Choy skidded the car to a halt and Captain Hop got out and started back along the roadway. There was no sign of life in the crumpled bundle spread across the dirty cobbles.

When he returned to the car he climbed back in and said, 'Make the next stop the Pootung Station House. I don't trust that bastard Lord.'

They drove directly to the Pootung Station House which was the combined headquarters of the Shanghai Police and Marine Police south of the river. It was situated a block to westward of the Pootung Ferry concourse.

Captain Hop entered the Inquiries Room accompanied by Sergeant Kee and asked to see Police Lieutenant Wu Tse-tan. He had first met Lieutenant Wu in Kunming where he had been attached to the Political Interrogation Staff at the railway station, under his own command.

When Lieutenant Wu entered the room he was clearly impressed by his old superior's unexpected visit. He said brightly, 'What do I owe this surprise to, Captain?'

Captain Hop glanced around the room. 'Is there somewhere we can talk?'

Lieutenant Wu evinced surprise. 'All right, Captain, This way.' He led the way into an interrogation cell in the outside passage, leaving Sergeant Kee in the Inquiries Room. He closed the door behind them. 'What can I do for you, Captain? Are you having trouble of some sort?'

Captain Hop had already established a story. He said with weary resignation, 'It's one of those political matters. Nothing exciting.'

Lieutenant Wu thought; who wants excitement when you boys make money like cows make milk? But he nodded his sympathy. 'So?' he said.

Captain Hop said, 'What I'm looking for is some help – discreet help. Somebody with the Marine Police was what I was after.'

Lieutenant Wu nodded his understanding. 'I know what you mean. And I know just the fellow – Sub-Lieutenant Hsiung. I'll go find him.'

Some minutes later he returned with a young Sub-Lieutenant of the Marine Police. He introduced them. Sub-Lieutenant Hsiung was even more impressed by the blue uniform of the KSS than Lieutenant Wu by his old superior. 'Is there something I can do for you, Captain?' He sounded extremely anxious to please.

Captain Hop met his gaze levelly. 'You understand this to be a matter in strict confidence?' he informed him unnecessarily.

Sub-Lieutenant Hsiung had thought as much. 'Of course, Captain. Naturally.'

Captain Hop said authoritatively, 'Then I'm interested in a Westerner called Harry Lord. Does the name mean anything to you?'

Lieutenant Wu was impressed. 'I know him by sight. He has something of a reputation as a tough boy that fellow. He works for The German.'

'Yes,' Sub-Lieutenant Hsiung agreed. 'I've seen him around the river. He has a launch called the *Jacaranda*. Quite a piece of machinery.'

'Well he'll be going downriver sometime this evening,' Captain Hop explained. 'My information is that it's unlikely he'll be coming back. However, I want to make sure that he doesn't do the unpredictable, and you can help by keeping an eye open for him. If you sight him then you report his position to KSS headquarters so that I can be informed immediately. Then follow him at a discreet distance and report where and when he docks. But don't intervene in anyway unless you receive explicit instructions on my behalf.'

'Of course, Captain,' Sub-Lieutenant Hsiung answered. 'Whatever you say.'

'And what do you want me to do, Captain?' Lieutenant Wu wanted to know.

Captain Hop said, 'If you could arrange to have somebody keep surveillance on the Carfax Oil Depot – say from ten o'clock onward? It's just a precaution against him perhaps slipping upriver past Sub-Lieutenant Hsiung.'

'I don't see any problem there,' Lieutenant Wu said. 'And should my man sight him you want him to call the Station House and I'll relay the information the same as Hsiung here?'

'Exactly,' Captain Hop affirmed. 'But as I've already said, it may not come to anything.'

'Nonetheless you can count on us,' Lieutenant Wu said authoritively.

'Of course, Captain!' Sub-Lieutenant Hsiung confirmed the pledge with enthusiasm.

Captain Hop left the Pootung Station House generally feeling a lot easier in his mind, and with Sergeant Kee climbed back into the car outside and started toward the Tienningshih Vehicular Ferry and breakfast.

* * *

It was noon and Harry Lord came awake the instant that the hand touched his shoulder.

Old Po's eyes started out of his head when he found himself staring down the barrel of the .38 Police Special that materialized in the hand under his nose. It looked as big as a drain-pipe.

Harry Lord relaxed when he saw who it was and squinted his eyes against the sunlight streaming in through the open doors to the veranda. 'Oh, it's you?' he said.

Old Po breathed a sigh of relief when he saw him put the gun on the bedside table. 'Some day you're going to shoot somebody with that thing,' he remonstrated.

Harry Lord sat up and looked at his watch. 'What's wrong? – did Mao arrive during the night?'

'No,' Old Po said solemnly. 'But somebody else has arrived.'

Harry Lord frowned as he swung his legs out of bed and reached his trousers from the floor. 'Like who?'

'She didn't tell me her name.'

Harry Lord stopped pulling on his trousers. '*She?*'

Old Po bobbed his pig-tailed head. 'Sure. And she asked for you by name too.'

'What does she look like?' Harry Lord always liked to know what they looked like; it was the legacy of a blind date when he was twelve years old.

Old Po grinned and with his hands described two curves through the air.

Harry Lord looked at him again and put the .38 Police Special into his waistband, thinking that if she really looked anything like Old Po made out then it wasn't a gun he wanted. 'Where is she?'

'Next door.'

She stood just inside the door to the hall.

Harry Lord studied her critically. Old Po hadn't over-estimated her any; that was his first thought. She was probably no more than twenty years old. Her face was pale and delicately featured, her hair short, black and thick. It was cut to follow the contours of her eyebrows so that it created the impression of her being in a permanent state of startledness. He couldn't remember having seen her anywhere previously.

She watched him uncertainly from the other side of the room, disconcerted by the unnerving blue-eyed gaze. 'Mr Lord?' she said at length.

'Uh-huh.' Harry Lord was equally at a loss.

The enormous black eyes stared back at him unwavering. She said by way of apology, 'I hope you aren't angry at me for coming here?'

Harry Lord had already decided he could excuse her *anything*. 'What can I do for you?'

'I'm looking for somebody.'

Harry Lord's gaze narrowed. 'I don't follow.'

Her black eyes became even more enormous. 'Then you don't know Mr Chang?'

'I've never heard of a Mr Chang in my life.' Among other things Harry Lord was a born liar.

Her uncertainty returned. 'But I was told you were inquiring about him only yesterday morning.'

Harry Lord's gaze narrowed further. 'Are you a friend of this Mr Chang?'

She hesitated. 'In a way, yes,' she said.

Harry Lord was curious. 'What sort of friend?' he said, surprised that Mr Chang could have known any such sort of girl.

'You know,' she said mysteriously, and smiled shyly. She had dimples and startling white teeth, as well as honesty.

Harry Lord thought; Jesus Christ up a gum tree. And took

a drink of what remained of the bottle of Haig & Haig, and thought he would never have placed Mr Chang as a womanizer in a thousand years. Recovered from his surprise, he said, 'Who told you I was asking about Mr Chang?'

She said, 'A boy in a bar on the Nanking Road. The Kimona.'

Harry Lord swore silently to himself. 'He told you that just for asking?' he said, and thought that with her looks she could have persuaded the President of the Shanghai Bank to reveal the whereabouts of his dollar-stuffed sock, never mind wheedle a customer's name out of an eavesdropping kid still wet behind the ears.

'Not at first,' she admitted with the hint of a smile. 'But then he said he had heard part of a conversation you had with some policemen and he remembered your name being mentioned along with that of the Red Fortune Hotel.'

Harry Lord's mind was now working on full throttle. 'When was this?'

'About an hour ago.'

Harry Lord wondered what had happened to him lately. He had began to take too many chances and it was asking for trouble. Instead of the girl it could just as easily have been the two cops who had been keeping watch on Mr Chang's office who had come calling. And when he thought about it, he saw that it was probably only a matter of time before they got around to asking the same questions as the girl had asked.

'Then you don't know Mr Chang after all?' She sounded depressed at the possibility.

'That depends,' Harry Lord said, suffering second thoughts. 'When did you last see him?'

She was impressed with his sudden interest. 'Yesterday morning when he left for the office. Not that there was anything for him to do there. He went simply for appearances sake, to disconcert the police. Then when I returned to the apartment in Nantao in the early evening after being out all day I saw two policemen leaving.'

'Did they say anything – ask any questions?'

She shook her head. 'I didn't give them the chance to say anything. When I saw their jeep outside the apartment I hid in the park across the street. But I wondered what had happened to Mr Chang. You see, I knew he had been trying to make arrangements to get to Hong Kong, and that he was waiting for his eldest brother to arrive from somewhere up north. So I thought perhaps his brother had arrived and that they had somehow succeeded in leaving Shanghai without the police knowing, and that the police were curious about what had become of him.'

Harry Lord was impressed. 'You knew about the cops watching him then?'

'Oh, yes. I even knew their names; Lieutenant Yang and Sergeant Soon. Mr Chang told me that they were after the money and bullion he had earlier drawn from his bank. They were quite blatant about it. They followed us on several occasions. Sometimes they parked outside the apartment for several hours at a time. Mr Chang was quite frightened by them.'

Harry Lord thought; three times over. 'And you?' he asked.

She smiled self-effacingly. 'What do I have that could possibly interest them?' she asked with open innocence.

Harry Lord wondered about that too. Along with her spectacular looks, her unabashed honesty had begun to intrigue him. And if Old Po's face was any measure of his admiration, then she intrigued him too. 'So you started looking around to see if you could find out what had happened to him – is that it?'

She smiled, all dimples and teeth and enormous black eyes. 'That was what I was doing when I heard about you.'

Harry Lord's mind was elsewhere. 'Did you see anything of those two cops on your travels?'

'No. But then I didn't go back to the apartment last night, because I didn't think it prudent.'

Harry Lord's eyebrows rose upward. 'You didn't think it *what?*'

'Wise,' she answered innocently.

Harry Lord grinned his magic grin. He had never met a girl quite like her. 'You've certainly got it all figured out. What do you say, Old Po?'

Old Po bobbed his pig-tailed head and beamed his toothless grin. 'Sure,' he said. 'She's a bright girl, all right. Number damn One.'

Harry Lord studied her contemplatively. As well as brains she also had looks, and a figure too, indisputedly. It was only now he realized just what sort of a figure she really had, and the yellow cheongsam she wore did it full justice. It also appeared to be about all she possessed, along with a flimsy pair of high-heeled slippers and a brocade bag. 'Have you been walking around all night on your own dressed like that?'

She glanced down at herself with genuine perplexity. 'You don't care for the dress?' She appeared hurt at the possibility.

Harry Lord started to say something, then ran a hand through his hair in embarrassment of her straightforwardness. No woman had ever asked him such a question. 'Well what I mean is with the way things are at the moment it's lucky you didn't come to any harm,' he said clumsily, and began to wonder if maybe or not he was dreaming all this and was going to suddenly wake up back in bed and find that none of it had ever happened. Then for some unaccountable reason the question of her welfare was suddenly vital to him. 'How about friends?' he asked. 'Have you got any friends in town?'

She shook her head. 'The only person I know in Shanghai is Mr Chang.'

'Where did you get here from?'

'Changchow.'

Harry Lord knew Changchow. He had once passed through it and had never experienced the urge to return. It was a drab town in the north which lay beyond Wusih, straddling the Shanghai–Nanking railway. He glanced sideways at Old Po and saw they were both obviously thinking each other's thoughts.

In reply Old Po beamed his toothless grin. 'I'll go and make ready the room next door.'

The girl stared at them both in bewilderment, started to open her mouth.

'Don't worry about me,' Harry Lord told her flatly.

'Sure. Don't worry about him,' Old Po announced happily. 'He's a good boy – even with a face like that.'

'Get out of here, you sugar-happy Chink,' Harry Lord told him. 'And see if you can fix us breakfast at the same time.'

Old Po grinned happily as he set himself in motion. 'Sure thing, Major!'

'You can eat breakfast?' Harry Lord asked.

'But I can't possibly accept such hospitality,' she protested in embarrassment, her delicate hands holding the brocade bag in front of her. 'Besides, it isn't necessary. I've been taking care of myself for a long time now.'

And Harry Lord wondered about that too. The way she had set him thinking so early in the day he wondered if he wasn't maybe going to fall over suffering from mental fatigue.

'Did you hear what I said, Mr Lord?' she asked with that unabashed innocence he found so appealing.

'Harry,' he told her.

Her former perplexity returned.

'My name,' he said. *'Harry* Lord.'

'Harry. Harry Lord,' she said in a reflective tone.

Harry Lord watched her with the magic grin all over his face. The manner in which she pronounced his name had given it a ring it had never known. It had sounded almost the sort of name which brought to mind a winner of the Nobel Peace Prize, or maybe an equerry of the King; or on the other hand – a first cousin of Captain Morgan.

A grave line returned to her face. 'Then you really *do* know Mr Chang?'

'Did,' he corrected her.

'Then something bad has happened to him.'

'On the contrary. I fixed it so he left town yesterday afternoon. He's probably in Ningpo right now making arrangements to get to Hong Kong.'

She said happily, 'Is that true?'

It was Harry Lord's turn to show perplexity. 'What are you so happy about? – it's *Mr Chang* who's in Ningpo.'

With wide-eyed innocence, she said, 'But why shouldn't I be happy at such news?'

Harry Lord suddenly had the impression that she was unware of her good looks and their appeal. 'Well if he'd told me at the time I could've fixed it so you could've gone with him.'

She answered earnestly, 'But I'm not envious of Mr Chang's good fortune. I'm just grateful for the kindness which he showed me when he found it possible. Now I must face less providential times again. One can't expect the rewards of life to come their way continually without acquainting oneself with its hardships. You see, I don't wish to accept your hospitality because I don't have anything of value with which I can repay you. It's really quite simple, Mr Lord. This is China.'

Harry Lord was as near dumbfounded as he had ever been. It was Old Dragonsville all over again; where everybody went bravely to meet their Fate with stoic calm and resignation. Only he thought; to hell with China. And he said arguably, 'But you don't owe me or Old Po anything. Besides, I'm pulling out tomorrow morning and the least I can do is take you as far as Ningpo. I got your friend Mr Chang out and it isn't any trouble. I've got my own boat.'

For a moment she was silent, non-plussed. 'But why should you wish to do something like that, Mr Lord?'

'Let's say it just occurred to me, that's all. Does there have to be a logical reason for everything? Most of the time I do things just because I want to do them. That's the way I am. But there's no ulterior motive involved – if that's what you're thinking. There are people around town here who say I'd go to hell for a pastime.'

She smiled involuntarily. 'But you don't even know me, Mr Lord. I'm unimportant.'

'Maybe it's the unimportant people I most like to do things for,' Harry Lord stated flatly. 'Besides, do you have any idea what could happen to you if those two cops catch up with you? With your Mr Chang having disappeared they'll be looking for blood. No – you're staying right here till I can ship you downriver.' When he was through he felt vaguely like the hero in an old swashbuckling movie where everybody dashed around waving rapiers and blowing their noses in handkerchiefs they kept up their sleeves.

The enormous black eyes stared out at him for a long moment from beneath her fringe before the hesitant smile shyly returned. 'I'm afraid I don't know what to say in answer to that, Mr Lord,' she admitted gracefully.

'Then it's settled,' Harry Lord stated flatly. 'Now it might help matters if you told me your name.'

'Annie,' she said shyly. 'Annie Kim.'

'Then why don't you sit down and make yourself at home, Annie? Breakfast should be along soon.'

Watching her cross the room to sit into a corner of the rattan sofa, she seemed to him as near bodily perfect as any Chinese woman he had ever seen. The width and squareness of her shoulders narrowed to a small waist which flared to tight round buttocks that pouted seductively out below the curve of her spine. Her belly was also rounded, pronounced in a way a woman's belly should be pronounced to his way of thinking, and then the thighs, long, rounded and muscular, tapering to long slim calves above neat ankles. And when she had walked across the room her movements hadn't contained any of Zephyrine Wan's designed sensuality; her walk had been entirely natural, more concretely arresting. All of her had moved. Her breasts had jounced and her buttocks had quivered on her high-heels. As far as he was concerned she was all woman, indisputedly so.

'What were you going to do with the gun, Mr Lord?' Annie Kim was looking at him from the corner of the rattan sofa.

Startled from his thoughts, Harry Lord grinned, took the .38 Police Special from his waistband, and hefted it in his hand. 'In this town you never know,' he said cryptically, and went through to the bedroom and put it in the coat pocket of his white cotton suit.

When he returned, Old Po entered the room carrying a large tray which he set on to the table in front of the sofa. 'I hope you're both hungry,' he beamed. In the polished dishes were kidneys, slabs of cured ham, bacon, eggs, fresh baked bread and a pot of coffee.

'Her name's Annie,' Harry Lord told him. 'Annie Kim.'

Old Po started for the door. 'Then I'll have your room ready in a few minutes, Miss Annie.'

'You'll see she doesn't want for anything while I'm gone tonight?' Harry Lord called after him.

Old Po stopped in the doorway, his grin fading. Ever since he had learned how Harry Lord made his living he had looked on him with awe and wonder. 'You're going out on that river again?'

'I'll only be gone a couple of hours. 'It's nothing to get excited about. Then we'll be pulling out for good. I want to be clear of the Whangpoo by daylight if possible.'

'I'll take care of her,' Old Po promised. 'But you watch out for those guns.'

'I'll keep an eye on them,' Harry Lord promised, and watched him close the door. Glancing at his watch, he had a vision of Sztykgold impatiently pacing the floor of his apartment on the Avenue Lafayette, and was unable to suppress a grin. He had never known anybody worry more than Old Heinie Sztykgold where money was concerned, especially somebody else's money.

Annie Kim watched him with concern. 'I hope I'm not keeping you from an appointment, Mr Lord.'

'Forget it,' he told her. 'It isn't anything important. Let's eat.'

They started breakfast and he saw her eat with such devotion it was obvious she now felt more at ease in his company. 'Like I said,' he explained. 'We'll be pulling out before daylight tomorrow morning if everything goes like it should. I can drop you at either Ningpo or Chinhai. It's much the same to me. At least it'll get you out of town before the Communists move in. Things'll no doubt get pretty rough around here when that happens.'

'But you really don't have to concern yourself about me, Mr Lord,' she protested. 'Besides, I'll never be able to repay you.' In her face and in her voice was reflected something equally of hope, despair, and the sad wisdom of age in youth.

In embarrassment Harry Lord fumbled for his cigarettes. 'You want to forget all that stuff about paying anybody anything. You hear?'

Very quietly she said, 'But this is—'

Harry Lord raised a weary hand. 'I know, I know. This is China. But let's forget about China for a time.'

He was on his second cup of coffee when Old Po returned. 'The room's ready now if you wish to rest,' he informed Annie Kim.

'Thanks,' Harry Lord told him. 'Now listen – if anybody comes asking about her you don't know anything.'

'Sure thing!' Old Po beamed a grin like maybe he had heard word that an aunt with a flourishing laundry business had just passed away and left him $500,000 and the monopoly on San Francisco's dirty linen. 'Old Po understands – damn right he does!'

Harry Lord turned to Annie Kim. 'You'll be all right. Old Po'll take good care of you. I'll be back sometime in the early morning.'

'I just heard in the bar,' Old Po quietly put in, 'that the Communists moved into Luikiahang and Yangkiachwang during the night and that fighting is taking place in the streets.'

Harry Lord understood the implications of Old Po's statement only too well; the Communists were now ready to open their offensive against remaining Kuomintang territory in South China. It was very probably no more than the matter of a few hours away. 'Well, we'll be gone by daylight,' he said.

'If I were you I'd be thinking about leaving right now,' Old Po commented sombrely. 'Never mind before daylight.'

'I don't know what you're worrying about,' Harry Lord said with an explosive grin. 'What you should be doing right now is nailing up a few pictures of Mao in the front hall before he gets here.'

Old Po looked at him wistfully. 'You could be right.' Although he was far from looking forward to making Mao's acquaintance he was too old to take revolution seriously. Prominent figures had come and gone down through the centuries but China still very much remained China.

Harry Lord rose and went to the bedroom for his coat. 'I've got to go and see somebody now,' he informed them both; and to Annie Kim said: 'I'll call you when I get back in the morning.'

*   *   *

Heinrich Sztykgold was pacing the floor of his apartment on the Avenue Lafayette. It had already gone 2.00 p.m. and there was still no sign of Harry Lord. He could have seen him in hell as a result. Yet he consoled himself with the satisfaction he felt with the events of the past few hours. It had required more than just ordinary effort and ingenuity to have organized everything. After Harry Lord agreed to make the trip he had returned to the apartment and gone over everything in final detail with the others before Tadatoshi and Nakamura left to make their way through the Communist lines north of the city to Lang Dok. He had no worries about that part of it. Harry Lord was the real problem. The man was a law only to himself, showed no respect for anybody. If there had been anybody else in Shanghai equipped to make the trip he would never have used Harry Lord.

Prowling to the window, he peered down at the avenue.

The trees lining the pavements were very green in the sunlight and the tables outside the cafés had began to fill as the afternoon advanced. He sighed, swore, freshened his drink, and deliberated whether to risk calling Harry Lord at the Red Fortune Hotel. He had been half considering it for the past hour but had so far resisted the impulse in case he upset him because out of sheer cussedness he was as likely as not to tell him to go to hell and that he had changed his mind and the deal was off. That was the maddening thing about Harry Lord, his self-reliance and unpredictability. He had no respect or consideration for anybody.

But Harry Lord wasn't his only problem. It was a far from ideal time for somebody of his own substance and position to be alone in Shanghai, and he would have felt a great deal easier in his mind if it had been possible to have left for Ningpo before nightfall. However, the success of the entire operation depended on Henry Wan remaining unsuspecting to the end. There was also Tzu Hsun. So far he hadn't seen any sign of Tzu Hsun although he was undoubtedly around somewhere watching him, for he was Henry Wan's insurance against anything going wrong. But he had come a long way in his fifty-seven years and he wasn't going to make any mistakes now. There had been a very great deal of success packed into those years too. When he thought about it he supposed his determination for that success stemmed from the cheerless existence of a childhood spent in an old Bavarian lumber camp.

He had been in his twenties before seeing anything of the outside world, when conscripted into the Kaiser's army at the outbreak of the Great War. He had been lucky in that respect too, serving out the duration playing servant to a Home Front Commander whose only troops were sixty mules and their drivers. Nonetheless he had benefited from army life, it had given him the urge for travel. Not for him was the return to a life behind the counter of his father's hardware store in Bavaria. Instead, ten months after Armistice he was on the other side of the world working as a clerk with a Dutch exporter in Singapore. Four years later it was Hong Kong, working for a Portuguese shipowner on the Connaught Road, a position which had further opened his eyes to the limitless opportunities awaiting those ambitious enough to grasp them. As a result he had taken passage to

Shanghai a year later determined to make his own mark on the Orient.

Yet it was only with the outbreak of the Sino-Japanese War that he first began to meet with any real success, when he was regarded through nationality as an ally of the Japanese, irrespective of the fact that he was an Austrian-Jew glad to be as far removed from the Fatherland as humanly possible. Consequently, with none of the restrictions on himself and his business so rigidly applied to his competitors, he made startling progress during this period, setting up a complex arrangement of blackmarket dealings between the Japanese and the wealthy Chinese landlords whose provinces bordered the Yangtze. By 1942 he had practically taken over the notorious Yangtze Run for himself, so that when the Japanese Empire collapsed at the end of the War there hadn't been a serious contender in sight.

But now, now he was about to bring off a coup that would be his grand farewell to the Orient. In a week he would be in Spain along with Tadatoshi and Nakamura, retired to the pleasant sunshine of the Mediterranean to grow oranges. He had harboured an ambition to one day be able to grow oranges ever since as a young boy he had been snowed in by the long winters in that desolate Bavarian lumber camp. And now he saw it as a novelty which would complete the realization of his every ambition.

So far all that he had ever been interested in was the acquisition of money, and the only time he looked at anything with interest and satisfaction was when his bank statements arrived from Europe. Yet even with wealth he had never experienced the desire to own property, to buy a suburban villa or a country mansion. Instead he had lived in the Roebaud Apartment building since 1936. His actual expenditure was meagre, and although he appreciated good food he ate little. His clothes were expensive but conservative, all alike. His acknowledged weaknesses were Turkish cigarettes and wines, with a preference for Bordeaux and Champagnes. It was nine years since he had taken a woman to bed, and apart from the black Mercedes bought out of momentary nostalgia for the Fatherland, his material assets were nil. Yet while most men would never have entertained thoughts of attempting to pursue a childhood ambition or dream, he didn't consider such eccentricities in any way frivolous.

It was for this reason that he was sitting lost in his distant Spanish orange grove when startled by the ringing of the phone. He moved quickly. 'Yes. Sztykgold,' he acknowledged.

'I thought I'd better call you to say there's been some trouble.'

Sztykgold recognized Po-han's voice instantly, and his heart slowed. His first thought was that he had called to report some major defect of the *Sungari*'s motors and that she would be unable to sail. 'What is it?'

'Yang Sen's dead.'

The words came like a hammer blow. Sztykgold drew a sharp intake of breath. 'What do you mean – *dead?*' he asked, his mind jarred by the knowledge that Yang Sen had known his plans in minute detail.

When Po-han answered his voice was inordinarily calm. 'I only heard about it half an hour ago. His body was found this morning in Godown Way. But I don't think it's anything to worry about – it was a motor accident.'

Sztykgold felt weak with relief, then anger took over from fear. 'What the hell was he doing in a place like Godown Way? That's way over behind the International Dock. When you left here last night you were returning to the *Sungari*.'

Po-han said easily, 'He stopped off for a drink when we left the Pootung Ferry. I didn't see any harm in it at the time. I didn't know he was going to get knocked down by a fucking truck. He must have met with a woman and was on his way back on board when it happened.'

Recovered from the initial shock, Sztykgold stared gravely at the phone. 'How did you find out about it – from the police?'

'No. Some junkmen heard about it in a bar this afternoon and stopped by to ask if I had heard anything.'

'So what do you intend to do about it?'

Po-han laughed. 'What the hell can I do about it? He was the one who was knocked down. Besides, I'm due to fuel at the Standard Vacuum Oil Dock in twenty minutes.'

Sztykgold sighed heavily. The news had unnerved him but he realized his plans were unendangered. Yang Sen had only been included in the final briefing because he was to have been in charge of the transfer of the bullion from the *Jaca-*

randa to the *Sungari*, and now his death wasn't the disaster he at first feared. 'You're certain everything's going to be all right?'

Po-han said coolly, 'You worry too much. Everything's going to be fine. See you tomorrow morning at Gough Hill Cove.'

Sztykgold stared at the silent phone when Po-han rang off. At least the man hadn't sounded unduly concerned, had in fact hardly even considered it an inconvenience. He put the receiver down, found his glass empty, and went to the bar. He was still immersed in thought when he was further startled by a robust pounding on the door. 'Who's that?'

'It's me – Lord,' the voice in the hall outside informed.

Sztykgold put his glass down, went quickly to the door, drew the bolts and self-locking catch, and edged it open.

Harry Lord pushed his way inside with a contemptuous glance at Sztykgold as he set about relocking the door again. 'Don't for Christsake forget the combination for that thing.'

Sztykgold countered sourly, 'You can say what you like – but caution's an investment in these times.'

Harry Lord said, 'Fuck the caution. You never took a real chance in your life.'

Sztykgold chose to ignore the remark, and returned to the bar. Hard on Po-han's shock news, Harry Lord's belated appearance, even with his deliberate insultingness, imparted a glowing feeling of relief. 'Can I get you something?'

'Scotch.' It was the first time that Harry Lord had been in the apartment without the two Japanese bodyguards being in close attendance and he was curious about their absence. 'Where's the Kempei Tai today?'

Sztykgold handed him his drink. 'If you mean Tadatoshi and Nakamura, then they're out on business. There happens to be a certain gentleman in Nantao who's somewhat reluctant to pay for a favour already granted. However, I trust they'll be back soon.'

Harry Lord stretched out in one of the deep upholstered chairs, unconcerned. 'Yeah – once they tip him in the river.'

Sztykgold decided against coming directly to the question of business. 'I'd begun to think you'd changed your mind about making the trip after all.' He sipped his drink with an adopted attitude of indifference. 'It's almost three o'clock.'

Harry Lord studied him narrowly. 'Never mind the socializing,' he said. 'Just let's get down to business.'

Sztykgold shrugged indifference. 'Whatever you say.' He sat into the chair opposite and spread a chart of the Lower Reaches of the Yangtze out flat on the table between them. It was all he could do to contain the excitement he felt now that everything was finally getting under way. 'See here?' He indicated some canal workings and the dotted cottages of a village on the south shore between Hupukow and Funshan, some forty miles upriver from Woosung. 'This is Lang Dok. The village and canal workings were abandoned some years ago. That's where the junk's tied up. She's crewed by a family called Liang, husband, wife and three sons. It was the fourth boy who returned to Chungking with news of what happened. The bullion's buried somewhere on shore close by so it shouldn't be too difficult a problem to transfer to the *Jacaranda*. The Liangs will be expecting you and everything will be ready. I gave explicit instructions regarding this so there shouldn't be any unnecessary delays.'

Harry Lord glanced up from the chart. 'Who went north?'

Sztykgold had his answer ready. 'A certain young woman and her husband,' he replied glibly. 'To all appearances two peasants returning home.'

Harry Lord accepted the explanation unquestioningly. He knew Sztykgold and he hadn't exactly expected him to bicycle his own way northward. 'Well I hope they got through because I'd hate to make a trip like this for nothing.'

'They'll have got through all right,' Sztykgold confidently predicted. 'The young woman's parents still happen to be here in Shanghai.'

Harry Lord knew what that particular comment implied; in straightforward terms – hostages. If there had been a medal for a man completely without scruples then Old Heinie Sztykgold would have won it hands down. He returned his attention to the chart. 'Go ahead.'

Sztykgold put a manicured finger on the junction of the Whangpoo and the Yangtze at Woosung. 'I learned from a River Commissioner this morning that two Kuomintang gunboats took up station here during the night in order to maintain surveillance on all shipping entering and leaving Shanghai. They're lying at anchor off the northern breakwater above the Spit, so you'd be well advised to show caution down around there. If they see you headed up the Yangtze they'll probably attempt to blow you out of the water. Therefore if you take my advice you'll wait for darkness before starting downriver.'

'And what time am I expected at Lang Dok?'

Having gained in confidence, Sztykgold now felt in command of the situation. 'I suggested eight o'clock. That's time for you to be well on your way back downriver before moonrise should it be a clear night.'

Harry Lord didn't see any problems so far. 'Where do I tie up when I get back?'

'The arrangements are that we all meet at the old Henderson Wharf out at Lunghwa. It's been derelict for years so we shouldn't have to worry about any curious eyes being around. I've also arranged to have a truck ready in one of the godowns, and along with Tadatoshi and Nakamura, Tzu Hsun will help you off-load.'

Harry Lord grunted approval. He knew the old Henderson Wharf, and as Sztykgold said, they were unlikely to be disturbed while off-loading. 'That suits me so far – but I don't want any fart-arsing around when I get in. I want that stuff off fast. I'm counting on being headed back downriver for good before daylight.'

Sztykgold nodded, his expression one of sympathetic understanding. 'Naturally. I don't want to be kept waiting around out there half the night either. Nor does Mr Wan. I might add that the bullion's going straight out to Lunghwa Airport where an aircraft will be waiting to fly it and the Wans to Hong Kong. And that must also be accomplished before daylight.'

'That's fine with me,' Harry Lord enthused, and stopped, struck by another thought. 'Just for the record, what does this stuff weigh in at?'

'I'm told something a little over a ton. At eighty dollars the ounce you can work it out for yourself.'

'I'll take your word for it. And the money? What about the money?'

Sztykgold leaned back in the chair with his Scotch and water. 'Mr Wan will have it ready. He was carrying one hundred and eighty thousand dollars in US currency when he came in from Chungking. I've seen it. Of course, if you want, you can have it like I'm taking my cut, in bullion.'

'No, money's all right by me. I don't want no fucking around with bullion. I don't know where I'm headed yet and there's always too many questions asked when trying to pass bullion.'

Sztykgold answered with a shrug, 'Whatever you say. I'll tell Mr Wan to have the money ready.'

Harry Lord eyed Sztykgold speculatively across the table. He felt vaguely uneasy. Sztykgold had never easily agreed to anything, had never capitulated over even the most minor point without offering some form of argument to his own advantage. He said obliquely, 'You seem pretty anxious to please all of a sudden.'

Although still confident, Sztykgold was finding it an increasing strain to maintain pretences. He chain-smoked another Turkish cigarette. 'Why not? It's not as if the bullion were mine. This is the last deal we'll make together and I'm only in this for my share the same as yourself. If Mr Wan hadn't approached me when he did I'd now be in Hong Kong. I make no secret about that to anybody. And if you're bothered in anyway with these arrangements you're quite at liberty to check them out with Mr Wan himself. He has the Peking Suite at the Great Eastern Mansions.'

Harry Lord thought it over, decided it was fair argument. 'Then there's only one thing more – how are you going to know when I'm headed back upriver?'

'That's also been arranged,' Sztykgold answered readily. 'Tadatoshi and Nakamura will be in a hire boat off the Nantao shore. When they sight you they'll blink the running lights and escort you up to Lunghwa. The boatman's worked for me before so there's no problem with him. Myself, I'll be on the Nantao Bund and when I have their signal I'll call Mr Wan at the Great Eastern Mansions then pick him, his wife and Tzu up in my car and drive them out to the old Henderson Wharf. We should be there within minutes of you and that way none of us will have previously been seen together during the evening – a simple precaution against the possibility of somebody finding a sudden interest in our association.'

Harry Lord was unable to find argument in any of it. 'I guess it makes sense,' he conceded.

'Naturally,' Sztykgold riposted with a smile. 'When I plan something I take care of everybody.'

Harry Lord gave him a jaundiced look. 'Don't give me that. You've never taken care of anybody in your life, except yourself.'

Sztykgold stared at him frostily. 'Then I'm disappointed if that's your considered opinion of me after the profitable years we've spent together.'

Harry Lord climbed to his feet. Old Heinie Ten-To-Me-One-To-You Sztykgold they called him around Shanghai, and it wasn't without good reason. 'Is that it?' he asked.

'I think so, yes,' Sztykgold answered coolly, still wearing a mortally hurt expression on his long grey face.

'Then if you haven't forgotten the combination for that door maybe I'll get out of here.'

'Of course.'

Harry Lord stopped in the hall outside and grinned back crookedly at Sztykgold as he was about to close the door. 'You know, Heinie – if you had a parrot you'd steal fucking birdseed.'

The malevolent grin was still on his face when he caught a taxicab leaving Mireille's Restaurant and started back toward the old International Settlement. Money was all right but always the people involved in the accompanying conspiracy gave him a pain in the arse. None of them ever took a real chance. And they always made everything sound so easy it was difficult to understand why they never went through with any of it themselves.

* * *

Captain Hop was standing by a window in the vacated offices of the Honan Assurance Company on the third floor of a building on the opposite side of the Avenue Lafayette from the Roebaud Apartment building, overlooking the tables outside Mireille's Restaurant. He glanced across at Sergeant Kee where he was concealed from the avenue by the drawn curtains in the empty room, a smile of satisfaction on his face. 'There's no doubt that everything's going our way.'

Sergeant Kee stared after the departing taxicab bearing Harry Lord. Then from the corner of his eye he saw Tzu Hsun put down his newspaper at the table he occupied outside Mireille's and make his way inside to the pay telephone in the window. 'It would seem that Tzu's about to make the same report to Mr Wan,' he observed.

On the other side of the room Corporal Choy was sitting with his back against the bare wall staring distantly out of the window beyond his two superiors. The subtleties of surveillance and the intricate technicalities which might lead to the apprehension of a suspect held no interest for him. What he enjoyed most was to be let loose on the person in question after he had been detained, when he could feel the give of gristle and bone under his fists and see the warm splash of blood.

But now, bored with the inactivity of the long day's surveillance, he emitted a loud belch and shifted his feet restlessly. 'How long will it take Lord to make a trip like that, Captain?'

Captain Hop glanced at the huge squatting frame. 'Oh, four, perhaps five hours. It's difficult to say. It'll all depend on what happens out on the river. He'll have to be careful.'

Sergeant Kee said, 'What worries me is the way Tzu's poking around.'

Captain Hop lifted his eyes from the avenue to Kee's worried face. 'It was obvious from the outset that he was going to stay close to Sztykgold, but we'll take care of him when the time comes. And should he get in the way we'll move more quickly.'

Sergeant Kee's anxiety was in no way lessened by his superior's obvious confidence. 'I don't like it,' he said. 'I don't like the way that Sztykgold went about it. It worries me. What if Yang Sen wasn't telling us the truth?'

'In those circumstances?' Captain Hop scoffed.

'Then why didn't Sztykgold take Lord into his confidence? It would have been much more simple, and he wouldn't have had to depend on Po-han. Lord could have ran the bullion straight down to Hangchow Bay.'

'Sztykgold isn't taking such a risk with Po-han,' Captain Hop assured him. 'You forget that Tadatoshi and Nakamura will also be on board the *Sungari* to look after his interests once they transfer the bullion from the *Jacaranda*. No, he obviously knows Lord better than you. The man might well be insane but he isn't idiot enough to trust Sztykgold, and Sztykgold knows that. With a cargo like that at stake all he would be likely to get out of it for his pains is a bullet through the head. No, using Lord would be a far bigger risk than using Po-han.' While talking he collected his cap, gloves and riding-crop from the window-ledge. 'Well I don't see any point in our remaining here. Nothing's going to happen here for a while. Instead I think we'll take a drive out past the Passel house just to let him see that we haven't forgotten him.'

Corporal Choy pulled the door shut behind them and they started downstairs. 'Is it really as much bullion as you say, Captain?'

Captain Hop laughed indulgently, 'Yes, Choy, it's really as much bullion as I say. And before tomorrow's more than a few hours old you'll be rich beyond imagination.'

Outside they walked northward to where the car was parked around in the Place Durantin. When they pulled out into the stream of late afternoon traffic they left Tzu Hsun at his table on the pavement outside Mireille's with his newspaper unaware that he himself had been the subject of discreet surveillance.

Twenty minutes later they were in Nantao, out on the west side where the buildings of the Old City looked across the river, out toward Lunghwa Airport and the western suburbs of the city. André Passel's villa was situated midway along the Shing Wong Road. A neat plasterwork structure, it sat on the embankment to eastward and looked down on the roadway from within a screen of shrubbery. Corporal Choy parked the car directly outside the drive. There were two cars parked in the drive, Passel's grey Ford, and a battered green sedan. The latter they knew belonged to an employee of Passel, an American flyer named Eddie Prudham who had flown with General Chennault's Flying Tigers before he decided to remain over in China.

Captain Hop lit a cigarette, and while he watched the two small children playing in the garden, he saw Passel's pretty Chinese wife come around the gable of the house. She stopped the moment she saw them, raised a hand to her breast, then ushered the children quickly into the house. André Passel appeared at the long open window seconds later. While he stared uneasily at the car, he was joined by the bulky figure of Prudham. For a lengthy moment all five men simply stared at each other, then Passel turned away from the window with a mumbled word to Prudham and emerged from the house.

Captain Hop watched him come down the drive, his face

almost as white as the open-necked shirt he was wearing. Behind Passel, Prudham remained at the window, a silent witness. Captain Hop stretched out in the deep upholstery, drawing leisurely on his cigarette as Passel approached. 'How's the family, André?'

Passel cleared his throat nervously. 'Is something wrong, Captain?'

Captain Hop's face assumed an expression of innocent surprise at the question. 'What on earth could be wrong, André? We just thought to call past and see how you and the family were doing.'

'We're still here,' Passel said lamely, 'if that's what you wanted to know.'

'Then I'm glad you took my advice.' Captain Hop glanced smiling at the villa's long open window flipping the half-smoked cigarette languidly into the roadway. 'What's Prudham doing here?'

Passel hesitated, glanced from one to the other of the cold, watching faces of Sergeant Kee and Corporal Choy. 'He's going to take the other plane out to Hong Kong with my wife and children as soon as I clear Shanghai with you and Sztykgold. I thought that would be all right with you.'

Captain Hop lifted his blue custom-tailored shoulders in a shrug of indifference. 'Of course – but don't be tempted into doing anything foolish.'

'I gave you my word on that,' Passel said stubbornly.

'Just remember that, André. Because I'd hate there to be any unpleasantness.'

Passel glanced back up the drive uneasily. 'Is there anything else, Captain?'

'Yes. Have you heard anything further from Sztykgold?'

'No, nothing. But I had a visit from a friend of Mr Wan early this morning out at the office. Somebody calling himself Mr Tzu. He checked out the arrangements Sztykgold made with me.'

'What did you tell him?'

'Only what I was told to tell him. It was all that I could tell anybody. You know that, Captain.'

'And?'

Passel shrugged. 'It seemed it was what he expected to hear. He left right afterward.'

Captain Hop again glanced at the villa. 'You'll probably

see Sztykgold in the early morning. We'll be right along with him.'

Passel's face darkened in a worried frown. 'Will there be trouble?'

Captain Hop laughed. 'Sztykgold never believed in risking his own neck. I thought you knew that, André.'

Despite this assurance, Passel remained uneasy, worried more for his family than himself. He didn't want trouble of any kind. All he wanted was to get the whole business over with, knowing there was no way he could get around it short of a miracle, and join up with his wife and children in Hong Kong where they would be waiting with Eddie Prudham. 'Have you any idea of our destination, Captain?' he ventured.

Captain Hop saw no reason not to tell him. It might ease Passel's mind sufficiently for him to co-operate more enthusiastically. 'We're going to pick up a cargo down on Hangchow Bay for Hong Kong. Only Sztykgold won't be making that part of the journey with us.'

Passel glanced at the other two watching faces. 'Just the three of you then?'

'Yes – just the three of us,' Captain Hop affirmed.

'And no trouble?' Passel couldn't quite bring himself to believe it.

'No, no trouble, André.'

An expression of heartfelt relief showed on Passel's sweating face. 'I was worried about there being trouble.'

'You worry too much, André,' Captain Hop informed him, and inclining his head to Corporal Choy, watched him put the motor in gear and swing the big open car out into the roadway.

Standing on the pavement, André Passel stared after them until they disappeared from view, a feeling of foreboding weighing him down, and not wanting to think about any of it.

* * *

The clock above the India Building showed the time was 4.00 p.m. On his way back across town Harry Lord stopped the taxicab in the old International Settlement's Garden Road and went into the Manchukuo Bar and Restaurant. One of the more fashionable uptown bars, it was frequented mainly by local Western businessmen and upper middle class Chinese secretaries who in their spare time were amateur whores. Harry Lord found a vacant seat at the bar and ordered a beer, four packages of cigarettes, and a bottle of Haig & Haig, Along the bar, on the corner, two girls perched on stools sipped their drinks, smiled in his direction, and shifted their crossed thighs to afford him a better view. Answering with the shadow of a smile, he pocketed the cigarettes, and drank a long swallow of the chilled beer.

He had left the Avenue Lafayette without intention of returning to the Red Fortune Hotel but once in the taxicab, after he had gone over the trip in his mind, his thoughts had turned to Annie Kim. He didn't know why, only that for some unaccountable reason she had dropped into his life out of nowhere and for some equally unaccountable reason she fascinated him. He was certain it wasn't just her looks, nor her straightforward honesty either; it was something of everything about her. And he found he could remember every little thing about her, like the way she had crossed the floor. His throat constricted at the thought of it. 'Jesus Christ,' he murmured aloud, and wasn't aware that he had spoken aloud until he saw several faces turn to look at him oddly, and he scowled toughly back at them and saw them quickly find interest elsewhere, as if it had all been a mistake and they hadn't really heard anything after all; that was the effect he had even on complete strangers.

After a further beer and two scotches he was no nearer finding an explanation for the strange fascination Annie Kim exerted on him than at the outset. But his life had always moved in odd cycles, without apparent rhyme or reason. Although he was aware that he had been looking for something all his life without ever being aware of what exactly it was he was looking for, he knew it had to be *something*. There had to be a meaning somewhere. He had roamed half the world as if possessed by the migratory instinct of a bird. But it had never occurred to him that that *something* might be a woman. He had looked for a great many things in his time and had even found some of them. The trouble was he was no longer certain about money. The only thing a man could do with money was spend it, or else count it, and he couldn't see himself counting money for the rest of his life like Old Heinie Sztykgold. For him the feel of money was passionless. That had been the way with everything he had so far found in life; when he found it the allure of looking for it vanished. But whatever it was he was really looking for he knew he would know it when he found it.

The next time he ordered he saw the two girls on the corner of the bar glance past him toward the door, then climb down off their stools and leave. Then a voice at his shoulder said, 'Hello, Harry. I thought it had to be you. There's only one pair of shoulders like that around Shanghai.'

He knew immediately why the girls had left, they were Helen Wong's girls. Although she was somewhere in her late forties she didn't look it. Physically she was tall, lean, had a firm youthful figure and long elegant legs. Nobody seemed to know why she had turned to whoring in order to make a living for she was obviously from a family of some means, and along with an air of breeding she had been educated to the extent that she spoke several languages fluently, including French and English. He had first met her two years earlier in Nanking where she had owned a bar on the Taiping Road, and had later brought her and three of her girls down to Shanghai where she had taken a house out at Eight Fairies Bridge.

He watched her climb up on to the stool at his side. 'Can I get you anything?'

She smiled and put her bag on the bar. 'A scotch would be appreciated.' She studied him with some concern while the bartender brought her drink. 'When I hadn't seen you around these past few weeks I thought you had left town.' Her English was as beautiful as her Chinese, musical.

'I've been pretty busy lately. You know how it is with the way things are going.'

'And I thought I'd lost yet another friend.'

'Who'd you lose lately?'

She moved close to his shoulder. 'I heard Jacques Roullet left this morning. I believe certain policemen didn't take too kindly to it.'

Harry Lord rubbed his cigarette out. 'It's good to hear he made it. I was in the club last night and he told me.'

Helen Wong sipped her scotch. 'I'm leaving for Ningpo this evening. It's all been arranged. I'm taking five girls along. I sent those two to get ready. I have passage booked from

Ningpo to Hong Kong on board the Lavender and Walker steamer *Palambang*.'

'It's nice to know you have connections. I hear they're watching everybody leaving.'

'And you?'

'I'm still trying to make up my mind about where to go.'

'Why not come to Hong Kong? From what I hear you could do big business in Hong Kong.'

Harry Lord pulled a wry face. 'I'm not so sure. Cops are bad business anywhere, but Limey cops in a Crown Colony are worse. I believe you've got to swag out pretty hefty squeeze to work Hong Kong, even a Chink.'

'And I'd hoped you might come and visit me.' The disappointment in Helen Wong's voice was unmistakable. 'I intend to open a place in Kowloon City.'

Harry Lord was curious. 'Just how the hell did you ever become involved in *that* business?'

Helen Wong smiled, lifted her chin. 'Through listening to the hypocrisy of others. I wanted to laugh at the world and its values. It isn't so complicated. This is China.'

Harry Lord grinned magically. 'I seem to have heard that somewhere before.'

Helen Wong studied his tough, dark face intently. 'Did you have a visit from a girl called Annie Kim today?'

Harry Lord was startled. 'You know that?'

'Mm-hmm. One of my girls was in The Kimona on the Nanking Road this morning and heard her asking about a man called Chang. The bartender later mentioned your name to her. It was only when I heard about it that I knew you hadn't left town after all.'

'How come you know her?'

Helen Wong smiled conspiratorially, her high, tight little breasts thrusting against the blue silk of her cheongsam. 'I believe she's grown to be a very beautiful girl.'

'Oh, so-so.' Harry Lord gave nothing away.

'She was also a very beautiful baby,' Helen Wong said. 'She was born on the pavement right outside the apartment building where I lived on the Taiping Road. I remember that day quite vividly. Her father was a rickshaw coolie. He and his wife were very poor. They lived in a lean-to in a nearby alleyway. I sort of semi-adopted her until they moved out to the riverside shacks above the city. The last time I saw her was in 1937, just before the Japanese Expeditionary Force arrived. I left then for Wuhu. When I returned two years later I heard that her parents had died in the Rape of Nanking, bayoneted in the street. But nobody seemed to know what had happened to Annie. You can imagine my surprise when an old amah I knew from Nanking days told me she had seen her here in Shanghai, that she was living with a man called Chang out in Nantao.'

Harry Lord was intrigued. 'When was that?'

'About two months ago. I was going to pay her a visit but eventually decided against it. She may not even have remembered me. And who was I to interfere in her life? I was told she seemed to be quite happy. And Chang wasn't without money.' She paused to search his face. 'How did you know him – Chang?'

'It's a long story.'

'But she was asking about him in The Kimona.'

'I know. He left for Ningpo yesterday.'

Instant concern showed on Helen Wong's face. 'And Annie?'

'I told her about it when she called earlier today. I also offered to ship her out.'

'Where is she now?'

'Back at the Red Fortune Hotel.'

'And you like her?'

Harry Lord held her searching gaze. 'I was debating that same question when you arrived.'

'Can you really ship her out?'

'I don't see why not.'

'I'm glad.' Smiling softly, Helen Wong laid a hand on his arm. 'And take care of her. From what I remember she was a very nice girl as well as a very beautiful one. But if anything should happen that you need help – well you know where to find me. That train doesn't leave until late this evening. And I would gladly see to it that she got safely to Hong Kong.'

Harry Lord watched her climb down from the stool. 'I'll remember that.'

With a somewhat sad, wistful smile, Helen Wong offered him her hand, allowed it to linger in his. She had known a great many men from all walks of life, but Harry Lord was the only one for whom she had ever felt admiration. 'Make sure you take good care of you both, Harry.'

'You too, Helen,' he told her, and watched her go out

through the glass doorway to the street. He heaved a sigh, and in his selfishness suddenly regretted having met her. He hadn't wanted to share his experience of earlier that day with anybody. Now in her kindness and generosity, Helen Wong had committed him to himself.

Without finishing his drink he went out and caught a taxi-cab back to the Red Fortune Hotel with the express intention of telling Annie Kim about his meeting with Helen Wong and her offer to help, but when he reached the door of her room his resolve deserted him, and instead he went to his own rooms and took the bottle of Haig & Haig out on to the veranda. It wasn't something to be lightly considered. For some obscure reason it seemed vitally important that he keep her to himself. He felt bemused even thinking about her, could feel the blood surge through him and his heart pound in his chest. He tried to tell himself the whole thing was ludicrous. He had only known her for the matter of a couple of hours. They were strangers really, absolutely. He knew Old Po's fat cook Ang Ah Mui more intimately than he knew Annie Kim.

He took a drink from the bottle and in effort to distract his thoughts, turned his attention to the city. The sun had slipped westward although its heat still clung to the unmoving air of late afternoon. He lit a cigarette and watched the river sparkle in the hard sunlight. He was going to miss Shanghai for she had been good to him in her own way, a period of his life he wouldn't easily forget.

'I hope I'm not disturbing you from your thoughts, Mr Lord.'

He turned startled to see Annie Kim watching him from the veranda doorway. He got to his feet clumsily. 'No. No, you're not disturbing me.'

Annie Kim glanced down at the too large pale blue towelling robe she wore wrapped around her. 'Old Po found it for me.'

'It looks better on you than it would on him.' Harry Lord's grin was slightly inane.

She smiled with him, turned her attention to the river. Its waters had darkened a shade in the lengthening sunlight. 'It's quite beautiful out here.'

'Yeah, I suppose it is.' Harry Lord sat one hip back on to the veranda rail. 'I thought you'd be asleep.'

She turned to face him. Her face was pale and fragile in the declining sunlight, her eyes enormous under the dark fringe. 'After bathing I didn't feel quite so tired.' She glanced back at the river. 'Where's your ship?'

Harry Lord motioned his head toward the south shore. 'Across in Pootung, the other side of the river there. Only she's a launch, not a ship. If you're watching you'll see me go downriver before it gets finally dark.'

She was curious. He was the first Westerner with whom she had ever spoken. She thought his eyes incredibly blue for a man so dark. 'How long have you lived in Shanghai?'

Harry Lord ran a hand through his lank black hair. 'Since '46.'

'And before?'

'Oh, around.'

She devoted him her entire attention. 'Then you came to Shanghai?'

'That's it.'

'And now you're a very successful businessman,' she announced happily.

Harry Lord laughed, showed startling white teeth in his crooked grin. 'There are a number of conflicting opinions about that.'

She tilted her head a little to one side, unable to make up her mind about him.

Harry Lord found that she put him in mind of the very appealing alabaster china dolls on display in the windows of uptown stores, except that she had even more appeal.

She said suddenly, her inquisitiveness overcoming her shyness, 'How do you come to have such a strange-sounding name?'

Harry Lord said woodenly, 'My mother lived next door to a synagogue in Golders Green.'

She showed a perplexed frown. 'Golders Green?'

'Uh-huh. London.'

She was impressed. 'I once saw pictures of London in a book. They were very beautiful. One of them showed the King and Queen riding in a golden coach. Have you ever seen the King and Queen?'

'They weren't exactly what you'd call near neighbours.'

The inclination of her head steepened. He disconcerted her. At times he seemed to say one thing and mean another.

She had never seen any man so handsome. But what truly enraptured her were his eyes. His eyes were bluer even than the sky. He also had a beautiful smile, although it was a little crooked. But on reflection she decided that was perhaps the beautiful thing about it, it being crooked.

Harry Lord suddenly found that he couldn't remain silent any longer on the subject of Helen Wong. The knowledge of her offer to help lay on his conscience like a sackful of bricks. 'I was talking a little while ago to somebody who knew you back in Nanking. Do you remember Helen Wong?'

Annie Kim raised her eyes, showed in them a trace of wistfulness. 'Yes, I remember her. It was a long time ago. She lived in an apartment building on the Taiping Road and it had a man on the doorway with a green uniform and gold buttons. I remember that time very well.'

'You don't have to talk about it. Helen told me.'

Annie Kim's gaze drifted out across the river. The sunlight now shone gold on the darkening waters. 'It wasn't all sadness in those times,' she reflected. 'There was one Japanese officer in particular who was very kind to me. A number of us children were sent to live in a school-house and he used to visit us whenever he found it possible. He was an artist and he would take us for long walks in the countryside and paint for us. His name was Major Hamaguchi. He wasn't a warring soldier, and some days he was very ill. He could speak several languages. He had attended Nanking University some years before the fighting began and he had many friends in China. Then one day he took me aside and told me he was sending me to Changchow where an old Chinese friend of his lived. His friend's name was Professor Chen. He had taught languages at Nanking University for many years and had known Major Hamaguchi while he was there. It was Professor Chen who taught me to speak English.'

'What about your friend the Major?'

'It was very sad. I learned later that he died. Professor Chen told me that he had suffered for a long time with an incurable blood disorder.'

Harry Lord studied her with an expression of grave concern on his tough, dark, high cheekboned face. 'And the Professor?'

'He was an old man when I first went to live in Changchow. He died last autumn. It was then I went to work as a maid in a hotel at the railway station. But later, when everybody began running from the Communists I decided to come to Shanghai. It seemed the only thing to do.'

Experiencing a feeling of inadequacy, Harry Lord remained silent.

Annie Kim said simply, 'That was when I met Mr Chang. It was in the Hankow Park. When he learned that I had nowhere to live he very kindly offered to give me shelter for a few days.'

'He did?' Harry Lord said without surprise, and wondered why it had never occurred to him to visit the Hankow Park.

'It meant a very great deal to me,' she impressed with unabashed honesty, as if it was imperative she put everything into its true perspective, that nothing should be misconstrued, whether acceptable or not. And her honesty only provided for the two extremes. She had always vindicated her actions as merely an exchange of mean values. Annie Kim was only acceptable to herself as Annie Kim.

Out of his silence Harry Lord said, 'Helen Wong has a place out at Eight Fairies Bridge. She's leaving for Ningpo tonight with some of her girls. They have passage booked to Hong Kong. She'll take you with her if you want.'

Annie Kim's gaze was so honest that it forced Harry Lord to drop his own awkwardly in embarrassment to the bottle of Haig & Haig. 'But I have already committed myself, Mr Lord. I owe that in return for the hospitality I have already received from you.'

Harry Lord suffered a sudden longing to reach out and draw her to him, put his arm around her. 'But you don't owe me anything. If you want to go with Helen Wong I'll take you out to Eight Fairies Bridge right now. You could be in Hong Kong in a couple of days.'

Annie Kim shook her head, raised a hand to her breast. 'But I don't feel it so here. Somewhere I'm moved differently, as though it is predestined.'

Confused, Harry Lord said, 'But I don't even know yet where I'm going. All I know is that I'm going to refuel at either Ningpo or Chinhai before crossing to Taiwan. That's one place I've got to go because of the money I've got put away in a bank in Keelung. I could certainly take you to Keelung, but what're you going to do there?'

Annie Kim answered serenely, 'Whatever is intended for me.'

'Christ,' Harry Lord said out of bewilderment. 'You can't go around believing everything in life's mapped out for you.'

Annie Kim smiled at him calmly. 'But this is—'

Harry Lord shook his head dumbly. 'I know, I know. This is China.'

Annie Kim said quietly, 'I'm sorry, but I believe that one must at all times present oneself in one's true light.'

Harry Lord got instantly to his feet, motivated by a feeling of responsibility for her that he had never felt for anybody else. 'Listen,' he said in a voice he didn't recognize. 'You stay right here till I get back. Don't even step outside to the Bund. I'll call you the moment I get back. You hear?'

Without waiting to hear any argument on her part, he left her on the veranda and outside took a taxicab and headed west toward the Hire Boat Jetty on the Shanghai Bund still clutching the bottle of Haig & Haig. And every detail of her standing looking after him on the veranda in the too large pale blue towelling robe in the declining sunlight was engraved on his mind.

When he paid the taxicab off he went down along the jetty and climbed into the first water-taxi he saw and told the boatman, 'The Carfax Oil Depot.'

Captain Hop and Sergeant Li leaned on the rail of the Shanghai Bund some way to westward of the Hire Boat Jetty beneath the sawing palms lining the waterfront and watched the cream and green water-taxi pull out across the river.

Captain Hop glanced at Sergeant Kee with a triumphant smile. 'It seems he's on his way.'

Sergeant Kee's solemn gaze followed the water-taxi as it headed out across the darkening waters of the river. 'Isn't he ahead of schedule?'

'What does it matter? He'll know what he's doing.'

Sergeant Kee didn't possess the same confidence but remained silent as he watched the water-taxi put in to the Pootung shore. 'I just hope that nothing goes wrong we don't know about.'

Captain Hop's smile faded. 'What can go wrong? We've

taken every conceivable safeguard on that score.' Then, tight-lipped, he raised the Zeiss glasses and focused them on the Tungkow shore. Below Henning's Wharf he saw the *Sungari* leaving the Standard Vacuum Oil Company dock, tacking her cumbersome bulk downriver under a spread of sail, her motors silent. Dropping the glasses down, he said, 'Come on. Let's get back to the Avenue Lafayette. From now on we don't let Sztykgold out of our sight.'

Together they walked briskly back to where the car waited on the far side of the northern carriageway and climbed into it and sat back while Corporal Choy swung it out into the stream of traffic and headed back toward the old French Concession.

The sun was lying red on the horizon when Harry Lord dropped down into the *Jacaranda*'s cockpit with the bow and stern lines. Then, thumbing the electric starter, the twin Issotta Fraschini motors exploded with a roar that came back off the dock like a clap of thunder. He allowed them to turn over, warming them for a couple of minutes, the dock reverberating with their roar, then took her away, nosed her out across the dock, eased her around the pilings of the jetty and out into the Whangpoo.

The sun had almost gone and lights were beginning to show on both sides of the river, and downriver a lane of lights glittered in the evening haze as the long hills that rolled south to the shores of Hangchow Bay lost themselves in the distance. In midstream he put the glasses on the Hongkew Bund and looked back at the Red Fortune Hotel, and through the haze saw Annie Kim on the fourth floor veranda, saw her wave until the silhouette of the Yangtzepoo Pilot House intervened. Then, opening the throttles back, he watched the bows rise while the stern thrust itself into the mauve water to throw a wash plume high as he went down past the sprawl of shanties fringing the precincts of the Shanghai Water Works. Soon he was below the last of the lights and on the stretch of river leading down to Woosung Spit, passing the lights of traffic on the Chungkung Road. Below the wreck buoys leaning in the current around the hulk of the *Cameroon Highlander* he came up on the *Sungari* with the dragon's head on her bows glaring wrathfully ahead. He passed down her starboard side and saw Po-han deliberately ignore him. But the bald-domed Manchurian was the least of his worries. He had never entirely trusted Wong Peng Yin's hero, had kept his dealings with him to a minimum, and if he was on his way south, then he had no regrets at seeing the last of him.

When he was around south clear of the forts at Woosung to northward he left the blacked out silhouettes of the two Kuomintang gunboats at anchor above the greystone pier breakwater and pounded down into the Southern Waterway. Minutes later he came up on the scattered lights of the fishing village of Yangkiachen on the south shore, passed them to starboard, and headed out toward the high-humped island of Tsungming Tao where it squatted in midstream to dominate the estuary to southward.

In time he came up on the cluster of lights that was Tsungming on the south shore of the island, left them behind, then saw the black rock shore of the southernmost tip of the island come into view where Yawo Sha and Heng Sha lay to southwest along with the Tsungsha Banks and Fairy Flats. Only then did he slacken speed and bring the *Jacaranda* around into the Northern Waterway. With the night-glasses he scanned the waterway ahead that had been closed to all river traffic except junks since 1931, then turned his attention to the long stretch of the east shore that was Communist-held Kiangsu province. Nothing showed anywhere except to southward, where the lights of some junks far out in the estuary pricked the Pacific skyline like a frail scattering of stars.

Satisfied that nobody had him under surveillance, he eased the throttles open, pushed the *Jacaranda* out into the waterway, and headed upriver toward Lang Dok, the intervening silhouette of Tsungming Tao shielding him from the prying eyes of the two gunboats lying off Woosung.

* * *

In the Peking Suite of the Great Eastern Mansions, Henry Wan finished dressing while two waiters laid the table in the big room for dinner. When he went through into the room the two waiters were making ready to leave. 'Did my wife order?'

'Yes, sir. Mrs Wan ordered.'

'Then I'll ring the dining-room down when we're ready to dine.'

When the waiters left he relocked the door, poured himself a brandy, and carried it out to the balcony. Standing in the pool of light that emerged from the open doors, he glanced at his watch and saw that it read 7.30 p.m. Sipping at his drink, he turned his attention to the scattered lights of the river. It was going to be a long evening, and he wasn't going to be able to relax until he knew that the bullion was safely downriver, even more to his peace of mind, was safely on its way to Hong Kong. So many things could go wrong, so very many things. Yet it wasn't Harry Lord who worried him most, it was Sztykgold. Lord was too frank and straightforward a man to possess a devious mind, but Sztykgold's projected honesty wasn't exactly reassuring. Again, thinking about it, he reasoned it might only be something due to his aloof and ultra-confident manner. After all, he had introduced him to Lord, left the final decision to him, and had also allowed him to check out the arrangements for their flight to Hong Kong with André Passel. Tzu Hsun's report had been to his entire satisfaction, yet the feeling that he was somehow at a disadvantage remained nagging at the back of his mind. But he was committed, and all he could do now was to try and contain his worries and trust that everything would go as planned. According to Tzu Hsun, Sztykgold's behaviour at least furnished no grounds for undue concern.

'Henry?'

He heard his wife's voice carry out through the open doors. I'm out here – on the balcony.'

Zephyrine Wan appeared in the open doorway, silhouetted against the light within. She was wearing the only evening dress she had brought with her, a French gown of black velvet which showed her figure to its fullest advantage. 'Shall I ring down and tell them that we're ready to dine?' she wanted to know.

Henry Wan returned his attention to the Racecourse, its trees inked in darkness, their greenery dappled with light where their foliage overhung the Nanking Road. 'In a moment,' he told her

She joined him at the parapet of the balcony. A long way below, the glare of light reflected itself from the walls of the Nanking Road while the sound of evening traffic reached up into the night. The moon hadn't yet risen but stars showed in the clear sky, bright, shimmering above the city. 'It was in the spring of 1936.' She sounded surprised at her own discovery. 'That was when I was last in Shanghai. I stayed with an old school friend whose family had an estate up near Luikiahang. It was such a beautiful place.'

Henry Wan glanced her way but said nothing. He remembered the first time he saw her at a dinner-party given by her lawyer brother Charles Yeh, his business associate. Twenty-two at the time, she was stunningly attractive, the focal point of attention. Born in Szechuan and brought up in Hong Kong by an uncle after the death of her parents, she had arrived in Chungking the previous week to live with her brother. She was the most beautiful girl he had ever seen, and he had jokingly remonstrated with her brother for conspiring to keep her out of the limelight for so long. Determined to win her attention, he had swept her off her feet during the following weeks, overwhelmed her with expensive gifts, and had taken great delight in showing her off to friends and business associates at every opportunity. And in turn, despite the difference in their ages, she had become fascinated by him, by his aggressiveness and confidence, by the respect he commanded.

With neither himself nor the Yehs being true Old China, they had considered themselves outside the conventional code of conduct and when they weren't travelling in high social circles they were seen swimming, playing tennis and horse-back riding in the various exclusive clubs of Chungking. Then in the summer of 1940 they had married and moved to the hilltop house out at Ta Er Wo. Sexually she had turned out to be the most uninhibited woman he had ever taken to bed. In the mornings she would wake ready to be serviced, and at night only fall asleep when physically sated. Happily, between her and business he was completely immersed, so that with the War far removed from the mountain fastness of Chungking, he wouldn't have known it existed but for the Japanese bombing raids. And if it hadn't been for the death of Charles Yeh as a result of one of these raids when a bomb hit the Russian Club killing twenty-nine people, then the War would have passed unnoticed.

But in early 1948 the idyllic period had come to an abrupt end. Although the Communist menace had been growing in the north for a long time, he had been inclined to treat it with the same indifference as the high-ranking Kuomintang officials with whom he met around Chungking. In their confidence in Chiang's ability to deal with the Communist threat, they hadn't awakened to the truth until too late, when the Communist troops were already sweeping across the country from the north, with Kuomintang troops either in full retreat or else deserting *en masse* to join the enemy.

Zephyrine Wan said vacantly, 'I wonder what Charles would have thought if he had lived to see this day – when the country's on the verge of falling into Communist hands.'

'I wouldn't like to say who I consider worst,' Henry Wan reflected bitterly, 'the Communists or Chiang and his Kuomintang bandits. If his stooges were to find out how we've been outwitting him and his taxes over the past few years, then you'd soon find out just how mean he can be. No, it's every man for himself, and I won't rest easy again until I feel Kai Tak runway beneath our undercarriage.'

Zephyrine Wan stared out at the city from a long way away, eyes veiled, the subtle fragrance of her French perfume wafting in the cool, dew-damp air. Secretly she was dreading the evening and the charade she was forced to maintain. It was draining not only mentally, but physically; to sit and talk and listen to a man who within a matter of a few hours would be dead, a man who was her husband. She tried not to think about it, but the thoughts of him dying somehow returned again and again no matter what she did or tried to think about, and she wished desperately that it was over and done with and that she was in Tzu Hsun's arms.

When she remained silent, Henry Wan turned to look at her where she stood framed against the glow of light above the city. She made an impressive picture, her fragile face in shadow. He saw that her beauty hadn't faded with the passing years, and from the past he remembered again what had strangely added to her allure had been the knowledge that she possessed a complete lack of bodily hair. And at thirty-two she was as physically attractive as ever. She was lucky in that respect for there were few women who improved with age, certainly not in the physical sense. Only her breasts had grown a trifle out of proportion with the rest of her figure, but they had always been a little over-large, a special attraction to him. Nor did they appear to have lost any of their firmness, although it was more than a year since he had last touched them. As if awakening, he was surprised at his thoughts. It was the first occasion he had thought of her in such a context for a long time, and he felt sullen anger at himself for this unexpected show of weakness.

But there had been a time when she had never been *out* of his thoughts. He found it almost impossible to accept that now. At the very least she had become a stranger. Had her betrayal been gradual he could have accepted it, but it had been a thing of brutal hurt. The vividness with which he remembered the events of that day was seared on his mind forever. It had been late afternoon, two days before the *Tunting Explorer* was due to sail, and he had returned to the house unexpectedly and had walked in on them. They had been lying on the floor of his study, so carried away with their lust that they had been oblivious of his presence. She had been on hands and knees between Tzu's spread-apart thighs, her clothing in obscene disarray, and he had stared at the scene in horror and disbelief, had witnessed the awful expression of hungry intensity on her face. Worse had been her moans of pleasure, her obvious urge to gratify her partner's desires, and the greedy sounds her mouth had made. But more degrading was the fact that there had been no alternative but to turn away, for without Tzu Hsun's help it would have been impossible to continue with the conspiracy to have the bullion shipped downriver before engineering their own escape.

He had lived with the shameful vision ever since, and more to his discomfort had realized it hadn't been the first time it had happened, that Tzu Hsun had taken the risk of calling at the house on other occasions when he had been at the bank. Commonsense told him it had been too shameless and unhibited for a first encounter, and he had wondered ever since just how many others there might have been during the latter years of his marriage, especially toward the end when he was devoting himself to the hazardous task of secretly converting the bank's securities and negotiable bonds into bullion on the black market. Despite the overpowering rage and anger he had felt, he had known instinctively the hand to be played if his own safety and continuing survival was to be secured, a hand he had played masterfully ever since, restraining every impulse he had felt to the contrary. And he was certain neither of them even suspected that he was aware of their secret. Now his burden was beginning to weigh heavily. To preserve an outward façade of ignorance had caused him to suffer a great deal emotionally along with his other problems, but now the opportunity to exact revenge wasn't so very far off. Once in Hong Kong he would be in a position to secure a whole new future for a mere few hundred dollars paid to the right people.

'Do you suppose we're really safe here?'

He sent a glance quickly to his wife's concerned face. 'I'm sorry – I was thinking about something else. But, yes, I think we're probably safer here than most other places. But nobody can prove that we've done anything criminal, as yet. We're merely here visiting for a few days, booked into a hotel like anybody else. Besides, as Tzu said, it must be extremely doubtful if anybody would attempt anything in such a prominent place as this even if they knew our reason for being here.'

Zephyrine Wan said wistfully, 'I just wish it was all over and we were on our way to Hong Kong.'

Henry Wan reached out a hand to hers. 'I couldn't agree with you more.'

With a fleeting smile, Zephyrine Wan stooped her head and touched her lips to his sagging cheek. 'And life will become fun again, too.'

Henry Wan smiled with her, although she didn't see its true nature in the gloom. Then glancing out across the city, he tilted the glass to his mouth and finished his drink. 'Shall we ring down to the dining-room now, and tell them that we're ready to dine?'

They were at table, in the middle of dinner, when the phone rang. Henry Wan rose and took the receiver from its cradle.

It was Tzu Hsun who spoke. 'I thought I'd let you know I'm at the Yacht Club on the Soochow Creek. Sztykgold's at dinner inside. He appears to be something of a regular visitor here.'

Henry Wan sent a glance at the table where his wife sat watching him intently. 'What about the bodyguards?'

At the other end of the phone Tzu Hsun said, 'There's no sign of them. However, the lights in the apartment were still burning when he left so I assume they're at home.'

Henry Wan reflected on the information. 'Do you know if he's spoken with anybody?'

'Not that I know. He's quite alone.'

'Then stay with him. I don't want us to be taken unawares if anything goes wrong. And let me know the moment he leaves for the Nantao Bund.' Returning the receiver to its cradle, he turned back across the room.

At the table Zephyrine Wan said anxiously, 'Is anything wrong?'

Henry Wan resumed his seat, smiled at her brightly. 'On the contrary. Everything's just fine. More wine?'

Zephyrine Wan smiled with him in her own secret knowledge, and suddenly the evening became agreeably less overcast.

* * *

When Harry Lord angled the *Jacaranda* in on the south shore the cockpit clock showed the time was exactly 8.00 p.m. With the motors barely turning over, he held her steady with one hand while he focused the night-glasses on the shore with the other. He had come in to the shore upriver of the village and in the darkness there was no sign of life to be seen anywhere. Allowing the *Jacaranda* to drift with the current, he kept her head pointed upstream, ready to slam the throttles open at the first sign of any trouble. Wedged in its clips on the underside of the dashboard was the .505 Gibbs, and the .38 Police Special jammed into his waistband, his light-suited figure a bulky shadow in the cockpit. Meanwhile the black edge of shore slid past etched against the starlit sky whose silver sheen reflected on an endless expanse of kunai grass which moved gently in a breeze that was scented with a mixture of rotting vegetation and the flowers of the purple bean and plum tree.

Slowly the *Jacaranda* slid past a clump of willows leaning themselves into the river, then down past the first of the greystone cottages with its broken walls dark and silent. Several more cottages followed, close to the water's edge, all of them in ruins, their interiors, open to the elements. On the south side of the village a large mound of dirt and rubble dredged from the river in a forgotten attempt to cut a canal came into view, its slopes grown with weeds and kunai grass. It was then that he saw the junk, starlight limning her silhouette. She was a forty footer, rigged for square sail, her midships living-quarters roofed by a hooped bamboo shelter. He was below her when he suddenly heard himself hailed by a voice out of the darkness.

'*Jacaranda*, ahoy!' The second time the voice sounded more certain of itself, and the glow of a carbide lantern rose up out of the kunai grass close to the water's edge.

'Put that fucking light out!' he yelled back, and saw it promptly extinguished. 'Stupid rice-eating bastard,' he went on aloud, knowing from previous experience that there was nobody as witless as an ordinary Chinaman when it came to matters of conspiracy. Then he saw the figure start into the river and he edged the throttles open fractionally so that the *Jacaranda* immediately held her way against the current.

The boy, his gaunt face showing uncertainty, stopped some way astern, the black water swirling around his shoulders.

Harry Lord peered astern at the starlit face. 'Who're you?'

'My name's Liang.' The boy gestured toward the shore. 'We've been waiting for you. Everything's been made ready.'

Harry Lord could just discern the line of a granite jetty astern of the junk, and easing the throttles open further, took the *Jacaranda* in toward it as the boy turned to struggle ashore.

There were four of them waiting on the jetty, a stooped old man, two more boys, both of them younger than the one who had been in the river, and a straw-hatted old woman whose face was lost in the wide shadow of the brim.

Harry Lord peered around the shore alertly, saw only the dull gleam of kunai grass, and hefted the .38 in his hand to make certain that they saw it.

It was the old man who spoke. 'We've been waiting for you. Everything's ready. See?' He pointed in the direction of a cottage which stood back off the jetty. 'The boxes are inside.'

Harry Lord beckoned him to board the *Jacaranda*, gestured at the bow and stern lines, and after watching him throw them ashore to be secured to a pair of ring-bolts by the two boys, he cut the motors and followed him ashore.

The silence was disturbed only by the dry rustle of kunai grass as it moved in the breeze, and by the restless swirl of the river. Harry Lord watched the eldest boy arrive with the dead lantern. 'You're on your own here?'

The old man dragged his eyes from the .38 in Harry Lord's hand. 'Yes. Take a look and see for yourself.'

'Then what happened to those people who brought word I'd be here tonight?'

'They left this afternoon, started back to Shanghai.'

Harry Lord stared cautiously into the sweet scented darkness which lay in a heavy cloak across the shore. Somewhere a bird called, long and plaintive.

The old man reached out a scrawny hand. 'You must load quickly and go. Sometimes Communist patrols come along without warning. Come – this way.'

They started along the jetty with the old man in the lead. All five of them wore black cotton work-suits and walked barefooted. Harry Lord followed in the rear trying to calm the sense of apprehension that troubled him. Yet he hadn't seen anything suspicious, nothing to indicate that anything was amiss.

When they stopped by the broken gable of the cottage the old man pointed inside. 'See?' His dark eyes flitted across his shoulder uneasily. 'Everything's ready.'

Harry Lord saw the stacked cases in the gloom, heavy, iron-bound cases with rope handles. He glanced once more along the shore, jammed the .38 into his waistband, then clambered over the rubble to try a case for weight. He had the case in his grasp for only a second when something hit him a blow that brought his skull crashing in on him, and in spite of an attempt to reach out and prevent himself falling, he felt himself begin to float down a long velvet tunnel of darkness.

* * *

Annie Kim lay awake in her room staring at the stars that showed in the patch of sky outside the window. After Harry Lord left she had stayed on the veranda to watch darkness fall. The sun had gone down to leave the sky the colour of blood and in the gathering dusk she had seen the launch go downstream on a river that had turned to flow mauve in the afterglow. She had waved to it until it had disappeared from view, and had known then that it was a day she would never forget, and in the afterglow everything had been turquoise, mauve and violet. She was in love. Her own simple logic told her that the peculiar conflict of emotion she was experiencing couldn't be anything other than love. Yet she was uneasy. In spite of the kindness and consideration which he had shown her he had given no indication that he expected any sort of payment in return, and in China such an arrangement was almost unknown. Nobody in China gave favours without first demanding far greater reward in return.

Suddenly the possibility occurred to her that he might be looking for a virgin. In panic she sat up to find the light switch. Quickly she crossed the room and stood up with her hands on her hips in front of the mirror. She turned first one way, then the other. She studied her reflection with sombre doubt. Yet she couldn't see any outward indication that betrayed the fact she *wasn't* a virgin. What was hidden beneath the dark triangle that reached up from between her thighs was, if anything, on the small side. Mr Chang had informed her of that fact one evening when she had paraded up and down his Nantao apartment naked. That was all she had ever done for Mr Chang, walk around, or sit around, naked. Only on rare occasions had he touched her, and then it had only been with his hand; an exchange of mean values.

Her eyes misted when she considered the possibility that he might only be interested in a virgin. She had only first given herself the previous year, at the hotel in the railway station in Changchow. It had been one of the conditions of employment, and had she refused she would have had to give herself sooner or later on the streets if she wasn't to starve. The more she thought about it the greater consolation she found in the fact that being a virgin surely had its accompanying disadvantages. There were so many things a man would have to teach a virgin before she was any good at making love. It stood to reason, was only logical. But she would have to show him how unimportant it was to be a virgin, how they could even be an encumbrance to a man. Yet uncertainty never left her eyes; and suddenly from outside, from the direction of the old International Settlement, the crackle of rifle-fire carried across the upturned eaves.

* * *

Harry Lord didn't know how long he had been unconscious, and it took him several moments to realize where he was when he regained his senses. Fighting a sea of nausea that threatened to wash over him, he rolled his eyes up to see the cockpit canopy above him.

'On your feet!'

He turned his head and saw Tadatoshi's face staring coldly down at him from behind the sights of a Russian machine-pistol, and he realized immediately that Sztykgold had been one step ahead of him from the outset. That was his first thought; his second was that he wasn't a man of such marked vision after all.

Tadatoshi again gestured at him with the machine-pistol. 'I said on your feet!'

Harry Lord emitted a groan and hauled himself upright with the aid of the wheel.

'Get over there – in the corner!' Tadatoshi, shoulders bulging from a tattered black shirt, a broad sweat-band knotted around his forehead, looked even more mean than he had ever done in any of the expensive suits he had worn around Shanghai. 'And no tricks. Make one wrong move and you get the whole magazine,' he warned.

Harry Lord backed into the starboard corner of the cockpit, his head clearing slowly. The *Jacaranda* was already well loaded, with the youngest Liang boy hauling the cases inboard across the port gunwale while the rest of his family man-handled them down along the jetty, stooped low and sweating, their eyes mirroring their fear and uncertainty as Nakamura goaded them to greater efforts with threats and curses. Harry Lord shook his head, eyeing the cargo narrowly. There was a sight more bullion already on board than $3,000,000's worth. The cases were stacked double, filling the entire stern-quarters, and as a result the *Jacaranda* was lying lower in the water than she had ever done on any previous trip.

Tadatoshi's baleful eyes flitted over him suspiciously. 'What're you thinking?'

'Fuck you,' Harry Lord said.

Tadatoshi took a step nearer, eyes narrowing to mere slits. 'You heard me!' he snarled. 'What're you thinking?'

Harry Lord said sullenly, 'I was thinking you're going to be lucky if she doesn't go under with all this weight in her belly when she gets under way, because if my guess is right there's a lot more bullion here than three million buck's worth.'

Grinning, Tadatoshi spat across the side. 'Let me do the worrying. Besides, we're almost through loading right now.'

Harry Lord cast a glance at the dashboard clock and saw that it showed the time to be a few minutes after 9.00 p.m. There was no disputing the fact that they had made good time loading what looked to be more than a couple of tons dead weight. But this time he was really in it; Shit Creek with a broken paddle.

'All right – finish!' Tadatoshi clambered across the cases and sent the youngest Liang boy ashore with a backhanded blow as his family were herded down along the jetty by Nakamura who took up the rear with a submachine gun.

Apart from the two Russian-made weapons which Harry Lord decided they had probably picked up while making their way through the Communist lines north of Shanghai, he also saw the butt of his .38 Police Special protruding from the waistband of Nakamura's black work-suit. That was when he remembered the Gibbs. There was no sign of it anywhere on deck and unless they had dumped it across the side while he was unconscious, he saw the remote possibility that they had overlooked it and that it was still in its clips beneath the dashboard.

Tadatoshi came forrard on the cases gesturing aggressively with the machine-pistol. 'The motors! – start the motors!'

Glancing up at the snarling face, Harry Lord forgot the Gibbs temporarily and touched off the electric starter so that the exploding roar of the twin motors echoed out across the river and the adjoining countryside with a shattering crash. Then he saw Nakamura from the corner of his eye hurl the bow and stern lines on board, and with the *Jacaranda*'s head beginning to swing with the current Tadatoshi clambered up on to the foredeck as Nakamura leapt into the stern-quarters. And then before anybody realized what was happening, Tadatoshi opened fire with the machine-pistol, and through the oily pound, jolt and clatter of brass hulls on the deck, Harry Lord saw three of the Liang family go down under the hail of bullets, leaving only the old man and the eldest boy on their feet, their faces dull and uncomprehending. Then Nakamura shot the old man point blank in the chest, and as he was hurtled back across the jetty under the force of the shots, the eldest boy came suddenly to life and threw himself sideways off the jetty into the black water close under the *Jacaranda*'s stern as it swung away clear of the shore. For a long moment there was no sign of him, and then they all saw his head break the surface further astern as he struck out downriver. On the foredeck Tadatoshi stood straddle-legged and fired over Harry Lord's head, a flame in the muzzle of the gun as he sprayed the river. Then back astern Harry Lord saw the boy jerk suddenly upright in the black water, lift his face skyward, and disappear beneath the surface.

Tadatoshi started back toward the stern, his attention focused anxiously on the shore that was still echoing the commotion of the previous few minutes. 'Get her moving!' he screamed. *'Get her moving!'*

Slamming the motors in gear, Harry Lord opened the throttles to bring them around to starboard, and swung her out wide into the stream, expecting the countryside to erupt with searchlight and star-shell at any instant.

In the stern-quarters both Tadatoshi and Nakamura watched the shore quickly lose itself in the darkness, then they relaxed, grinning at each other. Tadatoshi yelled down into the cockpit, 'One wrong move from here on and you're dead!'

Harry Lord didn't turn his head, although he doubted if either of them would be prepared to shoot him unless he pulled something utterly stupid. And it was for that same reason that he wasn't already lying dead along with the Liangs at Lang Dok; because he was their insurance against anything going wrong with the motors. In that particular field he knew for certain that they were out of their depth, but he had to remain careful. He had got the drift about Tadatoshi's and Nakamura's past a long time previously. Rumour put it, and he had never found reason to dismiss it, that they had served at one time in Shanghai with the military police, the dreaded Kempei Tai, with full powers of arrest and investigation over both the civil population and military personnel. Later they were supposed to have moved to Hong Kong, then south to Dutch Borneo where stationed at Sourabaya they were said to have been prominent parties to atrocities against the civilian population during 1944 before having fled back to China as the American Campaign in the Pacific progressed northward. Prior to Japan's surrender they had arrived in Shanghai and were provided with shelter by Sztykgold with whom they had struck up an acquaintance when stationed earlier in the White Sun Barracks. And it was just the sort of trick that Sztykgold would have pulled, the sort of trick that could be bought with a few dollars paid to the right quarters in Chungking. There was nothing that money couldn't buy, when one thought about it; even sanctuary for war criminals.

When he considered it, it was spine-chilling to be faced with the possibility that morning might dawn with him no longer there to see it. He hadn't thought much about death before and now that it was literally looking over his shoulder it spooked him to realize just how abruptly everything could come to an end, to go suddenly out blackly with a bullet in the head. That was providing one *did* go suddenly out blackly, because there was just the remote possibility that one might go gaily on his way with sprouting wings and a harp under his arm straight to the Promised Land of Dortmunder fountains, cigarette trees, and women who never said no. The trouble was nobody had ever come back to give a guarantee about it one way or the other and he wasn't therefore in a hurry to embark on an unknown journey.

But so far he still had life on his side, and with life he was still in with a chance, although it could have been argued to be less than a Chinaman's chance, and there were only two chances considered to be worse than a Chinaman's; slim, and none. What he really had to do was think constructively. In passing he wondered what somebody else would do in his position, like maybe Hannibal, or Napoleon, or maybe Garibaldi.

And he thought; who the fuck was Garibaldi?

Then he forgot about Garibaldi and started to think about the Gibbs again. With his body shielding his movements he stealthily edged his hand in beneath the dashboard and felt his fingers touch the oil-polished stock of the big weapon where it still lay snug in its clips. His spirits soared instantly, and a slow, crazy-mad grin spread across his face, although he knew he was going to have to wait for precisely the right moment before he stood any chance of using it. Five, maybe six seconds was how long it would take him to get it clear and start shooting. But from the way they were watching him he realized he would be lucky if he got it halfway clear before they gunned him down.

Instead he forced himself to control his impatience, and soon afterward something else claimed his attention. A sudden long flickering light broke to play along the horizon to westward. From the river it looked like the fitful play of an electric storm. 'See that?' he remarked across his shoulder. 'It looks as if the Communist artillery's just opened up on the Shanghai defences. They could be running around town by the time we get in.'

Tadatoshi gave him a leering grin. He had never cared for Harry Lord. He had always made him somehow uneasy. The crazy-mad grin had a way of unnerving him at times, just as it unnerved Sztykgold. And the man was mad enough to try almost anything. Only this time he had a gun on him. He said with relish, 'Who's worried about Shanghai?'

Harry Lord frowned. It wasn't the reaction he expected. For some reason he had never doubted that Shanghai would be their destination. 'Then where the hell are we headed?'

Nakamura put his head back and laughed. 'Where you're headed you won't be greatly concerned!'

Harry Lord's bleak features never altered. 'Is that so?' he said toughly, angered by Nakamura's confidence.

The smile disappeared from Nakamura's face and his eyes glittered. 'Keep your eyes on the river or I'll shoot you right now!'

Harry Lord stared back at him calmly. Nakamura didn't worry him. He was an ox, numb from the ankles upward. And it was odds-on that he wouldn't try anything opposed by Tadatoshi. He said calmly, 'Listen, Fuckface. Get trigger-happy now and we'll all end up floating down the river.' And grinned his sudden, crazy-mad grin.

Tadatoshi turned on him snarling. 'Shut your mouth, and do as he tells you!'

Still grinning crazily, Harry Lord turned back to the wheel full of frustrated anger and resentment. Even so he knew they would only shoot him now as a last resort, that they would put up with almost anything from him until they reached their intended destination. But that destination could be any of a dozen places on the south shore between Yangkiachen and Hangchow Bay. At least that was the most likely area where they would put the bullion ashore, somewhere down along that forty-five mile stretch of stunted shoreline and mud-flats, because he seriously doubted if Sztykgold would risk running the *Jacaranda* too far south because of the danger of them being intercepted by a Kuomintang patrol boat. Yet from the way everything had gone so far he realized that Sztykgold would have left very little to chance, if anything.

That was what rankled him more than anything else, the way Sztykgold had calmly set him up. Sztykgold had been laughing up his sleeve right from the moment he had set eyes on Henry Wan. It was little wonder he had been quick to agree to any arguable point he had made that afternoon; he had set the Wans and himself up like a windowful of tailor's dummies.

Halfway down to Woosung the moon rose to light the river clear as day, and he saw it was now Tadatoshi and Nakamura who were on edge. Back in the stern-quarters they scanned the river anxiously, knowing there was next to nothing they would be able to do if another craft put in an appearance, for due to the danger of the *Jacaranda* swamping herself in her own wash she was unable to make much more than twenty knots, and even then her backsuction was curling in around the stern so that only a few inches of freeboard showed.

Casually he glanced around him at the river, his mind on full throttle as he tried to devise a means where he could take both men off guard long enough to get the Gibbs clear. 'You know,' he remarked off-handedly. 'Henry isn't going to like this.'

Tadatoshi laughed. 'He doesn't have much choice – does he?'

Harry Lord said evenly, 'I don't know so much about that. Maybe you won't get away with this as easily as you think.'

Tadatoshi came back quickly. 'Is that what *you* think?' Now that they hadn't seen any sign of a patrol boat they had gained in confidence again.

Harry Lord glanced astern at them, disappointed to see that neither of them had relaxed their vigilance. 'I'm not thinking anything.'

'Good,' Tadatoshi announced. 'Because all the thinking in the world isn't going to help you now.'

'That's right,' Nakamura put in. 'By daylight this stuff will be in Gough Hill Cove and there won't be anything that can be done about it.'

Tadatoshi turned on him with a scowl. 'You've said enough!'

Nakamura put his chest out belligerently. 'What difference does it make?' he argued. 'There's nothing he can do about it. He's going to have a bullet in his head before he's another hour older.'

'You've said enough, just the same,' Tadatoshi insisted, returning his sullen attention to the river, wishing secretly he could feel dry land beneath his feet again. He had never cared for boats, not boats of any kind. Everything about them was foreign to him. And he knew that Harry Lord knew it too. That was the reason why he hadn't wanted Nakamura to goad him into doing anything rash. The man was mad enough to try almost anything, especially with his back to the wall. So from now on he wasn't going to take his eyes off him for a single second.

Harry Lord was perplexed. Hangchow Bay was still a long haul to southward and he couldn't understand what Nakamura had meant when he said that he would have a bullet in his head before he was another hour older. Gough Hill Cove was north of Ningpo, and at their present speed it was doubtful if they would sight the lights of Ningpo much before 4.00 a.m. He couldn't make sense of that remark, whichever way he looked at it. There was something that he wasn't taking into account, and it worried him. And meanwhile he saw the sprinkle of lights that was partly blacked-out Woosung begin to take on a sharper definition off the starboard bow, while ahead lay the moon-silvered silhouette of Tsungming Tao out in midstream.

With the current astern they had made good time despite the heavy weighted cargo, and then he felt the first trace of panic when he caught a glimpse of a light, very small, wink in the darkness above the northern shore of Tsungming Tao. Tadatoshi saw it too, and with an excited shout, indicated its position to Nakamura. Harry Lord swore. Time was running out and no matter how he went about it, he saw it would still take him five, six seconds to grab the Gibbs from its clips and swing it around, and he knew that he would never make it. And then he saw the junk. At some point in the past few minutes it had detached itself from the darkness of the island's shoreline and moved out into the Northern Waterway, shielded from Woosung by the intervening bulk of the island. His heart fell even more sharply away when he recognized her as the *Sungari*. Big and black, her sails furled, her motors creamed a phosphorescent wash astern as she stood off the island. It was all clear to him now; it was Po-han who was headed down for Gough Hill Cove, not the *Jacaranda*.

'Never mind the *Sungari*!' Tadatoshi shouted excitedly. 'Make for the bay below where the light shows!'

Harry Lord saw the bay right ahead, lying inside a jutting channel of rock, the water flat, calm, moon-silvered. They came up on the channel fast with the current astern and he closed the throttles over and moved into it while the *Sungari* angled across astern of them. Once in the bay he closed the throttles still further and felt the sodden lift of the stern under the weight of the bullion. Then he saw a sampan headed out from the beach that showed a narrow silver strip under the overhang of black cliff. He counted five men in it besides the one who stood in the stern working the sculling oar. They were about thirty yards off when he brought the *Jacaranda* around to starboard so that they were now lying broadside on to the beach.

His heart was pumping blood in his ears as he watched the sampan approach on the beam. When he looked astern he saw Tadatoshi was also watching the sampan, while Nakamura's attention was focused on the *Sungari* as she closed on the entrance to the channel. It was then that he saw the only chance he believed he was ever likely to see. But instead of going for the Gibbs he snatched the throttles all the way back over open so that the motors hooked with a roar, the *Jacaranda* surging violently ahead. He held her for an instant, motors thundering at full power, then slammed the throttles over almost shut.

When he wheeled around he saw Tadatoshi's startled face staring back at him as he disappeared across the stern still clutching the machine-pistol in an outflung hand. In the same instant Nakamura lost his balance, stumbled, and sprawled forward on to the cases. Clearing the cockpit in a single stride, he grabbed the submachine gun from Nakamura's hand and swung it like an axe when the Japanese came up off his knees, jack-knifing him back into the cases face foremost. Then, hefting the weapon in both hands, he drove it down on the unprotected skull, and only then, when Nakamura flattened out on the cases, did he realize that they were shooting at him from the sampan which had turned to follow astern and was lying about twenty yards back off the port quarter. Levelling the submachine gun on it, he emptied the magazine as bodies tumbled over each other in a bid to throw themselves out of the line of fire, then threw it aside and was back in the cockpit, pausing only to snatch the .38 Police Special from Nakamura's waistband.

Hauling the *Jacaranda* back around into the channel where the *Sungari* was headed down on him, he cocked the Gibbs and laid it ready on the dashboard. Undecided about what sort of action Po-han would take, he waited tense and alert, adrenalin pumping through him, then saw her heel to starboard in an attempt to force him into running the *Jacaranda* on to the western ledge of the channel. In reply he snatched the wheel around to his own starboard, shut the throttles down, and squeezed the *Jacaranda* across the *Sungari's* bows and on down along her port wall. Next he spun the wheel back around to port and opened the throttles again, and saw the dropping figures leave the high overhang of the *Sungari's* stern as he pulled out from under it.

He shot the first one with the Gibbs at waist-height, caught him in mid-air and cut him almost in half. The second one he shot with the big gun bucking higher, and blasted the body outboard before it made the stern-quarters. The other two made the drop cleanly, and he calmly worked the bolt on the big, ugly weapon, saw one of them rise to his feet, and shot him square in the chest. Then Po-han rose up off the cases, shaved skull gleaming in the moonlight, a US Army .45 grasped in both hands.

Harry Lord saw the muzzle flash right in front of his eyes and felt the blast as he hurled himself into the starboard corner of the cockpit, dropping the Gibbs and snatching the .38 Police Special from his waistband. The next heavy calibre bullet shattered the woodwork of the canopy close by his right shoulder and through it all he was vaguely conscious of Po-han walking steadily toward him through the noise and confusion yelling at the top of his voice in Manchurian. Holding the .45 straight out in front of him in both hands, Po-han aimed to shoot again, and Harry Lord ducked in the blast and muzzle flash as the bullet hammered through a metal vent on the canopy. Po-han was almost on top of him, bringing the .45 around again, when Harry Lord started shooting. He fired four shots at point blank range, the gun hammering in his hand, before the lumbering figure relaxed his grasp on the .45, lurching to one side with both hands clasped to his chest before pitching forward down into the cockpit.

Dazed and deafened by the thunder of gunshots, his heart pounding through his body with the force of a trip-hammer, his mouth dry with the realization of the very closeness of death, Harry Lord hauled the wheel around amidships and headed the *Jacaranda* out into the Southern Waterway with a scattering of shots from the *Sungari*'s decks following his wash plume. He held her headed out toward the sprinkle of lights that marked Woosung for three, four minutes before he next looked back to where the *Sungari* was lying about a quarter of a mile astern, a black shadow slanted at an angle on her port side, her bows lifted on the rocky ledge of channel, her deck a confusion of scurrying lanterns. Heaving a sigh of manifest relief, he eased the throttles, drawing down several deep breaths of clean river air, and let his gaze travel slowly around the *Jacaranda*. An overpowering smell of burnt cordite, blood, and death hung over her like a cloud, and in the starboard corner of the cockpit, Po-han lay hunched over where he had toppled. All expression had gone out of his ugly Manchurian face and his eyes stared sightlessly at the stars overhead. In his open mouth gold teeth glinted in the shifting light with the motion of the launch. Further aft, Nakamura lay on his face on the cases, while a third body sprawled half out of the launch across the stern.

Arming the sweat from his eyes, Harry Lord felt a flood of nausea rise in his throat. He had never killed anybody before, and now the reaction had set in. His limbs felt weak and sweat streamed down his body like it was a summer day without the whisper of a breeze to stir the air. The only consolation he could draw on was the fact that if he hadn't killed *them*, then they would have killed *him*. But more important, he couldn't go on thinking about it all night, and leaving the motors idling, he climbed out of the cockpit while the launch drifted broadside in the Southern Waterway with the current and went aft and tipped the body sprawled across the stern outboard. Next he got hold of Nakamura's feet and hauled him aft, rolling him outboard across the stern. Po-han he hauled upright, leant him across the starboard gunwale, and toppled him headforemost across the side. All three bodies floated placidly away downriver in the moonlight, eddying in the current.

Returning to the cockpit he then got the greased metal box of shells and the bottle of Haig & Haig he had bought that afternoon in the Manchukuo Bar and Restaurant from the starboard locker, and loaded both guns. By that time the *Jacaranda* had drifted downriver in the waterway so that she was just above the lights of Woosung on the south shore at the junction of the Whangpoo, above Woosung Spit. The two gunboats were also still in position, their silhouettes framed against the scattering of lights. But out there, so close to the shore of Tsungming Tao, he knew it would be impossible for their look-outs to pick up the *Jacaranda*'s low profile against the high-humped island.

Wiping his hands with a wad of cotton waste, he took another lengthy pull from the bottle of Haig & Haig, lit a cigarette, and leaned his arms along the after end of the canopy. He was below the northernmost shoulder of the island now, the *Sungari* hidden from view where she was aground in the channel. And above him, in the saddle between the hills, was the huddle of lights that was Miaochen, while to southward the river was deserted, the flat silver water pricked by the coloured winking lights of the fairway buoys.

Glancing at his watch, he saw the time was 11.50 p.m. All he had to do now was find the patience to allow the *Jacaranda* to continue drifting with the current until he was abeam the lights of Yangkiachen on the dark wedge of shore to southward, then cut across the waterway and make his run on the Whangpoo from southward, hugging the shore on low power to avoid throwing a wash plume. And meanwhile he saw a bank of clouds beginning to build in the north, beyond the glow of light that was Shanghai.

SHANGHAI

Sunday, May 22nd, 1949

MIDNIGHT. Chinese Communist crews of four short-range Russian-built bombers were gathering in the briefing-room at the utility airstrip at Nantung in Kiangsu province when Henry Wan put down the telephone receiver in the Peking Suite of the Great Eastern mansions.

'Was that Tzu?' Zephyrine Wan's anxiety caused a tremor in her voice.

Henry Wan turned to where she was looking at him out of a corner of the cushion-strewn sofa. 'Yes. Sztykgold's on the move again. He's just gone into a club called Jean Nicolet's Place.'

Relief flooded through Zephyrine Wan, and her face brightened. 'Then we've been worrying ourselves unnecessarily after all.'

'Perhaps.' Henry Wan's voice was guarded, carefully non-committal.

Zephyrine Wan rose from the sofa and poured herself a brandy. 'At least Sztykgold doesn't appear to be unduly concerned about anything.'

Henry Wan was no longer listening to her. He was plagued with doubt. Now that everything appeared to be going as Sztykgold had predicted, his wife's suddenly assured manner began to trouble him. It occurred to him that if she and Tzu Hsun really had made concrete plans to dispose of him, then they would almost certainly attempt to put them into operation before it came time to leave Shanghai. And the more he thought about it, the more he was convinced that his fears weren't without foundation. As he saw it, their most opportune moment would arrive after the bullion had been safely brought downriver, after it had been delivered out to Lunghwa. And he didn't even possess a gun with which to protect himself. Morosely, he began to ponder just how he might conceivably out-manoeuvre them.

Draining her glass, Zephyrine Wan sent a sly glance in her husband's direction, and almost as if she was aware of the trend that his thoughts had taken, she began to wonder if he didn't harbour suspicions about her and Tzu Hsun, and the uncertainty of it increased her uneasiness. Yet they had always been so careful in their association. But now she was worried by the possibility that they had taken too much for granted. And when she thought about it, she wasn't at all certain that his growing moroseness was entirely due to his concern for the bullion. Too many conflicting thoughts had passed across his face during the evening; she began to realize that now. They had both been playing games with each other, each trying to lull the other into a sense of false security. When she looked at her empty glass she saw that her hand was trembling.

'Is something worrying you?'

Startled by the sound of her husband's voice, she glanced up, tried to conceal any trace of guilt on her face, and found herself the subject of his intent gaze. Any confidence she had remaining suddenly evaporated. She knew that she couldn't remain any longer in the same room with him, not without Tzu Hsun. With forced casualness, she said, 'No, nothing's worrying me. It's just that I can feel a headache coming on.'

'Then why don't you go and lie down for a while?'

Zephyrine Wan found she couldn't meet her husband's gaze. She put her glass down, raised a hand to her temple, avoiding his eyes. 'Yes, I think I will.'

Henry Wan's smile was one of sympathetic understanding. 'Nothing's likely to happen yet. Sztykgold hasn't even returned to the Avenue Lafayette.'

Zephyrine Wan had to will herself to move. 'Yes, of course.'

Henry Wan watched her retire to the main bedroom, a frown darkening his face. Despite his close scrutiny of her he had been unable to read anything into her face, voice, or behaviour. He felt a growing sense of frustration with himself. Too much was passing through his mind. David Kow also worried him. Kow had never forgiven him for the manner in which he had acquired the bank, and Kow had always been a careful, vigilant man, and all it needed for him to do was to call at the bank over the weekend to realize that something was amiss. And if he drove out to the house at Ta Er Wo and found it hastily abandoned, then he would go straight to the police. He found that he had begun to sweat clammily, and he knew that he had to hold on to his thoughts, fight any trend toward panic. Above all he had to get his priorities in the right order, and his first priority was the bullion. Once it was safely accounted for he could talk to Sztykgold about his other problems. For a figure, Sztykgold was capable of furnishing an answer to any problem – even to one concerning the future of his wife and Tzu Hsun.

* * *

Harry Lord flipped his second cigarette across the side, opened the throttles back and listened to the motors pick up, deep-throated and dully rumbling, sending their reverberations through the deck beneath his feet. Easing the wheel around to port, he watched the bows swing around on to the patchwork scattering of lights that was Yangkiachen on the dark wedge of the south shore and began his run across the Southern Waterway.

When he was abeam of Yangkiachen he brought his head around back upriver, and keeping close to the south shore, moved in on the Whangpoo from southward. His problems had begun in earnest again and he was thinking in several directions at the same time. Gas was his first priority. As soon as he reached Shanghai he would have to top the tanks so that at the first sign of any further trouble he could turn the *Jacaranda* around and head back downriver. He wasn't so much worried about the bullion. He could call Henry Wan from Chinhai or Wenchow. Since the Communist offensive had begun he saw it would now be geographically safer to by-pass Ningpo as it was the southern terminus of the Shanghai-Hangchow-Ningpo railway, and the Communists would be certain to make a concentrated effort to push south in a bid to cut the Kuomintang's most convenient escape route to Taiwan.

Leaving Yangkiachen astern, he wondered if Sztykgold had already left for Ningpo to be on hand when the *Sungari* arrived at Cough Hill Cove. Although he would have had to leave Shanghai without arousing Henry Wan's suspicions, it would present no real problem after what he had already arranged. There was the possibility that he had even grown wings for the occasion. But he had caught Old Heinie Sztykgold on the wrong foot this time, and he wondered what his reaction would be in the cold light of morning when he waited in vain for Po-han and the *Sungari* to put in an appearance. The magic grin spread further and further across his face the longer he thought about it. But he wasn't finished with him. If he ever met up with him again he would run the .38 a yard up his *keister* before he pulled the trigger.

He was just below the southern shoulder of the Whangpoo, the beacons on the shore showing clear. With the motors at half power, their echo beat back hollow-sounding off the land as it coasted smoothly past on the port side. To northward the two gunboats had taken on the appearance of ghosts where they lay out beyond the greystone pier, and he kept a wary eye on them as he held the *Jacaranda* close in to the shore. Then he was clear around into the Whangpoo and he saw the stretch of water ahead was deserted, and easing the throttles open further, he left Woosung astern on the starboard quarter, and only then did he begin to breathe any easier.

He was abeam of the wreck buoys marking the hulk of the *Cameroon Highlander* when he began to meet with the first river traffic. In quick succession he passed three ocean-going junks to port, all of them blacked out, their sails furled. Then it was deserted again and the cool night air smelt of dew-damp and the river and the close by dark shore. He passed several more junks anchored off Henning's Wharf on the Tungkow waterfront where they awaited daylight, one of them with a carbide lantern lighting the midships living-quarters to show several figures gathered under an awning with one of them, a woman, eating rice out of a bowl. Only to the north was there any marked sign of activity, where occasionally the lights of traffic moving on the Chungkung Road would arc and sweep across the river as troops and armament hurried east to take up positions on the south shore above Woosung. Further north the bombardment he had seen begin earlier appeared to have slackened in intensity so that now the nervous flicker of gun flashes flitted across the horizon only spasmodically.

The sudden lance of a searchlight in the darkness out on the starboard bow took him unawares, for an instant startled him. He had come up on the orange beacons out on the end of the Luk Keong Godown Wharf in east Tienningshih, and his immediate reaction was to slam the throttles over almost shut. While the *Jacaranda* lost way against the current he stared hard into the glare of light, making out the high bridge and cockpit of a Marine Police patrol boat.

Seconds later her motors picked up with a dull rumble and she began to angle across the river southward. Up ahead he saw some river barges moored close in to the shore and he opened the throttles and spun the wheel over to cut in downstream to the cover they afforded. The patrol boat was less than two hundred yards away when she eased around to starboard to show the short-barrelled three-pounder gun mounted on her foredeck, the gunner lounging against the bridge casing smoking on a cigarette.

Lying under the steep shadow of the barges, he listened to her pick up speed and straighten out upriver, her searchlight flicking across the shore. He had been lucky, a couple of hundred yards further upriver and he would have been caught full in the open. But now, within a few minutes, near total darkness had descended on the river as the bank of cloud he had seen building earlier to northward drifted across the moon with the breeze in the direction of Hangchow Bay. Heaving a sigh of relief, his thoughts turned toward Annie Kim while he waited for the patrol boat to draw away. It was as if he had known her all his life, and not just for the matter of a couple of hours. She had had an unhinging effect on him right from the moment he first set eyes on her. When he thought about it, she had even appeared enthusiastic about him in an obscure way, and he regretted that he hadn't made at least some half-hearted attempt to let her know how he had an open mind on the subject. And the way he saw it, it would be a matter of personal failure if he couldn't get her downriver after he had given her his word. He couldn't get over how important she had become to him. Even more odd, it wasn't as if he was some fiddle-playing gypsy full of spiritual hunger. He couldn't even hum the Death March on a comb and paper. Vaguely, he wondered if this was the direction in which he had been headed all the time, destined to meet up with an amateur whore from Nanking. He didn't know, but in garrulous ecstacy he decided he was in over his head in any event.

When he pulled up clear of the International Dock he saw that *The Ladybird* had returned from Ningpo sometime after dark and was lying at the McBrayne Coaling Wharf in Yangtzepoo, her decks in darkness except for a shaded glow of light above her bunkering hatches. By the time he cleared

Tienningshih the patrol boat was up abeam of the Soochow Creek on the easterly end of the Shanghai Bund where the river swung southward around Pootung Point before continuing up to Lunghwa. The river was quiet now, dark, framed by the lights along the shore to north and south.

With the .38 Police Special and the Gibbs within easy reach, he crept up on the Carfax Oil Depot dock on the Pootung shore. When he eased his bows around into the dock he saw that the only lights showing in the office block were those in the windows of the Fuelling Master's office. Satisfied that everything appeared as it normally did anytime he came in during the night, he went on in to where the fuelling hoses hung coiled in their swivels with the bow line ready. Before the port gunwale brushed the pilings he cut the motors and scrambled up the iron ladder to the dock and hitched the line to the nearest bollard. The dock was quiet, and he quickly crossed to the office block expecting to find Tan-chu asleep at his desk, and stopped in his tracks when he opened the door. The room looked as if it had been swept by a typhoon. Everything of any value had been removed, and the safe stood with its door open and its metal drawers scattered nearby. He knew then the reason for Tan-chu's reluctance to meet his gaze when hinting of his future plans. The revolution now appeared to be paying dividends in the most unlikely quarters.

Returning across the dock, he wound down the swivel reels, dropped down into the *Jacaranda* to connect the hoses, then went back and started the compressor motor and wrenched open the fuel valves. Glancing about him, he thought the dock seemed unnaturally quiet, illuminated by the scattered arcs reflecting themselves from the flat oily water. Glancing at the swivel reels, he saw the hoses throbbing against the connections, and turned his attention to the river. There was no sign of the patrol boat headed back, gave it ten minutes, glanced at the hoses again, and from the corner of his eye caught a glimpse of movement back along the dock. Puzzled, but giving no indication of having seen anything, he turned back across the dock to lift a valve spanner before stepping into the shadows in rear of the office block.

The man had his back to him when he came around the octane tank the other end of the block. Tall and lanky, he was dressed in a blue custom-tailored suit, his oiled hair reflecting the gleam of the overhead arc. Weighing the spanner in his hand, Harry Lord stepped forward and brought it down across the brilliantined skull. The man went down without a sound, on to his face. Stepping around him, Harry Lord turned him over with his foot. Whoever he was, he had never set eyes on him before, but when he went through the man's pockets he found a wallet containing a Shanghai Police Department warrant card. A frown crossed his face as he glanced back down at the inert figure, puzzled as to what a cop could want around a place like the Carfax Oil Depot when three-parts of the city was in the process of either being liberated or looted. Commonsense said that even if the cops had arrested Tan-chu when he left with the contents of the safe it was doubtful if they would have continued to keep the place under surveillance. It didn't make sense, unless the cop had been waiting for somebody else to make an appearance. And thinking about it, he liked that idea even less.

Dropping the wallet, he headed back along the dock, turned the pump valves and compressor motor off, and dropped down into the *Jacaranda*. Quickly he uncoupled the hoses, and two minutes later had the *Jacaranda* headed back out across the dock, his thoughts now concerned with finding somewhere to lie up until he could contact Henry Wan. Ideally he had to find somewhere on the north side of the river, somewhere within reasonable proximity to the Great Eastern Mansions. Thinking about it, his gaze fastened on the blacked out *Ladybird* where she was headed upriver from Yangtzepoo, framed against the arcs on the Hongkew Bund, to her old berth at the Ropewalk Wharves, and as he watched her paddles cream a wash along the shore an idea suddenly came to him, an idea so simple and straightforward that it was impossible to fault.

Five minutes later he brought the *Jacaranda* around upriver off the north shore and nosed her up alongside *The Ladybird*'s bridge. Cupping his hands to his mouth, he yelled up against the thunder of the paddles, 'Ahoy – *Ladybird*!'

In reply Dutch Mary leaned her head out of a port wing window.

Harry Lord gestured upriver across *The Ladybird*'s bows

toward the shore. 'I'm going in under the quay ahead of you!'

Frowning, Dutch Mary peered ahead, then realizing what he implied, raised an acknowledging hand.

Easing the throttles open, Harry Lord forged the *Jacaranda* across *The Ladybird*'s bows and angled in toward the Ropewalk Wharves. Coming quickly up on No 3 Wharf, he cut the throttles back and turned the starboard spotlight on the underside of the Hongkew Bund, lighting the cavernous gloom of the high empty space beneath the quay. Apart from the fact that the cross beams allowed something like three feet of clearance to the low, raked cockpit, he saw from the watermarks on the pilings that the clearance would still be sufficient for him to get out if he was forced to remain hidden until high-water was reached.

Opening the throttles again, he crept the *Jacaranda* forward under the cross beams with the spotlight lighting the way, straightened her out, then cut the switches and took a turn around the cross beam with the bow and stern lines.

The Ladybird was close behind him, engines thudding, paddles threshing the water up white. With such a cumbersome vessel there was no latitude for mistakes while berthing, but Dutch Mary brought her calmly alongside, and with a creak and groan of timbers, touched against the Bund, shadowy figures moving hastily on her blacked out stern and stubby foredeck as they put the springs ashore.

Below the quay, Harry Lord nodded his satisfaction. Directly opposite the *Jacaranda* was *The Ladybird*'s starboard paddle wheel, so that only from right forrard of her bows, and from right aft of her stern, could he see out on to the river. And in turn there appeared no way whatever that anybody out on the river would be able to see the *Jacaranda* unless they came right alongside the quay to inspect its undersides.

Jamming the .38 Police Special more firmly into his waistband, he started back along the narrow cross beam until he came to an iron ladder, and climbed up on to the Bund. He was surprised to see a crowd of people already gathering around *The Ladybird*'s brow, all of them laden with bundled belongings, men, women, and children, clamouring to be allowed on board. Pushing his way through them, he found Dutch Mary and Ling in the starboard companionway.

'Not in trouble again you are?' The weary amazement in Dutch Mary's voice was unmistakable.

Harry Lord gave her the benefit of his magic grin. 'You know how it is by this time.'

Dutch Mary and Ling exchanged an understanding glance. 'Where you have been?'

'Lang Dok.'

Dutch Mary shook her head in disbelief. 'No wonder Mad Harry they call you.'

Harry Lord's magic grin was somewhat abashed. 'I've been thinking about *that* too,' he confessed, and glancing forrard, saw the patrol boat returning downriver, headed east along the waterfront below the Old Dock.

Ling followed his gaze. 'Are they looking for you?'

'I don't know – but I've got a load of bullion on board I don't want them to see – all of a couple of tons of it near's I can make out.'

Dutch Mary peered at him more closely in the semi-darkness. 'You are joking must be.'

'That's what I said. But it's jake. It belongs to a big-shot slopehead from Chungking.'

'Then your friend Sztykgold in this is too – eh?'

'He's part of it – only it's a little more complicated than that.'

'And what you intend now to do?'

'First I want to get in touch with the slopehead concerned and let him know I'm in town. Then I'll have to get the stuff off-loaded and pick up a friend I've promised to take south.'

Dutch Mary gave him a long searching look. 'Where all these friends are coming from you are finding so suddenly?'

With a mysterious grin, Harry Lord said, 'This one's of a different calibre from any others I've met so far.'

'Well your step you watch good,' Dutch Mary warned. 'Because once the crew with their families get back out of here I am anxious to get on my own account.'

Harry Lord glanced at the throng of refugees milling around the brow. 'And them?'

'We will take all for room we can find.'

'How long can you give me?'

Dutch Mary shrugged. 'An hour – longer a little maybe.'

In the next minute they heard the patrol boat drop down along *The Ladybird*'s port side, her searchlight flicking up over the superstructure. They listened in the semi-darkness of the companionway to her go on past, then saw her reappear out clear of the stern, headed downriver toward the mass of godowns on the Hall & McKenzie Wharf a quarter of a mile astern.

'Seems we're safe for the time being,' Harry Lord grinned, and starting down the brow, said across his shoulder, 'I'll be right back.'

In the companionway Dutch Mary and Ling watched him go ashore. 'We're never short of excitement with Harry around,' Ling commented, the expression on his long boney face giving the impression that he was far from certain about any of it.

Dutch Mary nodded thoughtfully. 'At least care of himself he can well take. But I hope no trouble he gets from those cops. Always they bad business have been.'

Harry Lord was headed east along the Hongkew Bund when the clock above the Yangtzepoo Pilot House sent its tinny strokes of 1.00 a.m. out across the river toward the Pootung shore.

* * *

Heinrich Sztykgold was in a confident mood as he returned by taxicab to the Avenue Lafayette. Before leaving Jean Nicolet's Place he had called André Passel at his office out at Lunghwa and informed him that he would be at the airport by 2.00 a.m., that he expected nothing to delay their departure. He thought it incredible just how smoothly everything had gone, that he had met with none of the difficulties he had been afraid he might meet with. The one disturbing aspect about the whole evening was the fact that he hadn't even caught a glimpse of Tzu Hsun, and he had expected Henry Wan to have at least taken the precaution of having him watched. Nonetheless he wasn't going to be fooled into relaxing his vigilance. His one regret was that he was without Tadatoshi and Nakamura, and their absence left him with a sense of vulnerability. He tried not to think about it, tried instead to think about Spain and his orange grove and the sun and the cool Mediterranean breeze. But it wasn't easy.

* * *

Unknown to Sztykgold, Tzu Hsun was also headed toward the Avenue Lafayette, although he was travelling by way of the rue Chanoinesse. The tough, twenty-seven year old guman from Chengtu wasn't so simple-minded as to follow his quarry in the first taxicab that came along. He had acted with foresight and cunning gained from experience. In the bustle of early evening traffic on the Avenue Lafayette it hadn't been difficult to follow Sztykgold when he left the Roebaud Apartment building and sit on his tail while they crossed town to the Soochow Creek. On the Creek Road he hadn't alighted from the taxicab until he saw Sztykgold enter the Yacht Club, then he had instructed his driver to drop him at the Wenshui Grill Bar half a block to eastward. There he had taken a table which gave an oblique view of the entrance to the Yacht Club, ordered several beers, and did nothing to draw attention to himself.

Sztykgold had been in no apparent hurry, and after calling Henry Wan to report his arrival at the Yacht Club at 9.10 p.m., it wasn't until 11.45 p.m. that he eventually reappeared again. Standing nonchalantly up on the pavement outside, he had lit a cigarette, declined the offer of a taxicab from the doorman, then started up the roadway toward Jean Nicolet's Place almost diagonally opposite the Wenshui Grill Bar. That had been the moment that Tzu Hsun had first become suspicious. To his practised eye Sztykgold had been deliberately exposing himself to anybody who might have been watching him. Unperturbed, he had called Henry Wan to report Sztykgold's movements, ordered another beer, and fully an hour later, at 1.05 a.m., had again seen him reappear on the pavement. Still Sztykgold had shown no urgency and had waited patiently for several minutes before the doorman found him a taxicab. And from his too obvious conduct, Tzu Hsun was certain it was his intention to return to the Avenue Lafayette, and he had allowed the taxicab to draw out of sight before he himself had left the Wenshui Grill Bar.

Once outside he had started casually eastward in the opposite direction to that which Sztykgold's taxicab had taken, then stepping suddenly out from the pavement, waved down a taxicab coming from Bubbling Well Road. Seated, he had brought a wad of US currency from his pocket, peeled several bills off, and thrust them at the driver.

'Get me to the Avenue Lafayette the quickest way possible and these are yours.'

The driver had required no further incentive. Putting his foot to the floor, the taxicab had leapt eastward in the direction of the Shanghai Bund, drove at a mad pace for three blocks on the Creek Road, then had hurtled around the corner on to the rue Chanoinesse in a diagonal dash across the heart of the old French Concession.

At 1.15 a.m. Tzu Hsun left the taxicab outside the Versailles Club, crossed the avenue past the entrance to the Roebaud Apartment building to vault the wall of the adjoining parking lot, then slipped quietly into the service entrance in rear of the building where it backed on to the rue Mouffetard.

* * *

Harry Lord had already decided on his next course of action when he left *The Ladybird*. Instead of going directly to the Great Eastern Mansions in an attempt to contact Henry Wan he headed east along the Hongkew Bund in the direction of Yangtzepoo. Luck had been with him so far that night but he didn't intend to put his entire trust in continuing good fortune. If Henry Wan was still at the Great Eastern Mansions, as according to prior arrangements he was supposed to be until receiving a call from Sztykgold, then he would get him to drive down to Yangtzepoo to finalize the deal, and if he was no longer there then he would have to think of something else. If the worst came to the worst he could call him from Chinhai and to hell with him. It was too dangerous to be seen running around town. After what had already happened there was no telling who might know the secret of Henry Wan's reason for being in Shanghai. Further, the cop's presence back at the Carfax Oil Depot still troubled him.

At an isolated telephone kiosk among the godowns on the Hall & McKenzie Wharf, he stopped and put a call through to the Great Eastern Mansions. 'Give me Mr Wan's suite. Tell him Harry Lord's on the line.'

The line went dead, then came alive again with the cautious answering voice of Henry Wan on the other end.

Harry Lord said, 'It's me. How's everything in town?'

'How's everything in town?' Henry Wan sounded confused and overjoyed in the same instant.

Impatient, Harry Lord snapped, 'I mean is everything fucking quiet!'

Henry Wan's voice was immediately inflicted with suspicion. 'Why, yes – why shouldn't it be quiet?'

A glint of perplexity showed in Harry Lord's eyes. 'What about Sztykgold?' he asked.

'Sztykgold? – I don't understand.'

Harry Lord lost patience. 'Listen, you stupid bastard, have you seen him tonight?'

Jolted, Henry Wan said quickly, 'Not personally, no. But Tzu rang me to say he had left the Yacht Club and gone into a club called Jean Nicolet's Place.'

'When was that?'

'A little over an hour ago – just on midnight.'

Harry Lord was startled into silence by Henry Wan's statement. He had expected Sztykgold to have already left for Ningpo, or at least to have heard Henry Wan say he had lost track of him. 'Are you sure about that?'

Henry Wan said uneasily, 'Perfectly sure. Tzu's been keeping a careful eye on him ever since we first talked together on Friday morning.'

'Then I've got news for you,' Harry Lord told him. 'Something's wrong. Those two Jap bodyguards of his tried to pull a heist job at Lang Dok. They were waiting for me when I put in. The idea was to transfer the stuff to a junk they had waiting at Tsungming Tao, then ship it south to a place called Gough Hill Cove north of Ningpo on Hangchow Bay. That's why I expected to hear you say Sztykgold's disappeared. I thought he'd have been on his way to Ningpo by this time, unless he's leaving it to the very last minute. He's obviously got it arranged for somebody to fly him down there – a Frog by the name of Passel if my guess's right. They've done business on more than one occasion that I know of.'

The ensuing silence transmitted Henry Wan's shock. 'Are you certain about that?'

Harry Lord said, 'You think I don't know when I'm being fucking shot at?'

Henry Wan discarded all caution in his anxiety. 'And the bullion?'

'It's here in town,' Harry Lord told him. 'And I'm going to speak to you about that too. There's a hell of a sight more than what I was told.'

'Please,' Henry Wan pleaded. 'That was Sztykgold's idea. I'll square it with you.'

'You've got that sort of ready money?'

'Yes, right here in the suite.'

'Then get a taxicab and ask for the Hall & McKenzie Wharf. It's down the back end of the Hongkew front, on your way out to Yangtzepoo. I'll be there. Only you'd better be careful. After what's happened tonight there's no telling who knows why you're in town. So make sure you aren't followed. And be here inside fifteen minutes.'

In his confusion, the germ of an idea caught at the back of Henry Wan's mind.

'Are you listening?' Harry Lord asked. 'I said be here inside *fifteen minutes*! I want rid of this stuff.'

'But, Mr Lord,' Henry Wan quickly countered. 'I'm still going to be in trouble. That man Passel was contracted to fly us and the bullion out to Hong Kong. What am I going to do?'

'How the hell should I know what you're going to do?' Harry Lord growled down the line.

'But, Mr Lord,' Henry Wan said tentatively. 'Couldn't you ship it further south for me? Anywhere will do as long as it's away from Shanghai. And you can name your own price – *anything*!'

A bleak scowl darkened Harry Lord's face. He didn't like the idea of going back downriver with all that bullion on board. The thought made him uneasy.

'I'll pay you anything you say, Mr Lord,' Henry Wan broke in desperately.

'I don't know. There isn't room for three passengers, and I'm taking somebody with me as it is.'

'But I'd be travelling alone,' Henry Wan urgently riposted.

'What about your wife and Tzu?'

'There's been an alteration to our plans,' Henry Wan said glibly. 'Tzu and she will be travelling independently.'

Harry Lord digested the information. Although his natural inclination was to refuse, the proposition wasn't without its attractions. For one thing he wouldn't have to waste time and run the risk of being disturbed while struggling to off-load the cases somewhere. And once he collected Annie Kim he could head straight back downriver. There was only the Marine Police patrol boat to worry about, and one boat couldn't easily cover the whole river. 'Okay,' he said. 'But you get on down here right now. You hear?'

Relief flooded Henry Wan's voice. 'I'll be with you as soon as I can find a taxicab.'

'I'll be looking for you,' Harry Lord said and cut the line dead, took a look at the waterfront, then made another call.

'The Red Fortune Hotel.' It was Old Po's voice.

'How's everything with you?'

Old Po relaxed. 'There hasn't been anybody asking for you or the girl, if that's what you mean.'

'Fine. Can you put me through to her?' Harry Lord waited, heard Old Po make the connection, then heard the phone in the room ring.

The answering voice was small and guarded. 'Hello?'

'It's me, Harry. Are you all right?'

Annie Kim's words tumbled out over each other. 'Yes. Yes, I'm fine. It was the phone that startled me.'

'Are you ready to leave?'

'I've been waiting dressed since before ten o'clock.'

'Then stay in your room till I get there. I shouldn't be long. There's nothing for you to worry about.' He hung up, and outside stood into the shadow of an adjoining godown to survey the long stretch of the Hongkew Bund. From that particular vantage point he would be able to see anything move half a mile away. Scrounging the collar of his coat up against the cool night air, he settled into the darkness to wait. He was still troubled by the news about Sztykgold, couldn't understand how he was still in town. But there was no way of guessing at the lengths which he had gone to in an effort to cover his true intentions. Sztykgold didn't allow his right hand to know what his left hand did half the time. But Sztykgold was the least of his problems now; what he was looking for was a single set of headlights headed east along the Hongkew Bund from the direction of the old International Settlement.

* * *

When Harry Lord hung up on him, Henry Wan replaced

the receiver with a trembling hand, mopped the oily film of sweat from his haggard face, then glanced at his watch. The time was 1.25 a.m. Harry Lord had said fifteen minutes, and there wasn't one to lose. Drawing a deep breath in a bid to steady his palpitating heart, he turned toward where the black metal document case stood ready beside the sofa with $180,000 packed into it, all the US currency which had been available in the bank when they pulled out from Chungking. And it was then that he saw his wife. She had so changed in manner she might have been a complete stranger. Her sculpted features were pinched, aged with hatred he had never seen before. And gripped in both hands, extended outright in front of her, was a silver-plated .22 revolver deliberately aimed at his chest. More disconcerting was the fact that she didn't offer to say anything, nor did she appear ready to give herself to hysteria. She simply stared at him with eyes that blazed hatred and contempt. He realized immediately that she had heard everything said between himself and Harry Lord on the phone, that it would be pointless to refute anything, and he shrugged resignedly. 'So I wasn't wrong about you and Tzu after all,' he calmly observed.

'It doesn't matter now.' Zephyrine Wan's voice was cold, measured, and level. 'And I heard everything that was said.'

Henry Wan said wistfully, 'But *not* where Lord has the bullion.'

'Maybe not. But I know that something's gone wrong, that Sztykgold's no longer involved. And I know you intend going to meet Lord, that you asked him to take you south.'

Henry Wan repeated his shrug of resignation. 'He also gave me an ultimatum – he said fifteen minutes and he pulls out.'

Zephyrine Wan flashed an anxious glance at her watch. 'Tzu will call. We'll still have time. Lord's bound to wait.'

'Maybe so,' Henry Wan calmly conceded. 'But you still don't know where we're to meet.'

'Tzu will make you tell.' The revolver in Zephyrine Wan's hands never wavered.

'Is that what you think?'

Zephyrine Wan's eyes narrowed and an odour of primal violence burned in the room.

Henry Wan said sadly, as if surprised that anything of such a nature could really have happened between them, 'I never suspected that you could really have hated me so much, that any persons knowing each other for so long could be capable of such emotion is bewildering to me.'

Zephyrine Wan began to show agitation. Her mouth tightened and she gestured at him with the revolver. 'Get over there – on the sofa!'

Henry Wan quietly complied. When he was seated on the sofa he looked up at the extended revolver. 'I suppose Tzu gave you the gun.'

A chill smile twisted the corners of Zephyrine Wan's mouth. The feeling of superiority and dominance imparted by the revolver added to her confidence. 'Yes – weeks ago.'

Henry Wan was silent, his haggard grey face inscrutable.

His lack of reaction added to his wife's desire to cause him visible hurt. 'You don't seem surprised about that.'

Henry Wan said calmly, 'I've known about you both for some time.'

Zephyrine Wan stared back at him steadily.

Continuing in an almost conversational tone, Henry Wan said, 'I came home early one afternoon and found you both on the floor.'

His calm, casual attitude only served to anger his wife further, and hatred flared in her eyes. 'There were others,' she coldly informed him. 'How do you think I amused myself while you devoted your time to playing the role of successful financier? There was even a bartender from a cheap little bar on the Tai Wan Road. He used to take me back to his room on the South Bank and fuck me till I ached. He was a puny little man but what a magnificent cock he had. He used to give it to me till I couldn't take it anymore.' She gave a short, mirthless laugh, mistaking the furtive dart of his eyes for embarrassment and discomfort. 'Doesn't that make you feel odious, Henry?'

Despite his façade of calm and resignation, Henry Wan's impatience and anxiety was quickly reaching breaking point. Precious minutes were slipping by. His tongue snaked over his rubbery lips as he searched desperately for a way out. Although the revolver was a puny weapon he knew that the tiny bullets would almost certainly stop him, if not kill him, if he made any abrupt move, and that his wife was equally capable in her present state of mind in shooting him out of simple reaction. He decided quickly against any attempt at physical argument, tried another tack. In a quiet, reasoning voice, he said, 'Listen to me. What's past is past, but the future can be altered. That bullion's only a short cab ride from here. We can be on our way downriver in next to no time. I told Lord he can name his own price.'

A shadow of doubt flickered across Zephyrine Wan's finely sculpted face, although she remained silent.

Henry Wan went on hurriedly, 'We can each go our own way, split the bullion into equal parts. I'll get Lord to put you ashore at Ningpo. From there you can get passage anywhere you want to go.' He saw her mind waver, the revolver wilt perceptibly. He pressed on urgently. 'Besides, how can you trust somebody like Tzu? How do you think it'll be when he gets his hands on the bullion? Afterwards? You appear to conveniently forget that you're a much older woman than the ones he'll want to play around with if he comes into a large sum of money. Have you thought about that?' He watched hungrily as her face began to betray her uncertainty. 'Think about it, Zephyrine,' he quietly urged. 'All that bullion between the two of us, enough for both our needs. And we can start again – each our own way—' He ended pleading, sensed his argument tremble on the brink of victory, and for an instant saw his wife's gaze falter, and he moved more quickly than he had ever done in his life.

Before Zephyrine Wan realized what had happened her wrists were pinned in her husband's grasp as he attempted to force the revolver down toward the floor. Then she stumbled and the revolver went off, a curiously innocent sound, muffled between their bodies.

Immediately Henry Wan's leg was clubbed from beneath him and he toppled to the floor as his wife pulled away. There was no pain, just numbness, but when he drew his hand away from the long muscle down the outside of his right thigh it was smeared with blood. He found he was trembling, but strangely, felt no anger and was surprised at the lucidity of his own mind. He realized immediately that he would never reach the Hall & McKenzie Wharf without help, and that that help would certainly not be forthcoming. Slowly he raised his eyes up to where his wife was leaning ashen-faced across the far arm of the sofa, the revolver still in her hand. He shook his head, extending mute sympathy. 'You fool,' he said quietly, without rancour.

Zephyrine Wan started back, backed off across the room. She raised a hand to her mouth, eyes wide and staring as if she couldn't comprehend what had happened. 'Shut up! – shut up!' she cried agitatedly.

A groan broke involuntarily from Henry Wan's lips. The numbness in his thigh started to ease and a burning pain began to throb in its place. He looked down and found the wound bleeding profusely, saturating his trouser leg, forming a pool on the carpet. With his right hand he clasped the wound tightly and tried to flex his leg. The pain stabbed all the way up into his groin, and he steeled himself to it and tried to lever himself into a crouch but there was no reaction from the muscles of his leg and he sank back on to the floor.

* * *

Captain Hop's eyes narrowed to slits in the cool rush of air as the big open car swept south on the Avenue Lafayette. He stared straight ahead, his mouth set in a determined line. For the first time he was worried, undecided about whether or not he had just made a mistake, and for the first time since Lieutenant Huang confessed his secret, doubt began to gnaw at him. Tzu Hsun had caught him unprepared when instead of following Sztykgold from Jean Nicolet's Place as he had expected him to do, he had instead unaccountably ignored him and had picked up a taxicab and headed east on the Creek Road. They had been keeping watch on both men from the roof of the Country Club Boathouse on the south shore of the Soochow Creek when it happened, and by the time they returned to where Corporal Choy had the car waiting in the parking lot of the Belvidere Restaurant, Tzu Hsun's taxicab had lost itself in the bustle of traffic on the Creek Road.

But Captain Hop wasn't alone with his worries; Sergeant Kee was also perturbed. He hadn't expected they would lose Tzu Hsun at such a crucial moment, and a swift glance at his superior's tight-lipped face showed it wasn't exactly a study of enlightenment and confidence. Captain Hop had remained silent since the moment he had instructed Corporal Choy to forget about trying to pick up Tzu Hsun's taxicab on the Creek Road and to return to the Avenue Lafayette instead. Finally Sergeant Kee could withstand the silence no longer. 'What do you think caused Tzu to forget Sztykgold the way he did, Captain?'

Surprisingly, Captain Hop confessed ignorance. 'I don't

know – unless he and Wan decided that Sztykgold was on the level after all. He certainly hasn't acted suspiciously. And from the direction Tzu was headed he could have been on his way back to the Great Eastern Mansions.'

Corporal Choy slewed the big open car to a halt beneath the greenly lighted overhang of foliage on the avenue to northward of the Roebaud Apartment building. From where they were parked they could just see the lighted windows of Sztykgold's apartment and the entrance to the building. And in the adjoining parking lot Sztykgold's black Mercedes was also partially visible.

'Do you suppose he's really up there?' Corporal Choy's hawked face was shadowed with doubt.

Captain Hop stared up at the lighted windows impassively. Because of Tzu Hsun's unaccountable behaviour they had lost contact with Sztykgold, had been at least seven, eight minutes behind him, and as a result hadn't witnessed him enter the building. Glancing back along the avenue, he saw the telephone kiosk on the far corner of the Place Durantin. He opened the door and alighted on to the pavement. 'Don't take your eyes off that entrance till I get back.' Then he turned and walked back along the pavement, crossed the avenue to the telephone kiosk.

He knew Sztykgold's phone number by heart. He dialled and waited, hearing the phone ring. Several moments elapsed before it was answered, when Sztykgold's voice said hesitantly, 'Yes? —hello?'

Captain Hop smiled relief. 'I'm sorry. I seem to have the wrong number. I wanted the Café Edouard.' He heard the line go dead and, smiling, returned to the car. 'He's at home. He just answered the phone.'

Sergeant Kee relaxed back into the upholstery. 'Now I feel better.'

Captain Hop resumed his seat, gestured at the apartment building. 'There's a back entrance on the rue Mouffetard. Maybe it would be better if somebody kept an eye on it just in case he decides against using the Mercedes.'

Sergeant Kee started up with his former enthusiasm. 'I hadn't thought about that.'

Captain Hop watched him cross the light-dappled avenue, walk toward the apartment building, then saw him swing over the wall of the parking lot.

'Do you think there's going to be any problems, Captain?'

Captain Hop turned to see Corporal Choy's questioning face the other side of the front seat. 'None that we shouldn't be able to solve.' Dropping his gaze to the two submachine guns on the floor of the car, he saw it simply as a matter of playing the game out to its inevitable conclusion. They would step in the moment that Sztykgold arrived at Lunghwa Airport, take him down to Ningpo with Passel, and collect the bullion when it arrived. The two submachine guns would take adequate care of Po-han and his crew along with Tadatoshi and Nakamura when they put into Gough Hill Cove. Then once the bullion was safely loaded on to the aircraft he would take care of Choy, leave him behind with a bullet in the head along with Sztykgold. Choy's usefulness would have reached its limits and it was the only solution. As for Kee, there were other factors to be taken into consideration. There was certain to be rumour and speculation in more than one quarter when Sergeant Pao realized they had disappeared on him, especially if he opened his mouth wide enough for word to reach Chungking. And with the fall of the Kuomintang inevitable there would be men prepared to follow up even the most frail rumour in the hope that they might be able to uncover a concrete lead, and Kee's companionship would be invaluable, for a time.

He had already given the subject of their eventual destination considerable forethought. The reason for his choice of Hokow was based purely on its geographical location. It was small, yet had a cosmopolitan flavour that wouldn't attract undue attention to their presence, and it lay on the border of Indo-China within easy access to the Kunming–Hanoi railway. It would have the same effect as if they vanished. And he knew the place well, had visited both it and Lao Cai on several occasions when stationed in Kunming, and if the reason for their disappearance was discovered he was confident that nobody would associate them with such an illogical destination.

The immediate area also provided ideal facilities to conceal all trace of their flight. Kunming had been the terminus of the Burma Road and there were numerous disused airstrips in the vicinity. He knew one amid the hilly country just to the north where both the aircraft and André Passel could be disposed of without difficulty. The journey south would be simple and straightforward, a change of clothes and the acquisition of a truck in Kunming, and they would be in Hokow by nightfall on Tuesday at the latest. Not that he harboured any intention of settling permanently in the wilds of Indo-China. It would merely be a period of respite while he could buy the time to decide the direction in which his real future lay. He had already given thought to Europe, to France in particular. He had always been impressed by the French. They were civilized, and knew how to enjoy the best in life. The old French Concession was testimony to that fact. Its luxury and grandeur had always appealed to him.

Suddenly he was disturbed by the squawking of the radio in front beside Choy: 'KSS Control to car 3D4 – do you read? Acknowledge, over.'

Choy grabbed the handphone, glancing at his superior. 'Car 3D4 to KSS Control – go ahead, over.'

'KSS Control to car 3D4 – message reads – suspect arranged to reach exit point at 2.00 a.m., over.'

Captain Hop took the handphone from Choy. 'Roger, AK, over.' Then returning the handphone to Choy, he said, 'That's Passel been in touch with Pao. Sztykgold's arranged to be out at Lunghwa by two o'clock. He's cutting it fine, so things should start happening pretty soon.

Both men returned their attention to the Roebaud Apartment building where they saw the lights of Sztykgold's sixth floor apartment still burning in the windows.

Corporal Choy said almost absently, 'What are we going to do about Pao, Captain? Are we taking him with us?'

'I've been wondering about that too, Choy. Maybe we can get to him before we leave. What do you say?'

'We can get him on the phone and have him come out to Lunghwa. We could take care of him out there. It wouldn't be any trouble.'

'All right, but let's think about that when the time comes. First I want Sztykgold.'

* * *

Heinrich Sztykgold had been unnerved by the phone call. Although it had obviously been a mistake, it had nonetheless served to bring the cold reality of the outside world into the apartment. He poured a drink, a large one, neat. Unfortunately it didn't produce the desired effect, and he poured another, finished it, then took yet another one into the bedroom while he changed into a stone-coloured tropical suit. Afterward he removed the contents of the wall-safe and returned to the lounge where he crammed everything into a brief case. Then, finishing his drink, he returned to the window. He knew exactly what he had to do, down to the last detail. He would take the service stairway, leave by the rear entrance, walk two blocks north on the rue Mouffetard, then take a taxicab from the Parisian Brasserie. Even giving himself such a circuitous route he still had ample time to be at the airport by 2.00 a.m.

Ready, he took a last look around the apartment, left the lights burning, and eased the door ajar. The hall was deserted, and closing the door quietly behind him, he started toward the service stairway. Not even the muted sound of a radio pervaded the quiet of the building. At the end of the hall he stopped, drew a deep breath, straightened his shoulders, and took a firmer grip of the brief case.

He hadn't covered the first flight of steps when a voice out of the gloom said, 'Going somewhere, Mr Sztykgold?'

Sztykgold froze in his tracks, a hopeless, frightened look entering his eyes.

'Now turn around – slowly.' The voice in the gloom was flat, chilled, emotionless. 'We're going back the way we came.'

Sztykgold felt himself disintegrate physically when he saw the silencer-fitted pistol in Tzu Hsun's hand. He wavered visibly.

Tzu Hsun took another step out of the gloom toward him. 'Come on – *move*!'

Sztykgold fought fear and panic, and when Tzu Hsun put the muzzle of the silencer to the small of his back he found difficulty in controlling his limbs.

'Those bodyguards,' Tzu Hsun demanded in a whisper when they neared the apartment. 'Where are they?'

Sztykgold's mind raced in a petrified circle. 'The Bund – the Nantao Bund,' he blustered weakly. 'They're waiting to escort Lord out to Lunghwa just as planned.' In the space of a few seconds he had become an incredibly old man.

Tzu Hsun reached past him to push the door of the apartment open, prodded him inside, and quickly ran his free hand over his coat where he stood passively in front of him, his alert gaze darting around the apartment at the same time. Then he backed off, kicked open the doors of the bedrooms, the bathroom, and the kitchenette to satisfy himself that they were alone.

'This is nonsense! I can't think what you expect to find!' Sztykgold's attempt at indignation failed dismally.

Tzu Hsun studied him impassively, aware that there was just the chance he was wrong. 'Then why were you sneaking out the back way?'

The basis for an alibi had half formed in Sztykgold's mind. 'I happened to be on my way to the Nantao Bund. I had a phone call from a River Commissioner just a few minutes ago to say that Lord was on his way upriver. He said he had seen the *Jacaranda* headed upriver off the Tungkow front.'

Doubt flared briefly up in Tzu Hsun. He glanced at the phone, backed toward it. He gestured at Sztykgold with the unwieldy pistol. 'Get over there – away from the door!' With the pistol covering Sztykgold he called the Great Eastern mansions and asked for the Peking Suite.

'But you have this all wrong,' Sztykgold blurted out. 'I told you—'

'Shut your mouth!' Tzu Hsun cut him short, then hearing Zephyrine Wan's answering voice, said: 'This is Tzu here. I'm at the Roebaud Apartment building. I've just stopped Sztykgold from leaving. He said he was on his way to the Nantao Bund, that Lord was sighted coming upriver a few minutes ago.'

In desperate urgency Zephyrine Wan said, 'You've got to get back here, Tzu! Now – right now!'

Tzu Hsun snapped, 'What is it? What's happened?'

Zephyrine Wan's voice wavered through tears and fear. 'It's Henry, he's shot, in the leg. He had a call from Lord and tried to leave with the money.'

Stunned, Tzu Hsun said, 'Lord's in town?'

'Yes. Henry has it planned to meet him somewhere. He's going to take him downriver. I heard them talking.'

Panic surged through Tzu Hsun. 'Then don't let him make a move. I'll be with you in a few minutes –just as soon's I can get across town.' He slammed the receiver down, his chill gaze still on Sztykgold's long ashen face which was now showing bewilderment through its fear.

Sztykgold stared at the pistol as if mesmerized, then

started back in terror. 'What are you going to do?' His voice sounded disconnected. His back came up against the wall and his eyes opened wider when he saw Tzu Hsun begin to bring his hand upward. '*Wait*!' he pleaded. 'Whatever has happened I don't know—' His voice trailed into a disconnected whisper as he stared at the unwieldy pistol. He had half raised his hands up in front of him when it made an abrupt popping sound which sounded like a damp paper bag bursting. Instantly he was clubbed back on his heels against the wall, swayed momentarily while his long ashen face registered an expression of rank disbelief, then subsided slowly to the floor.

Tzu Hsun stepped forward, aimed, and shot a second time; and Heinrich Sztykgold died before he had time to repent the fact that he would never realize his dream of a distant Spanish orange grove fanned by the cool Mediterranean breeze.

* * *

In the same instant that Sztykgold died, Captain Hop was lighting a cigarette in the big open car parked beneath the foliage of the trees lining the Avenue Lafayette a short distance north of the entrance to the Roebaud Apartment building. His attention was focused on the lighted windows of the sixth floor apartment. Instinctively he had begun to feel that something was wrong. Then he saw Sergeant Kee vault the wall of the parking lot and call out, 'He's dead – Sztykgold's dead!' And then Kee threw himself into the car breathlessly. 'Tzu was up there all the time! I saw him leave and I went upstairs and Sztykgold was dead – shot!'

Captain Hop felt as if he had been hit by a club. 'Which way did he go?'

'The rue Mouffetard – down the rue Mouffetard!'

Captain Hop turned on Choy, face twisted, eyes ablaze. 'After him!' he raged. 'Get after him!'

Corporal Choy slammed the big open car into a tight U-turn, took the turning into the Place Durantin, then hurtled around south on to the rue Mouffetard. They saw Tzu Hsun almost immediately, down near the far end of the roadway, climbing into a taxicab at the intersection with the Avenue Bertrand Aubusson.

'There he goes!'

Choy pressed the accelerator to the floor, cleared the rue Mouffetard, and hurtled the car around on to the Avenue Bertrand Aubusson to narrowly avoid a tram-car as they slewed across the roadway.

'There – up ahead!' Sergeant Kee held to the side of the car and gestured at the rear lights of the taxicab where it raced toward the old International Settlement. Then turning his agitated face on Captain Hop, asked, 'What do you think happened back there?'

'I don't know – but they must know something about the bullion or Tzu would never have risked shooting him.'

Sergeant Kee couldn't bring himself to consider the possibility that the bullion was destined to elude them. 'Then something must have happened out on the river!'

Up ahead a snarl of traffic clogged the roadway on the south side of the intersection with the Fat Tseung Road and both men were hurled against the rear of the front seat when Choy applied the brakes. In the chaos he yelled back over his shoulder, 'The taxicab – I've lost the taxicab!'

'Forget the taxicab!' Captain Hop screamed at him. 'Just get us to the Great Eastern Mansions!'

Choy wrenched the wheel around, and with the horn blasting, swung the car into Shu Kuk Terrace toward the waterfront. Minutes later they were threading their way through the congested stream of night traffic on the north carriageway of the Shanghai Bund, tyres screaming and bystanders staring after the hurtling car as Choy grimly hit it back across town toward the Nanking Road.

* * *

The moment that Zephyrine Wan heard the three distinct raps she allowed the silver-plated revolver to drop from her hand and ran out to the hall to unlock the door. When Tzu Hsun came through the doorway she threw herself weeping into his arms. 'What took you so long?' she babbled. 'I thought you'd never get here!'

Tzu Hsun brushed her aside. 'Never mind that – what happened here?'

Zephyrine Wan followed him into the big room where Henry Wan lay looking up at them with a strangely calm, almost detached expression on his sweating face, blood oozing from between the fingers of his right hand where it clasped his thigh. 'Lord called. I heard them on the phone. Henry was to meet him somewhere.'

'How did you come to shoot him?'

'He tried to get the gun from me and it went off.'

Tzu Hsun took the pistol from beneath his coat, screwed the silencer to the threaded barrel, then pointed it at Henry Wan's head. 'Where were you going to meet Lord?'

Henry Wan had began to think with a strange, cold clarity which he hadn't thought with in a long time. It produced an almost exhilarating effect. He said calmly, 'You must think me as simple-minded as she does.'

Tzu Hsun's arm flashed downward and the unwieldy barrel of the silencer-fitted pistol connected with Henry Wan's cheekbone. 'Try again!'

Dazed, Henry Wan struggled to raise himself from the floor, blood pumping from the gash that had opened across his cheek below the left eye. The room swam in front of him and he closed his eyes tight, trying to still his wheeling vision while blood splashed warmly down his shirtfront.

Across the room, Zephyrine Wan turned away, hiding her face in her hands.

Tzu Hsun grabbed Henry Wan's necktie and jerked him halfway to his feet. 'Talk, you bastard! Where's Lord?'

Determinedly, Henry Wan held on to himself, raised his left arm feebly to protect his head. 'Do you think I don't know that you'll kill me even if I tell you?' he gasped.

Tzu Hsun wrenched the necktie around so tight that Henry Wan's eyes bulged and his face darkened. 'I said *talk*!' he snarled, shaking the choking face back and forth. 'Come on – talk you—' He broke suddenly off, startled by the crash of a door hurled violently back on its hinges. He half turned, half straightened upright, pistol in hand, and catching a glimpse of blue-uniformed bodies in the doorway, saw a gun flame, and within an insect blink of time an even greater flame exploded inside his head.

Neither Henry Wan nor his wife saw Tzu Hsun's head explode across the room. In the confusion of the shot and the scramble of bodies entering the room it was over with before they realized what happened. Then, tearing his shirt collar loose, gasping for breath, Henry Wan was vaguely aware of the three uniformed figures crowding him.

Revolver in hand, Captain Hop glanced from Henry Wan to his wife. 'What was happening here?'

Sergeant Kee motioned at Tzu Hsun's sprawled body on the far side of the sofa. 'I thought he was going to shoot.'

Captain Hop ignored his half apology. 'You,' he said across the room to Zephyrine Wan where she stood against the wall with a blank, uncomprehending expression on her face. 'What happened here?'

Zephyrine Wan's gaze fell on Tzu Hsun's body and her teeth caught at her lip.

'He's been shot.' Sergeant Kee was standing over Henry Wan. 'He's shot in the leg.'

Henry Wan said vacantly from the floor. 'Who sent for you?'

Captain Hop walked over to him, holstered his revolver. 'Nobody sent for us – *Mr Wan*.'

Henry Wan stiffened, glanced from one face to the other. 'I don't understand.'

'Then don't strain yourself,' Captain Hop snapped. 'Just tell me about the bullion.'

Henry Wan's face froze instantly. 'Bullion?'

Reaching again for his revolver, Captain Hop took a step toward him. His eyes glittered cruelly in the crystal light of the chandelier. He snapped impatiently, 'Don't fuck us around! We know why you're in town. We've been watching you since you arrived. We picked up an officer of the KSS who followed you from Chungking. Your friend Tzu put a knife in him. Only he didn't die until he told us your secret.' He saw the shadow of defeat and resignation pass across Henry Wan's broken face. 'We put his body back on the Racecourse where Tzu found it.'

Henry Wan's shoulders slumped. Then somehow to know they had been under surveillance since their arrival in Shanghai, that they had been destined to lose everything in any event, suddenly made it so much easier to accept that same loss now. He didn't even experience a sense of disappointment. If he felt anything, then it was a sense of disillusionment and betrayal. He said wearily, 'You appear to know everything there is to know, Captain.'

'Except the whereabouts of the bullion,' Captain Hop corrected.

An indecipherable smile appeared on Henry Wan's

broken face, twisted it askew. Somebody had once expressed the opinion that the taste of revenge was never so sweet as when cold. Now he intended to find out whether it was true. 'I'm afraid I can't help you, Captain.'

Captain Hop's eyes narrowed suspiciously. 'What do you mean? We know for a fact that Lord must have the bullion here in town at this very moment, and that he's been in touch with you, or else Tzu would never have risked killing Sztykgold. We know that. We followed him here from the Avenue Lafayette.'

Almost serenely, Henry Wan said, 'Then perhaps you should ask my wife about it.'

Zephyrine Wan stared in bewilderment as the hostile faces turned on her. Then suddenly she realized the answer to the indecipherable smile on her husband's face, and felt at once numb, sick and empty. 'He's lying! I don't know anything about it!'

Captain Hop said icily, 'What is this – some sort of game?'

Henry Wan put in quietly, 'When something becomes a matter of life and death it's never a game, Captain, certainly not for the person concerned. And if you hadn't arrived when you did, *I* was the one who would have died, *not* Tzu. I had just tried to prevent my wife from leaving with him. They were on their way to meet Harry Lord, running out on me. If you look in that document case you'll see they intended to take every last dollar I owned.'

Zephyrine Wan took a step toward them, panic-stricken. 'Don't listen to him! He's making it all up!'

'That's not the case, Captain,' Henry Wan calmly countered. 'I was in the bathroom when she answered the call from Lord. Only she and Tzu knew where to meet him.'

'No!' Zephyrine Wan screamed at him. 'That isn't true!'

Captain Hop silenced the room when his riding-crop whiplashed against the length of his riding-boot. He snapped his fingers at Sergeant Kee and motioned at the document case. 'Open it up!'

All eyes were on Sergeant Kee when he opened the document case on to the telephone table and raised up the lid to expose the neatly packaged bundles of US currency.

'Fifty thousand dollars of that was Harry Lord's,' Henry Wan explained. 'For bringing the bullion downriver.'

Captain Hop considered Henry Wan's statement through

a lengthy silence. His policeman's natural suspicion, already aroused, was now further antagonized. Instinctively he felt that something was wrong. 'You seem peculiarly reconciled to the loss of a fortune which only a few minutes ago must have appeared firmly in your grasp.'

Henry Wan said philosophically, 'What can I do about it with a bullet in my leg, Captain?'

For a further minute Captain Hop remained thoughtfully silent, then, almost casually, turned his attention to Zephyrine Wan. 'Well?' he said.

Zephyrine Wan felt an icy hand grasp her heart. 'He's lying!'

'*Somebody* is lying.'

Zephyrine Wan drew back against the wall again when she Corporal Choy take a step toward her. She stiffened involuntarily as his gaze dropped down over her, raised a hand to her throat. 'What're you going to do?' Her voice fragmented and a look of naked terror entered her eyes.

A drooling grin spread slowly across Corporal Choy's hawked face when he saw how her upraised hand accentuated the shape and size of her breasts, pushed them up against the décolletage of her dress. Nor was she some downtown $5 bone-heap, but one of the unattainable ones. Even the fragrance of her perfume threatened to overwhelm his senses.

Captain Hop said chillingly, 'Get her over here.'

Before Zephyrine Wan could fend him off, Corporal Choy reached out a hand and sent her sprawling across the room into the far corner of the sofa. Then, pinning both her wrists to the rear of the sofa above her head, he glanced across his shoulder at Captain Hop, saw him incline his head sharply, then reached down with his other hand to grasp the neckline of her dress.

When the dress was wrenched from her body, Zephyrine Wan's cry was more from shock and disbelief than from pain.

A low, rumbling chuckle rose in Choy's throat as he watched her writhe and twist first one way, then the other, in a struggle to hide herself. Beneath the dress she was naked, and her breasts leapt and jerked as she tried to bring her legs up to cover herself. 'Look at that!' he chuckled hoarsely. 'There's no hair between her legs!'

Captain Hop said curtly, 'Well – what are you waiting for?'

Choy returned his attention to Zephyrine Wan. His face was strangely slack now, bloated with anticipation. He leaned over her, rammed his knee between her squirming thighs, and fumbled at his clothing with one hand while he held her wrists pinned against the sofa with the other.

Zephyrine Wan's face froze in horror and revulsion when she saw the enormous column of swollen muscle rear itself in front of her. When he arched his lower body at her she made a frantic lunge to turn away, so stunned and frightened that her cry of protest was only a strangled whisper.

'No – turn her on her belly.' Captain Hop's voice chilled the room.

All eyes swivelled to him, and as if it was only then that she realized the terrible implication of his words, Zephyrine Wan's mouth opened with a cry which was immediately silenced by Choy's balled fist. Dazed by the blow, she offered no resistance when he turned her effortlessly over so that her face was buried in the cushion against which she had been pinned. And then he mounted her, and although muffled by the cushion in which her face was buried, her scream was grotesque, demonic. Then he drove all the way into her and her legs flailed while the pain and anguish forced her head upright out of the cushion into which her fingers were dug like talons.

On the far side of the sofa Sergeant Kee averted his face when he saw Zephyrine Wan's limbs stiffen convulsively as her eyes glazed and rolled upward into her skull.

Choy stared at the naked body with outraged disbelief as it went limp beneath him, feeling cheated, like a child whose toy had inexplicably broken after only a few moments of pleasure. Then with a sullen growl he pushed himself reluctantly to his feet and adjusted his clothing without another glance at the obscenely sprawled body.

Captain Hop's frigid gaze moved from Choy to Kee, then to Henry Wan, who having lain cradling his gunshot thigh throughout his wife's humiliation and debasement, his mind locked and barred to every hideous sound uttered, was now startled by this new, menacing silence which had descended on the room. He looked up, glanced from one hostile face to the other, his eyes wide.

'You were lying, Mr Wan.' Captain Hop's voice was low with menace, the muscles quivering beneath the shaved flesh of his jaw.

Henry Wan turned cold and his flesh crawled. He inched away from the three men and his lateral vision caught the glint of silver-plated metal beside the liquor cabinet. Suddenly scrambling around on to his hands and knees, he started across the floor like a wounded rabbit. He was almost within arm's reach of the .22 revolver when Captain Hop's riding boot descended on his right hand, crushing it into the carpet. 'Take him outside and get him some fresh air.'

In the next second Henry Wan felt himself snatched to his feet by Corporal Choy and bundled toward the balcony. His right leg went from under him and he screamed aloud in pain.

Captain Hop and Sergeant Kee followed a few steps in rear, crowded into the doorway as Choy dragged Henry Wan out on to the balcony.

Henry Wan stumbled and fell against the parapet when Choy relinquished hold on him, and his face came apart in terror when his gaze fell on the garish chasm of light that was the Nanking Road eight floors below. He turned away, grabbed in desperation at Choy, then slumped to his knees, looking pleading up into Captain Hop's impassive face. 'The Hall & McKenzie Wharf!' he blurted out. 'I had to meet him at the Hall & McKenzie Wharf!'

Captain Hop studied the broken face dispassionately, then with his head made an almost imperceptible motion.

Corporal Choy saw it, and as Henry Wan struggled to his feet with a supreme effort and tried to push his way back into the room, he caught him by the collar and with a casual sweep of his arm, tumbled him out across the parapet into the darkness above the Nanking Road.

* * *

Harry Lord's watch showed the time was a few minutes after 2.00 a.m. and there was still no sign of Henry Wan. With a last look at the Hongkew Bund he returned to the telephone kiosk and called the Great Eastern Mansions. 'Give me Mr Wan's suite.'

The answering voice was hesitant, guarded. 'Mr Wan's suite?' It queried.

Harry Lord's face darkened. 'That's right. I spoke to him earlier this morning.'

'Oh, yes. I remember.' The voice remained indecisive, then in a more assured tone said, 'I take it that you're a friend of Mr Wan?'

Harry Lord stared at the phone with mounting apprehension. 'That's right – a personal friend.'

The voice again expressed hesitancy, lowered to a conspiratorial key. 'I was instructed to say nothing about the matter, but, well, there's been an accident.'

Harry Lord stiffened, threw an anxious glance at the Bund outside. 'What *sort* of accident?'

'I don't really know. The police were here. Apparently Mr Wan fell from the balcony of his suite. And I believe there are some other people dead up there – one at least. But I'm not conversant with what—'

Harry Lord didn't wait to hear anything further. Two minutes later he was headed west along the Hongkew Bund, his attention focused on the wide stretch of cobbled roadway ahead, the unenthusiastic heir to more than $3,000,000's worth of bullion. But this news was the biggest shock so far in an already over-eventful night when everything had gone wrong. He knew intuitively that it was Captain Hop who was involved. And earlier events also began to fit together; the lurking patrol boat out on the river, and the cop across in the Carfax Oil Depot. It had been more than coincidence. Captain Hop had somehow been in on it right from the beginning. Worse, he would have made certain Henry Wan had talked before he died.

He was up past the Ropewalk Wharves when he saw the fast approaching glare of headlights from westward. Ducking into the nearest doorway, he flattened against its shadow and watched the big open car sweep past on its way eastward, the unmistakable figure of Corporal Choy haunched over the wheel while Captain Hop and Sergeant Kee leaned their heads into the slipstream.

When he arrived at the Red Fortune Hotel a few minutes later he was met in the hall by Old Po. The old man's eyes widened when he saw he had the .38 Police Special in his hand. 'What happened to you?'

Harry Lord ignored the question. 'Is everything still quiet?'

Perplexed, Old Po said, 'Yes, why?'

Harry Lord armed the sweat from his face. 'It's the cops. Is she ready?'

'Yes. She's been waiting in her room since you called.'

Harry Lord snatched the switchboard phone from its hook and was jamming the lead into the room number when he heard the roar of a vehicle terminate outside with a screech of tyres.

Old Po grabbed his arm. 'This way!' Quickly he ushered him into the passage which led back to the kitchen in rear of the building, then returned to the front hall.

Harry Lord heard the slam of car doors followed by the clatter of feet. There were two of them.

One of them said authoritatively, 'Who are you?'

'My name's Old Po,' Old Po said out in the hall.

'Are you the owner of this place?'

'Such as it is,' Old Po airily replied.

'Never mind the humour, old man,' the voice directed. 'Does a Westerner called Lord live here?'

'Not anymore,' Old Po answered.

'What do you mean – not anymore?' a second voice demanded.

'He left yesterday afternoon.'

The second voice said, 'Did a girl come asking for him?'

'A girl?' Old Po said. 'Girls came asking for him all the time.'

'I told you never mind the humour,' the first voice instructed. 'If I shove this gun up your arse you won't think it so funny.'

Listening, Harry Lord realized that the voices belonged to the two cops he had seen in the jeep outside Mr Chang's office on the corner of Kwong Lee Road on the Friday morning; Lieutenant Yang and Sergeant Soon. Apparently they had finally gotten around to making the same inquiries as Annie Kim had made the previous day. It was all he needed; his luck was as far out as the tide at Dragon's Head Point at low water.

Out in the hall Lieutenant Yang said, 'Let's take a look upstairs, old man.'

Harry Lord listened to them start upstairs. He had no alternative now but to wait it out, and after they completed a search of the first floor, he heard them go on upstairs again.

'I tell you there's no girl here,' Old Po protested as they made their way upward.

Harry Lord waited, heard them search the rooms on the second and third floors, then move on upstairs. Tightening his grip on the revolver, he started cautiously after them. He was on the third floor when an excited shout and the hurried tramp of feet announced Annie Kim's discovery. He swore, and through the commotion heard another vehicle approach on the Bund. Opening the door of the nearest room overlooking the front, he crossed to the veranda and saw the big open car pull into the kerb behind the Police Department jeep. Captain Hop and Sergeant Kee hit the pavement before Corporal Choy cut the motor, entering the downstairs hall at a run as Choy propped a submachine gun on to the car door to cover the entrance.

Lieutenant Yang and Sergeant Soon were on the third floor with Annie Kim and Old Po when Captain Hop and Sergeant Kee met them on the way upstairs.

'What's going on here?' Captain Hop demanded.

Lieutenant Yang hesitated, surprised by the unexpected appearance of the KSS, and holstered his revolver. 'We wanted to ask this girl a few questions, Captain.'

'In connection with what?'

Lieutenant Yang's nervousness increased under Captain Hop's unflinching scrutiny. 'She's the friend of a suspect we wanted to take in for questioning. He disappeared on Friday and during our inquiries we heard there was the possibility that the girl was being sheltered by a Westerner living here.'

Captain Hop grimaced contempt. 'I suppose you mean a man called Harry Lord.'

Lieutenant Yang said innocently, 'Do you know him, Captain?'

Captain Hop said brusquely, 'You might say that.'

Lieutenant Yang spread his hands in an obsequious gesture. 'Then if we can be of any assistance.'

Captain Hop turned on Old Po. 'You!' he barked. 'Where's Harry Lord?'

Old Po looked even more downcast.

'So the old bastard's deaf now is he!' snapped Sergeant Soon, holding tight to Annie Kim's arm.

Captain Hop grabbed Old Po by the front of the gown and

raised him up on tip-toe, so that their faces almost touched. 'Has Harry Lord been around here this morning?'

Old Po swallowed heavily. 'He left yesterday afternoon.'

Lieutenant Yang said, 'That's what he told us. Only I'm not so sure about it. When we found the girl here she looked as if she was waiting for somebody to call.'

Captain Hop dropped Old Po and snatched Annie Kim's face toward him. 'Were you waiting for Harry Lord?'

Sergeant Soon wrenched on her arm. 'Answer the Captain!'

Annie Kim gritted her teeth and remained obdurate.

Captain Hop dropped his hand from her chin and stared at her for a moment, an idea forming in his mind. 'Take them back upstairs,' he instructed Sergeant Soon. 'Maybe Lord intends to call on her after all. It's just the sort of thing he'd risk his neck for.'

Sergeant Kee cut in, 'It could be that he doesn't even know we're here yet, Captain.'

Captain Hop found an emotionless smile. 'Then we'll arrange a surprise for him.' He turned on Lieutenant Yang. 'You go and cover the rear of the building and my men and I will take care of the Bund. Kee, you go down and help Choy run both vehicles off the front so that everything looks normal.' Next he said to Sergeant Soon, 'And see they keep their mouths shut. If Lord does wander in here I don't want anything going wrong.'

In the darkness of the nearby room Harry Lord listened as Sergeant Soon herded Annie Kim and Old Po back upstairs while Captain Hop and Lieutenant Yang followed Sergeant Kee back down to the hall. Then returning to the veranda doorway, he watched Sergeant Kee and Corporal Choy drive both vehicles off the Bund into Sai Woo Lane and return carrying submachine guns to join Captain Hop in the shadows along the front. Cursing, he started to turn back into the room, then stopped as the growing sound of aircraft motors reached him. Two searchlights down around Woosung had already jabbed pencil-slim beams into the sky, their glare diffused by the bank of low cloud moving southward in direction of the Pacific. Two minutes later the shriek of bombs carried upriver. The orange-yellow flash of the first explosion occurred downriver, on the north shore, a little way west of the Shanghai Water Works. Three more explosions quickly followed as the falling stick crept its way upriver along the Yangtzepoo waterfront.

When the first of the second stick hit the Hongkew waterfront, Harry Lord ducked clear of the open veranda. The next two bombs fell almost simultaneously, the first in the river just west of the Ropewalk Wharves, the second on the Bund. The crash rocked the building on its foundations and he hugged the floor as the hammer blow of concussion sent shattered glass and debris through the air. Then again the building shuddered, and then the detonations began to recede westward along the front toward the old International Settlement.

In that moment Harry Lord realized that whatever move he intended to make it had to be made right then, or never, and shielding his face in the cloud of dust and plaster fogging the room, he rose and went for the stairs. The first dim figure he saw when he shouldered the door of Annie Kim's room open was that of Sergeant Soon. He was gathering himself to his feet, and stepping forward, he slammed the butt of the .38 down across his skull. And then he saw Annie Kim and Old Po stumble toward him from the other side of the room. 'Are you all right?'

'We're fine,' Old Po answered in the gloom. 'But what happened outside?'

'Those were bombs,' Harry Lord said, brushing past them to the veranda. Several fires had already taken hold on the Yangtzepoo waterfront, and outside on the Hongkew Bund a gaping crater had been torn in the cobbles the other side of Sai Woo Lane. When he turned back into the room he thrust the wad of US currency which remained from the Chen-kou trip into Old Po's hands. 'That's for everything you've done for me while I've been here,' he told him. 'But now we've got to get away and I'm going to ask you one more favour.'

Old Po nodded. 'Whatever you say.'

Harry Lord found Sergeant Soon's revolver beside the sprawled body. 'This's what you do.' Cocking the revolver, he put it into Old Po's hand. 'Give us time to get downstairs and then aim it out through the veranda doors and pull the trigger. That's all you have to do. Then spread yourself on the floor and play dumb.'

Old Po scanned Harry Lord's tough, dark face in the gloom. 'And you?'

'I'm counting on that shot bringing Yang in from out back.'

Old Po reached out and grasped his hand. 'I hope everything goes well for you both. I won't forget the days we shared.'

'Sure.' Harry Lord put his arm around Annie Kim's shoulders and guided her toward the hall. 'S'long, old man. Look after yourself.'

'And you,' Old Po called after them, the look of wistfulness in his old eyes concealed by the gloom. It seemed with their leaving that yet another age had passed and now he would have to bring himself to face the uncertain beginnings of still another, one that would perhaps prove even more severe than its predecessor. And he wondered if he would be able to summon the necessary will-power to make what promised to be a transition from one extreme of politics to the other. But he had long since learned in life that nothing was ever easy. It was a pity that at times the hands of the clock didn't move in reverse.

Balancing the revolver in his hand, he raised it to head-height and aimed it very deliberately out through the veranda doorway at the sky above the upturned eaves of Hongkew and Yangtzepoo. It was the first time ever that he had held any kind of weapon in his hands, and he shut his eyes tight, averted his face, and pulled the trigger.

Harry Lord and Annie Kim were in the kitchen with their backs to the wall behind the door when the sound of the shot thudded through the building. Close behind it came the sound of running feet in the alleyway outside, then the door burst open and Lieutenant Yang exploded into the kitchen to disappear headlong into the passage.

Harry Lord didn't hesitate, grabbing Annie Kim's hand, he hustled her outside into the alleyway, broke running across Sai Woo Lane past the two parked vehicles, and sprinted into Chuk Lin Lane which ran parallel with the Hongkew Bund eastward.

* * *

Only Corporal Choy remained on the Hongkew Bund while the others converged in a rush on the top floor of the hotel.

Sergeant Kee was first into the room, saw the sprawled

bodies of Sergeant Soon and Old Po, but saw no sign of Annie Kim. 'The girl – she's gone!'

Captain Hop was right behind him, already suspicious about what had happened. In a smouldering rage he crossed the room and grabbed Old Po to his feet. 'Where's the girl?'

Old Po stared back at him dazedly. When he made no effort to answer Captain Hop hit him a blow to the temple that jarred him to his toes. 'Answer me!'

Old Po stared back with an even more dazed look about him.

On the other side of the room Lieutenant Yang was helping Sergeant Kee to his feet. He tottered unsteadily then straightened upright with a hand to his skull. 'Somebody hit me,' he groaned.

Captain Hop relinquished hold of Old Po so abruptly he sat back down on the floor. 'It was Lord! And it was this old goat who fired that shot to bring us up here!'

Lieutenant Yang couldn't believe he had been so easily made to look foolish, even incompetent. 'Do you mean he was in the hotel here all the time?'

'You don't know that bastard!' Captain Hop raged, fighting to control the violence which gripped him. 'He went out past you when you came in from outside, and the girl with him. They were waiting downstairs when the old man fired that shot.' Thrusting them aside, he started back downstairs, his teeth gritted, the blood pounding in his skull.

When they emerged on to the Bund Corporal Choy was waiting in front of the entrance. 'What happened?' he asked.

Captain Hop holstered his revolver and scowled at the Bund. 'They went out the back way – both Lord and the girl. Now get the car.' He turned his attention to the river. The violence that gripped him a few minutes previously now simmered just beneath the surface in cold fury. But to lose control of himself now was the last luxury he could afford. What he had to do was out-think, out-manoeuvre Harry Lord. One factor already on his side was that there was only one way for Harry Lord to take the *Jacaranda*, and that was *downriver*. Wherever it was he had her put away, that was the way he would go when he made his break, downriver. More important, he would have to make his break before daylight if he hoped to get away. Behind him he heard Choy drive the big open car lurching across the debris-littered roadway. 'Get Marine Police Headquarters on the radio and tell them to direct River Patrol Three to the Hongkew Bund opposite the Red Fortune Hotel.'

Sergeant Kee said quietly, 'Do you suppose he's heard what happened at the Great Eastern Mansions, Captain?'

'Probably. But there's nothing we can do about that now.'

Lieutenant Yang cleared his throat self-consciously. 'Can we be of any further use to you, Captain?'

Captain Hop said evenly, 'He has a launch, Lieutenant. The *Jacaranda*. My guess is it's hidden somewhere along this stretch of waterfront, between here and Yangtzepoo. I suggest you take a look along the front and around the Hall & McKenzie Wharf. We've already been down there and didn't find anything but it won't hurt to go over that area again.'

Corporal Choy stood up in the car. 'Here comes the patrol boat.'

They saw the running lights of the patrol boat swing in line as she angled in from midstream toward the Hongkew Bund, headed up from way of Tienningshih.

'You and your Sergeant go ahead,' Captain Hop instructed. 'We'll work our way down along the front with the patrol boat.'

Lieutenant Yang nodded, his hand on the flap of his holster. 'And if we find him?'

'Fire two shots and we'll be right with you. But don't shoot him. I want him alive. This is a political matter. He's wanted for questioning.'

Lieutenant Yang said hopefully, 'And the girl?'

'You can do what you want with the girl. She isn't worth a fuck to us one way or the other.'

The roar of motors reached a crescendo and died as the patrol boat bumped her port gunwale against the pilings of the Bund.

Captain Hop dragged Henry Wan's black metal document case from the car and dropped it down to the gunner waiting on the foredeck, then quickly followed it.

'Captain?' Lieutenant Yang was peering down across the edge of the Bund as Sergeant Kee and Corporal Choy dropped down on to the foredeck.

'What is it now?' Captain Hop's voice showed his irritation as the motors caught and hooked with a roar.

Lieutenant Yang called down through cupped hands, 'How do we we know this man Lord? The only description we have of him was from a bartender and a whore on the Kwong Lee Road.'

'There's only one Harry Lord, you fucking idiot!' Captain Hop yelled back at him. 'And if you don't see him first you'll be past caring what the hell he looks like!'

Outraged and ridiculed, Lieutenant Yang stared bleakly after the patrol boat as it swept clear of the Bund in a cloud of exhaust and upflung wash. 'To hell with these Blueshirts! That's all they're any good at – waving guns and shouting orders!'

Fingering the bruised welt of flesh and bone at the base of his skull, Sergeant Soon looked at his superior in sympathetic agreement. 'Yes, Lieutenant.'

Dusting down his light tan uniform coat, Lieutenant Yang stared morosely after the patrol boat. 'Just the same we'd better make a move or else that bastard's going to have our heads rolling.'

* * *

Harry Lord drew Annie Kim close to him in the shadows at the mouth of Yin Chong Street where it met the Hongkew Bund opposite the Ropewalk Wharves. On the far side of the stretch of cobbled roadway the blacked-out *Ladybird* sat at the quay like a three-tiered wedding cake in a dimly lighted banqueting hall. The milling throng of people around her brow had increased in number considerably since he had left her and their clamour carried high-pitched across the waterfront. A flicker of recognition showed briefly in Annie Kim's eyes as her gaze passed over *The Ladybird*. 'I know that ship. I saw her many years ago in Nanking. She belongs to a foreign lady who wore a uniform with gold buttons and had a braided cap.'

Harry Lord took a firmer grip of her hand. 'It still belongs to her. Dutch Mary's a friend of mine.' When he started across the Bund he saw Dutch Mary wave across the heads of the throng from the starboard companionway.

She met them, giving a warm smile to Annie Kim, when they pushed their way through to the brow. 'Your fine calibre friend?'

Harry Lord nodded. 'Annie Kim.'

Dutch Mary took in their dishevelment. 'You had trouble?'

'Yeah. I'm going to have to pull out with that stuff still on board.'

'And how downriver you are going to get?'

'When are you leaving?'

Dutch Mary glanced at the crowd of pleading faces around them. 'When these people on board they can get.'

Even with his own troubles a look of incredulousness still passed across Harry Lord's face. 'You mean you're shipping *that* lot out? Where are you going to put them all?'

Dutch Mary said with magnificent unconcern, 'Oh, somewhere they can find. First stop Wenchow.'

'Jesus Christ,' Harry Lord said.

Dutch Mary smiled happily. 'Him too I take He wants to come.' She turned her smile on Annie Kim. 'And your calibre friend – she on board wants to come too?'

Harry Lord shook his head. 'There's a couple of cops looking for her too. She's an old friend of Mr Chang. And there's just the off-chance you might be boarded.'

Dutch Mary caught suddenly at his arm as Ling hurried aft along the companionway. 'Wait,' she told him.

Ling gestured westward along the Bund. 'There's two cops headed this way. I saw them from the wheelhouse. There's also a police patrol boat running her searchlight across the Wharf Road boat-slip.'

Dutch Mary looked at Harry Lord and Annie Kim with concern. 'You better hurry,' she told him. 'And take care. From the companionway I will call to you when these people on board we get.'

Harry Lord pushed his way back through the surging crowd around the brow and swung over the edge of the quay on to the iron ladder astern of *The Ladybird* just as they began to jostle and push their way up the brow, spilling into the starboard companionway and flooding between decks. 'Take your time,' he told Annie Kim when he had her between himself and the ladder, then started down into the darkness until his feet touched the cross beam between the pilings. 'Mind where you put your feet. It's slippery as hell down here.' Once balanced on the cross beam, he guided her along until they were abaft the *Jacaranda* where she lay in under the quay. Then he took her around the waist and lowered her down on to the bullion cases in the stern-quarters, and dropped down to join her. In the darkness he found her hand and helped her down into the cockpit. Her hand was cold and he felt her shiver. He drew her down into the starboard forrard corner below the dashboard. 'Are you all right?'

Annie Kim sat passively into the corner. 'Yes, I'm fine.'

It was black dark in under the quay, the damp air raw with the stench of sewage and river debris. Out beyond the pilings it was equally as dark and the only sound that reached in from outside was the swirl of the river and the muffled whine of *The Ladybird*'s dynamoes carrying through her hull.

Harry Lord saw the pale smudge of Annie Kim's face in the darkness as he took the Gibbs from its clips and slipped the safety to off. 'They won't find us in here. They were past this way already and didn't see anything.'

'I'm not afraid, Mr Lord.' Her voice sounded small, lost beside him in the darkness.

Silence descended, dark and uncommunicative. Somewhere a rat squealed and scampered for a footing.

After some minutes she said tentatively, 'Why were those policemen looking for you?'

Harry Lord nodded toward the stern. 'Those cases back there are full of bullion, more than three million buck's worth.'

Annie Kim couldn't believe it. 'So much money?'

'So much money,' Harry Lord affirmed. 'It belonged to a big shot slopehead from Chungking, or did, until somebody pushed him off a balcony in the Great Eastern Mansions.'

Annie Kim was aghast at the thought. 'Somebody did *that* to him?'

'Well he didn't jump because he thought he had rubber legs.'

'And now the police want the bullion.'

Harry Lord eased the .38 Police Special from his waistband and squinted out at what little could be seen of the river beyond *The Ladybird*'s bows now his eyes were accustomed to the darkness. 'In a nutshell,' he said.

'Then you took a very great risk in coming to the hotel to collect me.' There was a detectable tremor in Annie Kim's voice.

'It was a promise,' Harry Lord said with deliberate carelessness.

'And you always keep your promises?'

He looked down at the pale smudge of her face in the darkness of the cockpit. 'It isn't so difficult – I don't make many.'

In the ensuing silence the ticking of the dashboard clock sounded abnormally loud in the cockpit.

By way of an apparent afterthought, Annie Kim said, 'All my life I seem to have been running.'

'Politics,' Harry Lord announced. 'There's always somebody around who's convinced that he knows what's best for everybody else. That's politics.' And he thought; all the woes of the world can be directly attributed to politicians. They had it by the balls. Politicians, bankers and hot-shot Union officers, they all had the same motto; Fuck you Jack, I'm inboard.

In the darkness the water sucked and slid around the weed-grown pilings of the quay, and Annie Kim thought his very size and the aggressive and determined set of his head and shoulders imparted a sense of security she had never before experienced. 'Do you think we will get away, Mr Lord?'

Harry Lord was surprised by her calmness. There was no trace of anxiety in her voice, just a tone of general inquiry. 'I wouldn't worry about it any,' he told her, already worrying about it enough for both of them. The last thing he wanted to tell her was that it was a cast-iron certainty that now Captain Hop had lost them he would pin everything on watching the river for them to make a dash for the Yangtze.

Annie Kim was more certain than ever that she was in love. She had never felt so complicatedly overcome with anxiety and tenderness and yearning in her life, and she was convinced that such a disconcerting complexity of emotion couldn't be anything other than love. And she was also afraid. She didn't know how she would ever again be able to face up to life if he didn't see anything in her; if he was unaware of her other than her immediate presence.

Suddenly Harry Lord saw the Marine Police patrol boat come into view out beyond *The Ladybird*'s bows, her searchlight flicking across the shadows on the Bund. Tense and watchful, he waited while she drifted down outboard of *The*

Ladybird to reappear out beyond her stern with Captain Hop and Sergeant Kee plainly visible where they stood on the foredeck following the probing beam of light.

Moments later Dutch Mary's voice reached down into the darkness from the starboard companionway. 'Below!'

Harry Lord leant across the port gunwale and put his head out under the cross beam. 'What is it?'

'You ready to leave?'

Harry Lord peered up at where Dutch Mary's face showed above the bulwark capping forrard of the starboard paddle wheel casing. 'Where's the patrol boat?'

'Headed toward the Hall & McKenzie Wharf.'

'All right. Give me a blast on your whistle to drown the motors and I'll come out on your starboard side here so's you're between me and the patrol boat.'

'Fine. A few minutes you give me.'

Harry Lord turned back to the cockpit. 'This is it. A couple of minutes and we're on our way.'

Even as he spoke he heard the dull thud of the brow overhead as it was hauled inboard, then the muffled jangle of telegraph bells carried through *The Ladybird*'s hull as her engines lumbered into life. Above the commotion they heard Dutch Mary call instructions from the starboard wing of the wheelhouse, heard the springs hit the river, then saw the bows begin to swing away from the quay. Suddenly the three giant wooden paddles set themselves in ponderous motion, their cumbersome blades tearing sheets of water into the air, threshing the river up white around her black hull, like an ungainly duck trying to set herself in motion. In acknowledgement of this maritime feat, a ragged cheer broke from her upperdecks as the tightly packed ranks of passengers craned their necks for a last look at the quay where it drifted away.

Rocking dangerously in the turbulent water swept in below the quay, Harry Lord waited ready to thumb the motors into life, and heard the asthmatic blast of steam hiss and splutter a miniature rainstorm across the upperdecks before it finally summoned the energy to break into a deafening blast. Even so the exploding roar of the twin motors in the enclosed space sounded loud enough to him to be heard in Woosung. Quickly he throttled them back, put them in gear, and went slowly ahead. Clearing the overhead timbers, he held the wheel to starboard in order to keep his port side clear of the threshing blades of the starboard paddle wheel. Then, as if it was thought part of the fun and games of leaving harbour, another cheer arose from *The Ladybird*'s packed decks when the grinning faces spotted the *Jacaranda*, and arms raised waving happily.

And Harry Lord thought; Jesus Christ on a bicycle.

Bodies were crammed, perched and clogged into every conceivable nook and cranny, and under a pall of black smoke belching from her spindly smokestack, *The Ladybird* turned around out in midstream and set out from Shanghai for the last time with newly acquired pride at again having achieved the impossible. With his best magic grin Harry Lord turned to Annie Kim where she sat huddled in the starboard forrard corner of the cockpit. 'With any luck we should be down around Hangchow Bay by daylight!'

* * *

Incensed at not having uncovered any trace of Harry Lord or the *Jacaranda* on the stretch of river between the Red Fortune Hotel and the Hall & McKenzie Wharf, Captain Hop was forced to consider the possibility that Henry Wan had lied about his telephone conversation with Harry Lord. Worse, he now saw that it had been a grave error of judgement to have disposed of him so prematurely, and he regretted his shortsightedness bitterly. Then as they cleared the Changsha Jetty he saw Lieutenant Yang and Sergeant Soon appear on one of the wharves. 'Did you find anything?' he called out.

Lieutenant Yang pulled a sombre face and moved his head negatively. 'We couldn't find a trace of either him or the launch anywhere along the front, Captain. Besides, I don't see where a launch could be easily hidden around here. There are only these wharves and jetties.'

Captain Hop knew that what Lieutenant Yang said was true; there was nowhere that a launch the size of the *Jacaranda* could be easily concealed. He glowered up at Lieutenant Yang balefully while he deliberated his next step. It had to be Woosung; he had to get down somewhere around Woosung Spit where they would be in a position to surprise Harry Lord when he made his break downriver. Almost in way of reply a blast of noise echoed across the river and he turned to see the ungainly silhouette of *The Ladybird* etched against the lights of the Tienningshih waterfront as she moved slowly downriver.

'What do you want we should do now, Captain?' Lieutenant Yang wanted to know.

Captain Hop swung around – and stopped – struck for the first time by just how the glare of their searchlight lit the underside of the wharf on which Lieutenant Yang and Sergeant Soon were standing. And as he stared at the exposed cavern beneath their feet he realized they had been ignoring the most obvious of all hiding places. He stood transfixed, mind racing, wondering if it was really feasible; that Harry Lord and the *Jacaranda* had been lying concealed by the bulk of *The Ladybird* beneath the quay at the Ropewalk Wharves all during the time they had searched their way downriver. He saw no other answer. 'There!' he cried, gesturing with the riding-crop at the underside of the wharf. 'There's your hiding place!'

At his shoulder, Sub-Lieutenant Hsiung gaped at him, uncomprehending.

'There – in there – you fool!' Captain Hop screamed at him. 'He had her lying beneath the quay at the Ropewalk Wharves concealed by *The Ladybird* when we came downriver. I should have remembered he was a friend of Dutch Mary!'

Slowly, as if nobody was quite prepared to believe him, a range of faces turned to stare vacantly after *The Ladybird*'s ungainly silhouette where it passed down along the Tienningshih waterfront toward Tungkow.

Captain Hop turned on Sub-Lieutenant Hsiung with a lunge. 'What the hell are you waiting for?' he screamed, his neck corded with rage. 'Get her moving – get her moving! He's on his way downriver!'

Sub-Lieutenant Hsiung was stunned to immobility by the outburst, then like a man shaken suddenly from a deep sleep to find himself faced with a major crisis, he turned and made a dash for the bridge. 'Get her around!' he yelled at the startled helmsman. 'Give the motors full power! Make her move!'

Seconds later the patrol boat heeled to port in a new surge of power, her screws churning the river up white under a dirty cloud of exhaust fumes.

Unable to contain his excitement, Captain Hop scrambled up the iron ladder to the bridge where he seized the night-glasses from Sub-Lieutenant Hsiung's hands. Hurriedly focusing them on *The Ladybird*'s stern, he held them locked to it while they came around in a wide turn out in midstream, swinging in astern of the bulky silhouette up ahead. He saw the *Jacaranda* the instant that their bows settled on *The Ladybird*'s stern. 'There she is!' he called out in a yell choked with the excitement and relief of finally being able to see his prize directly ahead. He studied the *Jacaranda*'s sleek silhouette hungrily. 'Give me every revolution you can make!' he exulted. 'There's no way he can get away from us now!'

* * *

They were down past the lights of Tienningshih, past Henning's Wharf, off the Tungkow waterfront, when Harry Lord saw Dutch Mary reappear at a window on the starboard wing of the wheelhouse above them.

'Astern!' she called down, cupped hands to her mouth. 'Back astern!'

Harry Lord dropped his gaze back astern and immediately saw the lights of the patrol boat settle on *The Ladybird*'s stern. 'It looks as if Captain Hop's had a sudden inspiration,' he called to Annie Kim who rose looking astern. Then easing the throttles back open, he sent the *Jacaranda* smoothly ahead. As they swept up past *The Ladybird*'s wheelhouse Dutch Mary and Ling were waving them urgently on. With a sweep of his arm Harry Lord drew the *Jacaranda* in ahead of *The Ladybird*'s bows and settled to watch anxiously aft where the undersuction threatened to boil back in across the stern.

Annie Kim stood close to his shoulder. 'Can they catch us?'

Harry Lord scowled grimly astern. 'Normally they wouldn't stand a chance but with this cargo we've got on board it's just possible they might be able to match us for speed, maybe even have the edge on us. But only time's going to tell. At least we've got something like a mile start on them.'

They passed the Luk Keong Godown Wharf with its orange beacons, then passed the wreck buoys around the hulk of the *Cameroon Highlander*, and were well out ahead of *The Ladybird* when they again picked up the running lights of the pursuing boat. Harry Lord experienced bitter disappointment when they pitched into view. Not only had she them matched for speed, but had already closed the gap noticeably.

'They're gaining on us,' Annie Kim shouted above the roar of the motors.

Harry Lord nodded. The gap had closed to something like three-quarters of a mile. With the patrol boat having moved in ahead of *The Ladybird* her running lights showed framed against the black wedge of the bows. It passed through his mind that if they made it safely into the Yangtze the patrol boat might call off the chase for it was unusual to see any Marine Police boat even as far downriver as Woosung Spit. On the other hand he decided that with a cargo of bullion on board there was every possibility that she would be prepared to tail them clear across Hangchow Bay, especially if Captain Hop had anything to do with it.

A little later he picked up the beacons out on the south shoulder and edged the wheel around starboard to run the *Jacaranda* in toward the shore, then held her on course parallel to it while the roar of the motors beat back muffled off the land. Then, to the north of Woosung, he saw the first gun-flashes light the darkness and a long burst of tracer shells climb to arc and sway across the surrounding countryside.

The lethal display held Annie Kim fascinated. 'What's all the shooting?'

'That's the Communists pushing down along the Yangtze's south shore. They can't be more than three, four miles north of Woosung by the look of it.'

Out beyond the mouth of the Whangpoo the broad expanse of the Yangtze was beginning to take outline in the darkness.

'Once we're around into the Yangtze I'll jettison some of those cases. If they follow us then maybe we'll be able to hold our own, maybe even gradually out-run them.'

Annie Kim turned her attention astern. 'Their lights have disappeared.'

Harry Lord shook his head. 'They've only put them out. They're worried in case Woosung might open up on them. But they're still there. See the bow wash?'

Back astern Annie Kim saw the phosphorescent glow hard on their own fading wash. 'They're much closer than they were when I last saw them.'

Harry Lord's attention was focused on the river ahead. For a brief instant a fragment of moonlight showed itself through the heavy bank of cloud moving southward. They were on the shoulder, following it around to southward, and he saw that the two Kuomintang gunboats had cleared anchor and were nowhere to be seen. Then they were around into the Southern Waterway and he saw it was empty of lights except for those of the fairway buoys. Motioning Annie Kim to him, he straightened the *Jacaranda* out parallel to the south shore of the Yangtze. 'Take the wheel and hold her just as she is,' he told her.

Annie Kim took a determined grip of the wheel and watched him clamber into the stern-quarters where he started to tip the after cases outboard. Meanwhile the shore buffeted past on the starboard beam and up ahead she saw the sprawled lights that was Yangkiachen begin to form a pattern along the water's edge.

Harry Lord had the sixth case out across the stern when the patrol boat swung around into the Yangtze and put her running lights back on. She was no more than half a mile astern now, and almost immediately the pencil beam of her searchlight jabbed across the intervening darkness. Caught in the glare, he realized that any attempt to jettison enough bullion to enable them to make any noticeable increase in speed was going to be in vain. Then he saw the muzzle flash on the patrol boat's foredeck, and caught in the blast of the exploding shell he was sent sprawling to the cases where he watched with detached fascination as the column of displaced water fountained in the glare of light no more than twenty yards off the port quarter.

The next shell exploded some way ahead to raise a column of water on the port bow, and scrambling back into the cockpit, he snatched the Gibbs from its clips.

'That one was closer,' Annie Kim called to him.

Scowling astern, Harry Lord grimly worked the bolt on the big, ugly weapon. 'Don't worry about the shells. They aren't shooting to hit. Hop wants us in one piece.'

The third shell caused them both to duck instinctively when it exploded directly ahead. This time the *Jacaranda* lurched dangerously in the turbulent patch of river as she ran through the subsiding column of water.

Leaning against the cases, resting the big gun into his shoulder, Harry Lord took aim astern. The first and second shots produced no visible effect, but with the third, the searchlight was abruptly extinguished. In the resultant darkness it took several seconds for his vision to readjust itself, then aiming into the narrow patch of darkness between the running lights, he sent away several speculative shots before he saw the blurred shape of a body hurtle outboard from the foredeck.

On the bridge of the patrol boat, Captain Hop hammered the remaining shreds of glass from the windshield with the butt of his revolver and saw Sergeant Kee and Corporal Choy lying flat on the foredeck. 'Tell the gunner to put another shot ahead of them!'

'He's gone, Captain!' Sergeant Kee called back over his shoulder. 'Lord got him!'

Sub-Lieutenant Hsiung saw rage and frustration contort Captain Hop's face. 'I can shoot that gun, Captain.'

Captain Hop considered the offer, then changed his mind. 'Maybe we can manage without the shooting after all. I don't want to risk sinking them.' Narrowing his eyes against the slipstream, he sent a long calculating look at where the *Jacaranda*'s stern showed above her wash. 'How long will it take us to run down on them?'

Sub-Lieutenant Hsiung peered into the darkness. 'At the speed we're overhauling them I'd say somewhere inside the next fifteen minutes.'

'Then stay hard on their stern.'

In the drab glow of the instrument panel, Sub-Lieutenant Hsiung's face showed curiosity about the *Jacaranda* for the first time. He had learned early after his entry into the Marine Police about the smuggling and the running of contraband that went on in the waterways around Shanghai, and it hadn't been long before he was accepting his own bribes, but he couldn't understand Captain Hop's consuming interest in the *Jacaranda*. But he knew Heinrich Sztykgold, and he knew Harry Lord worked for him, and that they were under the direct protection of Chungking, and as far as he was concerned it was sheer idiocy to become involved in any Chungking enterprise. And it was for that reason he knew the prize had to be a big one. Further, the *Jacaranda* was built for speed, he had seen her make speed too, only she was low in the water and laden so that she couldn't even out-run a police patrol boat, and in the circumstances he saw only one logical explanation. In a voice that was shakey and uncertain, he said, 'He must be carrying something pretty important, Captain.'

Captain Hop wheeled on him, eyes glinting dangerously. 'Never mind what he's carrying! All you have to do is keep hard on his stern!'

The sly curiosity on Sub-Lieutenant Hsiung's face vanished. He grinned self-consciously. 'I didn't mean anything, Captain. I was only curious.'

Captain Hop returned his attention to the foredeck, his face bleak. 'Give him a burst from time to time to keep his head down!'

On the foredeck Sergeant Kee and Corporal Choy obediently settled down to take aim on the *Jacaranda*'s wash plume, and the first short burst of automatic fire rattled out across the flat expanse of black water as they cleared to seaward the last of the lights that was Yangkiachen.

When the second burst of automatic fire cracked past low overhead, Harry Lord grabbed Annie Kim down into the cockpit and held the wheel steady with his other hand while he concentrated his attention on the pursuing boat. It was less than three hundred yards astern and still gaining. To add to the discomfort at least two bodies had settled themselves with submachine guns on the foredeck where the muzzle flames etched themselves above the dark wedge of the bows from time to time. 'What we need right now is ten minutes of Gasper Ruiz with that cannon on his back.'

Annie Kim frowned. 'Who's Gasper Ruiz – a friend of yours?'

'I wish to hell he was.' Harry Lord glanced toward the shore. It lay some four hundred yards away, a thin dark line of a slightly darker intensity than the surrounding night. 'Can you swim?'

Annie Kim raised her gaze to the starboard gunwale. 'We're going to swim for the shore?'

'It seems our only chance. If we can get close enough in

and slip across the side they'll go on after the launch.'

Annie Kim searched his tough, dark face. 'Whatever you say, Mr Lord.'

He had begun to edge the bows gradually in toward the shore when his attention was suddenly caught by a set of lights about a mile distant. Grabbing the night-glasses, he stood up and focused them downriver. Despite the fact that she was blacked-out everywhere apart from her steaming lights, he was in no doubt that he was looking at the high-rising bulk of a freighter headed upriver out in midstream of the waterway, between the beacons on Yawo Sha and Heng Sha. She was in ballast, high in the water, her outline as tall and formidable as the Shanghai Racecourse grandstand. Watching her, he suddenly saw the opportunity to take one last gamble. He had no illusions about the risk they would be running, but it was either that or Hop. Spinning the wheel around to port, he altered course abruptly and headed at an oblique run out across the waterway.

On the patrol boat, Sergeant Kee turned to look back at the bridge. 'He's altered course, Captain!'

In his panic, it took Captain Hop several moments before he picked up the sudden alteration in the *Jacaranda*'s wash.

Sub-Lieutenant Hsiung jabbed an arm to southeastward. 'There! He's making for the lights of that freighter!'

Captain Hop snatched the night-glasses from him and screwed the approaching lights into focus. 'Is he seriously thinking about trying to stop her?'

Sub-Lieutenant Hsiung shook his head. 'She won't stop out here. He must have something else in mind.'

'Like what?'

'I don't know, Captain. I think the man's mad.'

Captain Hop saw Sergeant Kee send another burst of automatic fire across the intervening expanse of darkness. 'Then stay right with him. He can't get away now. We should be on him in a few minutes, able to shoot directly down into the boat.'

Harry Lord knew they were going to make it even before the freighter took on sharper definition in the darkness up ahead. Twice bullets ricocheted off the cases in the sternquarters to drill spidery holes in the windshield alongside his head but he refused to risk a glance astern now the freighter began to grow in bulk by the second.

They were within fifty yards of her when he snapped on the running lights. With Annie Kim close at his side, he watched the freighter's bows lance a steady course through the black water, her bridge inked in darkness and with no sign of life showing anywhere in sight. Without taking his eyes from her, he watched the towering bows converge swiftly on their own. Solid, rust-pitted, and weed-grown, her plates climbed sheer from the water. He was half aware of her name in rust-streaked letters above them; *City of Rhadamanthus*. And then in the instant when collision appeared inevitable he spun the wheel to port, and lurching under the on-rushing forefoot, the wall of battered plates towering above the cockpit, the stern heeled and the *Jacaranda* thrust herself suddenly clear.

On the patrol boat the helmsman's hands froze on the wheel when he saw the *Jacaranda* disappear beyond the freighter's on-rushing bows.

'The wheel – the wheel!' Sub-Lieutenant Hsiung thrust the benumbed helmsman aside, rang the motors into reverse, and flung the wheel around to port.

Out on the foredeck a low cry of disbelief broke from Sergeant Kee's throat when he saw the wall of battered plates loom over them. Hurling the submachine gun aside, he scrambled to his feet as he saw Corporal Choy throw himself wildly over the port side of the foredeck. And then he started blindly aft, and everything seemed to go into terrifying slow motion.

On the bridge, Captain Hop was struck with paralysis as the freighter reared above them, the thunder of her bow wash drowning all other sound. Although the patrol boat's screws were biting into the river and their head already swinging to port, he saw that they would never make it in time and yet his mind couldn't accept that it would end in such a manner. Then somebody close by began a scream that rose to tear through his petrified mind. Yet even in that fleeting blink of time between life and death, when he was seized by the natural last desperate reflex for life, his first reaction was to grab the black metal document case from the deck before throwing himself against the bridge door.

He was on the bridge ladder, halfway to the deck, when the freighter drove her bows into the hull abaft the bridge, terminating the scream on his lips as he was pinned to the casing under a cascade of US currency bursting from the document case.

Harry Lord angled the *Jacaranda* down the length of the freighter's starboard wall and turned to see her stem drive into the patrol boat's hull abaft the bridge, lifting her bodily over onto her port side with a screaming and rending of timber and metal, forcing her deep under the forefoot. In the space of a second it was all over, and in the lurching cockpit he and Annie Kim stood side by side staring after the receding stern of the freighter, the pound of her engines already fading in the night.

'It's almost as if it were a ghost.' Annie Kim's voice was an awed whisper.

Harry Lord said solemnly, 'I'd hate to think what would've happened if we hadn't made it.'

Annie Kim stared at the debris-littered water. The silence was uncanny. It was as if the night had dropped an eerie veil across the river. Then she turned a searching look to Harry Lord's dark, brooding face. 'What are we going to do now?'

Harry Lord put a cigarette in his mouth and scratched a match alight on the underside of the canopy. 'We're going to get to hell out of here, that's what we're going to do. There's no telling who else might be skulking around out here on a night like this.' Then finding the almost empty bottle of Haig & Haig beneath the dashboard, he uncorked it and offered it to Annie Kim. 'Here,' he told her. 'Take a swallow of this and you'll feel a lot better for it.'

Annie Kim took two tentative mouthfuls, then handed the bottle back.

Harry Lord looked at it, drained it, glanced at it with disgust, then tossed it out across the side. He saw the current had carried them below Heng Sha, nodded approvingly to himself, and put the motors in gear and opened the throttles over. Spinning the wheel, he watched the luminous digits of the compass come around then settled the *Jacaranda*'s head on a course of south-south-west that would take them down on Hangchow Bay. Now nothing showed anywhere, not even a fragment of moonlight. Further, he caught the first damp breath of a rising fog that promised to close in from the ocean. At his side he saw Annie Kim shiver and stand close to him. Removing his coat, he draped it around her shoulders. 'Now why don't you settle down in that corner again and try to get some sleep? There's nothing for you to worry about now. Daylight should see us in Hangchow Bay.'

Annie Kim hesitated, allowed him to pull the coat more tightly around her, like a small child being dressed by a parent, but when she turned away her teeth closed on her lower lip and there were tears in her eyes. She didn't know what it was she had expected, but she had expected it to be so much different. And what made it so much more difficult to accept was the fact that she was in love with him, would always be in love with him. The hurt was of such intensity that it was physical. She didn't believe she would ever recover from her disappointment. Bravely she averted her face as she huddled herself into the corner of the cockpit, her tears lost in the gloom.

In embarrassment Harry Lord stared straight ahead through the splintered windshield, wondering what the hell had gotten into him. He had gone soft in the head. And it wasn't as if she hadn't made it plain how she felt. A couple of days ago he would cheerfully have banged her tail-end off and never have given it a second thought. But now he couldn't even bear to think about it. It was a hell of a way for a man to find that he possessed a conscience. On the way down from Lang Dok it had all seemed so easy, and now – now he knew what it was to possess a bloody conscience.

Stealing a glance at her he saw she was already asleep, huddled against the motor casing for its warmth, his coat around her shoulders. He wondered how many women would have found the courage to have been able to go through what she had gone through in the past couple of days, let alone what she had faced before. It required a very special brand of courage to accept just how inconsequential one was to the rest of the world, to accept one's insignificance. Yet he knew he couldn't go on feeling the way he did without he found some way to let her know. But maybe in the morning he would find the courage somewhere to tell her. Everything was always so much easier in the morning. But he was in a hell of a mess all the way around. His big problem was what he was going to do with the bullion, less what he had fed to the fishes back upriver. He had to get rid of it somewhere, find a way to unearth some information about what had happened at the Great Eastern Mansions, find out if Zephyrine Wan was still alive. Only he didn't want to be seen around with a boatload of bullion. He had been through enough trouble already without putting into Chinhai loaded down to the gunwales with the stuff. And he wondered if it was too much to hope that morning would bring an answer to that problem too. But when he looked astern at the fire-lit clouds lying across Shanghai and Woosung he saw that if the morning was going to bring any sort of answer to his particular brand of problems, then it promised to be one hell of a busy time ahead.

With daylight the *Jacaranda* was cutting smoothly through the flat oily swell of Hangchow Bay, her motors muffled and her superstructure wreathed in a damp grey blanket of fog.

They were somewhere to southwestward of the Parker Islands, with the Rugged Islands ahead on the starboard bow lost in the thick fog. The fog condensed into beads of moisture and trickled in rivulets down the superstructure and the bullet-drilled windshield, and glancing about him, Harry Lord decided that it wasn't after all the sort of morning conducive to solving problems, romantic or otherwise. Then, as if the situation wasn't already bleak enough, one of the motors chose that moment to stutter, cough, and lapse into unpleasant silence. Cursing, he cut the other motor and peered into the enveloping fog. While the *Jacaranda* lost way he strained listening through the damp, grey shroud but heard nothing more sinister than the lapping of the ocean against the hull. Spitting his cigarette across the side, he glanced at Annie Kim who was still sitting huddled asleep in the starboard corner of the cockpit, then slid back the motor casing and climbed down into the cramped machinery space with its humid smell of oil and gasoline.

Annie Kim awakened with a start, disconcerted by the movement of her surroundings, then sat upright when it dawned on her that she was on board the *Jacaranda*. As the events of the night flooded back on her she realized something was wrong, that there was no sign of Harry Lord in the cockpit, and that there was no sound of running motors beneath the deck. She rose looking anxiously about her, saw the open motor casing on the opposite side of the cockpit, and relaxed when the clatter of a spanner and an accompanying curse carried up from below. She started toward the open casing with a smile, only to stop abruptly as she became aware of the approaching sound of fog-muffled motors. The sleek grey shadow took shape on the starboard beam almost in the same instant, first the raked bows, then the heavy calibre machine gun on the dripping foredeck, and finally the uniformed figures on the open bridge.

Everybody appeared to become aware of the other's presence in the same moment, and with an excited shout carrying across the fog-wreathed water, Annie Kim threw herself toward the open casing. 'Mr Lord! A ship – there's a ship out here!'

It took Harry Lord only a few seconds to reach the cockpit, but when he hauled himself out through the open casing he found himself looking into the blued muzzle of a Thompson gun. And behind the gun the hostile face of a Kuomintang navyman glared down at him coldly. 'Easy! You take it easy!' The navyman backed off a step as the gunboat, with her White Sun Flag drooping from her masthead, bumped gunwales with the *Jacaranda* and allowed two more navymen with automatic rifles to leap from her foredeck into the *Jacaranda*'s stern-quarters.

Close behind the two men followed an officer. Grinning broadly, he skipped his eyes around the cockpit as Annie Kim stepped close to Harry Lord. 'Well, well, well,' he murmured. 'And what do we have here?' He was a Lieutenant-Commander, a portly man, in need of a shave, dressed in an ill-fitting uniform and a too large cap. The blue uniform coat was stained, its buttons tarnished, the braid discoloured by the salt-laden air. He carried a drawn revolver in one hand, and a half-smoked cigar in the other.

One of the navymen saw the .38 Police Special in Harry Lord's waistband, relieved him of it, and thrust it into his webbing belt.

The Lieutenant-Commander regarded Harry Lord critically, a half smile on his stubbled face, 'It's such an unexpected surprise to run into something like this in the middle of Hangchow Bay,' he mused. 'There's no doubt about it,' he purred, turning his attention to Annie Kim. 'A cosy little get together altogether, eh?' he slyly remarked as he ran his gaze down over her figure appraisingly. 'And pretty too.' He strode a step closer. 'Very pretty.' As he spoke he reached casually out and cupped her right breast in his hand. 'Nice titties too, eh!'

The three navymen laughed, and the Lieutenant-Commander smiled with them, to show teeth yellow with tartar and carious. The odour of decay on his breath hung in the unmoving air while his eyes again slid down over Annie Kim's belly and thighs.

'Look!' One of the navymen shouted excitedly, gesturing into the stern-quarters. 'Those are bullion cases!'

The Lieutenant-Commander came suddenly to life, wheeled on the three men where they stood gaping at the cases. He elbowed one of them roughly aside. 'Mind your feet!' he instructed the one on top of the cases, then raised his revolver and calmly shot the lock from one of them. Wrenching the lid open, his eyes grew wide. 'Well, well, well! The morning certainly is full of surprises!' A yellow grin spread across his face and he made a wild gesture at the three men. 'Get them on board the gunboat,' he told them. 'Hurry! And bring the others too, the engineers as well – everybody! I'll take care of these two.'

Harry Lord glanced at Annie Kim with a sinking heart. At that moment he had never felt so spiritually low in all his life.

The Lieutenant-Commander turned on him grinning. He had grown considerably in stature with the discovery of the bullion. He made an expansive gesture with the revolver. 'And who did this little lot belong to?'

Harry Lord said hollowly, 'The Commissioner of Shanghai Police.'

The Lieutenant-Commander laughed and slapped his thigh. 'A funny man, eh! A funny man! Well, well, well!'

Three-quarters of an hour later the three sweating navymen who had been joined by two engineers, the helmsman and the cook, trundled the last case down into the gunboat's welldeck and turned to look at their superior expectantly.

With a smile the Lieutenant-Commander gave a casual wave of his revolver and turned on Harry Lord and Annie Kim. 'All right – on your faces!'

Harry Lord hesitated. 'Wait a minute. What about the girl? You could put her ashore somewhere.'

The Lieutenant-Commander grinned. 'You think I'm stupid, eh? For her to have a mouth?' Then his grin vanished. 'On your face!'

Harry Lord scowled at the revolver, then reluctantly joined Annie Kim on the duckboards in the cockpit.

'And don't move if you know what's good for you!' The Lieutenant-Commander turned and climbed up on to the gunboat's foredeck where the three navymen were waiting with their guns at the ready, and motioned to the helmsman on the bridge.

When he heard the gunboat's motors come to life, Harry Lord exchanged glances with Annie Kim. He already knew how the end would come, that it wasn't the Lieutenant-Commander's intention simply to leave them in the middle of Hangchow Bay. Silence had to be assured as permanent. Twisting his head around to see the Gibbs in its clips on the underside of the dashboard, his hand squeezed tightly over Annie Kim's. 'Whatever happens stay right where you are.'

With her motors revving, the gunboat began to turn away, and when her stern swung into view Harry Lord saw one of the navymen standing on the starboard gunwale with a grenade in his hand poised ready to throw. Hurling himself backward, he snatched the Gibbs from its clips and cocked and fired all in the same movement. Clubbed startled back off the gunwale by the force of the heavy calibre bullet, the man in the same instant released the clip on the grenade, and in the following split-second Harry Lord saw it sail over backward into the gunboat's welldeck in a lazy arc. She was still pulling away, the fog closing around her, when the morning erupted with a blast that lifted the *Jacaranda* out of the water, almost turned her over. Everything had gone up in the same instant, the grenade, fuel tanks and ammunition lockers, showering the ocean with debris.

Stunned by the violence of the explosion, it was several seconds before Harry Lord raised his eyes to the lurching gunwale. All that showed was a cloud of ugly black smoke drifting slowly out across the face of the ocean with the fog.

At his side Annie Kim said dully, 'They've gone!'

Harry Lord nodded dumbly. 'Three times over,' he said, idly watching a red leather wallet drift along the hull in the oily swell. Leaning over the side, he fished it from the water. When he opened it a naked Chinese girl framed in a lewd pose on the edge of a rumpled bed grinned out at him from a photograph in the celluloid pocket. Tucked in along with her was $5 in single dollar bills. In a hollow voice he said, 'What about that – five lousy bucks out of three million!'

At his side Annie Kim began to laugh, a laugh which began out of the sheer relaxation of nervous tension, but which went on to grow in stature.

Harry Lord looked at her, puzzled. 'What're you laughing at?'

'Your face!' she said through a gale of laughter. 'It was so funny when you thought about losing all that money!'

Harry Lord dropped his gaze to the wallet, saw the funny side of it too, then flipped it across the side. Suddenly the morning didn't seem such a bad morning after all, even took on the glow of promise. And what the hell did money matter? He had all the money he needed in the bank in Keelung. After all, it wasn't money he was looking for, he knew that now, recognized it, and had so done since the trip downriver from Lang Dok. At his side, Annie Kim's laughter began to subside. Suddenly she became silent, aware of the look in his eyes. She felt her throat constrict. She swallowed tightly. 'What is it, Mr Lord?'

In a voice he didn't recognize as his own, Harry Lord said, 'Come here.' And pulling her to him, he put his mouth on her's, and she reached her arms around his neck.

When their mouths parted, she said, 'Oh, Mr Lord.'

'Harry,' he said.

She smiled up at him, offered her mouth. 'Yes, Harry?'

He kissed her again.

It was several minutes before they became aware of the fog-muffled bleat of a ship's siren. Then they saw the ghostly silhouette of a ship materialize from the bank of fog to southward. 'Jesus Christ,' Harry Lord said. 'It's *The Ladybird*. With the current astern she hasn't wasted any time.'

They climbed to their feet and watched *The Ladybird* waddle her overloaded frame laboriously down along the starboard side, her paddles threshing the water up white as she wallowed in the oily swell, every inch of deck space crowded with people. Then they saw Dutch Mary and Ling appear at one of the starboard wing windows of the wheel-house, waving excitedly.

'Ahoy!' Dutch Mary's voice drifted eerily across the ocean. 'Trouble again you are having?'

'We just stopped to admire the view,' Harry Lord yelled back.

'Then no assistance this time you need?' the cupped voice came back.

Harry Lord yelled back emphatically, 'Not this time I don't.'

'Then maybe in Saigon we will see you.'

'Not us you won't. We're headed for the South Seas.'

'Then to you both all my good luck,' Dutch Mary's voice drifted back.

Harry Lord raised an arm in acknowledgement, watching *The Ladybird*'s stern paddle and masthead disappear in the fog to southwestward. When all trace of her had vanished Annie Kim turned looking at him where he stood wreathed in curling tendrils of fog like some ancient sea-god risen from the deep. 'We're really going to the South Seas, Harry?'

'All the way,' he assured her.

She said hopefully, 'Then you think we can share happy times together?'

'Why not?' he asked.

Annie Kim dropped her eyes down. 'But all these things I've done before.'

Harry Lord grinned his magic grin and reached out his hand. 'Let's just say we've both been around.'

THE END

CAPE OF STORMS BY JOHN GORDON DAVIS

This epic novel of whales and whalermen in the Antarctic seas centres round James McQuade, a young marine biologist from South Africa. Every summer he went south with the whalers to the Ice, and this season the crew was a particularly flamboyant mixture of personalities. On board was a beautiful nurse, Victoria Rhodes, who rapidly became the target for frustrated male lust . . . Despite the mystery about her origins, McQuade fell violently in love with Victoria, and when the whalers returned to port, he could not bring their affair to an end . . .

0 552 10447 7 85p

FIRESPILL BY IAN SLATER

FIRESPILL . . . 600 million gallons of high-octane fuel poured on the windswept waters of British Columbia.

Flashpoint . . . one match will ignite a raging inferno.

Firestorm . . . burning with the fury of hell. Nothing will stop it.

Firespill . . . a blazing inferno of terror, totally out of control, threatening thousands of lives. An environmental disaster torn from today's headlines. A gripping, shockwave novel of total suspense, horror – and surprise.

0 552 10611 9 85p